THE ALPHA'S SAVIOUR

SHIFTERS OF GREY RIDGE
BOOK 1

REECE BARDEN

CHAPTER 1

HAYLEY

The loud squeal of tires skidding across asphalt disrupts the peaceful morning air, and I whip around to see where the noise is coming from.

Then I see him.

A young boy in a bright blue coat standing in the road, his little face frozen in shock, staring wide-eyed as a van hurtles toward him. My heart jumps into my mouth, and I step in his direction despite knowing I'm too far away to help.

Out of the corner of my eye, I see a blur of movement, and a man launches himself into the road. In a split second, he pushes the boy clear, but as he climbs to his feet to get out of the way himself, the van barrels into him with a sickening thud. His body flies through the air from the force of the impact. My stomach lurches at the sight, and I'm frozen in place; horrified at the scene unfolding in front of me.

The sound of screaming fills the air, breaking my stupor. A woman I assume is the little boy's mother races to his side, collapsing to her knees beside him, sobbing. Holding his chubby round cheeks between her two hands, she looks his body over for injuries. He's sitting up already, and even though he is crying and clutching his leg, he doesn't seem to be seriously hurt.

The driver of the van clambers out from behind the airbag with a loud groan then collapses on his hands and knees. Bright red blood pours down the side of his face from a gash above his brow.

Rushing in the direction the heroic man's body was thrown, despite dreading to think about what I might find when I reach him, I sprint across the grass verge at the side of the road. Scrambling down the steep slope, almost on my backside, I use my hands to keep my balance as my feet slip and slide on the loose rocks.

As I hit a gravel area at the bottom of the slope, I straighten and look around.

Where has he landed?

When I finally see him my blood runs cold. He is floating face-down in the river, arms spread and head bobbing in the slow- moving current.

Shit, shit, shit.

He is not moving and is clearly unconscious, if not already dead.

Don't think like that!

Kicking off my runners, I peel my hoodie and t-shirt over my head, and launch myself into the water. A beautiful sunny spring day with clear blue skies, the water is still shockingly ice-cold, and I gasp as I plunge into the dark river. My lungs constrict, refusing to work properly. I fight to keep my breathing even as I swim to him, grabbing the back of his shirt and rolling him over to get his mouth and nose out of the water.

Tipping his head back, I wrap my arm under his chin and swim back toward the bank. I'm swimming against the current now and am panting hard by the time I reach the edge. Grabbing him under the armpits, I plant my feet firmly into the mud and, using every ounce of strength I have left, haul him onto dry land.

He is tall and well-built compared to my slight frame, and I won't be able to move him any further than this by myself. It's probably not a good idea anyway, with potential spinal injuries to worry about. I drop to my knees beside him, hardly feeling the sharp stones beneath my knees; I've gone numb from the cold water. Bystanders watch, horrified, from the top of the bank, but nobody comes down to help me.

They probably think he's already dead.

I can't give up, though. I have to try.

I touch under his clean-shaven jaw to check for a pulse but feel nothing. I put my cheek to his mouth to feel if there is any air flowing past his lips or nose: nothing again. Rocking back on my heels, I focus on his muscular chest. I can't see any movement to show that he is breathing. It seems too cruel for him to die after committing such an act of bravery, but any other outcome seems unrealistic looking at him now, deathly pale and still.

I grimace at the nasty cuts across his forehead, right cheek, and jaw. His nose is clearly broken, and blood drips down the side of his face and into his dark hair.

And that's just what I can see on the outside.

I shake my head and refocus, silently thanking the gods for mandatory health and safety training, as I start CPR. My limbs feel tired and heavy from dragging him ashore. As I pray that the approaching sirens get here quickly, I'm vaguely aware of someone sinking to their knees in the muck beside me. Someone grips the man by his shoulders as I continue compressions.

"Cooper! Oh no, this can't be happening," the man beside me shouts, leaning over to take his pulse as I already have.

Suddenly, Cooper, jerks and coughs violently, choking and retching as his body expels the water from his lungs. Tears of relief prick my eyes as the man takes hold of his shoulders tilts him over to allow the water to pour past his blue lips and into the dirt.

"It's okay, you're going to be okay," I whisper with as much conviction as I can muster.

I smooth back his hair as he blinks slowly up at me, and I hear the rattle of a stretcher being carried down the bank. Paramedics surround us, crouching down beside him to take over.

I attempt to stand and give the emergency personnel more space, but I collapse backward, landing my ass on the hard ground. Strong hands reach under my armpits from behind, gently pulling me up and back a couple of steps so that I'm out of the way.

"Thanks," I mutter, looking over my shoulder at my helper, but he isn't even looking at me. He is staring at the man on the ground, Cooper. Judging by the look on his face, he must know this Cooper well. Pushing his jaw-length blonde hair back roughly, he's blinking back tears and cursing under his breath about this being a close call. I'm not as optimistic that his friend is out of the woods, so I say nothing.

Once my jelly legs work again and can hold me upright on their own, I step away, wrapping my arms around myself, and watch as they load Cooper onto a backboard.

My body shivers now that the initial adrenaline rush has passed and the cold that has seeped into my bones finally registers with my brain. My legs give way again, but the man behind me catches me before I hit the ground. He turns me to face him, holding me steady by my shoulders, and I stare dumbly into the brightest pair of blue eyes that I have ever seen. He bends down till we're eye to eye and looks at me with concern as my teeth chatter, slowly looking me up and down, taking in my wet hair and lack of clothing.

"Are you alright? Fuck, I think you need to get warm... What's your name sweetheart?" He looks at me, expecting me to move or at least formulate an answer, but my brain can't force any words through the fog in my mind. I just continue to stare. I don't think I even nod.

He frowns then sweeps me into his arms. My head rolls back to rest on his shoulder, and I flop in his arms, my energy spent. He adjusts my position and holds me tightly against his solid chest, turning to carry me up the hill behind the stretcher. A deep rumble reaches us, something weirdly like a growl, and the man carrying me jerks his head up quickly to stare at his friend, turning back to me with a curious look on his face.

Depositing me carefully on another stretcher parked behind the open doors of the ambulance, he cups my face and leans in close. His blue eyes are mesmerising, and a lock of his messy blonde hair falls forward across his face.

"Cooper would be dead without you; words aren't enough." He shakes his head. "Thank you..."

I grip his hand and give it a quick squeeze. "Is he going to be okay?" I stutter through chattering teeth as I am strapped down and loaded into the ambulance.

"He'll be okay," the man reassures me, giving me a little wink and nodding once. He sprints to the ambulance where they've loaded Cooper and jumps in beside him just before the doors slam closed.

A large crowd has gathered, drawn by the flashing lights, huddled around with worried faces and speaking in hushed voices.

So much for lying low and avoiding any drama.

All that work trying to find somewhere to hide and build a new life, something tells me I've just ruined it all. I shut my eyes, and, despite the paramedic beside me telling me that I need to stay awake, I feel myself drifting to sleep as the sirens turn on and the ambulances pull away.

CHAPTER 2
HAYLEY

I blink my eyes open to uncomfortably bright fluorescent lights, and my head pounds.

It takes a second to remember what happened and to realise where I am. Groaning, I close my eyes again and cover my face with my arm. I'm supposed to be living below the radar, not all over hospital and police reports.

"Welcome back. Headache?" A chipper nurse carefully peels my arm back from my face, handing me a cup of water and a little container with a couple painkillers. I tip the tablets into my mouth and take a few sips of water. Scooting up the bed into a sitting position, I pull the thin blankets up with me.

"How are you feeling? You've been out for a few hours," she asks gently, taking my pulse. I remember her; she's the same nurse who admitted me last night and took all my details. She's had a long shift.

"Fine," I answer, "I feel like a bit of a fraud for taking up a hospital bed, to be honest."

"You were in shock and nearly hypothermic when they brought you in. You must be exhausted. We'll keep you here overnight just to be safe. Anyone you need me to call?"

I pause for a second, shaking my head. I moved here to keep my mess away from my family; dragging them here now wouldn't make sense.

"No, I've just moved to town. I'll be home again before my parents can even get here." She pats my arm reassuringly, finishing her checks and quietly leaving me alone in the room.

My thoughts immediately turn to Cooper and my gut clenches as I wonder how he's doing. I should have asked the nurse.

An ache blooms in my chest as I wonder whether he survived. If he did, he must be here; I chose to move to Grey Ridge because it is a small, remote community; there isn't another hospital anywhere near here.

I'm normally pretty level-headed, but panic rises every time I replay the scene in my mind. It feels like an overly dramatic response but I can't help it.

I can remember his beautiful brown eyes looking up at me from under thick black lashes as the emergency services took over, and I was pulled away. He was so brave, willing to sacrifice himself, without hesitation, for that child.

A soft knock on the door distracts me from my thoughts, and a familiar pair of icy blue eyes peer into the room. It's my handsome helper from the scene of the accident.

"Is it okay if I come in?" he asks, pushing the door open wider.

"Sure."

He smiles brightly, shutting the door gently behind him and crossing the room in two long strides.

It didn't register at the river with all that was going on, but I now realise this man is quite good-looking. I'm normally a tall, dark, and handsome kind of gal, but nobody could fail to see how attractive this guy is. His biceps bulge from under the sleeves of his t-shirt as he moves, and how effortlessly he carried me earlier makes a bit more sense.

Suddenly, I feel exposed and self-conscious in my thin hospital gown, stinking of dirty river water. I'm grateful he isn't standing too close.

"How are you feeling?" His face is friendly, but his tone is serious, as though he's genuinely concerned for my wellbeing.

"Oh, I'm fine! They're just keeping me overnight as a precaution." I dismiss his concerns with a wave of my hand, and he frowns. "How is your friend?" Keen to divert the attention away from myself, I'm almost afraid to hear the answer.

When he hasn't spoken, I look up to see him gazing at me intently. I am never one to shy away from eye contact, but this is intense, as if he's trying to read the depths of my mind. The urge to look away is strong. I hold out, cocking an eyebrow at him, keen to know one way or the other. I get the impression that he's deciding what to tell me.

Maybe he's worried about breaking bad news to me? The thought has me feeling nauseous.

"Cooper's alive," he finally responds, "but he's pretty banged-up. Obviously. He had surgery for internal injuries, and he has some broken bones and lots of stitches; but, by some miracle, it's nothing that won't heal."

"Thank fuck!"

He smirks at my colourful language, and I exhale sharply in relief. Dropping my head against the pillows, tears well in my eyes. I quickly wipe them away, embarrassed at my emotional response. If anyone should be upset, it should be the man delivery the news, not me – a total stranger.

"Sorry, sorry, I'm just so relieved. I did everything I could, but..." I draw in a ragged breath. "He had no pulse, his breathing...I guess I just didn't expect him to make it." Shaking my head, I try to force those negative thoughts from my mind and pull myself together. The man stares at me again, as if trying to work out a puzzle, but just nods again and smiles.

"I wanted to stop by and thank you. If you hadn't done what you did, he would have drowned. If you need anything at all, anything, please just let me know. We are forever in your debt, Hayley," he leans slightly forward and grips the rail of my hospital bed, sincerity clear in his eyes.

We?

Who is "we"? Does Cooper have a girlfriend?

I shudder.

Or a wife?

Why do I care?

I don't even know this Cooper. Whether or not he is in a relationship is none of my business.

The blue-eyed man scribbles his name and phone number on a piece of paper, reaching out and pressing it into my palm, folding my fingers tightly around it.

"I'm just glad I was there to help..." I glance down at the paper, "Ethan."

He nods again, then turns and strides out the door without looking back.

Odd.

Was he was expressing his gratitude or hitting on me?

Surely a man as good-looking as that isn't shy around the ladies. If he was hitting on me, I am pretty sure I wouldn't have to wonder about it.

Or am I just that out of practice?

CHAPTER 3
COOPER

Beep, beep, beep.

The slow, steady noise beside my head drags me from my sleep and into what feels like the worst hangover I've ever had.

Slowly opening my eyes, I'm in a hospital bed. I try to sit up, but a sharp, stabbing pain in my stomach keeps me flat on the bed.

Moving my arms and legs, I'm in agony, and I wince. I hurt everywhere. I growl to myself, not liking this feeling of weakness one bit. So much for accelerated healing. It doesn't seem to be kicking in quite as quickly as I'd like. As a wolf shifter and an alpha at that, I pride myself in being strong and nearly indestructible.

Apparently, a speeding van is an exception.

"You're going to be a terrible patient, aren't you?" Leila stands in the doorway with her hand on her hip, chuckling to herself.

I ignore her and close my eyes against the pain. I hear as she lifts the chart at the end of my bed. I know her well enough to imagine her face, scanning over my stats, dark brows pulled together in a frown as she switches from annoying sister to serious doctor. She begins reading the litany of injuries catalogued on the clipboard in her hands – fractured skull, cheekbone, and jaw; dislocated shoulder; broken collarbone, arm, wrist, and ribs; ruptured spleen; shattered ankle; multiple lacerations.

I wish she'd stop, because I don't want to hear this. I can already tell that I'm a mess by how much it hurts. Finally, she whistles softly, and I open my eyes.

"You... you were very lucky. This," she pauses, blinking hard, and shaking the chart at me, continuing in a wobbly voice, "this would be enough to kill most people. Even you, Cooper. If that woman hadn't dragged you out of the river... I can't even think about it, it's too scary."

She keeps talking, lecturing really, about what a close call this was. As if she needs to tell me that getting hit by a van was a bad idea, but I've stopped listening.

That woman.

Flashbacks of what happened start running through my mind, but not the bad stuff. My wolf is pushing me to remember something else. An amazing scent. I smelled it just before the crash. I can remember it vividly, and my mouth waters at the mere memory.

Even after the crash, I can remember tingles all over my face and body. She was touching me, and a distinctive feeling of calm washed over me, despite my pain, as she whispered comforting words in my ear and her breath touched my neck.

My mate. She was there.

My mind keeps reeling. Another flashback. Long, tanned legs. A toned stomach. Drops of water running down a slender neck and into a tight sports bra as she stands a few feet away from me. A curtain of long, wavy hair hiding her face from view. Then, a much less pleasant image of her cradled in Ethan's arms, her face buried in his shoulder and her hand on his chest.

I clench my fists and grit my teeth, a growl building in my chest.

"Cooper? What was that? Are you in pain?" my sister asks, looking at me with concern as the heart monitor beeps rapidly, my blood pressure shooting up.

The thought of another man having his hands on my mate is making my blood boil with a jealousy unlike anything I have ever experienced. I've heard stories about the possessiveness that comes with finding your mate, but this intensity is shocking.

Agitated, I sit up and swing my legs over the side of the metal hospital bed, ignoring the searing pain in my abdomen where I have probably pulled open some stitches. Dark spots appear in front of my eyes, and my head swims in my now cloudy vision. Grabbing at the tubes and wires attached to my arms and chest, I begin tugging them off and ripping them out.

I need to find her.

"What on earth are you doing? Cooper?!" Leila shouts. When I don't answer, she bolts for the door ahead of me, but I don't care. No one can stop me.

What if she was hurt, too?

What if nobody knows who she is, and I never see her again?

My wolf lunges for the surface, urging me to keep going, to ignore the dizziness making the room spin. I push up onto my feet, grabbing the bed railing for support as my knees tremble.

Only when I try to take a step do I notice the cast on one leg, up to my knee, which will make walking too difficult. I reach down and slip my fingers inside the cast, pulling away lumps of the plaster.

"Woah, hold up Cooper. What are you doing, man?" Ethan rushes through the door and grabs my arm, trying to stop me from destroying the cast while simultaneously turning me back towards the bed.

I smell it. I immediately recognise that delicious scent, making my heart soar.

But it's all wrong. It's on Ethan; and it's recent.

In a split second, I pivot and grab him by the front of his shirt with two hands, shoving him hard against the wall, pinning him in place with a forearm across his throat.

"Where is she?" I roar, oblivious to the commotion I'm creating. Ethan slowly holds up his two hands in surrender and exposes his neck to show me his submission, asserting that he won't attempt to fight back. My wolf accepts his submission, but he's grinning like a fool, and it's infuriating. I don't care that he's my best friend of twenty years. At this moment, he's just an unmated male who smells like my girl – and I want to rip his head off.

"Cooper, you need to chill out. Hayley's fine, she's safe. I promise." His voice is low and calm.

Hayley.

Pride fills my chest as I hear my beautiful mate's name, and I loosen my grip. I feel Ethan relax as I remove my arm from his throat, and he takes a deep breath.

It's short-lived though. My joy in hearing her name is quickly replaced by a resurgence of jealous rage as I realise that he knew her name and I didn't. He wears her scent while I haven't even seen her face.

My anger roars again and I lift him off the ground, shoving him against the wall so hard a crack appears in the plaster behind him.

"Who is Hayley?" Leila interrupts. "Ethan, tell me what on earth is going on!" Confused, my sister stands a few feet away from us, knowing better than to intervene but nonetheless blocking the door from anyone else who might try to get in.

"Cooper! She's here," Ethan attempts to assure me. "She's in the hospital, but she's fine. I thought she might be yours, so I went to check on her. I knew when you woke up, you'd want to know how she was. That's all, I swear!"

I set him back on his feet and fix him with an icy glare, growling one last time as I push away and suck in a few deep breaths to calm down. Dragging a hand across my now-stubbled jaw and trying to regain some sense of control.

"Show me where she is," I order as I hobble around the room, searching for something more respectable to wear to meet my mate than the hospital gown I'm donning right now with my ass hanging out.

"No, Cooper. You can't...." Ethan starts, but before he finishes his sentence I'm rushing at him, snarling. Expecting it this time, he dodges me, darting sideways and putting the hospital bed between us. He rakes a hand through his blonde hair and exhales sharply, holding his two hands up in front of him for a second time today.

"Wait, wait, wait! Cooper. Damn it, stop trying to kill me for just a second! She's human!"

I stand stock still and he sighs, squaring his shoulders when I don't move to attack him again.

"She saw you get hit by a van, for fuck's sake. Yesterday! She knows how badly you were hurt. How are you going to explain this?" He waves his hand up and down at my mangled, but healing body. "How are you going to explain that you're up on your feet and walking around less than twenty-four hours later?" I pause and my stomach plummets.

He's right.

I don't want to scare her, and that means staying away. This hospital caters to both humans and shifters, but in different wings, ensuring there are no suspicions raised by our rapid healing.

"But she's my mate," I sulk. I hear Leila gasp from the corner of the room as she finally catches on to what is happening. I slump down, defeated, with my head in my hands.

This is unbelievable.

The second time being near her in the last twenty-four hours and I still can't see her.

I've heard all the stories about the mate pull, and I have longed for many, many years to experience it for myself. Now, I'm desperate to get to her. It feels like my skin is crawling with the urge to get up and go to her, to ignore the consequences. Logically, I know Ethan is right, but every fibre of my being is screaming at me to tear the building apart to find her.

My anguish must show on my face as both Leila and Ethan look like they're ready to throw themselves on top of me if I try to get out of this room again.

I twist to fix Ethan with a stare, pointing a finger at him. "You! You make sure she is safe. If anything happens to her, I will end you."

Ethan nods, still smiling despite my threats.

"And you," I face Leila and plead, "please get me out of here. I will tear this place apart if I stay here knowing she's in the same building."

She nods and leaves the room immediately, hopefully setting things in motion for my discharge. Given that most of the town's residents are wolf shifters, the staff is used to treating rapidly healing wounds, where making correctly setting bones is normally their greatest concern.

Before he leaves, Ethan places his hand on my shoulder, and, throwing back his head, he laughs as if seeing me so tormented is the best thing he has witnessed in a long time.

"Congratulations, man. You found your mate!" he cheers, laughing some more.

I try to console myself with the thought that this separation is only temporary and wince as I lie back down on the crisp sheets. Letting out a loud sigh, I wonder how long this torture is going to last.

CHAPTER 4
HAYLEY

The next morning, a nurse arrives after breakfast and hands me two plastic bags. They stink. She raises the first one and holds it out for me to take.

"Your hoodie and runners from the scene of the accident, Ethan dropped them off last night, along with your keys and phone, which were still in the pockets. He drove your car back here from the park rather than leaving it there overnight." She holds up the other bag, "These ... are the mucky, wet shorts and top you came in. You need something dry to wear home, so I brought you something fresh."

I wrinkle my nose and reluctantly take the bags. I hope I don't smell as bad as these.

"Oh, yuck," I say as I look at the wet dirty clothes through the plastic.

"Yep," she responds, obviously keen to get rid of the offending items. She hands me some green scrubs.

"Thanks," I mutter, mulling over what she has just said. "Wait, he drove my car here?" I stare at her in shock.

"Perks of living in a small town, honey. I don't think he minded helping the gorgeous young lady who saved the life of his Al... best friend. It's the least he could do."

A beep draws my attention to one bag, the dry one, and I fish my phone from the bottom. As I thought, I have one message and it's from my boss, Greg. That sad fact perfectly sums up the state of my social life since arriving here: there is lying low, and then there's becoming a complete hermit. I seem to have accomplished the latter.

Greg heard what happened and wants me to stay home tomorrow, which is fine by me. That the news of my hospital stay has reached him in record time doesn't surprise me. I grew up in a small town similar to Grey Ridge, and I know everyone has probably been talking about what happened. Living in a place where everyone knows everyone can be good and bad, but the strong sense of community that exists here just can't be found in a big city. I've missed that.

I change into the scrubs the nurse brought, along with my hoodie and runners, eager to get home for a long soak in a warm bubble bath and a decent sleep. I catch a glimpse of myself in the mirror and grimace. My lank hair badly needs a wash and I have dark circles under my eyes. I tuck my bag of wet running gear under my arm, and while tempted to throw them in the bin instead of dealing with the smell in my car, money is tight, so I carry them with me.

After visiting the nurse's station to sign some forms, I step out the front doors and laugh to myself as I spot my little red hatchback parked in the first parking spot, as close to the front door as it could possibly be.

How on earth did he manage that?

I thought I'd be wandering up and down the aisles of cars like an idiot, pressing my key fob until I spotted some flashing lights. Given how exhausted I feel, I'm touched by the sweet gesture.

Throwing my stuff onto the passenger seat, I lower myself behind the wheel when the sliding doors of the hospital open, and Ethan strolls out. His head snaps up immediately, like he could sense me, but his smile disappears the second he sees me, the colour draining from his face.

"Oh, hey, Hayley," he calls out awkwardly. He jogs over to me, glancing back over his shoulder twice, a tight smile on his face. It doesn't quite reach his eyes and it looks forced; his demeanour is anything but relaxed.

"You didn't have to do this, Ethan," I gesture to my car as we stand talking over the door, "but I appreciate it. Thanks."

"No problem at all, we have to look after the new town hero," he jokes, glancing over his shoulder again and positioning himself in front of me. I try to peer around him to see what has his attention, but he's conspicuously blocking my view of the hospital doors. And he's jumpy.

"Listen, I have to go, but I'll catch up with you later, yeah?" He winks, leaning over to give me a quick peck on the cheek, and darts away.

That's when I see a tall, stunning woman with long dark hair step outside; she's pushing a man in a wheelchair. Ethan rushes to the woman's side and slips an arm casually around her shoulder, whispering something in her ear. She looks around frantically, then locks eyes with me. Her face lights up in a massive grin even as Ethan takes control of both her and the wheelchair, hurrying them away.

Strange.

CHAPTER 5

COOPER

Grumpy doesn't even begin to describe my mood when my sister insists on pushing me out of the hospital in a wheel-chair. It's humiliating for an alpha shifter like me. It's only been 24 hours since the accident, but I'm perfectly capable of walking. I have general aches and pains where my bones have knit back together, and at the surgical incision, but all of that should fade over the next few days.

The gust of fresh air that blows across my face as she wheels me outside towards the car park feels wonderful. I hate being cooped up inside for long, and now that I am outdoors, I feel a bit more positive. I am alive. I have a mate who I am going to spend the rest of my days making happy, even if she doesn't know it yet.

My Luna.

As a human, she probably knows nothing about shifters. Ethan was right. If I had run to her and started talking about mates, declaring my undying love and devotion to her, she would have thought I was insane. She will feel a connection with me, but if I scare her out of her wits, that won't matter. I need to be clever and take things slowly.

"This way guys. Come on, quick, quick, quick," Ethan says as he reappears beside us at the front of the single-story red brick hospital, looking flushed and slightly guilty.

He steers the wheelchair in the opposite direction we were just going, pushing me along as fast as he can. I hear him whisper something to Leila, but my head is still pounding so I can't concentrate enough to pick up what it was. Ethan opens the door to the SUV parked at the end of the path and all but tosses me into the passenger seat.

"You'd make a terrible nurse. Do you know that?" I grumble, trying to re-arrange myself into a position that doesn't hurt my incision.

"What's going on Ethan?" I ask, picking up on Ethan's increased heartbeat as he slides into the driver's seat beside me. He's nervous, and my wolf is getting restless again. I can tell he's hiding something from me, so I glare at him, releasing a little of my alpha power to force him to fess up.

As Leila opens the door to hop in the backseat, a breeze blows in, and that amazing smell hits my nose again.

My mate.

Ethan is already driving by the time take another sniff. It's strong, and recent. I would have smelled it sooner if it wasn't for my busted face.

"Ethan, where is she? Why is her scent all over you?" I grit out, "Again?" and clench my hands into fists.

"She's here. That's why we need to go before you do something daft," he says. "I just kissed her goodbye, that's all. She's hot, dude. I must admit, I was kind of hoping she wasn't yours." He winks at me and laughs, moving as far away from me in his seat as possible, but I punch him hard in the shoulder.

"Ethan, what's wrong with you? Do you have a death wish?" Leila exclaims and smacks him on the back of the head, sitting back in her seat to laugh at his antics.

"Stop fucking touching my mate!" I shout and he winces, rubbing his arm, but he's still smirking as he seems to find great entertainment in my situation. I ignore him and stare out the window, trying to get a glimpse of her, but I can't see anyone.

My heart sinks as Ethan tears out of the car park and drives me away from my mate. Again.

CHAPTER 6

COOPER

Silence, for the entire thirty-minute drive home.

I'm trying to stay calm, fighting the urge to kick Ethan and Leila out of the car so I can race straight back to the hospital. I know Ethan is just winding me up, but I still want to tear his head off for daring to touch what is mine.

My old, beat-up blue pickup is parked alongside my small log cabin as we pull in; beside it, my dad's shiny brand new one. A loud sigh escapes my lips as I swivel and glare at my sister in the back seat, who at least has the good grace to look ashamed of herself.

"You told them?" I ask her in disbelief, "I haven't even met her yet, and you told them? What are we, seventeen again?"

"I was just so excited!" she says sheepishly. "And I only told Dad. I'm not stupid. Mum would already be in the hospital trying to fit her for a wedding dress if she knew."

I wish she were joking, but that sounds about right.

Hopefully, Dad had the good sense to keep it to himself. I climb gingerly out of the truck and walk slowly up my porch steps. Even with wolf healing, I still feel like I've been hit by, well, a van. I need to rest.

As I let myself into my home, I look at the rustic place with fresh eyes. Now it is potentially my home with my mate. No way am I bringing her to stay in the packhouse with all those unmated males wandering around. A small rumble starts in my chest just at the thought of it, and Ethan throws me a curious look as I cough to cover it up. I wonder what she'll think of this place. Is it good enough for her?

I immediately regret all the smart-ass comments I have made to the mated members of the pack when they do sappy romantic things for their mates. I understand the impulse now.

As soon as I walk through the door, my father stands and shakes my hand, pulling me into a man-hug, thumping my back. I can feel his pride as he beams at me as if I have done something epic – instead of stumbling across my mate. My parents are fated mates, and I know they are dying for us all to experience the same thing.

"It's good to see you home already, boy," his deep voice warm and emotional. "This is just wonderful. Not only are you in one piece, but you've found your mate. This calls for a celebration." He hands me a beer and, even though he has stepped away, his hand remains on my shoulder, squeezing repeatedly as he tries to contain his enthusiasm.

I shoot another glare at Leila, who shrugs. She obviously didn't give him the full story. Dad was probably planning his retirement on the way over here, working out how quickly he can hand the pack over to me now that I've found my luna.

"I must be the only one who doesn't feel like celebrating," I growl, sinking onto the couch and taking a long draw of beer. My father looks from me to Leila and back again, puzzled.

"She's human, Dad. I haven't even met her; she'd have seen that my injuries have already healed." My father's jaw drops, and, for a moment, the man who has known exactly what to do throughout my entire life is stunned into silence. "What the hell am I supposed to do? How do I explain all of this?" I gesture back and forth between us.

He can sense my misery, so he plonks himself down on the worn leather couch beside me, thumping his hand on my knee in an awkward attempt to comfort me. Any mated wolf understands the strength of the bond's pull, especially in those first moments of recognition. He knows how crazy my wolf must be to get to her.

I tip my head back and stare at the ceiling, throwing my feet up and wallowing in self-pity and frustration. Ethan and Leila are loitering just inside the front door, ready to pounce if I decide to make a break for it.

Thankfully, my father's silence doesn't last long, and he switches into Alpha mode, taking control of the situation. He just can't help himself and, for once, I am extremely grateful.

"This pity party is not very becoming of the future Alpha, Cooper. No son of mine is going to sit here and drown his sorrows," he says pointedly, snatching the bottle out of my hand. I sigh and raise my eyes to heaven, resisting the urge to remind him that he was the one who gave me the beer in the first place. Leila snorts, keeping her head down, trying to hide behind a curtain of hair.

"Right, practical stuff to start with. While I've never heard of an Alpha being mated to a human, I have seen it before in other wolves. It's rare. Your wolf is frantic, and he will remain so, tormenting you until you mate and mark her." Like he needs to tell me any of that. "You'll feel better if you at least know she's safe; so, find out where she lives and where she works."

I nod. I should have thought of that myself.

"Most importantly, don't tell anyone who she is to you until she knows what you are and has accepted you." He looks straight at my sister, "And for God's sake, don't tell your mother!" Sighing, he turns his attention back to me. "I don't care how excited you are. If anyone outside the pack finds out, she'll be in danger. And you'll have opened up the genuine possibility that your mother will kidnap her for you."

Ethan smirks, but nobody else laughs because we all know it's a distinct possibility.

"Go and see her. It should help your wolf relax enough to be tolerable. Just don't do anything stupid. Then stay away. Use that time to work out how you can woo her.

Ethan sniggers from where he's standing at the door, and I shoot daggers at him. My father and Leila try to hide their smiles.

"Woo her? For fuck's sake," I mutter, "what does that even mean? You are all loving this a little too much." I stab my finger in Leila and Ethan's direction.

THE ALPHA'S SAVIOUR   25

"It's okay big bro, we can have a rom-com marathon; you can get some pointers." A giggle bursts past her lips.

She knows I'm totally out of my depth. Wolf mating is normally straightforward: meet your mate, feel the pull, recognise each other immediately, mate and mark each other, live happily ever after. The relationship comes after; with a true mate bond, both wolves know they're meant for each other, perfect for in every way.

Except my mate. She hasn't a clue about any of this.

"Patience, son. I know it's going to be harder than you imagined, but she will be worth it. Fate has put you together for a reason." My dad thumps my leg again then stands to leave, ushering Ethan and Leila out in front of him.

Grimacing as I stretch out my long legs, I feel calmer now. Go see her, come up with a plan to make her mine, try not to come across like a stalker. Simple. Just be cool.

After dusk, armed with an address Ethan found, I leave my house without locking the front door, as always, and shift into my wolf. Bounding off the porch and into the trees, I know the house where she's living. It was empty for a while, and I hadn't realised someone bought it. It's crazy to think she has been nearby, and I haven't realised it sooner.

My sleek, black wolf glides silently through the forest, and in no time, we are sitting on the crest of a small hill that runs down to the back of her property. I can smell her everywhere; she must come out here a lot. The house is an old ranch-style wooden cabin that has seen better days. It needs a good bit of work to bring it back to its former glory. It's bigger than my place, too much for one person.

Does she already have a husband? A family? Is that why she needs all this space?

Running a lap around the house, I don't pick-up any other potent scents. In fact, it doesn't appear that anyone else has been here in quite a while, which is strange. I know she's new to town, but no one else has been here.

All the lights are off downstairs, only the soft glow of a bedside lamp shines from what must be the master bedroom. Satisfied that there is no immediate threat to my mate, or any other men around here to steal her from me, my wolf relaxes. I return to my spot on the hill and settle in for the night, happy knowing that my girl is safe.

CHAPTER 7

COOPER

lift my head from my front paws and stand to shake off some dead leaves clinging to my fur. I'm shocked to find that I've slept until dawn. Hiding in my mate's back garden isn't the ideal way to ensure a good night's sleep, but it did the trick, her scent comforting my wolf as I slept.

Standing slowly, I shake out my limbs, still marvelling at how much better I feel, when I hear the latch on the back door click, and the door swings open.

My heart jumps into my mouth as she steps out and turns to lock the door behind her. Her head tilted to the side while she slips on some headphones, waves of toffee-coloured hair cascade over her tanned shoulders, shimmering with natural blonde highlights from lots of time spent outdoors. I admire her slim, toned legs that seem to go on forever, and the tiny running shorts she has on. I never really considered myself a leg man, but I am now.

Staying away is going to be tough.

She finally turns toward the woods and my breath catches as I get my first glimpse of her face. She's stunning. I stare at her almond-shaped eyes and full, pink lips, and my heart soars. She's perfect.

Without realising what I'm doing until it's too late, I take a step toward her, and the movement catches her attention. Eyes locking onto mine, she freezes at the sight of me: a very large, black wolf standing in the trees only a few feet away.

Hayley

My mouth drops open, and I stare at the wolf in wonder. It's magnificent. I should probably be scared, but I know it's more nervous of me. I take a few slow steps backward, and my heart rate settles a bit as the wolf turns, bolting into the trees. My hands are trembling slightly as I open the door and step backward into the house, never turning my back until I am safely indoors.

Peer through the window, I can't see it anymore, but I've never seen such a beautiful creature that close before. The intensity of its stare had set my heart racing; yet, somehow, I wasn't afraid. The wolf seemed to be as stunned as me by our encounter.

I wonder if a jet-black wolf is rare. And the size of it! Was it unusually large, or had I just not appreciated how big they could be?

Deciding my run can wait for another day, I snatch my car keys and wallet from the kitchen counter and head for the front of the house. I have a never-ending list of DIY projects and I might as well take advantage of this unexpected long weekend.

"Hayley!" A familiar voice breaks my thoughts and I look up to see Ethan strolling towards me down the aisle of the local hardware store with a big smile on his face.

"Oh, hey there. How are you doing, Ethan?" I try to keep my tone casual, throwing some paint samples into the trolley.

"Great, but what are you doing here? I thought you'd be resting at home." He investigates my cart: tape, brushes, tins of paint, tiles, and grout. He raises an eyebrow.

"I'm fine. It was nothing a good night's sleep couldn't fix. I only just moved in, so I decided to do some bits around the house. I'm trying to do as much of it myself as I can."

He nods but doesn't look confident in my abilities. I try not to take it personally. I know I don't look like I'd be handy, but it's amazing what you can teach yourself when you have no money. Thank you, YouTube.

"I presume it's your place if you're doing all this work?" He trails along beside me as I move down the aisles.

"Yep. I'm going to turn it into a bed-and-breakfast, rent out a few rooms to get some extra income. But it needs to be a bit more presentable before I can do that." I gesture to the loaded trolley. He steps in front of me, blocking the way, and frowns, arms crossed over his muscular chest.

"So, you're going to have complete strangers coming and going, staying overnight… in your home?"

When I nod, he lets out a long breath and shakes his head as if this is the worst news he has ever heard. It's a tad dramatic.

"That's the general premise of a B&B. I won't make much money if I don't let people stay overnight." I am baffled by his reaction. He's making it sound like it's the most bizarre idea he's ever heard.

"It's not safe," he states flatly, and I swear I see his pale blue eyes darken.

I roll my eyes. Great, another guy who thinks he knows what I should be doing. My brother isn't in the country to give me shit, so the gods have sent someone else to do it.

"Oh, yes, because you regularly hear stories of bed-and-breakfast owners being killed in their sleep by guests," I say sarcastically, and his frown deepens. "Anyway, it's probably safer than a single girl living out in the woods all by herself. Not that it's any of your business." I push the trolley around him, still looking very disturbed, and start loading up my items at the cash register.

Ethan eventually follows, helping me to pack and load my purchases into the boot of my little car. It's only as I drive off that I realise he didn't buy anything or go back inside after I left.

Was he just in there looking for me?

CHAPTER 8

HAYLEY

When I arrive at work on Tuesday morning, it's immediately clear that news of my dramatic weekend has reached everyone in the office.

An enormous bunch of flowers and a hamper of muffins await me at reception. Everybody keeps hugging me, which seems over the top since I only started at this accountancy firm six weeks ago and have largely kept to myself.

Angela, the receptionist, has tears in her eyes as she goes in for a second squeeze, and I realise they aren't happy that I am ok, but that Cooper is. He appears to be equally loved by all my colleagues, and they appear genuinely shaken-up by the whole thing.

Who is he that everyone is so concerned about him, and why haven't I heard of him until now?

Letting me go, Angela hands me a stack of messages.

"Everyone wants to talk to you after that article in the paper yesterday. We've had reporters calling non-stop." She obviously expects me to be thrilled about being the local celebrity for a few days, but it's the last thing I want. If my cover has been blown, I'm not moving again. I've had enough.

"Thanks, Angela. Can you keep pretending I'm not here unless you know who it is? I just want to get back to work," I ask her, and she looks disappointed. It's probably the most excitement they've had in the office for a long time, maybe ever, and I'm shutting it down.

"Are you sure you're alright to be back in today?" Greg peers over the top of his glasses with concern, stepping out of his office to greet me.

"I appreciate you worrying about me, but I promise I'm okay. They only kept me overnight as a precaution." He smiles brightly and grabs one of my hands in both of his, a surprisingly warm gesture from my new boss, who has been friendly but quite formal since I started. Greg clears his throat and drops my hand as if remembering himself.

"Well, anyway, back to business. It just so happens Cooper's father, Jonathan Jones, has dropped in some documents for us to review ahead of a potential acquisition. The Jones's already have two spa resorts and are looking at buying a third. Could you have a look? That's more your area of expertise than mine."

"Of course. No problem," I say, delighted to get stuck into something interesting for a potential new client.

I have barely sat down at my desk when my office door bursts open and a glamorous lady with sleek brown hair barges in without knocking, closely followed by the dark-haired beauty I saw with Ethan at the hospital.

"Mom! You can't just walk in! Knock!" Up close, she is even more stunning. Shiny chestnut hair hangs to the middle of her back, and her gorgeous olive skin sets off hazel eyes and full red lips. I take in the other lady and, if she hadn't just announced this was her mother, I would have thought they were sisters. The benefits of good genes are clearly on display right in front of me.

"Hush, Leila, everyone here knows me. They don't mind!" She tuts, then faces me with a megawatt smile. My eyebrows shoot to my hairline as I'm fixed with her laser-like attention.

"Hayley! Oh, thank you, thank you!" With another hug, she hangs on to me for dear life, keeping me there a few seconds longer than I am comfortable with, especially since I have no clue who she is. I flick my eyes to meet this Leila's, who rolls her own and groans.

"Mum, get off her. She doesn't know who you are. You're going to scare her," Leila chastises, answering my silent plea for help.

"Forgive my terrible manners! I'm Cooper's mother, Marie Jones. This is his sister, Leila," she says, still holding onto my upper arms but pushing back enough to look me in the eye. She beams, again staring a little longer than I would deem normal, as she checks me out from head to toe. Leila shakes her head behind her mother's back.

"Ah, Mrs. Jones... or, sorry, Marie? Lovely to meet you," I correct myself when she scowls at my formal greeting.

"Would you like to sit down? How is Cooper?" I gesture to the two chairs in front of my desk, retreating to the safety of my chair. Leila tries to refuse, but Marie immediately sits down, prompting an exasperated sigh from her daughter.

"Mum let's go. I am sure Hayley has other things to do. Like her job." Marie studiously ignores her.

"Oh, he's doing great, isn't he, Leila? And it's all thanks to you." I shift in my seat, uncomfortable with praise for doing what anyone would have done.

"Ethan tells me you pulled him out of the water all on your own and brought him back to life. I will forever consider you family for what you have done for mine."

I am completely taken aback. That is quite a declaration.

"That sounds more like a punishment than anything else, Mum," Leila teases, and I have to stifle a laugh. Marie's lips tip up at the edges, but she ignores the dig.

"Wow, well, thank you for your kind words. I'm just glad I was in the right place at the right time. Please tell Cooper that I asked after him and wish him a speedy recovery. I'm sure I'll bump him at some point..." I need to wrap this up. The attention this has brought to me is already making me nervous. That his parents are wealthy business owners has no bearing on how I would have done things, but it explains why there is seemingly so much interest from the local press.

"Leila's birthday! You must come, I won't take 'no' for an answer. Leila, take Hayley out for lunch this week and let her know the plans," Marie insists, not leaving any opportunity for either of us to protest. I nod, and Leila grins encouragingly.

"That's a great idea, Mum. Now let's leave Hayley in peace."

I've been trying to keep to myself, but it's been nearly two months since I moved here, and I need to make some friends eventually if I'm going to stick around. Leila seems nice, and it'll be good to have some proper non-work conversation.

As they finally move to leave, a gigantic shadow fills the doorway, a deep, masculine voice booming out, "Hey, Hayls, I stopped by yesterday, but..." Marcus freezes the second he steps into my already tiny but now absolutely jammed office. He is a mountain of a man, six-foot-five and a wall of solid muscle. "Leila, Mrs. Jones, my apologies for interrupting." He nods politely, awkwardly holding out the cup of coffee he's carrying to me.

The tension in the room is palpable as I take it from him. It doesn't escape my notice that he looks everywhere he can but at Leila, who is wringing her hands in her lap and studying them intently.

Marcus clears his throat, "I stopped by yesterday, but they said you were taking the day off. I need to get your statement about the accident." We've already had this conversation on the phone, so I feel like he is justifying his presence to the others rather than to me.

I chance another look at Leila, who is blushing to her roots, and I suppress a grin. Very interesting. Marie looks back and forth between Marcus and me and grins, clearly getting the wrong idea about where the awkwardness in the room was coming from.

"Oh, I see! Don't let us keep you, dear," she laughs and winks, waving goodbye while Leila practically runs from the office. I turn to Marcus, who has a pained expression on his face, and laughter bursts from my lips before I can help myself.

"Marcus, what was that? You and Leila, eh?" The man looks completely lost as he rubs a hand along the back of his neck and gives me a one-shouldered shrug.

Marcus is the sheriff, and I went to visit him to explain my situation as soon as I came to town. He has been kind enough to check in with me regularly since then, and I suspect he drives by the house on his shifts as he always comments on the little bits of work I have done. He is as close to a friend as I have here.

"No. I mean... it's complicated." He obviously has no intentions of elaborating further. The big man doesn't look so tough now, flustered and desperate to change the topic.

"I bet it is." I wink at him and laugh when he groans out loud.

CHAPTER 9

COOPER

These have been the longest three weeks of my life.

Absolute hell.

But today, I have a spring in my step, because I can finally meet my beautiful Hayley. My nights have been filled with dreams of her. During the day, my thoughts return to her over and over, wondering where she is and what she is doing. I've spent more than a few nights sleeping on the hill overlooking her house, my wolf content the closer he is to her.

I am getting no work done, and my short temper is driving everyone around me crazy. Ethan has bumped into her a few times over the last few weeks, by accident-on-purpose, and some of the mated males from the pack have been keeping an eye on her house in the evenings.

While knowing she is okay has kept me sane, it has not been enough to satisfy my wolf. I am exhausted from fighting his urges to go to her. My mother's insistence that she saw 'a spark' between Hayley and Marcus when she accosted her in her office has done little to help.

I pick up last week's paper, which I have kept by my side, staring at it every day. Under the front-page article on the accident and my near drowning, there are pictures of Hayley and I, right beside each other. I must admit, I think we look good.

From what Ethan has told me, she still refuses to accept even the slightest bit of praise for what she did and was not one bit happy to see the story in the paper. She's not loving the attention at all, and I feel bad that it might make her uncomfortable.

Modest as well as beautiful.

I sent her a thank-you card, which included my number, a few days after the accident, but, other than that, I've stayed away. I hoped she would respond, but I haven't heard from her.

Hayley told Ethan that the house is hers, not rented. The knowledge that she has moved to Grey Ridge, intending to stay, laying down roots, cheered me up. At least she isn't planning on going anywhere in the short term.

Draining my coffee and pulling on my boots, I shake out my hands and force myself to remain composed.

This whole mate thing still has me reeling. My emotions are all over the place, but if I have any chance of winning her over, I'll need to make sure I don't come across as too aggressive. Alpha males are not exactly known for their patience. I'll have to temper my natural tendencies until I have her trust. I will have to tell her at some point, about what I am and who she is to me, but I want her to get to know me as a man first.

That's the plan, anyway.

My gut twists at the thought of her bolting.

I turn my truck into her driveway, and I take in the house properly for the first time through human eyes. It is in a spectacular location. I can see the potential, with the woods behind it, the large front lawn leading to the edge of the lake. A small, private jetty off to the side providing an amazing view from the full- length front porch. It just needs some love.

As I approach the end of the driveway, I spot her in the garden. In an instant, all thoughts of boring renovations go flying out of my head and there is only her. It feels almost surreal that my wait is finally over.

She is facing away from me, wearing shorts again, weeding the flower beds that run along the edge of the lawn. I groan as the sight of her bending over sends filthy thoughts racing through my mind. As she hears the truck tires crunching over the gravel, she turns to see who it is, raising a gloved hand to shield her eyes from the sun.

She blows a lock of caramel hair out of her eyes, and it might just be the cutest thing I have ever seen.

Stepping out of the truck, I can tell that she recognises me. Her expression goes from cautious to open in an instant. Her eyes open wide, and a warm smile spreads across her face, her delighted reaction filling me with joy. I know in that second that I will do anything in my power to make her smile like that every day for the rest of our lives.

"Hi there. I hope I'm not disturbing you. I'm Cooper Jones." I remember to walk a little gingerly, like someone recovering from surgery but not yet fully healed. Her gaze drifts over me from head to toe as she crosses the lawn, pulling off her purple gardening gloves as she walks. Her tongue flicks out to moisten her plump pink lips, and I clench my fists by my sides to stop myself from grabbing her and kissing her right there and then.

"Not at all. It's good to see you up and about. You look fantastic," she says enthusiastically. As soon as the words are out of her mouth, her cheeks flush. "Compared to the last time I saw you I mean!" she corrects, flustered by her blatant admission that she was checking me out. I try not to grin too hard, totally thrilled to know that she's not completely unaffected by me.

For the first time in weeks, I feel a bit more confident that I can make this work.

"So, what can I do for you?" she asks, gazing up at me now with a serious expression, and my short-lived confidence fades. She has no concept of mates, and it's clear that she isn't going to just leap into my arms as a she-wolf would. In a way I like it, I'm going to have to work harder, and wolves love a good chase. I rub my hand across the back of my neck like a nervous schoolboy as I try to remember what I planned to say, but any game I thought I had has completely deserted me.

"I wanted to thank you in person for what you did." I look her straight in the eye and I see her pupils dilate slightly, the eye contact feeling powerful and intimate, "And to apologise for my mother barging in on you at work, she can be full-on."

She lets out a big laugh at that but doesn't deny it.

"I should be the one thanking you. It's been great getting to know Leila. It's nice to meet someone else in town."

I must thank Leila for making her feel at home in Grey Ridge, but I notice she ignores my thanks. Ethan was spot on about the modesty part.

"Ethan mentioned you are doing some work on your place, and that just so happens to be my line of business." I nod my head towards my truck, which has Jones Construction and our logo printed on the passenger side door.

"You're here looking for business?" She tilts her head to the side with a little frown, and I wonder if she is disappointed to think that this is all I am here for.

"That's definitely not all I'm here for," I lean in closer, revelling in the little flush that shows on her cheeks at the subtle insinuation. "But considering what you did for me, I'd like to do something for you."

She squints her eyes at me suspiciously as she takes a step in, bringing our bodies dangerously close together. It's my heart rate that picks up this time as a waft of her delicious scent hits me. This is the strongest blast of it I have gotten yet, and it's heavenly.

"I'm not going to let you fix up my house for free," she states in a tone that leaves me in no doubt that she means what she is saying, and that bit of defiance turns me on more than I expected.

"I was going to suggest a friends and family discount," I lie through my teeth. I have no intention of letting her pay me for anything, but I need to get her to agree.

She hesitates for a second, pursing her lips, and I can nearly see her internal struggle between not wanting to accept help but still being tempted by the offer. Ethan told me how she is doing as much as she can herself on the weekends.

"You don't owe me anything. I was just in the right place at the right time," she hedges, but she taps at her lower lip with her index finger as if she is still pondering my proposal. I can't help but stare at the movement. I want to suck that bottom lip between mine and ravish her mouth until those lips are pink and swollen. Pulling my thoughts back out of the gutter, I look her straight in those gorgeous eyes, sneaking another inch or two nearer.

"I know, but please consider it. It would make me happy. Why don't you show me what you need to do and at least let me give you some quotes? If you decide to go with someone else, I won't hold it against you." I wink, and I see her resolve crack. She chuckles and smiles openly at me, blushing slightly again at my cheekiness.

"Some help would be great. I have been teaching myself some things as I go, with online videos, but some of it is beyond my skills," she admits. That she has nobody to help her with the work confirms that there is no other man in the picture. That thought makes my day. Looks like I won't have to fall out with Marcus after all.

"Great. Do you have time now to show me?" I am taking this as a win and decide to press on quickly before she has the chance to change her mind.

"Ok, yeah, sure. Just give me a minute to clean up." I follow her up the steps and onto the wide porch that runs the length of the front of the house – trying not to stare at her perfect ass when she bends again to toe off her mucky boots.

I bite my tongue and try to think unsexy thoughts to tame the semi that has appeared, making my jeans uncomfortably tight. Nothing like a raging hard-on to make things awkward with someone you just met.

"It's a beautiful house," I say, trailing along behind her as she heads in the front door and around the corner into the large kitchen.

"It is, or it will be again when it's finished. The roof is the only major thing that needs fixing, but I want to make some changes to the layout, open it up a bit. Then do some small repairs and painting. I'll try to do most of the garden myself." She keeps chatting as she washes her hands at the sink with her back to me, my gaze travelling over the curve of her hips and down her long, bare legs.

"I want to keep most of it open-plan downstairs, but I'll keep one ensuite bedroom for anyone who has problems with stairs, and one room I can use as a separate dining room for guests," she continues.

My attention is immediately drawn from her body and back to what she's saying.

"Wait... what?" I ask sharply, and she turns to look at me as she dries her hands slowly on the towel with a puzzled look on her face.

"I told Ethan, sorry. I'm turning this place into a bed-and-breakfast. There are plenty of rooms and it'll give me some extra income."

Oh hell no.

Absolutely no way. No way is my mate going to be living in a house, unprotected, with a stream of strangers coming in and out through those doors, sleeping just down the hall from her.

Over my dead body.

Concern and possessiveness rage through my system in equal measures, and I struggle to push down the desire to openly demand that she change her plans. I turn away, pretending to consider what changes she could make to the space so that she doesn't see my eyes, which have no doubt flashed to gold.

"Ethan never mentioned that," I say in what I hope sounds like a casual voice.

I'll kill him.

"But... are you sure it's safe?" I ask.

It's not safe!

My brain is screaming at me to tell her that under no circumstances can she have other men staying here, that nobody other than me should sleep under her roof, ever again. If she wasn't a human, that's exactly what I would say.

She walks around the island and stands just a foot away from me, and this near, her scent is intoxicating. I itch to pull her to me. She looks up and meets my gaze defiantly, with a subtle smirk on her face, as if she sees straight through my fake calm façade and knows exactly what I am trying so hard not to say.

"That's funny. That's the same thing that Ethan said. It's almost as if you boys think a girl like me isn't capable of taking care of herself," she muses.

She doesn't wait for me to answer as she turns and goes to step away again. Before she can, I grab her hand and pull her back; she's only a few inches from me, and sparks of electricity fly up my fingers at the skin-to-skin contact. A small gasp passes between her lips as we touch, and her eyes flick up to meet mine. I hope that means she felt it, too; not that I have overstepped the mark.

My answer comes quickly as a hint of her sweet arousal teases my senses.

"I didn't mean it to sound like that. I know you can probably take care of yourself, but there's nothing wrong with having other people looking out for you sometimes, too." I dip my head down so that we are eye to eye, and she can see my sincerity. She eyes me dubiously for a second, and unconsciously pulls her hand back, bringing it up to her chest, placing it right over her heart – which is pounding. Just like mine.

"Good, because I seem to remember I was the one who dragged your ass out of the river, not the other way around. You seem to be the one who needs looking out for around here." She rolls her eyes at me, but grins, letting me know she's not genuinely annoyed, and it makes me laugh out loud.

As the future Alpha of my pack, and a powerful wolf, there are very few people who have the nerve to roll their eyes at me or tease me. But, I suppose, my mate was always going to be someone strong enough to challenge me.

I spend the next hour following her around the house, taking notes as she points out the various jobs, making small talk about the town, restaurants to try, bars to avoid, and her work. It's pure bliss just to be in her company at long last. Every time she laughs it's like sunshine, and it makes me feel like a king to make her happy. When I see my card in her room, and it's covered in her scent, my chest swells. She's kept it, and picked it up over and over, even if she doesn't understand why.

It has to mean something.

I'm tempted to drag out the visit, because I never want to leave her side again, but I don't want to make her uncomfortable. I promise to get back in touch with some quotes and details of when I can spare a few of the young guys to help her out.

As I leave, I can't help myself and reach for the doorknob at the same time she does so I can 'accidentally' touch her again. I want to feel her small, soft hand underneath mine so it can set my heart racing.

I hear her heart suddenly beating loudly again, and she tilts her head up slowly, locking eyes with me.

The light-hearted atmosphere between us has transformed, the air suddenly thickens with sexual tension. I grab her roughly and haul her body tight to mine for a quick but searing kiss.

Despite every fibre of my body telling me to do the opposite, I force myself to turn away and pull the door open, stepping outside and jogging down the steps. I wave as I climb into my truck and I see her in my rear-view mirror, still watching me from the porch as I drive away, a stunned expression painted on her beautiful face.

CHAPTER 10

COOPER

As I push through the door of Greg's accountancy office, all heads turn to look at me and silence falls.

Even though I pride myself on being approachable and friendly to all pack members, most pack members are naturally submissive to the pack leaders. For those who rarely interact with me, the instinct to submit is hard to overcome and I can feel that they're on edge as soon as I enter the building. I smile politely, nodding at everyone I pass, greeting anyone I recognise by name.

She didn't call me, didn't text me asking what I thought I was doing kissing her like that, but I knew she wouldn't. So here I am, unable to wait any longer to see her again, with a thinly veiled excuse to visit her once more.

I knock gently on Hayley's office door, and, as it is already ajar, push it open slowly without waiting for a response. Hayley is sitting behind her desk, which is covered in a sea of haphazardly piled papers, brightly coloured pens and post-it notes strewn everywhere. Her shoes are under the desk, and her bare feet are tucked up underneath her on the office chair. With a pen jammed through it to keep it in place, hair is pulled up in a messy bun, and she's chewing absently on a highlighter as she gazes down at the pages in her hand.

The top buttons of her blouse are open, and I can see the edge of her lacy white bra, barely visible, but looking unbelievable against her tanned skin. Fuck me, she is sexy.

She is so deeply engrossed in whatever she is reading that she hasn't sensed my presence. I clear my throat to catch her attention.

"Oh gosh, Cooper, I didn't see you there. Come in." She gestures to the seat opposite her desk and unfolds her legs, slipping her pretty feet back into the high heels under her desk.

"Sorry to interrupt, you're busy. I just wanted to drop off these quotes. I was going to suggest we could grab lunch and run through them, but..." I gesture to the mess in front of her.

"Oh this, ha, it's always like this, organised chaos." She laughs. "Don't look so horrified!" She sits back and studies me for a second, then checks her watch.

"Lunch sounds great, actually. My brain needs a break. I've been looking at this for too long." Standing, rubs her eyes and arches to stretch her back, a movement that pulls her blouse tight across her breasts and makes my mouth water.

As she turns to grab a blazer off the back of her chair, her fitted skirt shows off her pert backside when she bends to pick up her purse, I bite back a groan. I turn away to get control of myself before I grab her and kiss her senseless right here in her office.

Or worse.

A smart professional woman might intimidate some guys, but not me. I can't help the thought of her bent over that desk as it pops into my mind.

"I couldn't cope with that mess; it's making me anxious just looking at it," I admit, placing my hand lightly on her lower back as she passes me on the way to the door. Any excuse to touch her and feel those sparks. She laughs again, amused, not offended, by my comment. She walks ahead of me as we leave the building, something a she-wolf would never do.

It's refreshing to be around someone who doesn't act differently just because of who I am.

"I know it drives some people crazy, but it works for me. I don't think my brain works in straight lines." She shrugs unapologetically and turns to me with a breath-taking smile. "So, do you have anywhere in mind?"

"Tina's?" It's a local café, very casual, not where I had originally planned, but now that I'm here, I realise that after my impromptu appearance at her office, the local rumour mill would go into meltdown if I took her anywhere conspicuous. It might do anyhow. I'm supposed to be hiding the fact that she is my mate, not announcing my interest in her to the entire town.

Unfortunately, my love life, or lack thereof, is a popular topic of debate around the pack.`

As I pull out her chair and she sits down, a subtle smell reaches my sensitive nose. I recognise it immediately.

Marcus.

That damn bear is still bringing her coffee. His scent on my mate is irritating my wolf. I need to find out why these two are such great buddies. He barely tolerates anyone else.

"I've listed all the jobs we went over. Let me know how it looks, and which jobs you want me to start for you." I push the papers toward her, and she frowns as she begins flipping through the pages, pursing her full lips adorably.

"Cooper, this is crazy. You're hardly charging me for anything." She looks at me as if I have lost my mind.

"Well, I'm out of action with time to kill, so I might as well make myself useful. Plus, I don't have any work for some of the crew right now, and this would keep them busy instead of temporarily laying them off." She gives me a look that says she does not believe a word that is coming out of my mouth, smart girl, but she doesn't contradict me. "I've priced the materials at cost, but, honestly, all you really need is some extra labour for the smaller jobs."

She still isn't buying it, so I throw some icing on the cake. "My mother doesn't want me to charge you anything at all, so this is a compromise." The mention of my mother seems to have made her soften, as though it's more acceptable to take a gift from a grateful parent rather than directly from me.

"It's far too much, but I'm not going to look a gift horse in the mouth. I appreciate it, and I didn't think I'd be able to afford some of this stuff until next year." She laughs and smiles at me. "My sisters will be eternally grateful that they don't have to earn their keep with hard labour when they come to visit," she adds, and my chest swells at how happy she looks. It's as if I've just taken an enormous weight off her shoulders.

"Sisters?" While I have the chance, I'm keen to know as much about my mate as possible.

"Yes, two. A twin, Zoe; she's a vet, lives in Dexter. My younger sister, Leah, is still finishing college. I have a brother, too, called Chase." She pauses and looks sad for a second as she stares into her coffee.

"Everything okay?" I reach over, putting my hand over hers, and she looks at me with a soft little smile. To my relief, she doesn't pull away from the physical contact. I wasn't sure how she'd react after our kiss yesterday, whether she enjoyed it as much as I did.

"Oh yes, fine. I just miss them. I haven't seen them for a few months. Since Christmas. My parents, too. It's... complicated, but hopefully, they'll be able to come visit soon." I can sense the deception in what she's saying. She's not lying, but there is more to this story than she's letting on.

"You've met Leila, obviously, and I also have two brothers," I try to lighten the conversation again by smiling and sitting back. "Rex is a couple years older than me; he's been travelling for the last year, but he'll be back in a few days." I grimace exaggeratedly and she chuckles at that. "Nathan's the baby of the family and acts like it, too."

"Are you going to come for Leila's birthday?" I ask, aiming to sound nonchalant, but as I meet her twinkling eyes across the table, I don't think I've succeeded.

She grins mischievously, whispering in a low, sultry voice that has my balls tightening in response, "I might be convinced."

She winks, and I chuckle at her playfulness, grinning back at her like an idiot.

The chase is on.

CHAPTER 11

HAYLEY

For the last week and a half, Cooper has arrived early every morning, before the rest of the crew, just to "keep me in the loop".

He appears just in time to enjoy a cup of coffee and a quiet chat on the porch before I dash off to work – and it has become the highlight of my day. Seeing his handsome, smiling face as he climbs out of his truck cheers me up without fail, and just being close to him sets my pulse racing.

I'm drawn to him, his raw animal magnetism doing funny things to my insides every time I see those chocolate brown eyes with flecks of gold that seem to be lit from inside. Strong cheekbones and full lips that I just want to bite, and that dark brown hair that curled a little around his ears, make me melt every time he appears.

No guy I have ever met has taken things this slowly, though, especially after teasing me with that kiss the first day we officially met. I would adore it if it weren't driving me crazy. I want him, and I think he wants me, so what's the problem? Maybe I'm reading the signals completely wrong?

My current predicament is a testament to the fact that I'm not that great at reading people's true intentions. I'm afraid to make a move in case I've got this all wrong. Being the focus of his attention is intoxicating. I bet I could just give myself over to a man like that and he'd know exactly what to do.

Maybe I've officially lost my mind, but maybe losing myself with Cooper Jones for a little while wouldn't be the worst thing in the world.

I already have two mugs in my hand when I hear his heavy boots hit the steps, and my heart skips a beat. He turns straight for the porch swing instead of coming inside, as has become our little routine. I look at the clock and can't help but chuckle: it's 7 am on the dot. I could set my watch by this man. I sit down beside him, a big grin on my face, and hand him his coffee. Tucking my legs underneath myself, we sit in companionable silence for a few minutes.

A light fog still hovers over the lake this early in the morning, and the birds fly low over the water.

He is dressed for a hard day's work in boots, khaki combats, and a white t-shirt, and there is something undeniably sexy about a capable man who can work with his hands. The white sets off his tanned skin beautifully. I want to reach out and touch those curls to see if they're as soft as they look. I want to grab his biceps and see if the muscles there are as hard as they look. I kind of want to bite him, and that's not something I've ever thought before.

He is just so handsome it makes me ache, but there is more going on between us than just that. I feel a connection to him.

He blows the steam coming over the top of the cup, and my gaze falls to his full lips, and I can't stop thinking about how much I want to feel them on my lips, on my body.

Why hasn't he kissed me again?

I sigh in frustration, louder than I meant to, and Cooper turns to me, one dark eyebrow raised in a silent question as he catches me staring at him. I feel my cheeks growing pink and shift awkwardly on the swing. He places his cup gently down on the floor and leans against the back of the swing. Wrapping one arm around my shoulders, he pulls me close and tucks me into his side like it's the most natural thing in the world.

I'm surprised by the gesture, and it takes me a second to recover, but I relax and rest my head on his shoulder. We sit there for another ten minutes, enjoying the peace and quiet, as if it's always been this way.

It feels so right.

That little gesture seems to state an intent. The kiss was about the chemistry between us, but this is about more.

The sound of a pickup truck breaks our little bubble, and I hear laughter and joking as Ethan and Cooper's younger brother Nathan reverses by the side of my house to unload more supplies.

"What are you doing after work?" Cooper asks quietly, his breath tickling my neck while he draws lazy circles on my shoulder with his thumb. Just that small touch has my nerves singing and desire shooting straight to my core. I clench my legs together to ease the tension growing there. I'm still in my bed shorts and tank top with a thin dressing gown covering my pyjamas. Suddenly. I'm very aware that I'm not dressed, yet being pressed against this gorgeous man, and my panties are getting damper with each passing second.

"Nothing. Painting, I guess," I shrug.

"No painting tonight. Take a break. I'll cook dinner for us." He stands and leans over to press a soft kiss to my forehead. "I'll see you when you get home," he whispers close to my ear, and goosebumps cover my skin at the promise those words hold. I nod, still stunned when he steps away from me and heads inside the house as the others come around the corner and into view.

"Morning, gorgeous," Ethan says with a big smile. He is grinning knowingly as he comes up the steps, giving me a quick peck on the cheek as he passes.

"You don't have to let him do that, you know," says Nathan, laughing. "He's not European, he's just a pervert."

Ethan hits Nathan on the back of the head as they follow Cooper indoors.

"It's too good of a chance to wind Cooper up. It helps, of course, that you're cute, Hayley." Ethan winks at me, his blue eyes sparkling with delight as Cooper fixes him with an icy glare. He might be all smiles with me, but I've noticed this side of him emerge when any of the men on site pay attention to me.

It shouldn't make me happy that he seems to make it clear that I'm off-limits to all of them, but it does.

"I might have to get in on that action," Nathan smirks, backing up and pretending to make a move toward me.

"Ha-ha, hilarious, that's enough," Cooper shouts as Nathan gets within arm's reach of me. Nathan halts and lets out a loud laugh, shaking his head.

"Oh, man, this is way too easy. Whatever you have done to my brother Hayley, I love it." Nathan continues to laugh as Cooper throws a chunk of wood at him, cursing them both under his breath. With a big smile plastered to my face, I leave them to their good-natured teasing so I can get ready for the day. It has me feeling truly happy for the first time in a long time.

CHAPTER 12

COOPER

My restraint has been severely tested, every morning, as Hayley greets me in her tiny shorts and tank tops; light dressing gowns do nothing to hide her amazing figure underneath from my hungry gaze.

Something was different this morning, though. I could sense her desire and frustration as she watched me closely on the porch swing. Knowing those idiots would arrive at any minute was the only thing that stopped me from taking her in a kiss that would linger in her mind for the rest of the day. I didn't leave any room for argument when I suggested dinner this evening.

I let the crew finish work early so I could tidy up her place, go home to shower and change, then head to the shops to get the supplies I needed.

I didn't say anything to Ethan or Nathan about my plans, but they have been watching me like a hawk; I'm sure they know I have something up my sleeve. Ethan knows she's my mate, so while he's finding my antics extremely entertaining, at least he understands what's going on.

Nathan, however, ever the ladies' man, is completely gob smacked that I am so smitten with the little human. He already doesn't understand why I refuse to use my status like he does, indulging in countless beautiful women. My interest in Hayley, after years of refusing to even date anyone while waiting for my fated mate, seems like an about-face. I feel bad for not telling him the truth, but he doesn't take the mate bond seriously enough.

I'm worried that if I tell him, he'll make some stupid joke and expose my secret to the pack before I'm ready.

I considered making this dinner a romantic meal with candles, flowers, the works, but I shelved those thoughts pretty quickly. What has worked so far, is keeping things relaxed. I've settled on a simple pasta dinner with some salad and nice bread. Over-the-top, clichéd gestures aren't my thing anyway, so there's no point in pretending I'm something I'm not.

As I potter around the kitchen, preparing our dinner and waiting for Hayley to arrive home, I feel relaxed and happy. I never thought domestic activities would bring me such joy; I'm genuinely looking forward to sharing a meal and spoiling her after a hard day at work.

Maybe I am just getting old and boring, as Nathan and Leila would probably suggest, but I know it's more than that. It's the feelings I am developing for Hayley, more than just the mate bond. The mate bond creates the pull, no doubt about that, but my brother Rex is the perfect example of how a pairing can still go horribly wrong. If there isn't a meeting of minds, the bond can't guarantee a happily ever after.

I sense Hayley before I see her, her delicious smell perking up my wolf. She pushes open the door, her golden eyes sparkling, and flushes as she spots me in her kitchen, wiping down the counters and filling the dishwasher. She drops her bag and car keys onto the hall table and kicks her heels off, pushing them underneath.

Pulling her hair loose, it falls in caramel waves around her slim shoulders. The five-second transformation from professional Hayley to at ease Hayley makes me smile. Her posture relaxes in the time she takes to walk from the front door to the kitchen island.

"It's nothing fancy, so don't get too excited. It will be ready soon, but you have time to get changed," I say as I hand her a chilled glass of white wine. She sighs happily as she takes a sip, resting her hip against the countertop and looking up at me with a twinkle in her eye. I've completely taken over her kitchen, without shame.

"I might just do that – if you don't mind. I promise I'll come back and help you; it smells amazing." She stands on her tippy toes to look over my shoulder into the pot, trying to steal a piece of bread before I wave her out of her kitchen.

"Go, it's all done. Get comfortable and I'll dish it out when you're back."

She disappears up the stairs with her glass of wine, and I hear the shower turning on, her light footsteps as she moves around. Ten minutes later, she re-appears in a simple navy dress, strappy flats, and a delicate gold bracelet on her wrist. Her hair is still down, but she has clipped back some layers at the front to keep them out of her face. She looks stunning as she watches me dish up and put garlic bread into a basket.

"I don't know what I did to deserve this, but I like it," she laughs as I pass by her with the food and set it down on the dining table. She follows me with the bottle of wine in a cooler and a glass for me, sitting down kitty-corner to me at the large rectangular table.

The conversation flows as we tuck into our food, and I laugh more than I can remember doing in years. At least since it was decided I would become the next Alpha of the pack – instead of Rex.

She's cautious when talking about her decision to move here and leave behind what sounds like a close family, a stellar career, and a fun lifestyle. I am guessing there is an ex involved, but she is keeping her cards close to her chest and, to be honest, I don't want to hear about another man. I'm just grateful that he obviously messed up whatever they had badly enough that she doesn't even want to broach the topic. He must be an idiot to let a woman like this get away.

The fact that her family has been absent since she moved here makes me curious, though. They sound like the kind of people who would enjoy helping her with the house renovations, and their conspicuous absence doesn't appear to stem from a falling-out.

After dinner, we move outside to watch the sunset behind the mountains, glasses of wine in hand as we lean against the newly repaired handrail. I can't help myself, and I put my arm around her waist, pulling her close to my side. I place a gentle kiss on her bare shoulder, her skin silky smooth against my lips.

She smells divine.

I use the chill in the air as an excuse to tuck her in front of me, between my body and the railing, and wrap my arms around her. I rest my chin on the top of her head, my chest pressed to her back, trying to get as close to her as I can. She fits against me perfectly.

I can feel her breathing becoming uneven, and sparks fly wherever there is skin-to-skin contact. Immediately, the sexual energy that is always simmering between us becomes palpable. I know she feels it as much as I do. She must feel the bulge in my trousers brush against her ass when I move, and she inhales sharply. I fight the urge to push against her harder so that she can feel exactly what she does to me, settling for holding her close.

I gently brush her hair to one side so that I can access her neck and press small kisses to the top of her back, then to the spot where her neck meets her shoulder – where I will, one day, place my mark.

Continuing along her delicate collarbone, I trail feather-light kisses up the side of her neck to just behind her ear. Goosebumps appear on her skin wherever I've touched her, and I am in love with the soft, breathy moans that are escaping her lips as she tilts her head to the side, letting me know without words that she enjoys this.

I gently turn her around to face me and place a finger under her chin so I can tilt her face up to mine. I keep looking into her beautiful brown eyes as I gently trail my fingers along her jaw and down her neck; along her collarbone, down her arm, and back to her waist. Even though it's all pretty innocent, the unbroken eye contact makes it the most intimate moment I've ever experienced.

Her pupils are blown wide, and her parted lips are just begging to be kissed. I lean down, agonisingly slowly, until our lips are millimetres away and pause, giving her the chance to pull back if this isn't what she wants. She moves only to rock forward ever so slightly, just enough to meet me.

That's all the encouragement I need. I close the gap and press my lips to hers. The kiss is firm but gentle, showing Hayley that I want her, but I also need her to know that this is not just about the chemistry between us.

As I pull her tight to my body, and she feels my hardness between us, she responds by parting her lips and deepening the kiss. She rubs against me as she reaches up to wrap her arms around my neck, pulling me closer and running her hands through my hair. A deep groan passes my lips, and she smiles, obviously enjoying the effect she has on me. I almost purr with satisfaction as her fingers run across my scalp, down my neck, and onto the front of my shirt, gripping it tightly.

Eventually, I force myself to lean back, breaking the hot and heavy kiss, gently placing my forehead against hers and closing my eyes. I take a deep breath, sighing in pleasure. I know that if we continue like this, I won't be able to stop myself from taking her upstairs to christen her new bed. My control is hanging by a thread.

"Holy shit," she whispers dreamily, and I laugh out loud at the bluntness of her comment.

"Exactly what I was thinking," I whisper as my hands roam up and down her back and luscious ass, around her waist and hips. I burn the feeling of her body into my mind, because it will have to do for the moment.

"I need to leave," I say softly. A frown creases the forehead of my little mate, and her nose wrinkles in confusion. "I don't want to, but after a kiss like that, I need to leave or I'll do something ungentlemanly – like throw you over my shoulder and carry you up to bed, right this second."

"Oh," she whispers, smiling as she realises that it's not a rejection, and the scent of her arousal grows stronger, telling me she loves the idea of me going all caveman on her.

Fuck, she really is perfect.

"Who says I want you to be a gentleman?" she murmurs, and I nearly swallow my tongue.

CHAPTER 13

HAYLEY

It feels like the words have barely left my mouth when Cooper lifts me, wrapping my legs around his waist as his mouth ravishes mine. His hands, lips, and tongue are everywhere as the passion that has been building between us explodes. We can't seem to get close enough.

I cling to him as he moves us backward and props me up against the porch railing. One hand massages my breasts roughly, giving me the firm touch I so desperately need, squeezing and kneading as his other hand seeks the hem of my dress, lifting it and gaining access to my drenched panties. He runs a finger over the thing material along my slit and my legs quiver, finally so close to getting his touch where I've wanted it for the last two weeks.

"Damn, you're so wet for me, Hayley." He growls his delight at finding my underwear soaked. "Does that pretty pussy of yours need to be taken care of?"

Cooper whispers in my ear as he licks and bites my neck, still just lightly stroking me over the lace. I've never been into dirty talk, but I nearly come at the combination of his words and his deep, husky voice.

"Cooper," I moan in frustration, wriggling to get him to apply more pressure where I need it.

"Say it, Hayley: do you want me to take care of you? Do you want me to make you come?" He stubbornly continues to deny me what I want. I nod, pressing my forehead into his shoulder as the pressure builds within me from his gentle caresses alone.

He pauses suddenly and I grab at his hand as he pulls away. He chuckles, bringing it back between my legs, but he still refuses to touch me where I want him.

Instead, he trails his fingers up along the crease where my thighs meet my pelvis, sending little shocks of pleasure through me and making my legs twitch in anticipation.

"You need to say it, princess," he warns, "nothing will happen until you do." This domineering side of Cooper is something new and holy shit, it is sexy.

"Please, Cooper," I beg, "Yes, I want you."

The second the words leave my lips, he kisses me passionately, yanks the lace to the side, and presses his finger inside me. I moan loudly as I squirm against the overwhelming sensations.

He pushes deep and uses the heel of his hand to apply firm pressure over my clit as he thrusts slowly in and out of me, curling his fingers to brush that sweet spot on each stroke. In no time, I can feel the pressure building within me, delicious warmth spreading to my fingers and toes.

"Yes, Cooper," I call out as I near my release, and I know it's going to be a big one. With one final grind of his palm against my clit, I shatter, mumbling his name over and over into his shoulder, where I think I bit him to stop myself from screaming.

That was the sexiest thing I've ever experienced. I'm dazed as waves of tingly pleasure continue to wash over me, and Cooper gently slows the thrusting of his fingers, straightening my dress and kissing the top of my head. I reach for his belt, but he grips my hands and brings them up to his lips instead, pressing kisses to the backs of my knuckles.

"Soon, princess, but not tonight. It'll be worth the wait, I promise," he whispers into my ear. He presses a gentle kiss to my lips and steps back with a groan. I can't help but laugh as he rubs his hand back over his forehead and curses quietly again while he takes in my mussed but content appearance. He drags me back to him for another brutal kiss, then steering me inside and waits to make sure I lock the door behind him.

Stand there, with my back against the front door, I feel thoroughly satisfied but weak as a kitten.

I briefly wonder if crawling up the stairs is too undignified. My legs are so weak after the orgasm-of-all-orgasms that he just gave me, I'm not sure I'll make it on two feet.

I can't wait to see what else he can do. I have a feeling it's going to blow my mind.

Where on earth did this man come from?

CHAPTER 14

HAYLEY

The alert going off on my phone wrenches me from the best sleep I have had in a long time, and I grin from ear to ear as I see Cooper's name pop up on the screen. After the orgasm Cooper gave me, I went to bed with a big smile on my face and a warm feeling in my heart. I think I was probably asleep before my head even hit the pillow.

Cooper: Fancy a hike this morning?

Last night we talked about going to a local beauty spot up in the hills. An outdoor date was probably a good idea this time. That kiss escalated quickly; it's like my body has a mind of its own around him. I can't believe I let him do that to me on my porch.

I'm such a hussy.

Hayley: Would love it. Give me 15 mins to get ready

I jump out of bed and hop in the shower. Steamy thoughts of Cooper fill my mind as I daydream about those kisses on my neck and shoulders, his hands running along my sensitive skin. Just remembering his soft lips on my back sends a shiver down my spine. Mentally, I shake myself as I step out from under the warm water and get dressed in black gym leggings, a tank top, and a light fleece.

I need to get a grip on my hormones, or I am going to pounce on the man as soon as I see him. I keep trying to remember to take things slowly, but then my traitorous body tells me to do the exact opposite. Maybe I just need to think of it as a bit of harmless fun and not take everything so seriously. If anyone deserves a sexy fling, it's most definitely me. I've never met anyone like this guy, though.

Am I kidding myself by pretending I'd be ok with this just being something casual?

I pad down the stairs and start pulling together some snacks and drinks to bring with us. I'm still in the kitchen when I hear his old truck rumbling into the driveway. I have to stop myself from running out the door to greet him, and I take a few deep breaths to calm myself down. Shoving the food into a backpack, along with a blanket, I open the front door.

Cooper is bent over at the side of my driveway, pulling weeds out of my flower beds, and the sight stirs something warm inside me. I can feel myself getting hot again just watching him gardening. I'm not sure this is normal.

Jeez, I have it bad.

I sit down on the bench and pull on my old hiking boots to distract my racing mind. He glances over at me with a cheeky smile on his face, as if he can tell my thoughts have fallen into the gutter.

"Morning," he says, beaming up at me as he leans against a wooden post, arms crossed over his muscular chest.

"Hi," I say shyly, fiddling with the zip on the bag, smiling but avoiding eye contact. Suddenly, I feel awkward about all but propositioning him last night. He reaches out and grabs my hand, pulling me to my feet. Stepping up the stairs to stand in front of me, he leaves just a few inches between us.

"Morning," he says again, pointedly.

My half-hearted greeting obviously didn't satisfy him, and he gently brushes his lips against mine, pulling me into his big arms. I melt against him, my nervousness disappearing.

"Better?" he says, inhaling deeply against my hair and sighing.

Did he just smell me? I kind of liked it.

"Yes, much better. I guess I'm just nervous," I admit with my face pressed into his firm chest. I feel his muscles move under his skin as he chuckles.

"Nothing to fear here, princess. And it's a bit late for nerves, anyway. Come on." He steps back and takes the bag, leading me by the hand toward his truck. Opening the door, he tries to buckle me in, but I swat at his hands, laughing at the attention he's lavishing on me. As we drive towards the start of the trail, we chat easily and any tension I felt fades within minutes.

"I'm meeting Leila tonight for some drinks. She's bringing me to Taaffe's. Is it any good?" I ask as I gaze out the window at the woods passing by, soaking in the beautiful scenery. He doesn't answer for a few seconds, so I turn to look at him. His jaw is tense, and his hands are gripping the wheel tightly. Interesting, it doesn't seem like he's a fan.

"It's okay," he answers slowly, "there isn't much choice around here I suppose, but I don't think it's the kind of place you might be used to. It's not exactly classy; rustic might be a polite way of describing it. What's the occasion?"

"Leila said that the party next weekend isn't really for her. It's just an excuse for your mum to invite everyone she knows. Leila wants to let loose a little on her own, I guess, and she was looking for a partner in crime." He laughs lightly, and the tension leaves his hands.

"Well, that's true. Leila's birthday is just another excuse for my mum to throw a party at the packhouse. It doesn't matter what it's for," he says, brow still furrowed.

"Packhouse?"

He flushes at my question. "Oh, it's just the nickname we have for the lodge where our office and accommodation are. Lots of the single guys on the construction crews have rooms there for when they're away on jobs."

"Hmm. Wolf pack, like in The Hangover, yeah? I probably don't want to know." I shake my head, laughing. "When does Rex get back?" Cooper seems slightly relieved at the change of topic. I dread to know what goes on there. It's probably like a big frat house.

"Tonight. I'm picking him up from the airport after dinner. Would it be okay if we swing by, if I can convince him to come along? I know he'll be dying to see Leila." He looks over at me hopefully and I smile brightly back at him, thrilled that he's already arranging our next date before this one has even started.

"I'd love that."

He seems relieved. How rough is this place that he doesn't want to leave us to have a girl's night there?

"You say that now. Rex isn't always the most sociable." He shakes his head a little. "He had a nasty breakup. His... fiancé dumped him when he told her he didn't want to take over... the family business. I guess she was more interested in the money than him. She got back together with some rich ex, pretty much immediately. He didn't take it well." He looks so upset on his brother's behalf that I reach over and place my hand on his leg, giving it a gentle squeeze.

"That's tough, but it sounds like he's better off without her." He smiles softly, placing his hand on top of mine, squeezing it back – and holding it in place on his leg.

"Speaking of the family business, Dad says you're doing loads of work for him on the Forest Spa acquisition. Don't let him work you too hard. He'll take advantage if you're too nice to him, he's not as helpless as he lets on." He winks, letting me know he is just teasing; his affection for his father, and all his family, is clear in the way he speaks about him.

"It's not too much. But I feel like I'm missing something. It's like I know I'm not making a connection that I should be, and it's driving me mad." I sigh, slumping back against the seat. "It'll come to me, but the Andersons are pushing to close ASAP."

"Yah, they seem keen to get it done ahead of the conference in two weeks, but I'm not sure what the rush is. I can't stand that Toby guy. He's a jackass. I don't have the same patience for listening to him you and Dad seem to." He smirks at me.

"Ha, that's just your excuse to avoid dealing with him! But yeah, he's not the easiest." I clasp my hands in my lap nervously, turning in my seat to face him.

"Your Dad mentioned going to that conference: two nights in a 5-star spa resort. I hope it's like this all the time. Or is this just a bribe to encourage me to get this deal done?"

It's an event being held in one of the Jones's resorts and I'd love to go, but I am testing the waters to see if Cooper minds me attending.

"Oh, did he now? Interesting. Definitely a bribe." His gorgeous brown eyes twinkle in amusement, but he also seems to be thinking hard on something.

"I've never heard of the event before, but most of the firms coming are massive." I had a look at the guest list they sent me, and it really intrigued me. The Jones Group is dealing with some of the largest private companies on the East Coast, and this seemed to be a jaunt for the rich-but-not-famous.

"Something like that. It's an annual thing. The heads of some large family-owned companies get together, talk business and socialise. It's kept quiet to stop it from getting out of hand. My mother is in her element at these things, schmoozing and trying to play matchmaker for all her children," he winces at the thought of it. "Hopefully, given that we're hosting it this year, she'll be too busy to cause any trouble. Leila normally dreads it; she'll be thrilled you're going."

I feel a twinge of jealousy as he mentions his mother trying to set him up with other women, even though he didn't seem happy about it. It's a ridiculous reaction to have over a man I had my first date with last night. He seems to sense my unease and begins rubbing circles on the back of my hand.

"I'm thrilled you're going, too." He brings my hand up to his lips and kisses my knuckles gently. "And my mum is generally harmless. If her kids are happy, she's happy. And believe me, I'm happy." He grins at me, and I can't help grinning back at him like a love-struck fool.

CHAPTER 15

HAYLEY

After an hour of walking up the well-worn trail, Cooper veers off the main path and holds out his hand to help me over some fallen branches, following some unmarked route through the trees.

It's unnecessary, but chivalrous all the same.

Although, when he picks me up by the waist to lift me over a stream, I suspect he's just finding excuses to touch me. And I am totally on board with that.

We break through the trees to an open area of flat rock jutting out of the side of the mountain, an amazing view down the valley on both sides. The bright green of the spring foliage in the morning light is stunning; mountains rise on both sides of the valley, some with snow caps remaining. The blue sky reflects off the ribbon of small lakes below.

It looks like a postcard, and I can't help but gasp as I look from side to side, taking in the beauty of it all.

"Nice, isn't it?" Cooper comes up beside me, standing close. "I run up here all the time."

"It's stunning," I say in awe. "Thank you. I never would have found this on my own. It's so beautiful." I turn to look up at his strong profile as he stares at the view and takes a deep lungful of fresh mountain air. He's so handsome. I can't believe I'm lucky enough to be here with him, in this special place.

"There are lots of viewing spots around here, but this is my favourite. Not many people know about it." He pulls the blanket out of my pink backpack, which he insisted on carrying, and spreads it out on the ground.

As he sits down, he stretches his long muscular legs in front of him and leans back on his elbows. I sit beside him, and we soak in the view together. A few minutes later, as he unpacks the food, we discuss the last few jobs to be done on the house, mainly painting and some tiling, and I cannot believe that he got it done so quickly.

"I'd love to take the credit, but Nathan is the brains behind the operation. He acts like a fool most of the time, but he's clever. He manages most of our sites and has a way of getting things done," he boasts proudly.

"Good for him. He has done a great job," I agree enthusiastically. "So, if he's the brains, you're just the hired muscle?" I tease, glancing down at his delicious shoulders and strong arms before I can stop myself.

"Have you been checking out my muscles, Hayley?" he grins when I blush. I roll my eyes and try to shove his shoulder, but my attempt doesn't move him an inch.

"I take it that's not normally your day job, then?" I change the subject, and he lets me pretend he didn't catch checking him out again.

"No, I'm normally in meetings or buried under a sea of paperwork at the office. Rex was on track to take over from Dad, but it never really appealed to him. I do genuinely enjoy it most of the time, so I'll take over when Dad steps down. Nathan is in his element in the construction side of the business; he'll eventually take full responsibility for that."

He rolls over onto his side so we're facing each other and, being this close, looking into his warm dark eyes, is enough to make my breath catch.

"Leila was clever enough to get into medicine; she escaped the family business altogether. Ethan helps me run a lot of the on-the-ground stuff, the hospitality business and a small brewery we own. Being the charmer that he is, he's good with people management," he laughs.

"So, if you're normally in the office, Cooper Jones, what have you been doing hanging doors and tiling at my house for the last two weeks? When you should have been recuperating!" I'm curious about why someone recovering from surgery would choose hard labour over a desk job. He looks guilty for a second, then smiles sheepishly and shrugs.

"At first, it was because I felt I owed it to you to make sure everything was done properly. I wanted to be the one to pay you back personally. But then those tiny pyjamas and robes you wear in the mornings kept me coming back."

I laugh out loud at that, and his cheeky little grin, and he edges closer, so that our fingers are touching.

"What will Rex do now that he's back?" I'm intrigued and a little scared to meet him. They all talk about him fondly, but there still seems to be an undercurrent of anxiety about him. He must have been in a bad way when he left.

"I'm not sure. Whatever he wants, I suppose. I just hope he stays around. He can be quiet and... gruff. But he's a good guy. I've missed him." Rex is getting more mysterious by the minute.

As we continue to demolish the little picnic I made, I can't help sneaking looks at Cooper. He hasn't shaved this morning, and he's getting a dark shadow across his firm jaw. He takes a big bite of a sandwich followed by a long swig out of a bottle of water, and I am fascinated by his soft, full lips and how sexy he makes eating look. I watch his throat work as he swallows, and an overwhelming urge to lick it comes out of nowhere. I blush as I wonder where the hell that thought came from.

This man can turn me on by drinking water. I've lost the run of myself.

"Thank you, Cooper. For everything. For this," I gesture to the view in front of us, "and for all the help with the house. Grey Ridge is feeling like home, and you guys have played a big part in that." I say suddenly, squinting over at him as I raise a hand to shield my eyes from the sun.

He looks stunned at my frank admission, but it's true. Cooper and his family, and even his ragtag bunch of workers that have taken over my house for the last couple of weeks, have made me feel welcome. The teasing and messing remind me of my own siblings.

"If me landing you with my crazy family makes it feel like home, I'm more than happy to oblige. You can keep them if you want," he jokes. "I'd do anything for you Hayley, you don't need to thank me. And it's not just because I owe you my life." I scoff at the dramatic statement, and he frowns at my dismissal.

Sitting up straighter, he leans in, his enormous frame looming over me. He moves closer to kiss me, wrapping a powerful hand around the back of my neck, tangling his long fingers in my hair to hold me in place. He pulls back and looks me straight in the eye, as if to show me how serious he is when he says his next words:

"Getting to know you has been the best thing that has happened to me in a long, long time." His deep brown eyes smoulder with intensity, and I squirm under the weight of his gaze. His eyes drift to my mouth as I bite into my bottom lip with my teeth to distract myself from the tingles spreading throughout my body. And the heat between my legs.

He's not a smooth talker like some of the players I've met before, but he pulls no punches and says it like it is. That worries me a little, because I know it's not just a line. Getting in deep with a man should not be in the cards for me with everything else I have going on. I'm not sure I can help it, though.

Before I can think too much about whether this is all going too fast, he uses his thumb to pull my lip free from my teeth and kisses it gently, sucking on it a little before kissing me full on the mouth. It's absolute bliss: the setting, the man, the sparks spreading through my body.

My head spins and I try to commit every second to memory.

A satisfied moan passes my lips as he pulls me against his hard body and his tongue delves further into my mouth as the kiss becomes more passionate. I allow him to roll me onto my back on the blanket and he lowers himself over me, keeping his weight off me with one arm.

His powerful, masculine energy makes me feel safe and desired; it's a heady combination.

For someone like me who is always on, always in charge and in control, it's nice to let someone else take the lead. Despite being out in the open, I can't stop myself from rolling my hips up against him. I need the contact to satisfy the ache in my core, but it's just not enough.

He strokes his hand down my side to my waist and back up, skimming over my breast, giving it a gentle squeeze, and swiping a thumb across my hardened nipple before going back to cup the back of my head. He seems to be almost lazily enjoying himself. It's a stark contrast to the hungry make-out session we had last night. He's stroking and touching me at a leisurely pace, while I'm being driven mad with need.

Maybe it is just like last night.

"Cooper," I whisper, almost a plea. I don't know what I want, but I know it's more, and I know he can give it to me. I know instinctively that he'll be able to play my body like a fiddle.

"Hayley." He breaks the contact between us but stays in position over me and leans our foreheads together. "I can't get enough of you."

He strokes his hand down my waist and along the outside of my thigh, trailing his fingers back up the inside, pausing tantalisingly close to my pussy. I groan again and lean my head on the blanket, sucking in a deep, shaky breath as our eyes meet again. I can see the fire of need in his, so dark now that they look almost black. But we both know this isn't the time or the place to continue this, despite what our bodies are telling us.

"I don't know what you're doing to me." As soon as we touch, I feel utterly helpless to resist this man.

"Me? Princess, I'm dying here." I glance down along our bodies, and I can see the evidence of his arousal pushing at his trousers as he tries to adjust himself. My eyes widen and I feel an unbelievable urge to reach out and touch it. It looks massive.

"Come on, we better get back," I sigh, scooting out from under him, "Leila is coming to my house for dinner before we go out." I pat his face in sympathy, hauling myself to my feet, gathering our things, and starting the trek back down the mountains.

I need to think.

My sexy fling is powering full steam ahead, and I wonder if one of us shouldn't be trying to slow things down before one of us gets hurt.

Damned if I know how, though.

CHAPTER 16

HAYLEY

Leila stares into my closet while I sit cross-legged on the bed, watching on in amusement.

I know that I have a ridiculous number of formal dresses for a girl who has moved to a small town in the mountains to run a bed-and-breakfast, but I couldn't bring myself to get rid of them all when they cost so much money. Hopefully, someone will get some use out of them at some point: like me and Leila at this conference.

"No, we're still going shopping," she argues. "It's bad enough that my parents make me go to these things when I'm not even involved in the business, the least I should get for it is a new dress or two."

"Ok, fine. We'll go shopping, but just for you!" I laugh. "I need a new fridge more than I need a new dress."

"Well, that's just sad," she looks horrified on my behalf. "And tell me again what was so bad about your old life again?" She turns back to rifle through the gowns again. Pulling out a particularly daring one, she raises her eyebrows and laughs at my face when I think about wearing it in a room of stuffy business owners.

My vague reasons for the dramatic changes in my life will no longer cut it now that she seems to have officially adopted me as her friend. She wants to know more.

"You should have been a lawyer." I scowl and she shrugs, unashamed of her persistent and blatantly obvious ways.

"You know anything you tell me is protected by doctor-patient privilege," she jokes before a more serious look fixes itself across her pretty features, letting me know that she suspects it wasn't something good that drove me to come here. I take a gulp of white wine and fiddle with the stem of my glass, steeling myself against the onslaught of emotions I work so hard to keep at bay.

"Hayley, you don't have to tell me anything if you don't want to," she backtracks. "It's not my business. I'm just being nosy."

I square my shoulders and sit up straighter, meeting Leila's eye where she leans against the wardrobe quietly, waiting for me to begin. "Just promise me you won't tell Cooper?" I ask hesitantly, "Any sane man would run a mile if he heard this."

She nods and smiles sympathetically, "No chance."

"It's a common story, really. I pride myself on being an excellent judge of character, and naively thought it would never happen to me."

Leila frowns, already guessing where this is going.

"James was charming and attentive at first but became more and more controlling. Deciding who my friends were, trying to stop me from going out without him. I realised he just wanted me as a bit of arm candy to drag around at his social events." I drink another gulp of wine for courage.

"I always wanted to move out of the city, and I had started putting money together, researching places to live, but James never took me seriously. And I never asked him to come with me when I went to visit properties, which, I suppose, says enough about the state of our relationship in my mind." I roll my eyes at my own stupidity. I should have ended things a long time before I did.

"Next thing I know, we're at a snooty dinner party with our friends and colleagues, and, out of nowhere, he announces that we're engaged. Without even asking me to marry him first!" I pause, Leila's jaw has nearly hit the floor.

"What the hell?"

"I know. It was crazy. James turned up the next day with this giant rock, expecting I'd just take the ring and be happy." My anger rises just thinking about his smug face, looking at me as though I was making a big deal for no reason. "Even standing there with the ring in a box, he still couldn't bring himself to ask. He really couldn't see the problem with what he'd done."

"I still don't know what he was thinking. Maybe he was trying to impress his boss, playing the settled family man and all that. Or maybe he thought my talk about moving was an ultimatum. I don't know. Nothing he had done up to this point was really *that* bad, but acting like I had no say in whether we got married was the last straw. I told him I couldn't, that it was over."

I twirl my bracelet round and round on my wrist as I attempt to push back the memories of what happened next. Leila stays silent but she notices my fidgeting.

"To say he didn't take it well would be an understatement. He wouldn't go, and started ranting on and on about how I was humiliating him. Nothing about loving or losing me, no sadness, just what it would look like to everyone else after his big announcement."

Leila moves closer but waits, letting me get the entire sordid tale out.

"When I'd had enough and told him to leave, he lost it. Shouting and roaring. He threw a glass and it shattered against the wall." I shake my head at the thought of his face bright red with rage as he lunged for me. Rubbing my sweaty palms on my thighs, I can feel my hands trembling. Leila grabs them and holds them still as I take a steadying breath.

"He threw me to the ground. I must have split my head open on the coffee table as I fell. He grabbed my hair, dragged me across the floor, and God only knows what he would have done, but my neighbour started banging on the door, complaining about the noise." I shudder, touching the scar in my hairline briefly before wrapping my arms tightly around myself.

"Oh, Hayley!" Leila sits beside me, throwing her arms around me in a tight hug.

"I did go to the police, but he's a lawyer; he knows the system and all the right people, so it didn't go anywhere. I spoke to work because that's how I met him – his company dealt with ours – and they offered me redundancy. It was decent of them, although maybe they just wanted to avoid any drama. In retrospect," I shrug, "all of that wasn't even the worst of it."

Leila looks equally horrified and confused by this admission.

"I planned to pack up my apartment and move home to my parents' house while I worked out what I wanted to do next, but James made my life a living hell. Following me, calling me, slashing my tires, breaking into my apartment, trashing my stuff, turning up at my parents. He even visited my little sister at college."

Leila's jaw drops again.

"It was terrifying. The guy is completely unhinged.

"He told me he knew nasty people who could make me disappear, and I couldn't bring that danger to my family's doorstep. But I couldn't hang around and wait to see if he'd make good on those threats, either. So, I left in the middle of the night with as much stuff as I could pack into my car." Looking up at the ceiling and blinking hard, I struggle to hold back my tears.

"I thought it would end when I was gone. Out of sight, out of mind. I know he still watches my parents' house, and, in the first week after I left, he tracked me to a motel where I used my credit card. Then he found me at the next place when I took out a lease, so..." I look out the window at the gorgeous view, really hoping what I say next doesn't come true. "If he wants to, he'll track me down here, too. I have to hope he's lost interest by now. That's why nobody knows I'm here. My family, my best friends."

"Oh, honey." Leila gives me a massive hug and while I don't do well with being pitied, it is nice having someone to talk to about it.

"When I moved to town, I let Marcus know, just in case anything happens, or anyone suspicious turns up. He's been checking up on me and keeping an eye out for anything weird, but I can't run forever. It's time for me to start building my new life here."

"Are you sure you're safe in this house on your own? You know my family has spare rooms at the lodge. There are always people around, so you'd never be alone. Or the hotel? You know my mother wouldn't mind," Leila offers, but I'm already shaking my head.

"I appreciate it, thank you, but I can't drag anyone else into my mess. I don't want to let him win by forcing me into hiding for the rest of my life. I just want a fresh start and to forget about him. Please don't tell Cooper yet, I will tell him. It's just a lot to dump on someone you've only known for a couple weeks and I'm only starting to get comfortable letting people in again. It would probably freak you out."

"Oh, you have no idea." Wide-eyed, she looks genuinely alarmed. "He would go nuts. I promise I won't say anything if you don't want me to, but only if you promise to ask for help if you need it. I don't care if it's me, Marcus, Cooper, Dad, whoever. And I don't care if you're embarrassed that it might be nothing, you ask us, ok?" I nod and hug her tightly, a tear slipping from my eye. "You're one of us now, and nobody messes with our family."

"I promise," I whisper and smile gratefully at her.

"Come on," she says, jumping up, "Let's turn these frowns upside down. I don't know about you, but I need another drink after hearing about that asshole." She pulls me to my feet and shoves the glass of wine back into my hand, determined to make me forget all about it, at least for a little while.

CHAPTER 17

COOPER

Rex's flight is late getting in, and I'm already impatient to get going when I finally see him saunter in. I realise I had forgotten how forbidding he looks in person. He's more tanned than before, and his black hair is now cut military short.

The black outfit of jeans, boots and a fitted t-shirt doesn't help to soften his look, and I see plenty of people giving him wary but admiring glances. He looks fit and healthy compared to the last time I saw him in person, which is a relief.

Being rejected by his mate nearly broke him, and he had faded away to a shadow of his former self, both physically and mentally. Never a big chatterbox to begin with, he became even more withdrawn and isolated. None of us were sure that leaving to go travelling had been the right thing to do, but we did agree it was worth a shot.

He smirks as he approaches us. I can't even call it a smile, and Nathan pulls him in a big, manly, back-slapping hug. Rex pushes him off, growling and grumbling, but I can tell he's happy to see us. I reach out and shake his hand, and he meets my eyes and nods, a silent acknowledgment of how good it is to be with each other again.

For two alphas in public, this is about as touchy-feely as it gets, but it's damn good to have my big brother back home. I can feel the power emanating from him, and I am shocked but thrilled to see his full strength is back. He is a formidable wolf, and it was painful to watch how weak he was in the aftermath of the rejection. It'll be great to have him at the next full moon run, the same night as Leila's party. Everyone will be there, and it'll be an enormous boost to pack morale to have him back among us.

"Come on, let's go." I turn and lead the way back to the car, striding along quickly ahead of Rex and Nathan.

"What's the rush, bro? Somewhere you need to be?" Nathan calls after me, laughing and elbowing Rex.

"Shut up, Nathan, just get moving," I snap. The delayed arrival means my mate is sitting in that dive bar with Leila, on a Saturday night, with nobody there to look out for them. Rex raises an eyebrow and grins, latching onto the fact that Nathan has some dirt on me – the normally calm Jones brother looking not so cool and collected right now.

"Cooper met a girl," Nathan snickers. "And Leila's taking her out drinking tonight, at Taaffe's. Someone isn't too happy about it. In fact, I believe the plan is to crash girls' night." He rolls his eyes as if ashamed of what I've become. Rex just stares, waiting for me to elaborate.

"I thought Rex might fancy a drink to welcome him back. And I don't like Leila being around all those unmated males," I lie. I know Nathan has his suspicions, but I've been careful not to reveal the truth. He only knows this is the first girl I've ever been serious about, and probably thinks I'm considering a chosen mate for the first time.

"Oh, yeah. It's Leila you're worried about." Rex ignores Nathan's sarcasm, making it obvious that he's waiting for me to tell the truth, leaving the silence to stretch out uncomfortably between us as we climb into the car.

"For fuck's sake, fine! I need to get there and make sure nobody puts their filthy paws anywhere near Hayley," I grumble. "Or even fucking looks at her. Is that what you wanted? Fucking Taaffe's. Every unmated male around will be there. What is Leila thinking?" I pound my fist on the steering wheel and glare at Nathan, who's laughter roars at my outburst.

"She's human." Nathan continues to explain. "She's the one who pulled him out of the river, and Leila is showing her a good time. She's new around here. It's only fair she gets to see who else this town has to offer."

I growl at Nathan, grinding my teeth together to stop myself from saying something I'll regret, and he laughs again, shaking his head.

Rex says nothing, but I can see from the glint in his eye that he's enjoying this as much as Nathan. His eye burn into the back of my head as I break the speed limit the whole way back to Grey Ridge. Rex has always been perceptive; I'd bet money he already has it all worked out.

As we push through the door to the bar, I already feel a little better as I pick up the faint smell of my mate. Rex watches me closely, but I don't care, immediately heading to where Hayley and Leila are sitting. Thankfully on their own, with their heads together, they're laughing like old friends.

"That's ok Cooper, I'll go to the bar and get this round in. You go sit down," Nathan calls out sarcastically as he heads to the bar.

"Hey," I say quietly as I join their table. The stunning smile Hayley gives me when she realises who's sitting down makes my spirits lift instantly.

"Hey, yourself," she says, and I can see she is relaxed and happy. I sit in the chair beside her, casually draping my arm over the back of her chair. I know it's a possessive gesture, and maybe I shouldn't be this obvious in public if I want to avoid questions, but my wolf doesn't care.

He wants to stake his claim, to block her from the view of all the other males. Until she's marked, he will not be happy about anyone but me being near her.

"You must be Rex." She nods and I realise Rex must be standing behind me. "I'm Hayley. Nice to meet you!" In my desperation to get to her, I completely forgot about introductions. She reaches over me to shake his hand. Rex smiles at her, then scowls at me for my lack of manners, smacking the back of my head, making Hayley laugh.

"Sorry, sorry," I mutter, as he eyes me knowingly. I want to deny it, but I know I've completely given my secret away to him. He braces himself and turns just in time to catch Leila as she launches herself at him. Rex envelopes her in his enormous arms.

We are all very protective of our only sister, and I know he must have felt guilty about leaving her behind. He sets her gently back on her feet and wipes away the tears spilling down her cheeks.

"Are you okay?" he whispers to her in a low voice.

"I am now. It's so good to have you back home, Rex. I missed you." She hugs him tightly again, releasing him to shove him into the seat beside hers. Nathan appears with beers, and Ethan arrives shortly after. Laughter and conversation flow easily around the table, and I feel content as I look around our small group.

Hayley fits in so well with my family and friends, it's like she's been one of us forever.

Rex clears his throat softly, and I look over at him. He stares pointedly at my fingers, which are unconsciously playing with a strand of her caramel-coloured hair. I shrug and grin like a fool.

CHAPTER 18

COOPER

The irritating sound of high-pitched fake laughter reaches my ears and I flinch. I know exactly who is coming our way.

Long red nails trail along my forearm in what I imagine is supposed to be a seductive manner, but it makes my skin crawl. I move my arm so that her hand drops away and I look up, unsmiling and, hopefully, unwelcoming. Carla. The fake, entitled, power-hungry, daughter of my father's beta.

"Hi. What can I do for you?" I ask politely but coldly.

She laughs again, as if I've said the funniest thing she's ever heard and tosses her bleached blonde hair over her shoulder.

"Just thought I'd come over to say welcome back to Rex," she says, but she never takes her eyes off me. She doesn't even glance in Rex's direction.

Silence has fallen over the rest of the table. Nobody else greets her or asks her to join us, but Carla doesn't take the hint and puts her hand back on my shoulder and strokes it down my arm, pouting her overly made-up lips.

"I haven't seen you since the accident. I thought you might need some nursing back to health, but you weren't there when I stopped by," she purrs, and I feel nauseous.

Leila shoots to her feet in anger at the disrespect Carla is showing to the future Luna, but I'm keen to avoid a scene. I turn in my chair, once again breaking Carla's physical contact with me.

"Thanks for your concern, Carla, but I've been well taken care of. Enjoy the rest of your night." As my hint hits her, she spots the recent addition to our usual table, finally looking at Hayley sitting by my side, my arm around her shoulder, our thighs touching under the table.

Carla looks furious and, for a second, like she'll lunge at Hayley right here in the bar. No doubt she would if Hayley were a wolf.

I can't see Hayley's face, but I feel her body stiffen.

She leans over and whispers in my ear, "I'll be right back, I'm going to the bar." She slips calmly and confidently away from the uncomfortable situation, leaving me to deal with it as I please. As I watch her go, I'm glad she's far away from this conversation.

"Is this some kind of joke," Carla sneers. "You're fucking the lost little human?"

Given her father's position, she has always felt that she has some sort of claim on me, particularly since I've never shown any interest in any female in our pack. She's seething with jealousy but trying to make it sound like a joke.

Nathan snarls at her, and Rex is quick to intervene, placing a calming hand on our little brother's shoulder, aware of the busy bar around us and that many ears are listening to the exchange.

"You should show some respect to the woman who saved your alpha," Rex uses his alpha tone to make Carla cower, "and show a little for yourself at the same time, Carla. It's becoming embarrassing."

Her face goes bright pink with anger and humiliation. She huffs in disgust but turns on her skyscraper-heels and stomps away. I hear a few sniggers around us from eavesdropping wolves who are delighted to see her put in her place so thoroughly by Rex, but I cringe at the position this has put Hayley in.

"Sensitively handled as always, Rex, it's good to have you back." Nathan claps Rex on the shoulder and grins.

I stand and scan the bar, keen to make sure Hayley is alright. I spot her leaning against the counter, right up against Marcus, one of his big hands on her shoulder as he speaks quietly into her ear.

She's so close to him, his thick beard is brushing against her jaw. Hayley smiles and nods up at him. It looks so intimate. A low growl escapes my lips before I can control it, and I hear the back of my chair crack under my grip.

"Cooper," Leila soothes quietly, "there is nothing between them." She tries to pry my hands off the splintered wood before I'm the one who creates a scene.

"Then why is that fucker always hanging around her?" I snarl, talking to myself more than Leila.

My siblings exchange concerned glances, but I fixate on Hayley, who is still all the way across the room, patting Marcus on the arm. Leila shrugs but seems relieved when Hayley puts some distance between her and the bear.

As she makes her way back, her path is blocked by a bitter and seething Carla; I watch in horror as she "bumps" into Hayley and spills her entire drink right down the front of Hayley's blouse.

Anger explodes from me at the sight of my mate being treated like this, and I can see every wolf cringe under the weight of my alpha aura as my emotions level the room. I force myself to stay where I am, as any over-the-top display of ownership towards Hayley will immediately disclose to everyone what's going on here.

Hayley looks down at the big stain and then up at Carla, who is watching Hayley with an amused expression on her face, waiting to see what kind of reaction she is going to elicit from her.

"Oops, sorry!" Carla giggles, then leans in closer. "He's out of your league, honey. You're just a bit of fun to him." Carla's voice drips with venom as she narrows her eyes, speaking loudly enough for every wolf in the room to hear what she's saying.

I'm sure Carla expected her status, her inherent dominance, to scare Hayley, but my little mate is completely unaffected. She looks at Carla with something akin to pity, as if her pathetic attempt at intimidation is nothing but laughable.

"At least I'm getting some 'fun', *honey*." Hayley winks at Carla, stepping around her and re-joining us. She is totally unaware that we could hear their exchange.

I am so proud of my little mate, and I can see the confused looks of the wolves around me as they consider her feisty response and her lack of submission to Carla. Hopefully, they put it down to her being human, where I know that it's because she is destined to be my luna, my partner and equal: a leader of this pack.

She doesn't have to bow down to anyone.

The barman, Sean, who also saw the exchange, nods to me and immediately steps around the counter, tapping Carla on the shoulder and pointing her towards the exit.

"That bitch!" Leila spits out as she looks down at Hayley's ruined top. Hayley laughs it off, seemingly unconcerned. She pulls the blouse off over her head, revealing a little silk camisole with lace edging the bust. I glimpse the pale pink strap of her bra peeking from beneath the delicate camisole and get a flash of her tanned, toned stomach before she straightens herself out. My cock springs to attention at the sight of her exposed skin.

I'm loving the view, but I'm not sure I love her exposing so much flesh in a place like this.

"Oh, just ignore her." Hayley crumples her destroyed blouse into a ball, flinging it onto her chair. and "Come on," she grabs Leila by the hand, pulling her onto the dancefloor. "Let's dance!"

I want to say something, but she conspicuously won't meet my eye.

"Well, well, well," Rex says slowly. "Nathan, if you had told me I was missing out on drama like this, I would have come back ages ago." Nathan grins at him and looks back at me expectantly. I don't know what to tell them, so I keep my mouth shut, refusing to admit anything.

Instead, I watch Hayley having a blast on the dance floor with Leila and Ethan. She's a brilliant dancer, enjoying every second out there. I'm mesmerised watching her hips sway and her hair spin as Ethan twirls her around the floor.

When my eyes fall back on the bar, Marcus is leaning against the counter watching them closely with beer bottle to his lips. He's a giant of a man, all muscle and built like a tank, with black hair and a thick beard. He looks more like a lumberjack than the sheriff, but I know he's a good guy behind the tough exterior.

I can't wrap my head around why he is here; I've never seen him willingly put himself in a crowd, and I've never known him to take interest in anyone romantically, either. He's a bit of a loner.

Walking up to the bar, I mirror his relaxed stance, leaning back beside him. Following his gaze to the dancefloor, I see Nathan and Rex shaking their heads at me. They're obviously expecting me to tackle the big man and are trying to convey what a terrible idea that is.

Like I don't already know that.

"What's on your mind, Coop?" Marcus asks after a minute of silence, still not taking his eyes off the girls. The bear shifter isn't a pack member, but we work well together, becoming friends as good as it seems possible with the solitary man.

"Don't see you here often. Any particular reason you're out tonight?" I turn to face him, but he doesn't look at me, his stoic expression doesn't waiver in the slightest.

"Could say the same thing to you," he deadpans, lips tipping up slightly as he takes another drink.

He's got me there.

"Fair enough." It's probably been six months since I've stepped foot in this place, and, even then, I hated every second of it. Everyone acts differently around me now that I'm set to take over, and it takes the joy out of socialising. Most wolves are nervous around me, finding my aura overpowering; others, she-wolves, want to ingratiate themselves to me because of my power and position.

A few probably hate me, seeing me as entitled and arrogant because sometimes I have to be the bad guy, the one to make some tough decisions no one else is willing to make.

"Just ask me whatever it is you came over here to ask, Cooper." He finally turns to meet my eye.

"Is there something going on between you and Hayley?" It pains me to have to ask him this, so I say it straight out. It makes me feel weak, and like I'm tipping my hand, but I need to find out. I blow out a breath.

From the look in his eyes and the openness of his body language, I know the answer before he begins to speak.

"Romantically?" He holds my gaze without blinking and I can tell there is no deception. "No."

"Then what's going on? And I don't just mean tonight. No offence, but you don't like anyone, but I hear you're bringing her lattes every Monday morning?"

"We're friends Coop. She's new in town and I'm looking out for her. It's not my place to tell you more than that, but your mate is something else." I freeze. "You're a lucky guy." I guess he's not the sheriff for no reason, but I'm impressed that he figured it out so quickly.

"Don't worry, I won't tell her. Or anyone else. But you should, and soon. She needs someone right now, and it would cut out all this nonsense," he says, referring to Carla's hissy fit. He drinks the rest of the beer in one go, slamming the empty bottle down on the bar. "Make sure she gets home safe," he calls as he pushes off the bar and walks straight out the front door.

My wolf bristles at the suggestion that we don't know how to take care of her properly.

I'm glad to hear there isn't anything going on between them, but he knows more about her life than I do, and it leaves a bitter taste in my mouth.

She needs someone right now.

What does he know that I don't?

CHAPTER 19

COOPER

As Hayley moves on the dance floor, looking sexy as hell, I scan the tables around us, and, in the gloom of the bar, I can see that I'm not the only one appreciating the view.

Possessiveness courses through my veins. I want to show them all who she belongs to. I want to walk out there, pull her close and dance with her myself, feel her body moving with mine. But I can't, and it's killing me.

When Hayley catches Leila's attention and tells her she's heading to the restroom, I can't help moving in that direction to intercept her. Just before she reaches the door, I catch her by the wrist and spin us into the dark hallway that leads to the emergency exit.

She gasps in shock and is about to push me off until I press her into the wall with the full length of my body and she realises who it is. I trace my fingers along the lace straps and delicate material running across the swell of her breasts, watching as goosebumps rise on her flesh in the wake of my touch.

"I like this," I press a kiss just above where the lace touches her chest, and she shivers. "She's nothing to me, Hayley. Just in case you're wondering. Never was, never will be."

"I don't want to talk about her," she mumbles as I skim my hands down her sides and lick and gently nip her neck. Right where I will place my mark, someday soon. I hear what she's saying, but I can feel her relax under my reassurance.

I lift the hem of her top, grazing my thumbs over her hips and along the silky soft skin at the top of her jeans, dipping slowly below the waistband to tease the skin there. She lets her head fall back against the wall and sighs in pleasure, looking up at me under hooded lids. I grab her face with both hands and lean down to kiss her, pressing my hips against her where my erection lines up perfectly to rub her clit.

She moans quietly, and I wrap an arm around her waist to keep her steady.

"Can you feel what you do to me, Hayley? Just being near you, watching you. Only you," I whisper into her ear, my stubble brushing against the delicate skin behind her ear. I rock gently against her, letting her feel just how turned on I am. I lightly drag my hands up underneath her silky top and over her toned stomach – something I've been dying to do since I glimpsed it earlier.

I feather gentle touches across the underside of her breasts and hear a sharp intake of breath as she arches her back. Pushing her breasts out and seeking more contact from my hands, I continue only to tease, trailing sparks across her skin as I slip my hands around her back and stroke them gently towards her shoulder blades, nibbling and sucking on her earlobe.

"Oh, Cooper," she whispers breathlessly, and my name sounds like heaven on her lips. I want to hear her scream it while I push inside her. She presses her pelvis towards me, seeking more friction.

From her scent, I can tell that she is already wet and ready for me, my mate so responsive to my every touch.

"I know you're wet for me Hayley. I want to take you right here, right now, up against this wall. I want to fuck you so hard you come screaming my name, so every fucker out there knows who's making you come."

She gasps in a combination of shock and arousal at the picture I paint for her, and I smile against her neck. My sophisticated little mate likes a bit of dirty talk.

"But I want to have all the time in the world for our first time,

Princess. I want to taste you and feel you come undone on my tongue. I want you to beg me to take my cock into your sweet, tight pussy." It's a promise as I grip her ass and squeeze hard. Letting my hands drift down across the sensitive seam where her ass meets her thighs, I let them drift in toward her core, where she longs to be touched.

She shudders and grips my biceps with both hands as her legs nearly give way, and I wonder if I could make her orgasm just by stroking her like this. I crush my lips against hers and she kisses me back fiercely, granting me access to her mouth when I nip at her bottom lip. Our tongues are stroking and tangling as we cling to each other, desperate to be as close as possible.

When I pull away, her eyes are bright and wild, pupils big and dilated with desire, and her lips are pink and swollen. The gentle flush in her cheeks fills me with delight, knowing how hot and bothered she is for me. I lean back and take her in, propped against the wall, looking slightly dazed and dishevelled. She looks so hot it's making my balls ache.

"Come on, we better go back before you get us into trouble." I wink, and she stares at me, gobsmacked, still gripping my arms for support.

There will be no witty comeback, it seems. I drag her back to the table by the hand, shooting daggers at any male who looks in her direction. As she drifts back into conversation with Leila, Ethan leans in closer.

"Jeez, Cooper," Ethan shakes his head at me disapprovingly. "You need to rein it in or go home. Your horny alpha vibes have half the wolves in this place humping in the shadows." He rolls his eyes and pretends to shudder.

"I feel like I need to go home and have a shower after that. I feel dirty," Nathan shivers and Rex laughs, shaking his head at their disgusted faces.

I just smile, because what else can I do? I'm just so bloody happy.

CHAPTER 20

HAYLEY

Leila steps out of the dressing room, twirling around in a beautiful emerald dress.

It sets off the green flecks in her eyes and her dark olive skin tone to perfection. She has lined-up a collection of jewel-coloured gowns to try on, and I'm curled on a sofa to watch the fashion show.

"You look gorgeous," I tell her honestly, but she would look gorgeous in anything. She smiles brightly as she twirls around, and I can't help but get swept up in her delight at trying on all these dresses.

"You need to pick something out for the ball," she says, and I laugh at her persistence. She pulls out a gorgeous, shimmering gold number, with a sweetheart neckline and fitted bodice that flows gracefully down to the floor with an elegant slit on one side. "Just try it on for me," she pouts.

I sigh and haul myself up, still exhausted from our late night. I don't know how Leila is so bright and perky.

"How are you not hungover at all? You drank as much as I did. It's infuriating," I ask as she hands me the dress and pushes me towards a cubicle.

"I don't get hangovers; good genes, I guess." She smirks when I scowl at her and close the curtain. "So, you and Cooper, eh? Going well, I take it?"

"Subtle Leila." I can't help but smile at her blatant attempt to fish for information. "Yeah, he's great, but it's very early. We're just hanging out." I try to sound blasé, though I am anything but. Last night was amazing, but the drama with the other woman, then letting him get me off in some dark, dingy hallway both show me I might be in way over my head here.

"I've never seen him so smitten," she admits. "It's cute. And there is some serious sexual tension going on there. Yowza!"

I put my head in my hands and groan while she laughs at how uncomfortable I am.

"Is it not weird for *us* to be talking about this?!" I exclaim. God, I hope nobody saw us in that corridor. My face burns just thinking about it. Hopefully, a small bar like that doesn't have CCTV.

"What? About you fancying my brother? Ok, yeah. A bit. But you're my friend, so you can talk to me about it. I just don't want to hear any actual details." She laughs again before emerging from her cubicle. I step out of mine and run my hands down the dress she has put me in, stepping into a pair of nude heels to check the length.

"It is beautiful." I admire the gown in the full-length mirror. "You are a bad influence," I tease. "And what about you? You and Ethan seemed cosy last night? Anything there?"

She spins around with a horrified look on her face and makes a gagging noise.

"Gross. That's like asking about me and Rex. Ethan is basically my brother. I could never, ever go there." She shivers before she looks at me in the mirror. "Get that dress, it's amazing, Hayley."

"Come on, you must have some romance going on. I'm not buying it. Look at you Leila, you're gorgeous. There were plenty of hot guys checking you out last night. Actually, seriously, is there something in the water here? There were *so many* hot guys," I ask, attempting to divert her focus away from convincing me to spend my last savings on a dress I don't need.

"Do not say that to Cooper. Ever!" she warns seriously as her face falls, and she looks down.

"Nobody around here will touch me. They all either work for Dad or are afraid of my brothers. The only ones that ask me out are the boring, rich guys we are going to meet at this conference. They're only interested in my family connections and having a pretty Stepford wife to push out some kids. They're not interested in *me*." She shrugs as if she doesn't care, but I can tell she's putting on a brave face.

"What about Marcus?" I ask softly, and I watch her reaction closely. Her eyes widen as she looks down guiltily, but then a flash of pain dulls her eyes for a brief second.

"Well, who wouldn't fancy that fine hunk of a man?" she jokes, but she's deflecting.

"Don't do that. He's a great guy. And he can't take his eyes off you. What's going on?"

She looks at me with pure agony in her eyes.

"I like him. I used to think he felt the same, but now he just avoids me. I guess I got it wrong. The man runs a mile whenever we cross paths." She shrugs.

I saw him watching her at the bar for as long as we were there, longing in his eyes. Her assessment just doesn't make sense.

CHAPTER 21

COOPER

I t's been three long nights since I had any quality time with Hayley, and that's far too many.

Between Leila stealing her away to go dress shopping, Dad burying her in paperwork for this Anderson deal, and my work that has piled up over the last couple of weeks, we have only managed to sneak in our early morning coffee dates.

By Wednesday, though, I am done, and my wolf has me snarling and growling at anyone who comes near me. I delegate as much as I can so that I can leave my office at a respectable time. Rex has rolled up his sleeves and is temporarily helping me as much as he can. We have an unsaid acknowledgment that I need time to focus on winning over my mate.

This was after he chewed me out for my possessive display in Taaffe's, correctly pointing out that I have now put her in danger by indicating she is someone special to me, even if it never crosses anyone's mind that she could be my fated mate.

By refusing to entertain relationships with the other female wolves in the pack, and then openly going out with Hayley, I've all but told them they're not good enough for me. Even though that decision was largely based on a decision to not shit where I eat, not the ladies in the pack themselves.

The last thing I wanted was to meet my mate and bring her home to a pack full of my ex-girlfriends and conquests.

Some might take their anger out on Hayley, as Carla did, and even try to scare her off. When dealing with the jealous power- hungry females in a wolf pack, a thrown drink would be the least of her worries.

Claws and teeth are a far bigger concern.

And if anyone blabs to another pack, someone could threaten Hayley to get to me. Most packs are much more inclined to use diplomacy to get what they want these days, but there are always those that revert to the old-school methods of violence and blackmail. We are animals, after all.

The full moon run after Leila's party is even more of a worry, though. Rex was right. I hadn't even considered it. I either need to get Hayley out of there before midnight, before everyone shifts and runs together through the forest as a pack, or I need to tell her about us before then.

She still hasn't trusted me with her reason for moving here, and Marcus's comment about her needing someone is playing over and over in my brain. If she doesn't feel she can tell me about her life before Grey Ridge, I don't think we're at the point where telling her I can turn into a wolf is a good idea.

Now that I think about it, I'm surprised Mum even invited her. She knows that the run would be on later the same night.

I race out the door without seeking my parents to say goodbye as I would normally do. Thinking about the party and the run has my mind reeling.

While I was delighted at first that my father invited Hayley to the Alpha's conference, now I'm angry he didn't discuss it with me first. I know she will be a great asset for him to have at business meetings, but it has put a definite deadline on me.

I need to tell Hayley about me, about the pack. She can't go without knowing about shifters.

Which is probably exactly why he has done it. And my mother.

And here I thought I'd kept this secret so well.

The pressure of trying to work out how to handle this situation has me agitated. Lately, the only thing that can calm me is seeing Hayley and being close to her. She's like a drug. I'm addicted to her and currently suffering from withdrawal.

It's almost 8 pm by the time I park my truck at my cabin and drop Hayley a quick text to see if she's free. Hopefully, she won't be offended by the last-minute request, but I don't want to wait another day. I hop in the shower and have a quick wash before throwing on a pair of jeans and running out to the living area, t-shirt in hand, to grab my boots and go.

I turn the corner and see the most breath-taking thing I could ever imagine, my little mate standing barefoot in my kitchen, dishing up dinner out of takeaway cartons onto plates, swigging from a bottle of beer. She's wearing a plain black t-shirt dress that skims her figure, and she looks deliciously at home in my house.

I could get used to this.

I drop what I'm carrying and rush over to her, wrapping my arms around her waist from behind, and drop a kiss on the top of her head.

"Hmmm, something smells good." I lean over and press my nose into her neck, taking a deep inhale. Her scent is just wonderful, and I can't get enough of it. She giggles and pushes me off so she can turn around in my arms.

"I hope you don't mind me just walking in, but your door was open. I didn't want the food to go cold." She looks nervous, as if I could be annoyed at her overstepping some boundary.

"When you asked about coming over, I just felt so bad that you have been working all hours but still coming to see me every morning, so I thought I'd do something nice for you instead." She stands up on her tiptoes to kiss me and I wrap my arm around her back to haul her closer.

Hayley's normally shy about initiating affection with me, but she's getting more confident. I understand coming over here to surprise me with food and making herself at home in my little cabin was a big deal for her. It pleases me to know she feels comfortable enough to do it, and my wolf loves the fact that she wants to take care of us.

"I don't mind at all, not one bit. Thank you." I give her another kiss before I remember I'm still shirtless. I step back and can't help but feel chuffed when I see Hayley checking out my body, eyes lingering on my muscular chest and abs.

Her eyes follow the trail of hair from my belly button down until it disappears into my jeans, where the top button is still undone. She goes a little pink and clears her throat. Pulling my t-shirt over my head, I grab the plates and head to the table.

Oh yes, I can tell this evening is going to be a good one.

CHAPTER 22

HAYLEY

Turning around to look at Cooper, I realise he's shirtless, and butterflies explode in my belly.

I can't help myself; I touch his massive pecs, leaning up to kiss him, and they're rock hard under my touch. I'm practically drooling when he steps back to pull his t-shirt over his head, his defined abs tensing and rippling, making my head spin.

My fingers itch to reach out and trace them, to trail my hands down the line of soft, dark hair that starts below his navel and disappears into his soft, faded blue jeans.

He looks like an underwear model, and I feel an uncontrollable urge to lick him all over. I take a deep breath to regain my composure and focus on setting the table. From the smile tugging at his lips, he knows exactly what effect he's having on me.

His home is warm and cosy. The décor masculine, all wood and leather, but the soft blankets and pictures of family dotted around the place make it seem lived-in and welcoming. I was worried it would seem too forward, arriving at his place with food and uninvited, but I know he has been burning the candle at both ends. I wanted to do something nice for him. He seems happy to see me, and I'm amazed at how natural it feels to get dinner ready, talking about our days as if we've been together forever.

Together? Relax, Hayley

We've only had three dates, and a serious relationship, when my life is still all over the place, is a terrible idea. While whatever this is feels so right and so easy, I need to stop myself from getting carried away.

This was supposed to be a sexy fling.

The "sexy" part seems to be working out just fine, but my brain can't seem to comprehend the "fling".

Relaxing on the couch after dinner, Cooper pulls my feet into his lap, giving me a foot rub while we continue our mundane chit-chat. I sigh, thanking my lucky stars for his magic hands as I melt into the cushions.

This man cannot be real. Hot, smart, funny, gives killer foot rubs.

What else could a woman want?

My dreams for the last three nights have been filled with replays of him, reducing me to a quivering mess in the bar with a few kisses and some naughty words. Rubbing myself against him like a cat, I don't think I've ever wanted someone so badly in my life. My insides clench as I think about it: the feel of his firm length pressed against my hip. It's making me wet again.

A nudge brings me out of my daydream, and I realise Cooper must have been talking to me.

Shit.

"Hayley? Where did you go? You completely zoned out." He looks me straight in the eye, taking a deep breath, and every muscle in his body tenses. His brown eyes glow a golden bronze in the soft light, but there's nothing soft about the hungry way he is looking at me. It's pure lust.

The relaxed atmosphere disappears in an instant. Suddenly nervous, I try to pull my feet away from the intensity of whatever is pulsing in the air between us; but, as I do, my toes brush against the now obvious bulge in the crotch of his trousers. He lets out a low growl, an honest-to-God *growl*.

While I want to think it's weird, it isn't, and I feel myself even more turned on as my desire continues to edge higher. He holds my feet where they are, takes another deep breath, and swallows slowly, returning to rubbing my feet in silence. Like nothing happened. I watch him cautiously as I try to steady my racing heart.

The sweet and innocent massage has ended. With each stroke of his hands against my feet, he drifts a little higher. He wraps his hands around my ankles and massages up my calves, then back down to my feet. Tingles are erupting everywhere he touches, and I am in absolute bliss, mesmerised by the heat between us as his magical hands send jolts of electricity straight to my core.

I tip my head back and close my eyes, his hands drifting higher still, tickling me as he skims over the sensitive spots behind my knees and up the outsides of my thighs.

I can feel him watching me, but I can't open my eyes. The sensations are already so intense and overwhelming that I can't focus on anything else. It's like when we were in the bar but amplified a thousand times.

His hands stroke gently from my ankles all the way to the top of my thighs, and I shiver as he reaches my underwear. He skims his fingertips along the edges of my silk panties and follows the hem all around to my ass. His fingers follow the same path back again, edging underneath the hem, teasing, stroking, and my sex quivers.

I'm spellbound by what he's doing. I've never had someone take their time like he does, focusing all of his attention on me, pleasing me with no rush. Like he has all the time in the world. Enjoying himself in my pleasure.

It makes me feel precious, cherished.

I subtly edge my legs wider, giving him better access, and I'm rewarded as he trails his fingertips along the edge of my panties, down the side of my lips, and around to the sensitive skin where my thigh meets the underside of my ass.

He strokes over my clit, and I gasp, I can't help but arch off the couch, seeking more pressure. The caressing touches drive me wild, but they're not enough.

"Cooper!" I call in frustration as he does it again and I twist my head from side to side, not knowing what to do with myself as my need for him builds. I could come from these delicate, teasing touches alone, but it's not what I want. He chuckles, obviously enjoying how much he's driving me mad with this sweet, sweet torture.

"Do you like that, Hayley? Tell me what you want," he whispers, still seated on the other side of the couch and stubbornly out of my reach. He dips a finger through the wetness at my opening without entering me. Every muscle in my core clenches in anticipation of the intrusion that never comes.

I feel like crying.

When he doesn't push his finger deeper inside but moves back to gently circling my clit, a little too softly, a little too far away, I pant, "Fuck, Cooper. Do whatever you want. More, I just need more!"

CHAPTER 23

HAYLEY

I'm practically begging, and I don't care one bit. He gently pulls my underwear down between my legs, flinging them over his shoulder. Suddenly, his mouth is on me, and I cry out in pleasure as his tongue licks and flicks at my sensitive clit.

Twirling and circling, delivering long, firm strokes that have me crawling up the couch and away from the strength of the sensations. He finally pushes a finger inside me, and my sex clamps down, so close its unbearable – then he adds a second finger, agonisingly slowly, increasing the sensation.

His hand drifts over my stomach, holding me in place as I writhe beneath him. Increasing the tempo of his fingers inside me, I'm on the verge of coming but am holding back, tensing to delay my release. He curls his fingers as he strokes in and out, the added sensation as he hits my g-spot ratcheting everything up another level.

No longer can I hold back. He throws me into the strongest orgasm I have ever experienced. I toss my head and call his name, my eyes flying open in shock at the power as Cooper pulls me to him, twitching and shuddering with the aftershocks, despite being wrapped in his powerful arms.

"That was amazing, Hayley. I need you right now. Tell me I can have you?" His breath on the shell of my ear is ragged. His deep husky voice filled with longing has my head spinning. I have no idea what's happening to me, but every inch of my body is begging for him to take me, to possess me.

I can't speak, so I nod. He grabs my chin, tilting my face to his and kissing me gently.

"I want to hear you say it, Princess. I need to hear you say you want this as much as I do." He speaks into my neck as he licks and kisses one spot that makes me crazy.

"Yes, Cooper, I want you. Take me," I whisper. He lets out an actual growl again and devastates me with a soul-deep kiss. His tongue tangles with mine, his hand cupping my cheek, with such devotion that my heart soars.

"I'm on the pill," I add for good measure, just so we're on the same page. He sits back for a second, looking at me spread out in front of him with undisguised lust, and nods. It's raw and carnal, like I'm the prey and he's the predator.

"I'm clean, I promise," he whispers, his hands ghosting over my heated skin.

"Me, too. I've never gone bare before." A glimmer of light hits his eyes, and the flash of gold in them is striking.

"I've never…" Cooper starts just as I cut him off.

"But I want to. With you." I bite my lip, a little shocked at my boldness, and he groans, his hands gripping my flesh a little tighter at my words.

"Fuck, Hayley; you're something else," he mutters, staring into my eyes. I am still catching my breath as he rips his t-shirt over his head with one hand and opens his jeans with the other, pushing down his boxer briefs and freeing his massive cock.

He shucks his jeans, and my dress and bra follow. Taking my two hands, he pushes them slowly up, pinning them on either side of my head against the cushions. As his eyes take in my naked body from head to toe, instead of feeling exposed and vulnerable, I feel sexy and desired.

He presses soft kisses to my breasts and stomach while his finger circles my clit, worshipping my already sensitive body, rebuilding my arousal. Sucking and nibbling at my nipples, tugging and pinching them as they pebble under his attention, he takes the weight of each in his hands and squeezes them.

"Open your eyes, Hayley," he commands, and, despite the desire to screw them tightly shut against the onslaught of sensations making heat spread through my body, I force my eyes open and my toes curl. Gazing down at me with pure, unbridled desire flashing in his eyes, he plunges his cock into me in one deep thrust.

"Cooper!" I cry out as I come again, the foreplay and build- up tonight, of the last two weeks, coming together in one explosion. Finally, having him inside me, filling me completely, feels better than I imagined. I cling onto him for dear life, and he pulls us both up to sitting so I'm straddling his lap.

When I'm coherent again, resting my head on the bulging muscles in his shoulder, I feel that his whole body is tense. His muscles are straining and the tendons in his neck are standing out in restraint. I feel his cock twitch inside me as I shift, and he pushes deeper inside me.

"Oh my gosh, Cooper," I whisper in disbelief, shaking my head gently, completely stunned at the power of what is happening. He kisses me tenderly, rising carefully, keeping us joined, he wraps my legs around his waist as if I weigh nothing at all.

Crashing his lips down on mine, he walks into the hallway, whispering how beautiful and sexy I am, how hot it was to see me break apart just for him.

I place my hands on his tanned, muscular shoulders and lift myself slightly, before lowering back down and rocking my hips as he hisses and bites my lip.

All plans of making it to a bedroom appear to be on hold as he growls and spins, pressing me against the nearest wall, shifting my weight to just one arm.

"Hayley, you feel so good," he moans, pressing his forehead to mine and thrusting once, deep inside me I rock my hips, desperately needing him to move again. I swear I can feel his cock pulsing inside me, and I want him to take his pleasure; to see him lose control as I have.

He smirks into my neck as I attempt to take matters into my own hands, pressing me a little harder against the wall, using his two hands under my ass to roughly squeeze both cheeks.

With a tilt of his hips, he pushes so deep that he fills me to the hilt. I moan loudly in pleasure at the sensation of feeling so full, so completely owned, as he begins pushing in and out of me. Every inch of him stretches me, his crown rubbing against that perfect spot with each roll of his hips. I rub my hands down his strong back, and I can feel his muscles bunching and moving under his skin with the power of his thrusts.

"Not here. You deserve a bed, Princess." He pulls us away from the wall and resumes the walk quickly towards the back of his cabin. I know he is a big guy, but I marvel at how he carries me so easily.

"Hayley, you feel so amazing, so tight," he breathes, kicking open the door and lowering us both to the mattress. "I wanted to take my time making you come again and again, but I can't." Gripping my chin, his eyes lock with mine. "I can't wait any more."

He kisses me deeply and grabs both of my breasts roughly and squeezes, kissing each one gently and licking over my nipples, rocking in and out of me. Slowly he builds the pace and the force behind each thrust.

I can feel myself inching higher on the bed, and I put my arms above my head to brace myself against the headboard.

"I have wanted this for so long, Hayley. To make you mine," he growls as he reaches between us and strums my clit in time with each thrust.

"Oh, Cooper. I can't... I can't again." He drives me toward another peak, and I whimper.

"Yes, you can. Just wait for me, Princess," he orders.

I'm moaning and panting as I feel my control slipping, the sensation of being completely owned by him making me delirious.

"I... I'm going to... I can't...," I cry, desperately clinging to him as I'm overwhelmed, swept past my limits. He lifts my hips to deepen the angle and thrusts hard, holding my hips and pulling me to meet him each time. I grip his thighs and dig my nails in as he powers into me once, twice, three times; I can't hold on any longer when he presses hard against my clit with his thumb.

My body shakes as I call out his name, another orgasm rocketing through me.

With one last thrust, I feel him shudder as he roars, releasing deep inside me, gripping my waist tightly to hold me in place while he empties into me. He pulses in and out slowly a few times, dragging out my release before finally collapsing over me, his head buried in the crook of my neck.

"Hayley," he whispers reverently, and my heart flutters with the emotion conveyed in that one word.

I reach up and trail my fingers gently through his hair and the curls at his neck, marvelling at this gentle, yet oh-strong-man who has turned my world upside down. Cooper has me enthralled; it might not be a good thing, but it feels amazing right now. He turns his head to mine, kissing my nose softly as his gorgeous face lights up in a soft smile, and his breathing evens out as our heart rates settle.

"That was unbelievable. I don't even know what that was." I'm dumbfounded, and he laughs. Rolling onto his side, he grabs my hands and brings them up to his lips, kissing each finger and my palm.

"You're unbelievable," he smiles at me with adoration like I've never received before.

"You have some serious skills, Mr. Jones."

He beams with pride, and I swear his chest puffs out. I have never had that much pleasure from sex – from anything. He brought me to ecstasy so quickly and easily, yet it was more than that.

I feel emotional, connected to him. Amid the passion and frenzy, something happened. Something deeper.

"I've never done that before," he admits, meeting my eyes.

For a second, I think he meant sex., but that can't be right.

"Yeah, me neither, it was pretty spectacular."

"No, any of it, Hayley."

I try not to look as shocked as I feel.

"You're my first. I've done some fooling around, but never all the way."

How has this hunk never had sex before?

"How are you that good?" I ask bluntly before I can stop the words tumbling out of my mouth, and he chuckles.

"The right partner, I guess," he whispers as he plants a kiss to the tip of my nose. "Will you stay here tonight? With me?"

He looks me in the eye and seems genuinely nervous. It's endearing after his very commanding performance, and a little something in me appreciates that even though things between us have moved so fast over the last week, he still takes the time to stop, to check in and ask me what I want at each step along the way.

A little voice niggles in the back of my head that staying tonight will blow any notion that this is still just a fling completely out of the water.

I'll worry about that tomorrow.

"Yes." It's doubtful I could leave even if I wanted to. My legs are jelly. I smile drowsily, and he plants another panty-melting kiss on me, wrapping me up in his big, brawny arms, and breathes deeply in and out into my hair. His smell and his warmth are comforting, and I'm so exhausted, I feel myself drifting off to sleep with a dopey smile on my face.

CHAPTER 24

COOPER

After what we did last night, it's like I can feel the mate bond becoming physically stronger between us, as if we have added another thread to the invisible connection that will bond us forever. Even though she hasn't moved yet, I know she's awake, and I feel a twinge of anxiousness flowing from her. I'm immediately nervous.

"Hayley, promise me that if we're going too fast, you'll tell me? Just talk to me. We have something special here and I don't want to ruin it," I say quietly against her neck, laying my cards out on the table, fear that I pushed too soon gnawing at my insides. Something in her face flickers, and I wonder if I've hit the nail on the head.

Damn it, I got too carried away.

Or maybe she's put off by my admission that she was my first? Is that too much pressure?

I kiss her shoulder, her golden skin too tempting to resist, then turn her gently to face me. She's wearing a sleepy little smile that settles my nerves a bit, but I still need to know.

"Are you sorry about last night?" I steel myself for her response. If she regrets it and pulls away from me, I'm not sure I'll be able to take it.

"Cooper, I'm happy about that, so happy, trust me," she whispers, as she moves to straddle me, sitting back on my thighs so I have a perfect view of her body in the early morning sunlight streaming through the windows. She rubs her hands across my pecs and trails them down my abdomen, then along the muscles running from my hips to my groin. She watches her hands as she dips them even further down, but I catch them in my hands before she touches me there.

"You're killing me here. Please, Hayley, we can take things slow, you don't have to..."

She cuts me off with a shake of her head as she bends down and plants a kiss on my collarbone. Her hair tickles across my chest, sending goosebumps over my skin as she wriggles lower, kissing and licking her way down my stomach.

"Hayley don't start that unless you plan to finish it," I growl.

She peeks up at me but looks down along my body at my now rock-hard dick.

"Maybe that's exactly what I want to do." She smiles and bites her plump bottom lip between her teeth as she sees how hard I am for her; how much she turns me on. She wraps her hand around my cock and applies some firm pressure, pumping her hand slowly up and down over my hard length, and my eyes roll back in my head.

With her other hand, she reaches for my balls and rolls them gently. I lie back and cover my face with my arm, a groan of pleasure leaving my lips. I can't watch or I'll go off in two seconds. She looks so fucking hot.

Sliding her tongue along the V reaching down to my groin, my thighs and ass tense as I struggle not to move, not to take back control of the situation. She chances a glance up at me, and I stare back from between my fingers.

My eyes must be shining where my wolf is pushing through, and I clench my elongated teeth behind firmly shut lips to stop myself from hauling her up the bed and embedding them in her neck.

I reach out to touch her hair, tucking it behind her ear as she moves closer to my groin. Gently licking the very tip of my cock, taking the bead of pre-cum waiting there, and swirling her tongue around the head, she flicks the sensitive spot on the underside.

"Hayley, you don't have to... fuck!" I moan as she slowly takes me into her warm, wet mouth as far as she can. My head falls back against the pillow with a thump, and I stroke her back as she bobs her head up and down over my length. She uses her other hand to stroke the base that she can't reach with her mouth and hums around me as I massage her breasts while she works.

The vibrations send shocks of pleasure straight to my balls, and I fist my hands to stop from grabbing her and shoving my cock down her throat. She looks like an angel as I watch her. Unable to look away as she sucks a little harder, she increases the pace and adds a second hand to the mix by stroking and massaging the spot behind my balls. My hips jolt up and I swear I won't be able to hold on any longer.

"I'm going to come, Hayley, come here to me," I warn, gently trying to pull her off and up my body, but she takes me further down into her throat and swallows. I growl, and fist the sheets beside me, thrusting my hips up into her mouth a second before I shout her name, coming hard. My seed shoots into her throat, and she takes each drop as I continue to pulse my hips with each release.

"Oh Hayley," I sigh, lifting her up to straddle my hips, pulling her down for a kiss. "What did I do to deserve you?"

"I don't know, but it must have been something pretty great," she teases in a sultry voice as she rolls her body up against me. I grip her hips in my large hands and move her harder against me. She looks down and grins, obviously impressed at the speed of my recovery.

"Cooper! Ready again? I'm impressed," she coos flirtatiously, smiling down at me. Her body is the perfect combination of lean muscle and gentle curves; her sexy bed hair that she hasn't bothered to fix, her plump parted lips, and eyes closed in pleasure. Her perky tits and small waist, those sexy little moans she makes as she rubs herself against me, are the hottest things that I have ever seen. She looks like a goddess, and I reach up to caress her breasts, to stroke over her flat stomach and her curved hips.

"Hayley, you're beautiful." I lift her by her small waist and stretch up, pressing a gentle kiss to her lips.

I pause for a heartbeat, waiting until she opens her eyes to look at me, and then plunge her down onto my cock, ready to take her again.

Her eyes open wide in surprise, and a deliciously soft moan escapes her lips as she relaxes, her head falling back in ecstasy. I feel her clench around me as I pulse my hips upward while holding her firmly in place. She places her hands on my chest and uses her thighs to move up and down slowly, riding me and taking her pleasure.

I reach up and stroke lightly around her dusky pink nipples, sitting up and sucking one into my mouth, licking and nipping it before moving on to the other. She places her hands on my shoulders for more leverage and picks up the pace, up and down, faster and faster. Her pussy squeezes every inch of my dick as she gets closer to the edge. She rolls her hips on my every upward movement, her clit gaining that friction she craves.

Her breathing gets shallow as she gets more excited, and her moans are louder. I love how she is uninhibited in taking what she needs from me, and she digs her nails into my shoulders as she climbs higher and higher.

With one hand around the back of her neck, I pull her face to mine, kissing her deeply, tilting her head sideways and kissing her jaw, neck, and shoulder. I push my other hand between us and stroke her clit, harder and faster. I grip her firmly and thrust up roughly to meet her, barely keeping my wolf in check.

"You're mine, Hayley. Say it."

Her eyes fly open in shock at the demand behind those words right as her orgasm hits her, and she cries out. Her insides massage my cock as each aftershock shakes her body.

So much for slowing things down.

"Yours, Cooper, I'm all yours," she whispers, smiling, touching my face as she comes down from her high.

My wolf is desperate to claim her, and her neck is too close for comfort to my mouth. He is ecstatic at her words, even though I can sense that she still has lingering doubts. I struggle to stop him from taking it as permission to mark her, so I flip her underneath me and nuzzle her breasts, kissing her stomach gently and taking a few seconds to push him back down.

Rising back up, sinking into her warmth again, it's a heaven I can't get enough of. I want to devour every inch of her.

"You're so beautiful, Hayley," I say as I thrust into her, gradually building up the pace and force of my strokes, caressing her ribs and waist with my hands. I grip her waist as I rise to my knees and pull her up onto my lap. I hold her tight to my chest and drive my hips upwards to bottom out inside her.

Grabbing her breasts and squeezing them roughly, I roll her nipples between my fingers, pinching them. She sucks in a breath, enjoying the pleasure and pain, and I feel her pussy twitch around me.

It's a sharp contrast to the gentle lovemaking of a few minutes ago. I continue to pump up into her, harder and faster, frenzied in my need to claim her, made worse because I know she doesn't trust this completely. I need to make sure she never wants to leave.

She groans as I flick her clit on each stroke and then I feel her tense, another orgasm ripping through her when I press firmly down on her clit.

"Hayley!" I shout as I empty into her, stream after stream of my come filling her up, and my wolf howls with joy inside my head.

We collapse, boneless, onto the bed, side-by-side, our fingers entwined as we catch our breath. This woman has turned my brain to mush, and I love it. I gather her in my arms and kiss her, trying to show her how much she means to me and when I pull back, she's smiling adoringly. I feel like a king.

"I don't think my legs work anymore." She wriggles her toes as if genuinely testing whether they are still functioning. I hop out of the bed and into my ensuite to turn on the shower. I lean in to test the water temperature and when I turn around, Hayley is lazing on the bed, unashamedly checking out my backside. Her brazenness makes me laugh.

"I'm all yours, princess. You can look all you want." I cross back over to her, lifting her bridal style and carrying her to the bathroom. I set her down just in front of the shower, place some fluffy towels into her hands, and kiss her gently. "You go first. I'll get breakfast." She steps under the water, and I pause in the doorway as I see the warm water cascading over her body, trailing over every dip and curve. I'm instantly hard again.

How on earth am I ever going to get anything done with her around?

CHAPTER 25

HAYLEY

had secretly been hoping Cooper would join me in the shower, but as I wash my body, I realise I'm quite sore and it's probably a good thing he had enough sense for the two of us to leave.

We'd never make it to work.

I smile when I get out of the shower and see the toothbrush and toothpaste that he has left out for me. Sexy and thoughtful. What a catch. I frown a bit as I wonder: why he is still single?

Those voices saying that something doesn't add up are back.

Is he too good to be true?

Leila's party. Will there be ex-girlfriends there that I should know about? I haven't asked him anything about his past relationships, because I really, really do not want to talk about mine. But something magical happened between us last night, and I'm letting myself think that this could be something special. I'm the first person he's slept with. Surely that means something. Right?

When I walk back into his bedroom, the dress and the underwear that were thrown across the sitting room last night are neatly folded on the bed. I dress quickly and stroll out to the kitchen, gingerly lowering myself down into a chair at the table in front of the delicious spread Cooper has laid out: pancakes, fruit, bacon, and juice.

"Mm, these are so good. You're a man of many talents," I say as I tuck into the homemade pancakes and berries. He groans when I lick some maple syrup off my fingers.

"Stop that." He shakes his head. "You're killing me."

I grin and he crosses over to me, placing a soft kiss on my lips. "I'm going to go hop in the shower and get going. You eat up and

stay here as long as you want." He stands, carrying his dishes to the sink then disappears down the hallway. Fifteen minutes later, Cooper comes back, dressed, clean-shaven, and gorgeous.

"I'll see you later." He emphasises "you" and somehow makes it sound like both a threat and a promise – and a sexy one at that. He snags a piece of fruit off the table, kissing me again and dashing out the door.

My phone rings, and I find it shoved down the side of the sofa, abandoned and forgotten in our haste last night. I flip it over and see the name I'd been hoping for.

"Hayley! Where the hell were you? I've been trying to get you all night!" Sam screeches down the phone and I can hear her fingers clacking away on the keyboard as she talks, probably already at work for hours by now. I don't think I've ever seen her doing less than two things at the same time.

"Sorry, Sam. I was, eh, having an early night," I struggle to keep the giggle out of my voice, but fail.

"What?! Don't tell me you're getting laid, up on some mountain in the back of beyond, and I can't get any in a city of eight million people!" I can feel her eye roll down the phone.

"They make them big and handsome here, Sam. You'd love it. If you ever take a few days off, come visit," I suggest, knowing full well that she never takes time off work.

"Yeah, yeah. Maybe just send me some pictures? Or at least tell me what or who is making you sound this annoyingly happy." She sighs. "Actually, that's for another time, with wine and zoom. I'm about to ruin your buzz."

"You found something?" I whip out a pen and notebook from my purse, settling back at the table.

"Unfortunately, yes, or fortunately I suppose, since they haven't signed yet. Those Anderson bastards are trying to pull a fast one."

I love Sam. She curses and drinks like a sailor, but she is fierce and loyal, and the only non-family person I've trusted with my current location.

"Just tell me."

"The builder they used for the Forest Spa, the one the Joneses are buying, is under investigation for cutting corners, jeopardizing fire safety requirements. Three other properties he constructed have been shut down and the remedial works has run into the millions."

I groan, pressing my fingers to my temples.

"Do they know? The Andersons, I mean." I had a gut feeling something was off, but I didn't think it would be this bad. If the Joneses were to buy this property and it turns out to have the same issues, it could ruin them.

"Hard to know for sure. There's probably no proof either way, but I'd be shocked if they hadn't heard something. You said they're in a rush to close? Seems suspicious. And maybe there are no problems, but just having that builder's name attached to the property will lower its value." A notification flashes on my phone as she sends me the information she has gathered.

"Crap. Ok, thank you so much, Sam. I owe you."

"Yes, yes you do," she agrees. "You can pay me back by setting me up with one of your hot mountain men when I visit."

God help them; they wouldn't know what hit them. Sam is like a whirlwind. I'm not sure the laid-back male population of Grey Ridge would know how to handle her.

"Deal! I better go and tell Mr. Jones. Talk to you later." I hang up feeling nervous. This information will probably kill the deal. It's not my fault, but sometimes the messenger does get shot. It's not the first impression I was hoping to make on Cooper's dad.

Time to pull up my big girl pants.

CHAPTER 26

HAYLEY

I call ahead and asked Kim, Jonathan Jones's assistant, to schedule a meeting with him as soon as possible.

She phones back a few minutes later and says Cooper's dad is there and available to see me whenever I can get there. So half-an-hour later, I'm sitting in my car outside their lodge, working up the courage to break the bad news to the head of my firm's largest client. A pretty blonde appears on the front steps and waves when she sees me climbing out of my car.

"Kim, I presume, lovely to meet you at last," I say as I walk up the steps and extend a hand to her.

She shakes it and smiles back, tucking her chin-length platinum blonde locks behind her ear. "You too. It's so good to finally put a face to the name. I'll show you to Jonathan's office. This place is a bit of a maze." She ushers me through the front entryway and down a long corridor. I glance through the open doors on each side as we pass, seeing a large kitchen and massive living space on one side, and what appears to be a dining hall on the other, with a breakfast buffet lined up along one wall.

"The lodge is three stories; the bottom floor has living areas and offices, dining and kitchen facilities for staff and guests, lounge, game room, library, and gym. The first floor is staff accommodation. A lot of our single workers live here, me included. Free accommodation and food, not going to turn that down." She winks and points out the various rooms as we move along, turning left at the end of the hallway. "Top floor has some guest accommodation, and the living quarters for the Jones family. Johnathan and Marie are at the front of the house, Cooper and Leila have apartments on the left; Rex and Nathan share on the right."

My steps falter for a second at that. Cooper has an apartment at the lodge. He's never mentioned it, which seems strange, although I suppose it must be convenient when he needs to work late. I wonder how often he stays here.

At the end of the hallway, Kim raps lightly on an open door and then pushes it wider, gesturing for me to go in ahead of her.

"Oh, Hayley. Come in, and sit," a deep voice booms.

When I walk in, Cooper's dad looks up from behind his desk, a friendly smile on his face. He looks just like Cooper with a few more lines on his face and grey streaking through his hair. We shake hands, and he grasps mine in both of his, warmth radiating from the deep brown eyes that are exactly like Cooper's. I take a seat in the chair opposite his desk and have a quick look around.

His office is decorated exactly as I expected: all masculine with dark wood, sturdy furniture, leather chairs, and paintings of the great outdoors. I can picture Cooper in here one day.

"How are you doing?" He sits back in his chair smiling gently at me, hands interlaced on his abdomen, the picture of openness and welcoming.

I wonder how welcoming he's going to feel in a few minutes.

"Good. Thank you for seeing me on such short notice. It's about the Anderson deal," I say seriously, getting straight to the point. "I'm sorry to be the bearer of bad news, but I had someone look into the builders. Unfortunately, they've had some issues with the previous developments they've been involved with. They're being investigated for repeatedly cutting corners with fire protection measures to save costs. The places are death traps, and the remedial works run into millions. The Andersons may know that they, potentially, have the same problems in this hotel, and may be trying to offload it before word gets out."

I sit straight and try not to flinch as Jonathan curses loudly. Clenching the fist that sits on the table, he pounds it once and, I swear, I hear it crack. He immediately schools his features and regains his composure, running a hand over his head.

"Forgive me, Hayley. Obviously, I am grateful that you've brought this to my attention. I've known the Andersons for a long time. To think that they would try to pull something like this..." He blows out a breath and shakes his head in disbelief.

"I assume you'll want to investigate yourself, but I just wanted to make sure you knew before you committed to the deal. At the very least, the valuation is off," I say, and he nods solemnly. "You know, Mr. Anderson hasn't really been involved. It's mainly that Toby pushing to get closed..." I don't finish that sentence; Mr. Jones can fill in the blanks.

Maybe Anderson's son-in-law left his old friend, Mr. Jones, out of the loop. He seems like a nasty piece of work, so I wouldn't put it past him.

"Thanks, Hayley. No wonder they were so keen to get contracts exchanged." He looks furious, knowing as well as I do that the rush to get the sale completed is surely a sign that they know the property is in trouble. He pauses for a second, considering something, clasping his hands in front of him on the desk.

"Don't say anything to Toby other than the deal is on hold. I'll get Kim to schedule a face-to-face meeting at the conference next Friday to discuss it."

I agree and go to stand, but he holds out his hand and gestures for me to wait.

"Anything else?" I ask tentatively, concerned by the frown he's wearing. Is he annoyed that I didn't catch this sooner? Is he angry that the deal is dead in the water now until we know for sure whether this property is affected?

"I never personally thanked you for saving Cooper. And now this. We owe you a lot."

I try not to fidget as he watches me closely.

"You'd be a great addition to the Jones family."

"What?" I look at him in confusion. He couldn't mean what I think he means, could he?

"You should work here. You'd fit right in, and we could do with someone in house who has proper financial experience. Consider it at least. You can tell me after the conference."

Oh. Family as in work-family. Not the please-marry-my-son kind of family.

I need to get a grip.

"I'll think about it." I smile back at him, chuffed at the offer, even if my heart is still beating a little faster at the thought that he means more than work.

If I wasn't dating his son – am I dating his son? – I'd take him up immediately, but I need to make sure it won't make things awkward with Cooper. I excuse myself and step outside the office, leaning against the wall for a second to gather my thoughts. I came here expecting to collapse a deal and ruin someone's day, not to leave with a job offer.

As I push myself off the wall to go, I hear the deep voice that fills my heart and my dreams. Cooper. It sounds like Nathan is with him.

I walk towards his office; the door is slightly ajar. I'm about to knock and say hi when I hear my name, so I pause. If they're having a personal conversation, especially if it's about me, I don't want to barge in unannounced.

I know I should leave, but I don't. I loiter and listen.

CHAPTER 27

COOPER

As I walk into my office after breakfast, Nathan is waiting for me. I leave the door open, and swing into my chair behind the desk.

"Out. Whatever it is, I'm not in the mood," I say rudely, pointing at the open door.

Last night may have been the best night of my life, but it made keeping my mate a secret even harder, and I'm sick of it. I don't want to leave her in the morning. I want her here with me, running the pack businesses, side-by-side. It's fraying my nerves, and, at 9 A.M., I'm already out of patience.

I hate lying to her.

I hate not knowing everything about her.

I'm completely on edge.

"Charming. What's up with you?" He perches himself on the edge of my desk, tossing an apple up in the air and catching it, up and down, up and down. I grit my teeth.

"Nothing," I grumble, throwing my phone into a drawer and slamming it shut.

I can feel Dad pushing at me through the mind-link, but I block him.

I just want some peace to clear the mountain of paperwork on my desk. Then I need to work out what the hell I'm going to do about Leila's party on Friday.

How can I make sure the whole pack doesn't find out that Hayley is my mate before I get a chance to tell her myself?

"Shouldn't you be in a good mood this morning?" he asks with a smirk, and I glare at him.

"What are you talking about, Nathan?" I ask with a sigh. He always talks in riddles instead of getting to the point. It drives me mad.

"Cooper. You reek of Hayley and sex. I would have thought that finally getting some action would have improved your humour." He chuckles to himself and raises an eyebrow at me.

"Shut the fuck up, Nathan," I snap, clenching my fists on the table.

"Jeez, Cooper. I mean, who is she that you're this worked up?" He tries to bait me into confirming she's my mate.

I hold my breath, trying to rein in my temper. I might love my brother, but, right now, I want nothing more than to wipe that stupid smile off his cheerful face with my fist.

"Nobody. It's none of your fucking business what I do."

I need to get out of here. I need to let my wolf run off his agitation before I shift in the office and tear the place apart.

"Good for you, Coop. It's good for you to have someone keeping your bed warm and your dick wet while you wait for the right one to come along. That's how it is, right? It can't be anything serious," he tries again.

My vision blurs as my wolf lunges forward to punish him for daring to speak about our mate like that. My canines extend and I struggle to push him back down.

"Something like that," I mutter, concentrating on keeping it together. "For fuck's sake, Nathan, just get out. Go and do some actual work."

"Fine. You're no fun. But, FYI, shower again before you meet Mum. She has your date for Leila's party in her office. The poor girl might not appreciate her future mate coming in smelling like another woman." He laughs as I groan, looking up at the heavens and praying for help.

"Who the hell is she trying to pair me up with now?" I demand. "Actually no, I don't care. This is bullshit."

I might not be able to tell Mum about Hayley, but I need to put an end to her setting me up. It's another headache that I just don't need right now.

"You're right, it is. How come Mum never sets me up?" he complains, rubbing his hand across his jaw.

"Maybe because you're a cold-hearted man-whore."

"Fair point." He grins, sliding off my desk and taking a big bite of his apple. "You know, you're a lucky man. Hayley's a good one. Better than you deserve, anyway." He thumps me on the shoulder and strolls out of my office without a care in the world.

If I thought he could take the whole mate thing more seriously, I'd tell him about Hayley. To Nathan, it's all just a game, and I can't risk him making some smart comment or joke that lets the cat out of the bag.

Deep breaths.

Go for a run.

Have another shower.

And stay away from Nathan so I don't kill him.

CHAPTER 28

HAYLEY

Nobody.

I'm just keeping his bed warm, and his dick wet until the right one comes along.

A crushing weight settles on my chest as those words rip my heart from my chest and shatter it into a million pieces. I think I might throw up. His conversation with Nathan replays over and over in my mind as I stumble out of the packhouse and into my car, tears threatening to spill down my cheeks.

I feel sick. And stupid. How did I read him so wrong?

I thought my awful experience with James was the reason I had been waiting for something to go wrong, for something to prove that Cooper couldn't be this perfect, and I couldn't be this happy. I was waiting for the other shoe to fall all along.

And boy did it. I shouldn't have ignored my intuition.

He isn't serious about me. I'm not his, despite his sexy, "You're mine" growing nonsense. He was just having a good time, telling me what I wanted to hear.

My joy has been blown to smithereens.

Was it too much to hope that something would go right for me?

How am I going to live in this small town, work for his father, stay friends with his sister?

One thing is for sure, I'm not letting another man run me out of my home.

I'm done.

Done with men. Done trusting them.

And I'm definitely done with Cooper Jones.

Ethan and Rex are already there when I drive in at half nine. This is the first morning I haven't been here already, having my morning catch up with Cooper. They exchange a knowing glance and grin at each other. Given I hardly know anyone else in town, they're assuming that there is only one place I could be coming from this early in the morning.

"Morning Hayley! You're up and about early!" Ethan calls to me as I climb out of my car. I grimace, knowing they think they've caught me red-handed, but where normally I would join in the teasing and the banter, today I keep my head down and rush past, unsure what to say. I swipe at my face and avert my eyes as Ethan looks a little too closely at me.

"Don't be a dick," Rex scolds him, wondering what's wrong. Ten minutes later, I'm leaving again, dressed to impress to make myself look better than I feel.

Again, I keep my face angled away, avoiding eye contact, and hop into my car before speeding off towards town. There's a car pulling in as I leave but I look straight ahead and keep going. I don't feel able to make small-talk with suppliers, or the postman, or Jerry who makes the deliveries for the local hardware store. I'm too shaken.

This town might be my new home but for today, I'm going to be rude and keep on going.

CHAPTER 29

COOPER

Distracted, I stare at my computer screen and groan. I can't focus.

Memories of last night mean focusing on the meetings in my diaries and the work I've let pile up while I hung out at Hayley's house is impossible. About to throw in the towel and go for coffee before a meeting with my dad about the upcoming alpha's conference when I feel Rex reaching out to me via mind-link.

Rex: Coop. What's up with Hayley? Cooper: Why? What did she say?

Rex: Nothing, ran in and out without saying hi. What did you do?

Cooper: Nothing, I swear.

Rex: Well, somebody did something. She looked upset.

Rex being rejected by his mate has him worried that the same thing could happen to me. For a wolf, their mate is everything. With Hayley being human, I'm under a lot of pressure to get this right. The fact he's looking out for me means a lot.

Admitting defeat, I turn off my computer and head down to the house, convincing myself that I need to see everything is done properly before the guys move onto a new site. It's a complete lie, but it allows me to do what I want.

Pulling into Hayley's house, I smile. The last of the work that I had them fast track on the house is now finished, and the place looks great. I walk around the property to make sure we have left the house tidy for my mate before we pack up the last of our equipment and leave for good. Pausing as I emerge from behind the shed, I see there's a tall man standing out front, looking up at the house.

Rex comes out of Hayley's front door at the same time I spot a pile of paint tins that need to be stored inside. Deciding to move them inside while I wait for Rex to deal with this guy, I stay back, my wolf feeling overly territorial about a house that doesn't even belong to me. Not a great idea when speaking to humans.

Pulling the door closed behind him, Rex nods in greeting, and I see the man's face tighten as he watches Rex pocket the key.

"Can I help you?" Rex asks him, crossing his arms over his chest and staring at him. The man's dressed in an expensive suit, and a dark rental idles on the road at the end of the driveway.

His black hair is slicked over to the side, and a forced smile full of unnaturally white teeth breaks out on his tanned face. Not from around here then. I take in the shiny shoes and flashy watch and immediately decide I don't like him. Although I doubt that I'd like any man walking up Hayley's driveway.

"Just wondering whether Hayley is home?" he asks, trying to appear casual and relaxed, but I can see the stiffness in his posture and the tension in his jaw. Something is off. It's the middle of the morning on a workday, and her car isn't here. She has a phone. Why is he here looking for her instead of just calling her? Ethan, who's just come outside, goes to answer, but Rex cuts him off.

"Hayley? Not sure who you mean, buddy," he says, pretending to be the clueless labourer he has probably pegged us for. I do not like this dude at all. Whatever he wants, or whoever he is, I am not helping this douche sniff around my mate. His smile slips for a second, as he doesn't get the response he wanted. I don't think he enjoys being called buddy either.

"No problem. I'm just an old friend, thought I would stop in and say hi while I was passing through. I'll catch her again," he says with a fake smarmy smile plastered back on his face. Ethan edges over to Rex, and we all watch as the stranger climbs into the passenger seat of the car and drives away slowly. So, he's not alone either.

"What's up?" Ethan asks Rex, wondering why he was being so frosty to the guy. He shrugs because I can't explain it.

"Not sure, he just seemed like a bit of a dick," Rex says, as if that was a good enough explanation.

Ethan and I laugh. "He was a dick," I agree.

"I don't think you can be objective here, Cooper." Ethan rolls his eyes and pats me on the shoulder. "And Rex, with those people skills, it's shocking you decided you aren't suited to being an Alpha." Rex laughs and I relax a little. Nobody can argue with that.

CHAPTER 30

COOPER

've been trying to get a hold of Hayley since Rex told me she was upset leaving, but she hasn't answer my calls or respond to any of my text messages.

Distracting myself by helping Rex and Ethan, I'm done waiting when my dad finally catches up with me and tells me what Hayley uncovered. She was at the packhouse to tell him, personally, but never stopped by to say hello.

After the night we had, I'm surprised. I have a gut feeling something is wrong.

It's enough to get me into my car and drive to Hayley's office to check in with her. I don't want to suffocate her, but I can't stay away and the closer I get, the worse I feel.

I'm getting worried and she comes first, now and always.

When I finally get to her office and push the door open, I'm not prepared for the sight that greets me. Hayley looks beautiful. She's polished and sophisticated, as always, in a navy dress with long sleeves and her hair up in a high ponytail. I was expecting her to be a mess, considering I can feel the jumble of emotions pushing and pulling across the bond. Her eyes are slightly red, as though she's been rubbing them, but it's the only sign that something might be wrong.

She looks up at me with frighteningly calm eyes. She doesn't smile.

"Hey Princess," I say cautiously, shutting the door quietly behind me.

She says nothing, just stares at me blankly; frankly, it's terrifying. She looks so composed, but I can feel a staggering rage radiating through the bond.

"I couldn't get a hold of you, and I was worried. Everything okay here?"

I stand awkwardly beside her desk, because I don't know where else to go. I don't want to sit down like I'm her client, but her frosty demeanour gives me the distinct feeling that going in for a hug and a kiss would not be welcome.

"I think you should leave," she whispers with steely authority, and my heart sinks.

This is not good.

"First," I say cautiously, "I'd like to know what I've done to upset you, Princess?"

Does she know? Did someone tell her I'm a shifter? Maybe this is the end. She obviously wants nothing to do with me.

"I'm not your fucking Princess," she snaps, her cool mask slipping for just a second. Fire flickers in those golden eyes of hers before she pulls the shutters back down and turns to the papers on her desk. "And I don't care what you want. Leave."

"No." The alpha in me is furious at being dismissed by my mate. "Not until you tell me what is going on. Everything was fine this morning, better than fine, amazing, and now you won't even look at me." I won't back down until I know what's wrong. I'll do anything to make her happy, but I can't begin unless she tells me what I've done.

"Everything *was* fine, for you, because you're just 'wetting your dick', waiting until the 'right one comes along'? Well, that's not fine with me," she hisses, firing her pen across the desk and onto the floor, spinning her chair to face away from me.

Oh no. This is worse than bad. This is a nightmare.

She doesn't let me see them, but I can smell her tears. She heard.

"Princess, no, no, no..." I grab her chair and spin her back around to face me, sinking to my knees in front of her. I grab her hands and hold them between mine.

"I told you, stop calling me that," she whispers sadly. "Please, just leave."

"No, I'm not leaving, not until you understand. I didn't mean that. Any of it. Nathan was just saying it to wind me up, and I was just trying to get rid of him." I can tell she isn't even hearing what I am saying. She has shut up tight, her body rigid as she stares at a spot behind me.

"You didn't disagree with him, Cooper. Did you?"

She yanks her hands out of my grasp and stands, grabbing her purse from the floor and tucking it under her arm.

"If you won't leave, I will." She marches past me and out the door, taking her delicious scent, and my heart, with her.

Hayley

"Hayley," he mumbles as he catches up to me on the street, pleading with me to stop. I can hear the sorrow in his voice and see the regret on his face, but I'm not about to feel bad for him.

He reaches for me, just as someone walks past us, and he freezes; he pulls his hands back and shoves them into his pockets instead.

The last piece of the devastating puzzle slots into place.

"You didn't tell me about your place at the lodge, because you don't want to bring me there. We'd be seen together." I shake my head at my own naïveté. "You don't want anyone to know we're dating." I can't believe I was so blind.

He flinches, and I know I'm on the money.

"Same reason you brought me hiking in the mountains. That you made me dinner at *my* place. That you only kissed me in that dark fucking hallway. You piece of shit," I shout at him, completely horrified now that I see it all so clearly.

He never brought me out in public. Even that night at the bar, he didn't touch me until we were out of sight. I had thought those things were romantic and special because he wanted me all to himself.

Oh, God.

"Why? Because you have a wife? A girlfriend? Or am I not good enough for you? No, wait, I don't care. I don't want to know. We're done." I march into the car park, rifling through my bag for my keys so I can get as far from Cooper as possible.

"Hayley, I..." he speaks, but I cut him off with a look.

He puts his hand on my arm, but I jerk away from him.

"Don't you dare touch me," I say sharply, and he startles as if I've slapped him.

Triumphantly, I hold up my keys, finally finding them buried in the bottom of my bag, but Cooper steps between me and my car, blocking my way.

"I'm so sorry, Hayley, I'm an idiot. Please, can we talk for a minute?" He sounds so desperate, moving to the side as I try to dart around him.

"Cooper, get out of my way!" I say through clenched teeth, my anger rising at being corralled like this.

"No." He crosses his arms, staring down at me.

"Are you seriously forcing me to stay here so you can try to feed me some bullshit about not understanding what I heard this morning? Or are you going to humiliate me some more by admitting that you like me enough to fuck me, but not enough to tell anyone?" Venom laces my words.

I need to get out of here before the tears that are stinging the backs of my eyes spill out. He doesn't deserve to know how much pain I feel.

I need to stay angry so that I don't completely fall apart.

He still hasn't denied anything I've said, but at least he looks as devastated as I feel.

"We did not fuck, Hayley. We made love." He steps toward me, speaking quietly, "And you mean everything to me. I really need you to listen, because it's not what you think. Let me explain." He gestures toward my car, like we're going to go somewhere so he can explain. Obviously keen not to have this conversation so publicly.

"Kiss me," I demand suddenly.

He pauses, looking panicked as he glances around us to see who's watching. I roll my eyes and push past him, yanking my car door open and jumping behind the wheel.

"Don't worry, Cooper, you can bring your other date to Leila's party. You don't have to worry about being seen with me – ever again."

As I reverse out of my parking space far too quickly, I see Cooper standing in the middle of the car park with his two hands on his head. He kicks the gravel, and a cloud of dust rises around him as he watches me turn the corner and speed away.

I'm such a fool, getting caught up in another whirlwind romance. How did I not learn my lesson? Not that I think Cooper would have physically hurt me, but as the tears fall down my face, I think this might be worse. I was falling in love with him.

CHAPTER 31

COOPER

I should have kissed her.

Screw who saw us. I should have grabbed her and kissed her with everything I had and never let her go. But I hesitated, and that hesitation may have cost me my mate. She's right to be pissed off; I'm furious with myself.

Nathan tried to goad me into admitting she was my mate, and I should have either admitted that she was mine and sworn him to secrecy or laid him out with a punch.

Agreeing with him just so he'd leave me in peace was disrespectful to Hayley, my soulmate, and the most precious thing in my life. The guilt is gnawing away at me, knowing how hurt she must have been to hear that. It would have devastated me if it were the other way around.

Damn it!

She doesn't know that I would do anything for her, that I love her with every bit of my heart and soul. Because I do love her. Even without the mate bond I'd want her, because she's perfect for me. She's just perfect.

And I have no idea how to fix this.

The door to Taaffe's bangs against the wall as I storm inside and

THE ALPHA'S SAVIOUR 131

head straight for the bar. My chest is burning, and I know it's her pain. I deserve to feel this way as punishment for what I've done, but she doesn't. My mate is hurting because of me. I'm supposed to take care of her and keep her safe, not make her cry.

What kind of man am I?

Sean sets a beer down in front of me and I shake my head.

"I'm going to need something stronger than that, Sean." I rest my forearms on the bar as I slide heavily onto a stool.

"Bad day, huh?" he asks while reaching to get me a bottle of whiskey and a glass.

"The fucking worst." He pours a drink and I knock it back in one. He fills it again, silently, moving off down the bar to give me some space, he leaves the bottle in front of me.

I pull out my phone and send a text to Hayley, asking her to give me five minutes. I don't know what I'm going to say, but I know the only hope I have of winning her back is to tell her everything.

It's do or die time.

As the evening goes on, I'm not optimistic about my odds, and as I finish my fifth drink, still with no response from Hayley, my brief glimmer of hope fades even further.

Nobody else is sitting at the bar; the anger and sorrow radiating from me keeps everyone at their distance. I know exactly who it is the instant a large body drops onto the stool right next to me.

"I fucked up," I say simply, taking another sip of my whiskey, glancing sideways at Marcus.

"I guessed that." He gestures to Sean for a glass. I bet Sean was getting nervous and asked Marcus to come by in case I got out of hand. Marcus is probably the one person in town, other than my dad, who has any shot at dealing with a raging alpha.

"It's bad. I'm not sure if there's any coming back from this."

I voice the words that I've been afraid to think, and they stick in my throat. I know it's true. Everything she said was spot on – even if for all the wrong reasons? Even if she could get past this, the bombshell that is my explanation will probably be the nail in my coffin, anyhow.

"You're mates, you'll work it out."

I scoff at him, knowing that he won't agree by the time I finish telling him what happened.

When I end my story with the way she tore out of the parking lot with tears streaming down her face, I know he's trying very hard not to lose his temper.

He grabs the bottle and pours another drink, downing it in one.

"Exactly," I mutter, and he blows out a harsh breath.

"What the hell were you thinking? You should have knocked him on his ass not agreed with him. Hayley does *not* need this shit. You have no idea what that girl has been through." He thumps his fist off the bar and Sean looks over with a raised eyebrow.

I knew it.

Sean's throwing stink eye because he called in Marcus to keep things calm. Marcus raises his hand in apology and lowers his voice. "This is exactly why I told you to tell her."

"I didn't want to scare her away. It was going so well I was afraid she wouldn't accept me." I put my head in my hands and sigh.

I've been here for hours, trying to think of any way to make this better. I can't. Marcus looks uncomfortable with my obvious despair, and I know he would rather be anywhere other than sitting here, listening to my woes. The fact that he is even here tells me he's not always the grouch that he pretends to be.

"I'm not exactly the best person to give advice about women. You know me as a grumpy bastard, but I wasn't always as bad at this." He chuckles wryly, shaking his head. "The only thing I will say is that Hayley is crazy about you, and once she's cooled down, she'll hear you out."

"Maybe I should go over there. I need to make sure she's alright." I go to stand, but Marcus puts his large hand on my shoulder and shoves me back down into my chair.

"No. Not only will you make it worse by turning up at her place, uninvited and stinking of booze," he looks at me sympathetically, "sitting outside her house morning, noon, and night until she talks to you will not work. You need to give her some time."

I eye him curiously, frustrated at not knowing as much about my mate as he seems to, but appreciating that he's trying to help me. My alpha nature is telling me to just make her listen, to show her I care, and that I won't give up. Marcus is telling me that's not a good idea, and I should trust him.

He keeps me company while I finish the bottle, deep in thought about whatever his own predicament is. We make a right pair. Misery really does love company.

"Did that work for you? The space thing," I ask, wondering who the mystery lady could be who broke this tough guy's heart.

"Fuck, no. I never even got to kiss her."

CHAPTER 32

HAYLEY

A soft rap on the front door drags me out of my depressed stupor and over to the window to check who it is. A broad back, that I can barely see around, clad in a red and black checked flannel shirt could only be one man: Marcus.

Who else turns his back on a door and still expects it to be opened for him?

"Hi, Marcus. What's up?" I crack the door open and lean against the frame. I'm trying to hide from view, given that I look a complete mess and need a shower badly. I've worked from home for the last couple of days, wallowing in my misery as I obsess about Cooper and what happened.

"Don't 'what's up' me. Open the door," he says sternly, using a massive hand to push the front door wide open, striding into my home like he owns the place.

"This isn't a great time, Marcus." I stand by the open door, arms folded in front of me to hide my bra-less-ness.

He ignores me as he looks around the living room, taking in the loose tissues, the empty bottle of wine, and the open tub of ice cream on the coffee table.

"Come on, Hayley, it's like a Bridget Jones set in here," he mutters as he lifts the fluffy throw off the couch and plonks himself down, making my three-seater look tiny under his massive frame.

"Seriously, Marcus, I think I'm coming down with something and I don't want to make you sick. It's probably best if you leave."

Staring down at my feet, I will him to just get up and go. I can't bear for him to see me in this state again. I bawled in his office when I first came to town and explained about James. He'll think this is a regular thing for me.

"Seriously?" he mocks, not buying my lies.

He already knows.

"Hayley, just sit down." He pats the seat beside him then leans back with his arms along the back of the couch, making himself comfortable and telling me he's not going anywhere.

"Fine, but you're not staying. I'm feeling sorry for myself here, if you hadn't noticed. I'm not in the mood for company," I warn him, then sigh because it's not his fault.

He's not Cooper, it's not fair to take it out on him. He's here being a friend. I wander over and slump down in the corner of the couch, pulling the blanket over my lap and tucking my legs beneath me.

"Are you alright? Have you slept?"

I tilt my head to look at him.

It's a strange question, not one I would have expected to be top of the list from him. Maybe I look so awful that it's obvious I haven't. I shake my head no, and he puts his thick arm around my shoulder, pulling me into the side of his big, warm body.

I haven't had any problems sleeping since I started spending time with Cooper, but last night, for the first time in ages, I couldn't drift off for longer than half an hour. Each time I did, my old nightmares about James following me, breaking in, and attacking my family, kept coming back.

"I'm a mess. I know this is ridiculous. We're barely even dating." I sniffle, frustrated that my tears are coming again at the mere thought of Cooper.

"It's not ridiculous, Hayley. When you know, you know," he says quietly.

I scoff. I thought I knew, but, apparently, I was completely wrong.

"I'm obviously not an excellent judge of character. How did I get it so wrong? Again!"

"I know you're not happy with him right now, but do not lump Cooper in with that other asshole," Marcus fixes me with a stern look.

"Fine. I know he's nothing like James. But even still, Marcus, I thought we had something." A little sob escapes me, and Marcus squeezes my shoulder with one arm and strokes down my hair with the other. It's something my father would have done, and it's comforting.

"I saw him; he told me what happened," he admits, and I stiffen, waiting for him to row in and defend Cooper. To tell me I was mistaken, that I heard him wrong, that it wasn't a big deal.

"He was totally in the wrong. He told me that himself."

I glance up at Marcus suspiciously, but there's only honesty in those soulful brown eyes.

"He is in bits, Hayley. He loves you. He has to tell you his side himself, but you have to believe me when I say he doesn't think of you like Nathan said. He knows how lucky he is to have found you."

"But..." I try to argue with him, but he shushes me before I can launch into a rant.

"I know he hurt you, and he knows it, too. He's completely torn up over it, but there are some things you don't understand, yet." He meets my eyes as he rubs his thick, dark beard thoughtfully.

"I don't think there is anything that can excuse it," I say quietly, shaking my head. "I would never speak about him like that." The pain feels as fresh as it was yesterday, and I rub my chest where it aches.

"I'm trying to get you to see that there might be more to it. Maybe you can't get over it, but at least hear him out and then decide. For your own sake." He levels me with a stare, "And you have some stuff you need to tell him too, Hayley." He's really going all-in on the tough-but-fair-dad act. "You can't say you're serious about someone while keeping big secrets yourself. Cooper won't run, Hayley. He'd want to know; he'd want to help."

I want to sit up and face him, to argue with him, but his arm is like steel, and he has me trapped.

"I've said my piece. Just think about it. He did something stupid, but you know in your heart how he feels about you." He pats the top of my head as a yawn escapes me. "Now get ready. I'll drive you up to Leila's party. She'll be gutted if you miss it."

"What about you? Are you coming, too?"

He shakes his head slowly. It would have been nice to have someone arrive with me. I'm not sure what kind of reaction to expect from Cooper's family. No doubt they've all heard at this point.

"Too fancy for a simple guy like me, I'm afraid. I'm not one for parties." He hauls me to my feet and points to the stairs. "Go beautify yourself. I'll wait."

"Marcus, you're one of the good ones, you know that?"

As I pass, I pat his arm.

"I know, I know. I'm a fucking saint." He winks, chuckling darkly. "Get ready to have some fun. Show him what he's missing."

CHAPTER 33
HAYLEY

By the time Marcus pulls up in front of the lodge, cars are already lined up everywhere, and people are milling around with drinks and food in their hands, laughing and chatting. I fiddle nervously with the hem of my dress. There are way more people here than I expected.

"Hayley, just enjoy yourself. It'll all work out." Marcus smiles reassuringly as I climb out.

"I think this is a bad idea..." I hesitate without closing the door. I convinced myself that I'd be able to handle seeing Cooper, that I'd just avoid him or something; that if I had to talk to him, I could be civil and stay calm. Now I know I was just fooling myself.

"I'm not letting you back in this car, Hayley," Marcus says, sensing that I'm ready to turn tail and run straight home. "You live here now, too, and no matter what happens with you and Cooper, you're not hiding anymore. Do you hear me?"

Nodding, I feel stronger. He's right, I can't go back to staying at home like I did for the first two months after moving here. I need to have a life if this is going to be my home.

I wave goodbye and wander around to the back garden where there is a big BBQ with picnic benches and a bar. The patio doors at the back of the house are flung open, with music drifting out and filling the evening air.

Everyone looks happy and relaxed.

Fairy lights are strung from tree to tree and around the gazebo; it looks magical in the dusk.

Leila makes her way over to me and brings me over to her family and I smile and nod at the friendly faces that greet me warmly. Since the whole rescue thing, everyone in town seems to know who I am. "Oh, yay, you came! Thank you," Leila says quietly, pulling me into a big hug as soon as she sees me. "My mother is already driving me mad about the conference, trying to get me to agree to some dates. You need to run interference for me."

"Oh, my heart bleeds for you. Your mother is trying to set you up with rich, eligible bachelors, boo-hoo." I roll my eyes at her dramatics. "Maybe I'll get her to help me out instead, if you're not interested." I hear a choking noise behind me and turn to see Ethan watching me while he thumps his chest.

"Drink went down the wrong way, sorry," he mutters.

Leila ignores my comment completely and drags me to the bar, snagging two glasses of white wine and clinking our glasses in cheers.

"I know you and Cooper fought; I've told him to leave you alone tonight. You don't have to talk to him if you don't want to, okay?"

I nod, feeling my throat tightening at the thought of having to face him. I wanted to come and prove to myself that I am okay, but I'm not. Far from it.

Sitting at a picnic table with Ethan and Rex, Leila and I are just catching up when Marie sneaks up, placing her hands firmly on Leila's shoulders. Leila flinches and I stifle a laugh. Her mother has a glamorous redhead in tow who is scanning the crowd over our heads.

"Leila, have you seen Cooper? This is Amanda. I wanted to introduce them, but I can't seem to find him anywhere."

In my peripheral vision, I see every one of Cooper's family go still. You could cut the tension with a knife. This must be the date Nathan warned Cooper about. I school my features into one of pleasant indifference as Marie continues speaking, oblivious to the stifling atmosphere around her.

"I do apologise for his tardiness, dear," Marie says to Amanda. "Let's get you some food; we'll find him. He's around here some-where." Amanda nods politely at all of us and follows, hot on Marie's heels, as she leads her away to find her missing son. Rex and Ethan continue to eye me without saying a word, waiting for a reaction, but that's not my style.

The last thing I want is to create a scene.

Ethan suddenly stands and strides quickly toward the main house, no doubt to find Cooper. I can't bear the thought that everyone is looking at me with pity. At this point, that's upsetting me more than anything else.

Leila puts her arm around my shoulder and gives me a squeeze, whispering in my ear, "I don't know what my mother is up to, but you know what she's like. There's no way Cooper wants anything to do with that girl."

Smiling weakly at her, I nod, but the truth is, I feel humiliated again.

"It's fine, Leila. We never said anything about being exclusive. He's a big boy. He can see whomever he wants." I smile at her, trying to keep my dignity intact in front of her family and friends.

"Oh, no. He's not seeing someone else; he doesn't want to see anyone else!" she insists, looking desperate to repair the situation as she looks to Rex for help.

"It's fine, forget it. It's not a big deal, okay?" She looks at me as if she might be the one to cry.

I try to push down my embarrassment and focus on not ruining Leila's birthday by creating drama. I look up at Rex, who touches my arm and changes the subject, like he can tell I just want the attention away from me. I smile gratefully and take another sip of my drink; I am going to need all the wine I can get if I am going to get through this night.

Once everyone is engaged in conversation, I escape from the table and make my way inside, getting away for a minute to put my head on straight.

As I round the corner, I see Cooper's broad shoulders and soft, tousled chestnut hair. He's leaning against the wall, speaking quietly with Ethan.

Thankfully, he's facing away from me, so I head in the other direction, not wanting to have this horrendous conversation right now. Somehow, though, he knows I'm there and whips around, fixing me with dark eyes that look very troubled.

As soon as he sees me, he comes after me, even as I try to hurry away, he catches up easily with his long strides.

"Wait, Hayley. Please, wait!" he grabs my hand and pulls me back towards him, looking panicked. He is usually so confident and charming; it's strange to see him flustered.

I look him in the eye, waiting for him to explain, but a man with long wavy black hair and a cocky smirk fixed on his lips interrupts us. He would be good-looking, but he seems to radiate anger. I step back from him instinctively; his presence makes me uncomfortable. Cooper places his arm on my lower back reassuringly, but just for a split second, dropping it again and distancing himself from me.

The action leaves me cold. It's the second kick in the gut.

Why am I even here? Am I a total glutton for punishment?

"Cooper, good to see you," the man grits out, but it doesn't seem to be good at all as they shake hands, gripping tight and looking like they are trying to break each other's fingers. The animosity between the two is clear.

"Reynolds, you came," is all Cooper can manage in greeting.

Not exactly a warm welcome.

"Well, it's very hard to say no to your mother, and we're neighbours after all. It's time we mend fences," he states, clearly less than enthusiastic about the prospect.

He is smiling, but it's so forced it's terrifying.

"And who do we have here?" he focuses his intense stare on me.

I feel Cooper tense beside me, and I can tell he does not want to introduce us.

"This is Hayley Walker. Hayley, this is Dean Reynolds. Hayley has been doing some work for my dad," Cooper says stiffly, gesturing to me dismissively, as if I don't warrant a proper introduction.

I raise an eyebrow at him, and even though he doesn't take his eyes off the other man, he has the grace to look ashamed.

"Ah, smart and stunning. Lucky Jonathan." This Reynolds speaks to Cooper as if I'm not here. It reminds me of the arrogant pigs I had to deal with in the city, who still seem surprised by women with brains.

The man, Reynolds, sticks out a large hand for me to shake and I grit my teeth, but accept it and shake quickly, not smiling at him or giving him any encouragement to continue engaging with me.

He holds on just a second too long as he looks me over appraisingly, and a whisper of fear courses through me as I wonder what he might do. Cooper doesn't like the guy, and I can see his jaw ticking the longer Reynolds's attention is on me. But Cooper doesn't say anything, doesn't claim me as his date or his girlfriend.

Because I'm not.

"Lovely to meet you, Mr. Reynolds, if you'll excuse me," I say coolly, turning and walking quickly towards the bathroom before Cooper can stop me. I close the door behind me and lean against it, sucking in a couple of deep breaths, finally letting a few tears fall.

CHAPTER 34

COOPER

Fury fills me that I have to stand here talking to this prick, Reynolds, and act as though I don't want to rip him limb from limb while my mate walks away from me. Again.

Hurt, again.

His father, the previous alpha of their pack, was a terrible leader and a downright sick person, if the rumours are to be believed. Relations between our packs have been tense for years.

My mother originally dated Dean's father and didn't take her leaving him for her fated mate too well. Over the years, his bitterness towards our family grew. He took every opportunity he could to make our lives difficult: blocking business deals, refusing to let any of his pack mate with anyone in ours, preventing them from working for our businesses or in our town. We also suspect he initiated constant small-scale attacks on our people and property.

Dean took over a couple of years ago, and, given his reputation for being even more cold and ruthless, this "mending fences" talk is hard to believe. I can't let him know Hayley is anything to me. He could easily see hurting her as an opportunity to weaken me as the future alpha of this pack.

My earlier delight that Hayley came tonight has all but vanished.

I make my excuses to get away from Reynolds. Following her scent to the bathroom, I stand outside to wait for her, even though all I want to do is break the door down and comfort her. I can hear her heart beating fast, a couple of sniffles, and I can smell tears.

It feels like my chest is being torn open.

As I pace up and down, I run my hands through my hair, getting more and more agitated. The door finally opens and Hayley steps out, looking beautiful but worn out.

"Hayley, I..." I start, but she turns and holds up a finger with a steely look in her eye that leaves no room for argument. She brushes past me, walking purposefully back to the table where my friends and family are gathered. I trail along behind, unsure what I can do to make things better.

Leila smiles when she sees us together, but it twists into a frown when she sees our faces and realises that we haven't made up. Quite the opposite. Hayley picks up her purse and folds her cream cardigan over her arm before she turns to my parents, smiling warmly at them.

It's unnerving how well she can put on a happy front.

"Marie, Jonathan, I'm afraid I have to leave early. Thank you so much for having me. It's a wonderful party, and I hope you have a great night."

I touch her hip gently to tell her not to go, but she subtly steps forward, out of my reach, to give Leila a tight hug. The rejection feels like a kick in the balls. She's slipping through my fingers.

"Sorry for dashing off early. Have a great night and I'll see you soon." She nods at everyone else with a bright smile on her face, giving Leila another big squeeze and directing a filthy look at me.

"Hayley, I'll drive you home...," I offer, but she looks at me with a face fixed in a frosty, neutral expression and shakes her head.

It would be better if she was furious and shouting. My beautiful mate, who was screaming my name in the throes of passion just two nights ago, is now looking at me as if I'm nothing more than an acquaintance. And one who she doesn't particularly care for at that.

"I'm not drinking, I'll drop you back home," Rex offers and looks at me for my reaction. I nod, grateful to him for suggesting it. It's probably the best solution. She's not going to let me drive her home, but at least I know she'll get there safely.

"I'll get my car and meet you out front."

"Thank you, Rex. That would be great," Hayley smiles at him, obviously relieved by his offer.

As she walks through the house, I catch her by the elbow and pull her into one of the empty lounges, needing to speak to her alone before she runs off. Needing to be close to her, to touch her.

I want to comfort and reassure her, but she takes a step back to maintain some distance between us, crossing her arms in a barrier. She looks up at me with big, sad, doe eyes and its agony to know that I've made her feel this way.

"Hayley, Amanda is not my date. I would never, ever do that to you. Please tell me you know that, at least." She rolls her eyes at me. "Believe me, Hayley, I don't want anyone else."

I step towards her again and she doesn't move away this time, letting me take her hand when I reach out to her. It's a minor victory. I rub circles on her palm with my thumb and I sense it calming her as she looks down thoughtfully at where our fingers are entwined.

"Cooper, it's humiliating. You're ashamed to admit that something has been going on between us. And introducing me to that Reynolds guy as if you couldn't care less about me..." She's shaking her head, getting worked up again as she talks about it.

"Look, maybe I read too much into what was going on between us. I don't know, we never talked about whether we were exclusive..." She trails off and tries to re-establish her distance from me. I force down the urge to growl at the thought that she would see someone else.

"Not *was*, Hayley, what *is* going on between us. I know it's only been a few dates, but I'm crazy about you. I am an idiot, and I'm so sorry that I hurt you. I want to tell everyone you're mine, it's just... complicated," I try to sound confident, but words sound lame even to my ears, and she shrugs. "I'll explain everything, I promise, just not here, not now."

"Sure, Cooper. But, for now, I just need to get out of here. Enjoy the rest of the party," she says sadly, dropping my hand and walking to where Rex is waiting, keys in hand. I stand on the steps and watch her walk off.

I wait, but she doesn't look back.

CHAPTER 35

HAYLEY

I feel bone-weary as I close the door to Rex's car and slump down in the seat. I can't wait to get home and be on my own.

I'm upset, but I'll wait to have my meltdown in the privacy of my own home, thank you very much.

"Thank you, Rex. I'm sorry for dragging you away," I say quietly, turning to look at Cooper's very handsome older brother. The resemblance to Cooper is striking. There is no denying that they are brothers, but Rex's almost-black hair is cut short, and his dark, serious looks make him look like he belongs in an action movie.

I haven't spoken to him that much, and, while he has an imposing presence about him, he's always been friendly to me.

"You're welcome, but you're actually the one doing *me* a favour. These things aren't my scene." He looks over at me, smiling, but his face softens, concern written all over his features. "Can I do anything to help?"

I shake my head, letting my hair fall over my face so he can't see my eyes glistening.

"Thanks, but no. I'm just not really in a party mood, either." I try a smile to lighten the mood, but it ends up more of a grimace. I had been hoping for a night of fun and laughter to cheer myself up; I had not planned on crying in a car on my way home by nine o'clock.

"That girl was not his date, Hayley. My mother tries to meddle in all our lives, but she would never cause trouble if she knew about you and Cooper," Rex tries to reassure me.

"Oh, I know that I do. That's the whole point, isn't it? She doesn't know, because Cooper didn't tell her, or anyone, and doesn't seem to want to, either. Maybe we weren't even dating? I don't know anymore."

The hurt blooms again in my chest, and I sniff to stop the tears from falling.

"He's crazy about you, Hayley; you know that right? Even though he's my brother, I wouldn't say that to you if it wasn't true," he turns to look at me as he parks outside my house.

"Just not enough to tell anyone." I sigh, feeling deflated and just plain sad. "Thanks again for the lift, Rex." I smile at him and climb out of the car, trudging inside.

As soon as I get through the front door, I kick off my shoes and head straight to the fridge to pour myself an enormous glass of wine. I should keep a clear head for when I speak to Cooper tomorrow, but I know I won't sleep because I'm too wound up. My brain will be spinning. He said it's complicated, but it shouldn't be, not if you love someone.

The idea of him not wanting me as much as I want him has me reeling.

I'm feeling conflicted about having "the conversation" given that I have my own mess, which I haven't told him about. He isn't the only person who has some explaining to do. Whatever complications he's talking about probably pale compared to the drama following me around.

Hoping that a soak in a bubble bath will help me relax and switch off my brain, I head upstairs and run the bath. Just as I pour in some calming bath salts, the doorbell rings. I turn off the taps, heading downstairs with butterflies already in my belly.

If Cooper has followed me here, I'm not going to let him in.

Liar.

Even *I* know I am talking rubbish. One look at that gorgeous face, into those sad brown eyes, and I'll probably melt.

I spot a bunch of flowers on the ground outside the door as I peek through the side window, and my heart warms a little. Cooper must have dropped them off but wanted to give me some space at the same time. I grin despite myself, opening the door and bending to pick up the beautiful bouquet.

The potent smell of cologne hits me, and I recognise it instantly. The blood in my veins freezes as I turn to my left and see the face I never wanted to see again standing in the gloom of the porch.

I knew this moment would come.

I knew that one day I'd have to face him again. That he is here, in the dark, hiding in the shadows, tells me he means business. Fear seizes my insides. I'm on my own and vulnerable, and he knows it.

"Hello, Hayley," he says, unsmiling.

Something hits me on the back of the head, and everything goes black.

CHAPTER 36
COOPER

Hiding is not very alpha-like behaviour, but that's exactly what I'm doing.

I'm so angry with myself for making such a mess of everything, and I know that if I go back out to that stupid party, I will do something regrettable.

A gentle knock sounds on the door and it opens wide to reveal Leila and Ethan, both looking at me with apprehension as I knock back yet another glass of very expensive whiskey.

This is becoming a bit of a habit.

I'm sure I make quite the picture, drowning my sorrows in the dark, leaning back in my leather chair, feet up on my desk amidst a sea of chaos. My computer, books, pens, and papers are strewn all over the room; a bookcase lies tipped on its side.

"Rex dropped her off, safe and sound. How are you holding up?" Ethan steps over the mess without acknowledging it, leaning against the fireplace, arms folded across his chest.

"Just great, Ethan. My mate hates me because she thinks I'm embarrassed to be seen with her." Bitterly, I pour another glass of whiskey, scowling at it. If Hayley were a wolf, this would all be so much simpler. We would already have mated. She'd carry my mark, and this party could have been our mating ceremony.

I've waited years to find her: visiting other packs, going to conferences I hated just on the off chance she'd be there. And I never gave up hope. I worked hard to be a man my mate would be proud of. I had assumed that finding her was the hard part that as soon as I met her, my happily ever after would begin.

That my mate would want nothing to do with me had not been a part of that picture.

I look out the window at the night sky, brightened by the full moon and the glow from the strings of lights outside. The evening is crisp and clear, music and laughter drift through my open window as the pack bonds and enjoys the anticipation of the full moon run. I can't seem to muster any enthusiasm.

My wolf normally loves the thrill of running as a pack, but tonight, he just wants to find Hayley.

"Okay, Coop. I think that's enough of that." Leila removes the glass from my hand, setting it down on the table. "You're not going to impress her by turning up tomorrow smelling like a bar."

I sigh; I know she's right, but I also don't know what else to do. I can't think properly and have a killer headache that won't go away.

"Look, Hayley cares about you, otherwise she wouldn't be upset," Ethan reasons. "She just doesn't understand that you're trying to protect her. You'll tell her everything tomorrow. Hopefully, she won't freak out, and then she'll get it. Simple."

I just stare at him – even he doesn't look convinced.

CHAPTER 37

HAYLEY

Something with a sharp edge is digging into my wrists and I have lost feeling in a couple fingers. A trickle of warm liquid runs down the back of my neck and shoulder, and the coppery tang of blood fills my mouth.

James.

When I shift in my seat, a blinding pain shoots through my head, and I wince. I tentatively try to move my lower jaw. It's sore but nothing worse, and all my teeth feel like they're intact.

I slowly open one eye to see that I'm in my own sitting room, on a dining chair, my hands bound with cable ties. While it's better than being dead, this is not good. Nobody is going to come looking for me tonight.

James is sitting opposite me on the couch; arms stretched out along the back cushions, he looks completely at ease in my new home. And it makes me so angry. This house is supposed to be my fresh start, and his presence here is tainting it. His long legs are splayed out in front of him, and he smirks when he sees me coming around.

It's completely dark outside now, but I can see the faint silhouette of a man standing outside the back door. There's a creak from the front porch as someone else paces along the length of the house. So, there are at least three of them. *Wonderful.* It figures that he would have brought men with him to do his dirty work. James wouldn't want to get his manicured hands dirty.

Groaning in frustration, I try to twist and loosen the ties, even though I already know that there is no way I can get my hands free. James says nothing as he watches me squirm, enjoying every second of my misery.

Looking at his hard face, I don't understand how I ever thought he was handsome. He is too groomed, too polished; it's all fake. Gym honed muscles rather than the kind that come from hard work. His is a sunbed tan rather than a healthy colour from time spent in the great outdoors.

Even though I know he turns heads walking down the street, all I can see now is a horrible person, inside and out.

Cooper is everything this man isn't, decent through and through. There is no comparison.

I might never see him again, thanks to this dangerous psychopath sitting across from me. Clearly, he is not here to win me back this time.

I genuinely didn't think that James would go this far. It appears I gave him too much credit.

"So, you found me." I want to get whatever he's going to do to me over and done with.

He smiles smugly, and it irritates me. He's getting the satisfaction of making me listen to his little victory speech.

"Did you honestly think I couldn't?" he mocks, jaw clenching at my disrespect as I raise my eyes to heaven.

"I knew you could if you tried. I just thought you'd have lost interest by now." I eye him carefully. "What do you want, James?"

He took perverse pleasure in scaring me with the break-ins at my apartment and messed with my head. Naively, I thought that even if he found me, he would just try to cause trouble for me at work or something like that.

This will not end well for me. I've watched enough crime shows to know that he can't let me live long enough to tell anyone about this.

"Hayley, you've made me look very foolish," he starts, shaking his head disapprovingly. His eyes are cold and unfeeling as he stares at me. He is speaking calmly, but I can tell his rage is bubbling just beneath the surface. "I treated you like a queen. I would have given you anything you wanted, and you threw it all away. For this." He sneers as he looks around him with distaste at my new home.

I bite back my anger at his condescension. It's not the time for that argument.

"Why do you even care? You're a good-looking guy, lots of money. Someone else will appreciate you. You don't want me." I try to appeal to his ego, knowing these are the things he thinks make him attractive and important.

"You're right. I did want *you*, but not anymore. Now I just want you to pay," he says, and a shiver runs down my spine.

"Your whining to the police has caused me some problems... They visited me at work, and your firm won't hire me anymore. I have certain clientele who are not happy that I've come to the attention of the authorities. I've lost a lot of business because of you."

So that's it; he's angry that I have cost him money and embarrassed him. Not that I left him.

"James, think about what you're doing. Murdering me isn't going to help win back those clients." This is hopeless. I can't even wholeheartedly try to reason with him.

"Oh, I am thinking about it, Hayley. I've been thinking about it for months now. It might not get my business back, but it's going to make me very happy."

In that moment, I know he has well and truly lost it.

He doesn't care about anything anymore.

He's never going to let me go.

CHAPTER 38

HAYLEY

I scan the living room, looking for anything I can use as a weapon, but, other than a few flimsy picture frames or a lamp, there's nothing with any potential.

My eyes drift to the hall table, and I see the small, red plastic handle of a screwdriver sticking out from behind a bowl.

Jackpot.

Except it's all the way over on the other side of the room.

"I've moved hours away from you James, I haven't contacted the police since they dropped the charges. I have a new job, and a new home here. I have no interest in making your life difficult." I continue my attempts to reason with him, even though I know it's pointless: he made his decision and is committed to whatever he has planned.

"I don't care, Hayley," he shouts; "Nobody makes a fool of me!" Standing suddenly, he steps in front of me, close enough that I can feel the heat radiating off his body.

James tucks a strand of my blood-soaked hair behind my ear and runs his thumb over my lips. His touch makes my skin crawl. I don't want him near me, but I fight the urge to pull away, knowing it will just make him angrier.

For a moment, I panic as I wonder what else he might have

planned for me – before he kills me – and adrenaline surges through my body as my fight or flight instincts finally kick in.

I won't ever let him touch me again. I'd rather die.

I realise that if I am going to get out of here; I need to do it soon, before the other two guys come back inside. James looks at his ridiculously expensive watch and towards the back door, raking a hand through his hair.

He isn't looking at me for the first time and even though it's not much, this slight lapse in concentration might be the best opportunity I am going to get.

I push up from my chair, and launch forward, shouldering him backward with all the force I can manage, grateful that they didn't think me enough of a threat to tie my feet as well. I turn and sprint towards the hall, hearing James's curse as he immediately gets back to his feet to charge after me.

If he gets his hands on me, he'll kill me right now. I've been on the receiving end of his temper once before, and I have no desire to experience that again. My fingertips brush the handle of the screwdriver, but he grabs me from behind, two gigantic hands gripping my waist, and yanks me back towards his chest.

Thrashing and bucking with all my strength, I throw my elbows back wildly, connecting hard with his ribs. I hear him grunt in pain and take a sharp breath. His grip on me weakens ever so slightly, enough that I can forcibly throw my head back. It connects with his nose in a sickening crack. Pain radiates through my already battered skull and spots appear before my eyes, clouding my vision.

I force myself to stay upright because I know I only have seconds. Those seconds could be the difference between life and death. He instinctively puts his hands up to his bloody nose and releases me from his grip, allowing me to take the last step towards the table and grab the red handle with my bound hands. Just as I get a good hold of it, one of the other men bursts through my front door, hearing the commotion no doubt, and pauses for a second to take in James, doubled over.

Then the thug lunges for me.

Without thinking, I spin and twist out of his reach, stabbing the head of the screwdriver up into his side as hard as I can, my hands still tied together. I pull back and the man clutches his side, bright red blood oozing between his fingers and onto his shirt. I plunge the screwdriver down hard into his thigh this time and he screams, collapsing in a big heap on the ground beside me, gripping his leg.

My brother always said that if you put someone down, you need to make sure they stay down. Hopefully, this guy isn't getting back up any time soon.

The back door banga against the kitchen wall as it, too, is shoved open. The third guy is coming. James rights himself, his eyes watery from the broken nose begin to clear.

I need to get out of here, right now.

Turning and bolting for the stairs, I dart up them as quickly as I can on wobbly legs with my arms still awkwardly bound in front of me. I turn right as I hit the landing and head straight for the master bedroom. I lock the door with shaky fingers and cross the room, pulling open the window and swinging a leg out through it. The bedroom window opens above the sloped roof over the kitchen and back door, but I can't see what's down there.

I say a silent prayer that nobody else is waiting for me at the back of the house.

"Hayley! Open the fucking door, right now! You've nowhere to go. You're just making this worse for yourself," James roars as he rattles the door handle violently and launches himself against the locked door.

In my mind, I can see the look of pure rage on his face when I refused to wear his engagement ring. I imagine he looks exactly the same now, red-faced and terrifying. If he gets his hands on me again, he'll kill me himself with his bare hands. The door splinters as he shoulders it again, and I hear the frame crack. It won't much longer.

One more kick and he'll be through.

I swing my other leg out of the window and slide down the roof tiles on my ass, wishing I was wearing anything other than a thin summer dress.

When I reach the edge, I realise I won't be able to hold on and lower myself down so long as my hands are still tied together. I'll just have to jump and hope I don't break my neck.

Clambering as close to the side as I can, I swallow my fear, and launch myself forwards, trying to brace myself as best I can for the hard landing. My fingers bend back awkwardly as I tip forward, landing with my hands in front of me, and a sharp pain radiates up my arm.

Falling heavily to my side, the impact knocks the air out of my lungs. Hauling myself, unsteadily, to my feet, I look around, half expecting someone else to appear from the shadows. I lean over with my hands between my knees to suck some air back into my lungs, wincing at the sharp pain in my side.

Think, Hayley, think.

If I go out onto the road or driveway, I'll be a sitting duck. They'll spot me immediately. The woods are my best chance.

Even though they are nearly, completely dark, save for the light of the full moon, they'll be just as difficult to navigate for them as they will be for me. I might be able to put some distance between us or find a good place to hide. I have a good sense of which direction will bring me out near Cooper's cabin, and even though he's not at home, his house is always open. I can lock myself inside and call the police from there.

I jog up the hill at the rear of my house, my bare feet sinking into the soft dirt and leaves of the forest floor.

As I move deeper, a deafening crack thunders from a large tree beside me, and I feel the sting of bark hitting my arm. I've never heard a gunshot in real life before, but there's no mistaking what that was. Ducking down in terror, I shrink behind a tree and twist to look behind me, up at the window I just climbed out of. One man is standing in my bedroom window, tucking a gun back into a holster; then, as both he and James turn to run back down the stairs.

So much for my head start. I need to make the most of the little time I have, so I turn and run, run as fast as I can.

CHAPTER 39

COOPER

"Smooth," Ethan says sarcastically, putting his face in his hands and shaking his head as I fill him in on how I introduced Hayley to Alpha Reynolds as a colleague.

"Just shut up," I snap, not needing Ethan to tell me I got it wrong. If Ethan winds me up anymore, I'm at risk of destroying everything that isn't nailed down. Not that there's much left untouched as it is.

"Leila, will you just answer your fucking phone?" I growl as the buzzing of her phone fills the air again. Leila looks at the phone anxiously and hesitates. Sighing, I tip the phone toward me and see Marcus's name flashing up on the screen.

"Marcus?" Leila ignores me and answers the call now, avoiding our curious stares.

"Leila, finally! Why aren't you answering your phone?" he barks down the line.

"Well, hello to you too," she snaps back. The brief glimmer of excitement I saw on Leila's face at seeing his name has been quickly extinguished by his rudeness.

"Is Hayley there? Or Cooper? I can't get in touch with either of them," he asks, and I'm instantly paying attention. He is all business. Something must be going on.

"What's wrong Marcus? Hayley left a couple of hours ago," Leila asks.

"Fuck!" he says, "Where is she? Is anyone with her?" The urgency in his voice comes through loud and clear despite the traffic noise and siren blaring in the background.

"No, I don't think so. Rex dropped her home earlier, but he didn't hang around." Leila glances nervously at me. After hearing my mate's name and the nervous tone in Marcus's voice, I'm paying close attention. Leila puts the call on speaker and places it on the desk so everyone can hear.

"Marcus, it's Cooper here. What's going on? Why are you looking for Hayley?" I ask, running a hand through my messy hair. Leila and Ethan fidget, my dominant aura building as I get tense, making the room stifling. Ethan moves to my side and places a hand on my shoulder, my best friend ready to stand by me, just waiting to see what needs to be done.

"Coop. Hayley's neighbour, old Jack Miller, called to say he heard some shouting, and what sounded like a gunshot, over at Hayley's place. But we've been out at a massive pile-up on the interstate. I'm on my way back now but it'll take me at least 15 or 20 minutes." He growls and curses, blaring the horn of the squad car as he races back through traffic.

"There's nobody else who can get there any sooner. You need to go, and I mean right now," he says forcefully, and I feel the colour drain from my face as I takes in what Marcus is saying, that my mate is in danger.

"Ethan, mind-link Rex and find out where he is. Tell him to get back to Hayley's house ASAP and we'll meet him there," I order, jumping into action even though I haven't a clue what is going on.

Wolves can't mind-link their mates if they're from outside the pack until they're fully mated. I don't even know how that'll work with Hayley being human, but my wolf is going ballistic that we can't contact Hayley and find out how she is.

"Marcus, do you think it's him?" Leila asks quietly. I whip my head around to stare at her, my wolf peeking through in my eyes and his rage, quite frankly a bit scary as he tries to work out what is going on and what she knows that I don't.

"It has to be. Shit, Cooper, this guy is a nasty piece of work. I looked at him before. He has guns, some really dodgy friends and a bad temper. Be careful. I'll get there as soon as I can." Marcus hangs up, and silence fills the room.

A split second later, Ethan and I are already moving out of the office. Ethan leads the way, already pulling his shirt up over his head, blond hair sticking up all over the place, and unbuttoning his jeans as he walks. My second in command would walk through fire for me without asking any questions. And I'd do the same for him. If anyone can help me find Hayley, it'll be him.

"Leila, fill me in right now," I snarl at Leila angrily.

I'm on the edge of wolfing out and losing control. Knowing that Hayley is human, and so much more fragile than us, is making my wolf even more volatile. That my own sister knows something about my mate that she hasn't told me, means she is in his bad books now.

"James is her ex. She was trying to leave him, and he hit her." She winces as I roar in rage, grabbing a table in the hall and tossing it across the room into a wall, breaking it into bits. People scatter and clear a path to the front door, keen not to be in the way of a crazed Alpha.

I take a deep breath and Leila continues.

"He started stalking her, breaking into her apartment and messing with her stuff, hassling her and her family, so she went into hiding. She had hoped by now he had lost interest, but it looks like he found her again."

It feels like I'm about to explode.

"Leila, why the fuck did you not tell me about this? I should have known!" I'm shouting at her but I'm not really angry at her, I'm hurt, and pissed off at myself that I haven't done enough to make Hayley feel safe enough that she could confide in me about something like this.

Jogging through the house, Leila runs to keep up with me. My gut twists.

"Because she didn't want me to! And you would have freaked out and camped on her doorstep for the last month and scared her off." I strip off, shoving my clothes at her, not acknowledging that she's right. I can't in this moment, because I know exactly who he is. It's the suit from earlier today. I have no reason to think that other than a gut feeling. One that I should have paid closer attention to at the time.

"I think we've seen him," says Ethan as he waits beside the front door. I nod. "He wasn't on his own. Someone else was driving."

"Leila, tell Rex what you just told me. Let him know we're on the way, then get your medical bag and go to Hayley's. Do not get out of your car without checking in with us!" I warn.

"Get Nathan to stay here and watch Reynolds. Tell Dad to keep the pack-run well away from Hayley's house." Pulling myself together and switching back into commanding Alpha mode so the panic doesn't take over, I take off across the lawn in front of the lodge. Shifting into my massive black wolf mid-leap, I run into the trees with Ethan's dark brown wolf hot on my heels. I pray to the moon goddess that Hayley is safe and nobody gets hurt.

Except for this James guy. I want to make him pay.

As I run, my anger and guilt build. Knowing that this guy scared Hayley badly enough that she fled gave me a good idea of how horrible things had been. Yet she still hadn't felt able to share this with me. My recent behaviour probably hasn't helped with building her trust.

Physically, without the ability to shift to defend herself, she is too fragile to be in a situation like this. My wolf is freaking out at the thought of her being in danger. If she hadn't left the party because of me, she wouldn't be home alone and vulnerable.

Ethan and I race through the woods at top speed, taking the quickest route that leads from the packhouse along the river and right down to the back of Hayley's house. My feet are barely touching the ground as I push myself to run harder and faster. I need to get to her like I need to breathe, and every second might make all the difference.

Rex: Cooper, I'm here, there are 3 male scents. One is the guy from the other day. Dark sedan parked at the side of the house. Bonnet is cold, it's been here a while. Hayley's tires are slashed.

He relays information to me as succinctly as possible as he assesses the situation and clears the property calmly, using the military training all senior ranking wolves receive as teenagers.

Cooper: We're coming from the rear, two minutes out, keep talking, tell me what you see.

Rex: Shit Coop, there's a lot of blood, mostly someone else's though.

He keeps the mind-link open as he searches and the wait to find out what is going on is torture. He said most of the blood isn't hers, meaning some of it is. I try to force myself to stay calm and focused on what he is telling us.

Rex: Ok one male in the hall, unconscious, stab wound to the side and thigh. He's bleeding pretty heavily.

Good girl. My wolf is so proud of our little fighter. She just needs to keep fighting till we can find her.

Cooper: Just find Hayley. Leila is on the way; she'll help him if she can.

Rex: Her blood is on the porch and in the sitting room. But she's not inside the house. Looks like she jumped out an upstairs window. I can smell gunpowder in her room, but there isn't anything to suggest she's been shot.

She jumped out a window. And someone shot at her. How dare they shoot at my mate?

A vision of her fleeing through the trees, with her wavy hair flowing behind her and tears in her gorgeous brown eyes, pops into my head, and it's so real, it makes me falter for a second.

Was that a vision or just my imagination running wild?

Rex: They've followed her into the woods out back. They've split up but are headed in your general direction; I'll track them from this side and keep you posted. They can't have gotten too far; they won't be able to see shit out here.

Ethan: Cooper, she's okay, she's probably found a hiding place. We haven't heard any more shots at least.

I can't answer him. He is trying to reassure me, to get me to focus on the positives. I concentrate on sensing her emotions, to get a fix on where she is. We're coming from the opposite direction and the wind is at our backs, so we have no scent trail to follow. I catch a glimmer of her dread hovering in the back of my brain. It's like a spark or a memory that I can't quite grasp, and I growl in frustration as it slips out of reach again.

We must be close if I can pick up anything at all with us not being marked yet. In the pitch dark, it would be hard for a human to pick their way through these trees. However, the sky is clear, and the moon is full and high, which would have allowed them some light to move by, albeit slowly.

Hayley knows these woods well.

She runs out here almost every day rather than on the roads, although usually, she sticks to the well-trodden forest trails.

Then it hits me. I know where she is going. She is running to my cabin. She's coming to me.

Cooper: She's heading for my place.

Rex: She's still bleeding, and she's barefoot. She won't be able to make it that far.

Cooper: She'll try, she won't wait for them to find her.

I veer off to intercept her route and have only travelled a few hundred meters when I pick up her delicate scent on a breeze. Then a man's, reeking of sweat and anger. I hear footsteps, heaving breathing, and loud heartbeats. Slowing down, I approach quietly, careful not to give myself away, and then I spot them through the branches, standing in a small clearing amidst the tall trees.

"You broke my nose you bitch!" he screams at her, spit and blood flying as he shouts. The urge to rip his head off for speaking to my mate with such disrespect is strong. Instead, I creep closer, staying as low to the ground as I can, stalking towards them, using the cover of the trees to hide me for as long as possible.

Hayley is squatting down, with her back pressed up against the bark of a tree. She is barefoot, her hair wild and tangled, with both her face and her blue dress covered in dirt and blood. A tall man, with black hair and his shirt hanging half out at the back, is standing in front of her. He has a revolver in one hand, hanging loosely down by his side, the other hand up to his face where his nose is bleeding and swollen.

"Go fuck yourself, James," Hayley spits out at him, and I flinch. While I admire her spirit, it's not the smartest thing to say to someone standing over you with a gun.

Cooper: I found Hayley, and her ex. He has a gun.

Ethan: I have the third guy in my sights. I'll take care of him.
Rex, go help Coop.

"Jesus, what a fucking mess. Nothing can ever just be easy with you. How am I going to explain this?"

"Oh, I'm sorry, did I ruin your plans to kill me quickly and quietly?!" she shouts at him sarcastically. She thinks nobody is coming and I can sense from her she is just resigned to her fate now, but I will always come for her. She pushes her caramel hair back from her face with her tied hands and glares at him defiantly.

James is pacing now, frustrated and confused about what to do next as she has laid waste to his plans. His injuries will make him the prime suspect in any investigation if anything happens to her. I can see him getting more and more agitated as he struggles to come up with a way out of this that will leave him in the clear.

I edge closer still, trying not to make a sound, but I see Hayley pick up on the movement as I get within a few meters of them. As she spots me in wolf form, stepping out from behind a tree trunk, she stares at me wide-eyed and gulps. James spins quickly on the spot and raises the gun, but I lunge, sinking my teeth into his forearm, snapping it with my teeth, but not before he gets a shot off. I feel a blast to my shoulder as the bullet hits me and knocks me backward.

He drops the gun and clutches his arm, screaming, and he falls backward, trying to scramble away from me on the forest floor. I lunge at him again and grab him by the lower leg this time, clamping down until I hear a loud crack. I release him, satisfied that he is incapacitated for the moment.

I want to kill him, to tear him to shreds and give in to my wolf's rage, but I hear Hayley's terrified sobs, and making sure she is ok is more important than giving in to my bloodlust.

As I turn, I see Hayley still pressed against the tree, but now she has the gun in her hands and is pointing it shakily at me, eyes wild with fear. She presses her finger to the trigger and pushes herself to her feet.

"Stay back."

CHAPTER 40

COOPER

A ll that Hayley sees right now is a giant black wolf who has viciously attacked someone in front of her.

She is confused and scared.

Her hands are trembling as her eyes dart wildly around and she tries to make sense of what just happened. I can't think of any other way to make her understand I am not a threat, so I back up a few steps and let the transformation happen. Within a couple of seconds, I am standing in front of her as a man.

"Cooper?" she whispers, and I nod, holding my breath.

I expect her to faint or scream, but she drops the gun and launches herself into my arms. Big sobs wrack her tiny body as she wraps her legs around my waist, buries her head in my neck, and clings to me.

Rex's giant, dark grey wolf emerges from the trees behind us and her entire body tenses in my arms.

"Don't worry. It's just Rex."

She watches silently as he pads over and sits down a few feet away, head down and ears flat in submission, trying his best not to look intimidating.

Cooper: Rex, stay with this guy till Marcus gets here. I'm bringing Hayley back to Leila to get checked out.

Rex's wolf nods and trots over to where this James guy is lying, groaning, drifting in and out of consciousness on the forest floor, and growls at him. I know he would also love to rip the guy to pieces rather than hand him over to the police, but he's restraining himself for Hayley's sake.

I adjust Hayley's position in my arms so that I can carry her more easily back to her house, and her grip tightens. I thought she'd be terrified of me, horrified by what I can become, by what I just did to James. His blood is still on my skin. That she is allowing me to comfort her gives me some hope for our future.

"Shh, it's alright Hayley, I'm not going anywhere. Leila is at your house. She's going to look you over, okay?" She nods into my shoulder.

Just having her in my arms and breathing in her familiar scent is making me feel calmer, but I need to make sure she isn't badly hurt. Leila meets me at the tree line with a t-shirt and tracksuit bottoms, which I pull on quickly, setting Hayley down gently. She winces as she looks down at her bleeding feet, torn up from running through the forest over rocks, sharp sticks, and tree roots.

"I won't leave you. I'm right here," I tell her as I pick her up again, carefully, and carry her around to the porch, stepping back to let Leila do her thing.

Leila snaps on some gloves and cuts the cable ties that are still wrapped around Hayley's wrists, placing them into an evidence bag for Marcus.

Hayley rubs her wrists and flexes her fingers, letting out a low hiss when she opens her left hand fully. Angry red welts circle her arms where the ties have chaffed her skin. Leila has a quick look at her hand, turning it over and pressing it on the back gently with her fingers. Moving on to look at the wound on Hayley's head, she treats her so delicately, and I am so grateful that my sister is here to help. There is nobody else I would trust to take better care of Hayley.

There are spots of blood on the porch and a trampled bunch of flowers. I inhale and stiffen when the familiar scent hits my nose. It's Hayley's blood.

I poke my head through the front door of the house and see a guy who was obviously stabbed, laid out on the floor. I can still hear a faint heartbeat. He has a tourniquet tied around his leg, and Ethan is pressing a towel to the wound on his side. I don't care one way or the other whether he dies, but for Hayley's sake, it'd be better if he survives. I'm not sure how she would deal with taking someone's life, even in self-defence. Looking at the amount of blood on the floor, though, it's probably touch and go for him.

The hall table is shoved out of place. A dining table chair is tipped over on the floor, a vase is broken, scattering bits of ceramic and flowers all over the floor. Pictures have been knocked off the walls, and the rug is all bunched up and pushed to one side. Bloody smears and handprints trail along the wall up the stairs and to the master bedroom.

I can see the damaged door to Hayley's room hanging on one hinge at an odd angle. The frame is cracked and splintered where it was rammed open. The faint metallic smell of gunshot powder lingers in the air.

They came very close to killing my mate, but she fought like hell. We may have gotten to her just in time, but whatever she did here is what really saved her life.

I pull the door over to block her view of the inside. She doesn't need to see all the blood. I had visions of us living here together, but she might never want to set foot in this house, ever again, after tonight.

My wolf is agitated being apart from her, the smell of her blood making me anxious, so I sit on the top step and lift Hayley into my lap, holding her tight to my chest. Leila frowns at me but says nothing, forced to finish her work with me in the way. She knows better than to comment. I'm still annoyed at her for keeping secrets from me.

I knew Hayley was hiding something; I should have pushed her more to tell me. If I had known about James, I could have found him and made sure he never came near her again. He would have been in no doubt who she belonged to.

As my anger builds, so I try to change my train of thought. I need to stay in control for Hayley and be her rock, not pass my anger down the mate bond towards her. I'll let my wolf out again later to work out his rage and frustration at not getting to exact vengeance on that scumbag.

"Hayley, honey, you're going to need some stitches for that cut on your head, or I might be able to glue it. But you need an x-ray on your hand. We'll go to the hospital in the ambulance and get you fixed up there," Leila says to her, but Hayley just clings to the front of my shirt.

"Hayley... if you want Cooper there, he can come, too. Do you want that?"

Growling, I pull Hayley closer to me. Leila frowns and glares at me, exasperated. I'm not making her life easy. Rationally, I know I can't just assume that Hayley wants me to go, especially after her seeing me shift, and the fact that she didn't want to talk to me just a few hours ago.

She could still freak out at any time.

Hayley nods again, but then she stiffens suddenly, and I think for a second that she is going to change her mind before she looks down at my arm and the gash running along the outside of my bicep.

"Cooper, you've been shot!" she exclaims, putting her hand to her mouth. "Leila, you need to look at this." She points at the wound and goes to stand up to make room for Leila to get closer, but I stop her from getting up.

"He's fine," Leila says, not the least bit concerned. She knows I'm not badly injured. The wound on my upper arm from the bullet is already closed over.

"Hayley, it's ok, I promise. It's already healed, see?" I lift my arm so she can see that there is no more blood, and the edges are knitting together. Her brows lower in a cute little frown as she strokes her fingers over the wound, trying to work it out.

"I'll explain later, all of it," I whisper, kissing her forehead gently and she nods slowly, looking up at me with those big, brown doe eyes of hers, like I am her knight in shining armour.

CHAPTER 41
HAYLEY

When we get to the hospital, Leila hurries us through to a private area, away from the noise and chaos of the main emergency department.

"Hayley, are you hurt anywhere else? Did they... touch you anywhere else?" she asks softly. Out of the corner of my eye, I see Cooper clamp his jaw shut and swallow hard, trying to be calm, but I catch the pain and fear in his eyes that they might have taken advantage of me while they had me tied up.

He rubs his thumb across my knuckles, letting me know he's there for me, that no matter what, he'll support me.

"No, no, nothing like that," I say adamantly. Cooper lets out the breath, and I can see his relief, even though every muscle in his body is still rigid and his jaw is clenched tight.

"Cooper, you need to wait outside for a minute."

He growls, and Leila scowls at him.

"Stop that. You're not Alpha in here. Hayley, I'll do a quick X-ray and take some pictures, then you can get into some clean clothes so Cooper can bring you home, ok?"

"I'll be right here. As soon as I can come back in, Leila is going to come and get me, right?" He crouches down in front of me and looks me in the eye, rubbing his thumb lightly over my tender cheek and jaw. He kisses me on the forehead, so gently it brings tears to my eyes, and backs out of the room.

I don't want Cooper to leave. I just want to cling to him and stay in his arms, but I also want to get this over with so I can go home as quickly as possible.

Home.

I'm not sure that I'll ever call that house home again, not for a long time, anyway.

"Can you hop up and sit on the edge of the bed?" Leila holds out her hand and lets me put my arm around her to keep the weight off my torn-up feet, before helping me up onto the examination table up. She stands over me, pulling on gloves, and looks at the gash on my head.

"I think I can get away with some glue on this cut, Hayley. No stitches. You won't be able to get it wet for twenty-four hours, so what I'm going to do is get pictures of your injuries for Marcus and then let you clean up as best you can before I fix this up. We'll x-ray that hand then, and I'll get you out of here." She leans over and hugs me, and I grip her tightly.

She takes out her camera and catalogues all the injuries and marks on my body, cleaning and bandaging them as she goes. She takes samples from under my fingernails and has me step out of my clothes, which she bags and keeps for the police.

She hands me some scrubs to change into and I suddenly realise how dirty and bloody I was when I see my once blue-dress in the clear plastic evidence bag.

"Thanks, Leila." I smile at her weakly as she ushers me into the bathroom, closing the door softly behind her. I strip off my underwear and throw them straight into the bin. I try to clean up as best as I can with a wet towel and clean my face with some wipes Leila left for me. When I go back out into the treatment room, Leila is sitting at a desk, filling out paperwork. She looks up when she hears the door opening.

"Better?" she asks with half a smile, twisting towards me and grabbing my good hand in hers. "Hayley, I am so sorry this happened to you. I'm so glad you're ok." She squeezes my hand and sucks in a deep breath.

"I know you saw Cooper... change... it's a lot to take in. Are you alright? You can tell me or ask me anything."

"Leila, I know this might sound daft, but I haven't processed it yet. All I know is that Cooper, Rex, and Ethan saved me. And here you are making sure I'm well looked after. I'm not afraid of you." I see her anxiety turn into relief. Maybe it was the knock on the head, but I'm just glad that my friend is here.

"Good, you have nothing to fear, not from us and not from James anymore." She wraps her arms around me and squeezes me tight, a wide smile on her face.

"Ok, now about Cooper... We're very protective of families and... partners. He might smother you a bit, but please try to be patient. I know you were mad at him when you left..."

I hold up a hand to stop her.

"Leila, that seems a million years ago. I can't be mad at him after what he just did for me." I swallow hard as my voice wobbles. "If he wants to mind me, I'm sure I'll cope. We'll sort out the rest later." I try to laugh, but wince as my ribs are still sore from my rough landing.

After confirming my hand is broken, she fixes it in place with a half cast and puts my arm into a sling.

"You'll only need this for a week, then I'll give you a splint. Is it ok if I let him come in?" she asks sheepishly. "He's wearing a track on the floor outside and driving the nurses crazy."

I have barely finished saying "yes" when the door swings open and Cooper is striding straight to my side, wrapping a big arm around my shoulder, and placing a tender kiss on my temple. He frowns and curses when he sees the cast, softly kissing the fingers that are peeking out from the top.

I gaze at him, this big powerful man with such a caring side, and I'm not upset with him anymore. His brown eyes and set jaw radiate possessiveness and concern, and, despite my unhappiness that he didn't feel comfortable telling people we were together, I can't pretend anymore that I have any doubts about how much he cares for me.

"Thank you, Cooper, for coming for me," I whisper, my voice strangled with emotion.

"Always Hayley, I'll always be there for you. I would do anything for you," he whispers, pressing his forehead to mine. I crawl into his arms and place my head against his warm chest. He wraps his arms around me tightly, and I feel like I can finally breathe now that he's here.

"I'm so sorry for dragging you and your family into this. He could have hurt you tonight. I should have told you before." I look up at him, and as I blink, the tears that I've been holding back spill down my cheeks. He looks dumbfounded that I'm apologising to him.

"Hayley, I'm not that easy to hurt," he says softly, with a wry smile. "And you don't have anything to be sorry about. I'm the one who should be apologising, for keeping secrets from you. I should have told you about this," he gestures to his body.

"You're safe now, Princess. I won't let anything else happen to you ever again," he promises. "Now let's get out of here. Let's get you home."

He brushes my tears away with his thumbs and kisses me lightly on the lips, hesitantly, as if he's afraid I'll push him away. Instead, I snuggle deeper into him and wrap my arms around his bicep as best as I can with the clunky cast on one arm.

"Take my car. I need to catch up with Marcus, anyway. I'll get a lift home later." Leila smiles softly at us as she drops her keys into Cooper's hand. Marcus arrives at her shoulder and takes the evidence bags.

"I'll come to see you in Coop's place tomorrow. We'll keep the questions until after you've had a rest." Warmth and concern radiate through his deep voice. He gives my shoulder a comforting squeeze and nods to Cooper, silently telling him to get me out of there.

Cooper doesn't need to be told twice and stands with me in his arms, hurrying to Leila's car and buckling me into the passenger seat. I look at him and an image of the black wolf standing amongst the trees flashes into my mind. It was him. The wolf I had seen in the woods before was Cooper. And the thought that he was watching out for me, even then, further reassures me.

I have a million questions, and I probably should be afraid of this man. But I'm not. He came for me when I needed him most.

When I thought that James was going to put a bullet between my eyes out in the forest, I was only thinking about Cooper. How our last words had been angry.

I love this man, and no matter what happens, if he'll have me, I'm keeping him.

CHAPTER 42

HAYLEY

Blind panic consumes me as I feel a heavy, immovable weight pinning me in place.

I feel trapped, claustrophobic, and in the pitch black, I can't work out where I am. I kick and thrash, desperately trying to get free. My brain is still foggy as an image of James standing over me with a gun, lodges itself in my mind.

The weight lifts away, I fight to get on my back, scrambling until I hit something hard. A chink of recognition filters into my brain as a familiar scent hits me.

"Hayley..." a voice says quietly, soothingly, reassuring me. My heart stops racing, and the adrenaline leaves my body in a rush. As my eyes adjust to the darkness, I can make out Cooper's handsome face staring at me with concern. He is sitting at a distance, hands up in surrender, giving me space to get myself together, careful not to crowd me.

"Cooper?" I whisper, launching myself at him and burying my head in his neck. I cling to him, big fat teardrops wetting his bare chest. Memories start to come back to me of the ride home from the hospital, and him force-feeding me toast before tucking me up in his bed.

We're in his cabin. I'm safe.

He holds me and rocks me gently, whispering in my ear, saying all the right words to comfort me. He tells me that James is gone, behind bars for the rest of his life, and that I never have to worry about him again.

Cooper tells me how he will protect me, take care of me, and I feel like I am being wrapped in a warm blanket of love and affection. All the tension leaves my body, and I drift back to sleep, feeling like, maybe, everything is going to be okay.

The smell of breakfast drifts down the hall, along with Cooper's out of tune humming, as he potters around the kitchen. I sit up gingerly, spotting a clean pair of tracksuit bottoms and a t-shirt sitting on the foot of the bed, along with some fluffy towels. I run my hand over the back of my arms, and I can feel where I'm still covered in specks of dried blood and muck. Heading across the hall and straight into the bathroom, I'm suddenly desperate to get clean.

I step into the shower and direct the warm spray at my body, letting the water wash the remaining dried blood and muck from my skin. The sight of red water swirling down the drain, stark against the sterile white of the tiled room, makes my stomach churn.

Nobody has told me whether the man I stabbed lived. I can't bring myself to feel bad about it, though, maybe, that the guilt will come later if he died. My spirits lift as the water, now running completely clear, seems to wash away the heavy fog in my mind.

The relief that I don't have to hide from James any more slowly hits me. It's scary to think how close I was to being killed. I had no fight left and just wanted him to get on with it – then Cooper found me.

I have no clue how he knew where I was, but I've never been as happy to see someone in my life. The sight of him standing in front of me, lit up by the silver moonlight filtering through the trees, with worry etched on his handsome face, is something that will be burned into my memory forever.

A gentle knock on the bathroom door lets me know Cooper is here and he pushes it open slowly. A low growl burst passes his lips at the sight of my battered body. Bruises like fingers mark the skin on my hips and upper arms, a nasty purple one developing on each knee from my fall.

"Sorry, it's the bruises. I am just so sorry I wasn't there with you to protect you, Hayley." He crouches down in front of me and kisses my bruised hips as he seems to wrestle with himself to stay composed. He rests his head against my stomach and wraps his arms around me, and I can feel the guilt and worry radiating from him. It makes my heart ache to see him so upset.

"Cooper, it's over now. You saved me. I can stop looking over my shoulder," I assure him. "I'm ok, look at me, I promise I'm okay." Stroking his hair and his shoulders, the tension slowly leaves his body. Still though, his overprotectiveness is clear when he scoops me up in his arms and carries me toward his gigantic sofa. Setting me down, he leans over and kisses my forehead.

A soft rap at the front door lets us know that Leila and Marcus have arrived to speak with us. I am still wearing the track-pants Cooper gave me, and they're ridiculously big. I've rolled over the waistband and tied the drawstring as tight as I can but they're still swimming on me. I need to get my clothes and shoes, but I've no idea when I'll be let back into my house. I am so angry that James has sullied it for me with his appearance. I'll think of him whenever I am there instead of all the improvements I've made and the happy memories I've created there with Cooper.

Leila bursts past Cooper as he opens the door and makes a beeline straight for me while Marcus enters slowly behind her, seemingly happy to hang back. But he is watching her closely, as always.

"How are you this morning? How is your head? Did you sleep at all?" She fires questions at me as I stand to greet her, she grabs my shoulders and dips her head to look me straight in the eye, obviously worried that I might have had a meltdown overnight.

"I'm alright, honestly." I sit down at the long rustic wooden kitchen table and gesture for them to join me as Cooper heads into the kitchen area to put some coffee on.

"Are you okay here? If you feel safer, I can bring you to a women's refuge. There's security there and it's free." Marcus sits down beside me at the table, putting his hand on top of mine. Cooper growls quietly from across the room, and Marcus laughs at him, amused, not offended or scared by his reaction.

"I'm not hitting on your mate, Cooper, or trying to steal her away.

Relax." He chuckles but pulls his hand back from mine and leans back, crossing his thick arms across his broad chest. Cooper's gaze flicks to mine as Marcus calls me his mate, and I store that away for later.

"Marcus, stop winding him up," Leila chastises, and Marcus just shrugs his huge shoulders in response as he looks in her direction, but she stubbornly avoids his gaze.

"James and his buddies are in custody and there is no way they are going to get bail with the seriousness of the charges against them. He's not saying anything, but that's not going to help him much with all the physical evidence and eyewitnesses." He scrubs an enormous hand over his thick, black beard and leans forward on the table.

"I still need to get a detailed statement from you, though. Do you want to do it here now or we can do it in private at the station if you'd prefer? Whichever you want," he asks gently, his deep brown eyes watching me carefully to see how I'll react to going back over the events of the last 24 hours and the months before.

"Here is better, thanks, Marcus. Record away," I say, gesturing to the device in his hand.

"You both need to leave," Marcus states bluntly to Leila and Cooper, who have positioned themselves on either side of me in support. He holds out a hand to stop them from speaking before they protest. "Sit on the porch, you'll be close by, and I know you'll hear everything anyway with that damn doggy hearing, but I have to at least attempt to follow procedures."

"I'll be right outside if you need me," Cooper assures as they walk outside, pulling the door gently closed behind them.

"You seem to be doing well. You're tougher than you look, kiddo. You did good."

I'm relieved he isn't treating me with kid gloves.

"Ha, I'm not sure about that. But it's over, at last," I answer, trying to take the only positive I can think of from last night as Marcus sets up the voice recorder on the table and turns it on.

"You have told me a lot of the background of your relationship with James before. If you don't mind, though, can you start from the beginning? How do you know James Morrow?" he asks. I calm my breathing, gathering all the courage I can and spilling the whole sorry story again.

I should have told Cooper all of this before now; he's out there with Leila, who knows it all, learning these details for the first time indirectly. It's completely unfair to him.

I tell Marcus about meeting James, about the charming side of him, and the real, nasty side of James that appeared as time went on. My anxiety is through the roof as I tell him about the 'engagement' and the first time he hit me, knowing full well how much distress that will cause Cooper. I cover how the police couldn't do anything other than warn him off. How he threatened me, and I suspected him of breaking into my apartment and damaging my car, and eventually how I had to run from him.

Marcus interrupts me at this point to tell me they found some of my parents' mail in James's rented car, and that it was likely he narrowed down my location based on the postmark on a card that I had mailed to them from a town 60 miles away. James also had clippings from the local newspaper article about me saving Cooper.

I knew I had drawn attention to myself by intervening, but I would do it again in a heartbeat to save someone's life. I swear I can feel the guilt rolling off Cooper when Marcus explains that part. He's blaming himself for James finding me, even though I always knew he would, eventually.

As I go through my movements yesterday, including leaving the party early after a disagreement with a 'friend', Marcus raises his eyebrows at my choice of words to describe Cooper, closely followed by cursing from outside.

He's listening.

We clearly have more talking to do later. Cooper paces and growls as I describe what happened the night before, from the flowers on the doorstep to the shot fired out the window. When it comes to the part about how I was rescued, I just say that Cooper tackled him to the ground when he saw James pointing the gun at me.

Unless I want to be laughed at, and for James to get away scot-free because I look like a crazy woman, mentioning wolves seems out of the question. Marcus is kind and patient and gives me all the time I need when I struggle to get the words out. He knows instinctively that fussing will make me feel uncomfortable, so he sits back and waits.

The second Marcus says the interview is over and hits pause on the recorder, Cooper runs straight towards me, wrapping me tightly in his muscular arms, tucking my head under his chin. He pulls me nearly off my chair, rocking me from side to side as he holds me close. I think he needs the hug as much as I do, although he'd never admit it.

"Marcus, when can I go back to my house?"

He shrugs apologetically and some tendrils of dark hair fall across his forehead.

"Not yet anyway. It could be a few days by the time they've fully processed the scene. If you need anything in particular, let me know and I'll see what I can do."

I notice Leila never came back inside. Marcus flicks a glance at the door as if he's wondering where she is, too, and it's obvious something is going on with them. As Cooper joins Marcus at the table to give his own statement, I head outside and plonk myself down on a porch chair beside Leila.

"You look like you could do with a hug as much as I do," I joke, and she glances at me from underneath the curtain of dark hair hanging around her face.

"I feel stupid even being upset about it with everything else going on, but I just feel a little fed up today." She smiles weakly at me, tipping her head back towards the cabin door. "We had a bit of a thing yesterday, but today he's back to freezing me out. I guess I need to move on." She sighs dejectedly and leans her head on my shoulder.

"It's his loss."

If he can't see what a catch the gorgeous, smart, sexy doctor is, then he is an idiot.

But he's no idiot.

I think he sees her very clearly.

I just have no idea what's holding him back.

CHAPTER 43

COOPER

After shooing out my sister, who has adopted my mate as her new best friend and couldn't care less about my desire to have some alone time with her, I spend the rest of the day trying to take care of Hayley.

I'm trying to make up for not protecting her from harm last night, as well as just being grateful that she has forgiven me for the mess I created with Nathan before. I just want to wrap her up in cotton wool and lock her away in my cabin. Partly to make sure that she is as ok as she is saying, and partly to ease my guilt.

Learning that by rescuing me from the river, she had led that low life right to her door has me twisted up in knots.

My wolf thirsts for the vengeance we held back from last night. Every time I see Hayley struggling to do things because of the cast, or when I see the cuts and bruises that cover her arms and legs, he surges forward, trying to tempt me to seek justice shifter style.

"Cooper, don't take this the wrong way, but you need to get out of here for a while." She sneaks up behind me where I have been sitting at the kitchen table staring into my now cold, undrinkable cup of coffee, and swings around to sit on my lap. "It's like I can feel your brain running a hundred miles an hour and the tension is pouring off you. It's suffocating. I am going to call my parents and fill them in on what's happened, and then take a long soak in the tub. Go for a run or something, work off some of that stress. I'll be here when you get back." She cups my face in her palm and runs her hand over my stubbly jaw before giving me a soft, sensual kiss that holds the promise of more.

"Fine, I'll go for a run, and then we can relax with a film," I concede, reluctant to leave, but not wanting my mood to affect her.

"Sounds good." She gives my bottom lip a playful nip before she disappears down the hall. I strip off and head straight for the front door. Rex is close by, has been since we got back from the hospital, so I don't need to worry about Hayley being left unprotected.

My wolf howls in anticipation as I let the shift take hold and give him the reins, allowing him to tear around the woods, checking to make sure there are no other threats to our mate out there and running till our lungs burn.

I'm a new man by the time I get back. My wolf brought me to Hayley's house, checking for himself that there was no longer any threat there. We ran throughout the pack territory; the land of my ancestors seeming to invigorate my soul and provide me with renewed energy. I slip back into the house and over to Rex, who is lying on the couch, keeping watch. He opens his eyes and nods, letting me know everything is ok, before standing and walking silently to the door, letting himself out without making so much as a sound.

Tiptoeing down the hall, I pause at the door to my bedroom, soon to be our bedroom. Hopefully. If I can convince Hayley to stay here. I don't think I could stand to be without her now, to not wake up beside her every day.

She's curled up on her side, fast asleep, honey-coloured strands fanned out across my pillow. I sit down beside her and stroke her hair back from her face, rubbing a thumb gently across her forehead, smoothing out a little frown line between her brows. She looks deep in thought, and I wonder if she is having another bad dream.

I strip down to my boxers and wrap myself around her, hoping my warmth and presence will give her some comfort. I soak in her scent and just enjoy being close to her. Hayley wriggles beside me in the bed and inadvertently presses her ass to my groin. I groan and then freeze, torn between not wanting to freak her out and my primal need to reconnect with her. It doesn't seem appropriate to be thinking like that, but it's like I need to reassure myself that she is ok, alive, here with me, mine.

Selfish, I know, and I feel like a jackass.

I inch back slightly so I can reposition without waking her, but then my naughty little mate scoots back and reaches around to hold my hips in place, pressing me tightly against her again. She's not asleep anymore. I can't help but moan as she rubs against me, and my hand on her waist moves up slowly under her t-shirt to brush along her belly and the underside of her breasts, the skin silky soft and deliciously warm.

Her small hand reaches down and strokes my thigh softly as she continues to rock slowly against my now rock- hard erection. I know I am a terrible person for not stopping this, but I am finding it extremely hard to care.

I nuzzle her hair out of the way, inhaling a lungful of her delicious scent, and press kisses from her shoulder, up her neck, and along her jaw, to her favourite spot just behind her ear. I feel her sigh and shiver as my breath tickles her skin, and I suck the spot where I will mark her as mine.

"Hayley, we shouldn't do this, you need to rest," I murmur beside her cheek, saying one thing but doing the exact opposite as I close the space between our bodies further, wanting every part of our bodies to be touching. I grip her hips and push my hard length against her, admitting defeat and giving in to the need burning through my body.

"No Cooper, I need you. I need to feel you inside me. I need to feel alive," she whispers breathlessly, sounding as turned on and desperate as I am. Craving skin-on-skin contact, I need to feel our bond like I need air. I reach down, grab the hem of the t-shirt she has on and pull it off over her head, careful not to tug on her cast. I rip her panties off and toss them away before pulling down my boxers and pressing back up against her, loving the feel of touching her body with my own from head to toe.

My hand that had been caressing her breasts drifts lower between her legs where I lightly trace the sensitive skin along the tops of her thighs before grazing her mound. She gasps and grips my thigh tightly, trying to pull me tighter to her. When I sweep a finger between her lips, and she tenses in anticipation, wet and ready for me, before grumbling in frustration when I move my hand away again to caress her breast.

"Cooper, stop teasing me, please," she begs. She wiggles against me, trying to tempt me into giving her what she wants.

"Hayley, you should know something else about wolves," I whisper in her ear, as I continue to stroke her waist, tummy, the side of her breasts, her legs, every touch making her wetter and wetter. The scent of her arousal is thick in the air and floods me with satisfaction.

"Cooper, not now..." she moans, trying to rub herself up and down my length to break my control. I ignore her and continue to whisper in her ear. Stroking her clit once, twice, I plunge a finger deep inside her and she sucks in a breath, before grinding down on my hand, seeking more.

Removing my finger, I lift her leg, positioning myself at her entrance, gritting my teeth, and forcing myself to pause, to hold back from sinking into the heaven that I know awaits me.

"Wolves mate for life. They find their perfect match, the one person who completes them, who fits them like a glove." As I say those words, I push my cock deep into her tight pussy in one firm stroke. Her head falls back to my shoulder with a moan, mouth open and a soft whimper escapes her lips as I stall again and hold still, buried to the hilt inside her.

"Wolves treasure their mates. They can't bear to be apart, and they'll do anything to make them happy." All the time I'm speaking softly, lips against her ear, I am languidly stroking in and out of her, making her feel every inch of me. I hold her hips in place so that she can't dictate the pace but can only accept what I am giving to her. Her breathing is quick, coming out in little pants as I continue to torment her with slow thrusts.

"You're mine Hayley, I've known it since the first second we met. You're mine and I'm yours." I growl, and I feel her tighten around me as the vibrations from my chest spread through her body and reach her core. I pump into her a little harder, keeping the pace slow and steady.

"Nobody else will ever get to see you like this, to feel your pussy clench around their cock and hear those sexy little noises you make as you come apart. Do you hear me, Hayley?" I pick up the pace now and pound into her harder and faster. "Nobody else will make you dripping wet like you are for me, Hayley. Nobody else will ever make you scream their name."

I growl louder and I feel her quivering as she hurtles towards her climax, her one good hand digging her nails into my ass as if she's afraid I'll stop.

"You're mine, Hayley, say it. Say it and then you can come," I demand in my bossiest Alpha voice. I rub two fingers up and down over her swollen clit and round and round, not staying in one place long enough for her to reach her climax.

"Cooper, yes, yes," she whispers. Her eyelids are fluttering shut and a little frown creases her forehead as she tries to move her hips to meet mine, pushing her core against my hand to get more pressure where she needs it, to get her release that is hovering just out of reach.

I know what she needs, but I want to hear her say the words first, even though she doesn't understand what I am asking her. My balls tighten and I can feel a tingle beginning. I won't last long, it's just too good.

"Say it, Hayley," I command, and when she pauses for a second, I wonder if I am pushing my luck, pushing her too far.

"I'm yours, Cooper," she breathes out, meeting my eyes over her shoulder and staring into my fucking soul. I put my thumb to her clit and stroke harder, pounding into her now at a punishing pace and instantly I feel her pussy grip my cock like a vice, pulsing as she finds her release with a loud moan, reaching her arm back to tug my hair as she arches against me.

Seeing her like this throws me over the edge as I thrust one last time as deep as I can and shoot my seed into her, coating her insides and filling her with my scent.

I bite back a roar and clench my teeth together, turning my head away from her shoulder to stop myself from leaning forward and sinking my teeth into her neck to mark her as mine forever, like my wolf is urging me to do. My canines have even descended, and I can taste blood where I've nicked my lip trying to keep them covered. I roll onto my back breathing heavily,

and Hayley flops beside me where we lie shoulder to shoulder, boneless and jelly limbed until we can speak again.

"Holy shit Cooper, that was intense," she mumbles, as she rolls and tucks herself into my side, flinging a leg over me and stroking her fingers across my chest and stomach. I chuckle at her dazed expression.

"Are you okay?" I say, guilt creeping in as I wonder if I was too rough. I look at her arm in the cast, but it doesn't seem to bother her too much.

"It was amazing," she says dreamily, and she sounds blissed out. "Is all of that true? About mates? I heard Marcus mention it. I wondered what he meant," she asks, uncertain.

"All true. We mate for life, and the connection between a mated couple is intense." I turn to face her and cup her face in my hands. "Hayley, I promise I was going to explain about shifters to you, and then you could decide whether you could accept it, whether you could accept me. I just didn't want to scare you off," I say quickly, nerves creeping in.

"Like turning into a wolf in front of me?" she asks, smiling into my chest as she teases me.

"Or from a scary wolf into a very naked human with no warning at all?" I joke.

"From a gorgeous wolf to a very sexy man, you mean," she corrects me, looking up into my face with wonder instead of disgust. "I want to see you do it again. I didn't take it in properly last time."

"Any time. He likes you a lot," I say with a grin, hope filling me after her positive reaction so far.

"After the other night, he's my hero," she laughs as she presses a kiss to my lips before swinging her legs out of the bed and standing up to stretch, pulling back the curtains to let sunlight flood the room.

As I look at this beautiful woman, gazing at me with adoration in her eyes, I just can't imagine what I did to deserve this.

CHAPTER 44

HAYLEY

Cooper is waiting on me hand and foot, and it seems to make him happy, so who am I to argue?

My mind inevitably keeps drifting back to the events of Friday night, but whenever my mood turns darker, Cooper pulls me back out of it with some light-hearted banter.

I have to keep reminding myself that James isn't coming back.

My mind also frequently returns to our earth-shattering lovemaking. I have never felt anything as powerful as that. Cooper is always dominant and likes to be in control, but this was more than physically taking charge. This was as if he was showing me that he owns my very soul.

I love my independence. I love being a strong woman with my own life, but there was something freeing about being able to relinquish control to someone you trust completely, to not have to think, to just feel.

I could get very used to it.

Cooper settles in on the sofa to return some of the many calls that I have seen him let go unanswered over the weekend. It's nice, comfortable, and I can imagine that this is what it would be like to live and work together if I join his family's company. He hasn't said anything outright yet, but his actions suggest he is intent on me staying here for the foreseeable.

Something about Cooper's tone turns my focus to what he is discussing with Kim, his father's assistant. The normally cool and collected blonde sounds nervous.

"Cooper, I have been getting lots of phone calls and I'm fobbing people off as best I can, but I can't do it forever. What am I supposed to say to people?" I hear her ask hesitantly.

"What do you mean?" he asks, but I can tell from the stiffening of his shoulders that he already knows what's coming and isn't keen to hear it.

"About Hayley. You lost it at the packhouse. Everyone knows you rescued her and wouldn't leave her side at the hospital and now she is living in your cabin. People were talking before, but they're demanding to know now." Cooper sighs deeply and pinches the bridge of his nose between his thumb and forefinger.

"Everyone should be safe in my territory and let's not forget I owe her my life." He is making it sound like rescuing me wasn't personal, that it was just his duty rather than anything else. I can appreciate not wanting to discuss your personal life with your employees, but it seems like the cat is out of the bag.

Why continue to deny it?

"And now she is staying with you..." Kim tries again.

"She's new in town and has no family here. Would you suggest I leave her to sleep at the side of the road? Or in a packed house full of wolves when she has only just found out about us?" I can sense he's getting irritated now, as can Kim, who quits trying to get him to admit something he is not willing to do. She sighs softly and tries a different tactic.

"Cooper, you can be with whoever you want, but people are asking if you are taking her as a chosen mate. Everyone is going crazy because you swore you never would, and now it looks like you're taking a human outsider. What should I tell them?" As she puts the crux of the matter to him, her voice shakes.

Holding my breath, I'm eager to hear what he says. I hadn't considered that his being with me would cause him issues in his job and with his friends and family. He has explained to me how his dad is the pack leader and that he'll take over when the time is right. It's an enormous responsibility. One that comes with scrutiny.

Is this what Marcus meant when he said I didn't understand everything yet?

"You can tell them that nothing has changed; I won't choose a mate. Other than that, it's none of their business," he states firmly and hangs up the phone. I can feel him struggling to rein in his anger, and he paces up and down a few times before coming back to me with a forced smile on his face.

"Is that why you didn't want everyone to know about us? Even Nathan?" I ask, as he leans down over me on the couch and grips my chin, pulling my lips up to meet his in a kiss. He nods and kisses me along my jaw.

"I knew the questions would start immediately, and someone would tell you about us before I got the chance to, just to cause trouble," he says, kissing his way down my neck and sucking lightly where my neck meets my shoulder, where he has told me a mating mark would go.

Whatever that is.

Squirming as tingles begin in my core, I feel the wetness growing between my legs.

Is having a human mate so bad that even when confronted with the fact that everyone knows something is going on, he still won't admit it?

His pack expects him to be with a wolf. They're not happy that he is even dating a human, let alone potentially mating one. He said he won't choose a mate. Does that mean he's not going to stay with me?

I think back to the utter contentment I felt at waking up wrapped in the strong arms of this man just a few hours ago, holding me possessively as if challenging anyone who might dare to pries me from his grip.

I said I would keep him if he'd have me, but is that selfish of me?

What will happen if he doesn't have the support of his pack?

Cooper slides down beside me on the sofa, tanned muscles on display under a white fitted t-shirt, dark brown hair mussed up, and very cute. He looks at me, a bit puzzled. He can read me so well; he can already tell something is wrong.

Reaching out, he wraps one big hand around my hip and pulls me across to straddle his parted legs. He holds me close and strokes his hands up and down my thighs, his fingers brushing closer and closer to my sex, sending goosebumps across my skin.

I close my eyes and just feel, leaning into him and enjoying the sensations, the feeling of being treasured, cherished.

Around his employees and what I now know to be his pack, he is friendly and charming, but there is no mistaking that he is the boss. There is a steeliness to him that screams don't mess with me. This softer side of him only seems to appear when we are alone together, and it makes me feel so special.

"Something wrong, Princess?" he mumbles into my skin, nipping slightly, and the sting sends another jolt of arousal straight between my legs. A gasp escapes me before I can stop myself. I have zero control over myself around this man. He's just too damn sexy.

"What's a chosen mate?" I ask. He pauses, and then pulls back to look me in the eye but continues to stroke and rub my thighs.

"There are two types of mates. Chosen, as the name suggests, is like your human marriage. You meet someone, figure you work well together, and commit." He holds my good hand in his before continuing.

"Fated mates are a whole different story. They're destined to be together, two parts of a whole, meant for each other. The connection is incredibly powerful, and a wolf knows by scent, from the first second they meet, that they are mates. It's magical. There's no denying it." He trails a finger along the palm of my hand and sparks explode there at this touch as if to demonstrate his point.

"And that's what we are, Hayley. You're my everything. There's nobody else for me." He looks me in the eye, and my heart skips a beat. There is nothing but sincerity and devotion there.

"You told everyone you would never choose a mate..." I continue, confused.

"I said I would never choose a mate because I was waiting for you. If a wolf takes a chosen mate, they won't recognise their fated mate if they meet. I decided long ago that I wasn't prepared to give that up. I want something extraordinary, something like this." He kisses me again and my brain scrambles. I am trying to stay focused, to learn what I need to know, but I can barely remember my name.

"But I'm just human." I gasp as he rocks up against me, and I can feel his erection straining at the front of his sweatpants.

"I am aware of that, and it doesn't make any difference to me. You're perfect Hayley, you're everything I've ever wanted."

"But what about your pack? Will they accept me? Are you even allowed to be with a human?" I ask tentatively and he scoffs, pulling up my t-shirt to kiss across my stomach and my breasts.

"I am the Alpha. I can do whatever I want." He means it and it's such a turn-on to see his confidence.

"Cooper," I groan, "seriously, though." I push back so my ass is on his knees rather than his crotch. He frowns as he watches me straighten my top.

"Fine, spoilsport." He sighs, leaning his head against the back of the couch. "To wolves, nothing is more sacred than fated mates. They would never interfere, and they will be ecstatic that I've found mine. It will make me a stronger, better leader. They'll welcome you with open arms. You can expect lots of questions about having pups."

"Then why not tell them?" I could understand him wanting to keep it quiet before when I didn't know about their secret, but not now.

"It's a lot of pressure, Hayley. They'll expect us to be mated and marked immediately to take over the pack. You've just had your life turned upside down by that asshole. I don't want to be the one to do that to you again." He puts his hands on either side of my face and pulls me back to him for a gentle kiss before shifting slightly and pressing our bodies together once again.

"If I was a wolf and not a human, what would you have done?" I frown at him, already having a good idea of what his answer will be.

"I would have taken you to bed the first time I met you. I would have thrown you over my shoulder as soon as I saw you standing in your garden in those hot little shorts and carried you inside. And you would have loved it because you'd have known I was yours too." He grabs my waist as if imagining exactly what it would have been like.

"I would have sunk my teeth into that sexy neck of yours, and watched you come on my cock over and over as I made you mine forever," he says calmly, biting down gently on my shoulder, making my pussy clench.

"Jesus Cooper," I whisper. This man has a wicked mouth.

"That's exactly what you'll be saying, Princess. It's supposed to feel incredible," he mutters against my skin.

"Were you disappointed that I was human? Is that why you didn't mark me before?" I ask quietly, a horrible feeling taking root in the pit of my stomach. He had to hold himself back because of me. Everything would have been easier for him if he were mated to someone else.

"What?!" He forces me to look into his eyes. "No, never think that. Whatever is going through that brain of yours, just knock it off right now, ok? I couldn't be happier. I just had to make sure that you wanted me too. There's no going back, Hayley. Once I mark you, you're mine forever." He growls out the last bit and rubs me along his thick length.

I can't help the quickening of my breathing or stop my body from repeating the movement, desperate to feel some friction.

"Then why not do it now?" I ask, and Cooper's jaw clenches. He's trying to remain calm and in control, but it appears he's not used to being questioned.

"Fuck, I want to. But the reason is the same. This is all new to you, Hayley. You've just been through something traumatic. I don't want you to regret it," he grits out, squeezing my breasts over my top, before pulling it up over my head.

Reaching behind me, he releases the clasp of my bra, freeing my breasts, and brushes his thumbs over each nipple. He watches intently as my nipples harden and he licks and sucks each one. It's like he's trying to concentrate on pleasing me rather than having this conversation.

"Cooper, I want you too. You said it's destiny, so why fight it?" I push again. He growls and presses his forehead to my chest.

"Because I won't force you into anything. I can't be like him." He shakes his head.

"Baby, you're nothing like him." I pull his face up and kiss his full lips, trying to convey how certain I am about him, about us.

"You need time to process what happened, to find out about what being with me means. I've waited this long. I can wait some more. When I come back from the conference, you can spend some time with the pack and see if it's a life you could be happy with."

He seems to have this all worked out, even though it seems to pain him to suggest holding off. And part of his plan seems to involve keeping me away from this Alpha conference. Well, that's not going to happen.

"You're talking yourself out of it, Cooper. I'm telling you I want you, but you're pulling back. If it's really what you want, then do it. Make me yours." Kissing him fiercely, I suck his bottom lip between my teeth and biting it before tangling our tongues together and gripping his hair tightly with my hands. I rub against him and grab at this t-shirt to yank it over his head, needing to feel his warm skin against mine. I feel desperate and overwhelmed by my need for him.

"No! Not like this." He grabs my hands and pulls them away from his chest, panting and leaning back away from me. I feel his words like a slap in the face. Even though I know he wants me, his refusal to mark me feels like a rejection. Like he's telling I'm not good enough or strong enough because I'm just a human.

I push myself back up to my feet.

"Fuck, you're the most stubborn man I've ever met! If you don't want me, just say it." I know I'm being irrational, but my emotions are all over the place. It's like my body craves his bite. I swear my neck is tingling in anticipation, and anger surges through me because he won't give me what I want. Aware that I'm being ridiculous, I try to rein in my reaction, but his bite is a need I can't describe.

"I'm trying to do the right thing here, to protect you," he shouts, putting his head in his two hands, looking frustrated that I don't agree with him.

"Fine." Stooping, I pick my t-shirt off the floor and pull it back over my head.

"Fine? It doesn't look like it's fine. Hayley..." He stands and reaches for me, but I step back and fold my arms across my chest.

"I need to go see my parents for a couple of days. They're worried about me, and they won't relax until they see me." I try to put some strength into my voice, even though my legs feel like jelly at the thought of leaving him.

Cooper's whole body stiffens, and he straightens to his full height. Leila has already warned me that his protective instincts won't let me be far away from him, but I need to get out of here. I feel out of control. It must be the mate bond, and it is driving me mad that he seems to be able to resist.

He tips my chin up with his fingers, forcing me to meet his stormy brown eyes.

"Princess, if you want to go see your parents, I'll gladly bring you." His voice is cautious.

"And how would I explain you coming to stay with me if I can't say that we're together?" I ask bitterly, shaking my head and taking a step back from him. Growling, he takes a predatory step toward me again.

"Princess, I don't understand exactly what is going on here. If something I have said or done has left you under the illusion that I don't want you, I am sorry." Prowling forward, his brown eyes turn almost black. "So let me be perfectly clear. I want you here, I want you in my house and my bed. Forever. And I will mark you, Hayley, just not right now." Cooper sounds like he is talking a crazy person down from the ledge and it makes me even more annoyed. I don't like feeling like this.

"It's not about marking me! It's about sneaking around like you're doing something wrong just by being with me. I just need some time to think and some space," I say, calming down slightly now. He frowns again but doesn't stop me as I walk out of the sitting room toward our bedroom.

"So, you don't want me to come with you to your parents," he says flatly, arms crossed across his broad chest as he watches me flit about the room, shoving anything of mine into my bag as I do my best to avoid meeting his eyes.

"No, I don't." The hurt in his expression tells me he didn't appreciate my bluntness. I sigh and turn to face him.

"I'm going. I'll call when I get there. I'll just stay for a few nights and then I'll be back." I kiss him softly but leave no room for argument in the way I say it. He doesn't say a word, just pulls his keys out of his pocket and holds them out for me to take.

"Your car is still out of action. Take my truck." He carries my bag out to the truck for me, tossing it into the back and hauling me in for a kiss.

"Don't forget that you are mine, Princess. Make no mistake, you will wear my mark and I will put my pups in that belly. If you're not back in three days, I *will* come and get you. We need to talk about this. All I want is for you to be happy, don't run from me," he warns.

I march straight out the door, turned on at his words, but furious at myself for loving it. The insinuation that he is letting me go for three days but will drag me back like a caveman if I dare defy him grates on me. I'd also secretly love to see if he would do it. Arrogant, handsome, sexy man.

CHAPTER 45

HAYLEY

By the time I have driven to my parents' house, I feel much calmer and have my emotions back under control.

This short break will be good for me. For us.

At least, that's the mantra I have been repeating ever since I pulled out of Cooper's driveway, and the dull ache in my chest continued to intensify. I focus on what's in front of me instead to boost my spirits. It will be good to see my family in person after so long. My dad, in particular, has been wracked with guilt that he had to leave me to fend for myself. He offered to come with me when I moved, but I couldn't do that to my mum, and he could have been hurt if James found him with me.

It doesn't even bear thinking about.

As I pull up outside, I don't even have the door open before my mum is running down the driveway, dragging me out and engulfing me in a tight hug. My Dad saunters down behind her, always the more chilled out of the pair, and gently pries her arms from around my neck.

"Let her breathe now, Michelle, she's here. Look, she's in one piece, almost," he coos as he turns her away from me and she presses her tear-stained face into his chest without letting go of my good hand.

My Dad wraps each of us in one of his arms and steers us back inside, winking at me over my mother's head as she continues to sniffle and then apologise for crying. Inside the door, I pull her back into a firm hug and then push out at arm's length to force her to look at me properly.

"Mum, look at me, I'm fine. It's over now." I press a kiss to her cheek and drag her towards the kitchen where Dad is already back at the oven cooking up a storm and my little sister Leah is sitting cross-legged on the kitchen island, stealing from the bowls of sides spread out across it.

"Get down!" my mum scolds, but the smile on her face that she's so bad at hiding gives her away. She loves Leah's antics and lets her away with murder, especially now that she's the only one of us living at home anymore.

"Oh, what, so I have to pretend to have manners now that Hayley's graced us with her presence again?" Leah says jokingly, rolling her eyes as she scoots over to the edge and hops down, before reaching up to kiss me on the cheek and a hug.

"It's good to have you back," she whispers, as if it's a secret that she might like me. "Although we have a spare, so you know, we don't *really* need you," she says louder and winks at me as Mum turns around and smacks her arm good-naturedly.

"And speaking of Zoe, where is my big sister?" I joke, as there are exactly five mins between us age-wise. She is way bossier than me, and I always joke that it started with her shoving her way out first.

"She wanted to be here, but she got an emergency call out, the usual. Hopefully tomorrow." Dad shrugs, but Mum sets her lips into a thin line. The life of a vet is tough, and it's not that Mum disapproves of her job. I know she is proud of her, but she worries about the unsociable hours she does and how little time she has for family or friends. Or dating.

"Can I do anything?" I ask, peeking over my dad's shoulder to see what's on the menu.

"Shoo. You're useless with that thing on anyway, so just sit down." He nods towards my cast, which I am hoping to get off the day before the conference. Leila is confident that the break will have set enough that I can get away with just a splint for the next few weeks. I'm praying she's right because it's driving me nuts.

Sitting down on one of the kitchen stools, I relax and just absorb the laughter and banter going on around me, and the warmth of being home.

I am so glad I came. This was something I missed a lot.

It might not have been the best way to leave Cooper and Grey Ridge, but it sure feels great to be here.

A family dinner and a good night's sleep in my old bed have done wonders for my soul. When I potter downstairs, I feel a hundred times better. Cooper has been tiring me out.

"Dad, has the paper come yet?" I yell through the house, reverting to a teenager who obviously can't walk to the front door herself to check. The sound of a throat clearing drags my gaze up from yesterday's news.

"Hayley, I found this young man asleep on our porch. I have a feeling he might belong to you." My dad has a smirk on his face as he leads a delighted-looking Ethan into the kitchen, and I can see his amusement as a flush I can't control spreads across my face.

"I'm very sorry. I didn't think you'd all be awake yet, and I didn't want to disturb you." Ethan is saying it to my dad, but his eyes flit around my home, taking in every little detail. He is being super polite and respectful. No wonder Cooper has him working with guests at the resort. This guy can ramp up the charm when he wants to.

"Come in and sit." My mother pushes him into the chair beside me before shoving a plate and mug in front of him, grinning from ear to ear. "Hayley, where are your manners? Introduce us."

Leah is grinning so wide her face is going to split open as she glances back and forth between the two of us, jumping to the wrong conclusion. I should have known I'd have company.

"Ethan, this is everyone, everyone, this is Ethan," I say grumpily before turning to him. "I take it Cooper sent you here to babysit me. This is ridiculous." My whole family is staring, not even pretending not to be fascinated by this drop-dead gorgeous stranger sitting in their midst.

"Yep." He smirks, before picking up some toast from the bread-basket and biting off a chunk. "Cooper is Hayley's boyfriend," he says by explanation to my parents, and they both turn to me with questions in their eyes.

"Oh really?" Dad says, grinning at me with one eyebrow raised, delighted with this nugget of information. God, this is torture. I feel like I'm being teased about my first crush.

"He couldn't come himself, but he asked me to tag along and keep an eye out for her. You can never be too careful, just for the time being." He is laying it on thick, and my mother, the traitor, is lapping it up, nodding along and smiling at him like he hung the moon. "Maybe he's being over-protective, but it's only because he cares."

That part is directed at me and I narrow my eyes at him.

"You're so right. And thank you." She pats his arm like he's an old friend. "No more sleeping on the porch. You'll stay with us while Hayley's here. Hayley, how could you let him sleep outside?" She looks at me, horrified. "And why do we know nothing about this boyfriend?"

"I didn't know he was here! If I did, I would have told him to go home," I grit out. Ethan just smiles, his piercing blue eyes dancing with amusement at my outrage. I ignore the question about Cooper.

"That would be wonderful, Mrs. Walker. This is delicious, by the way." He helps himself to just about everything on the table and my mother beams, fussing over him, getting him more food. Leah just stares at him, no doubt wondering how I know a man this hot, and she hasn't heard anything about him.

"Fine, stay." I sigh as I stand up to leave, still trying to be annoyed that he followed me here, but he's very hard to stay mad at. Ethan winks at me, knowing full well that he was always going to get his way. Even if I make him leave the house, he'll probably just sleep in the back garden, anyway. I curl up on my parents' sofa, under a blanket, and pull out my phone.

"Leila, hey. I just wanted to let you know that I'm staying at my folk's house for the next few days. But I'll be back in time to head to the conference with you." She pauses at the other end of the line, and I can feel her reluctance to comment because she doesn't want to get involved.

"Does Cooper know?" she asks incredulously. "He must be freaking out."

"Yes, he knows, Ethan's here," I say brightly, as if it's all fine and that we planned it that way. "Could you do me a favour? The house has been cleaned and fixed up. Could you swing by and just check it at some stage over the next few days?" I ask, keen to move the topic away from Cooper.

"I'll do you one better. Would you mind if I stayed there for a couple of nights? I need to get out of the packhouse, and Cooper's is out. I don't think he's going to be fun to be around until you're back," she jokes.

"Of course, you're more than welcome. Just maybe tell Marcus because he's probably still monitoring the place." Leila hesitates for a fraction of a second before responding.

"That's brilliant, thanks Hayley. I promise I won't make a big mess. I'll be your first official guest," she gushes, and I note she doesn't agree to contact the big sheriff.

"Perfect. I'll see you on Wednesday or Thursday then," I go to say goodbye, but then I can't help myself. "Leila, will he be alright until I get back?"

"Probably not, but he'll survive. You take care of yourself and don't worry about him. He's a big boy. But I'll get Nathan to check in on him," she offers, and I feel better about basically running out on him. This mate bond has me all over the place.

CHAPTER 46

HAYLEY

"Ok, spill."

My sister saunters in with a plate of biscuits and flops down on the couch beside me, with her back to the armrest, and stretches her legs out across my lap. Her mass of blonde curls hangs around her shoulders, and her brown eyes sparkle with curiosity.

"What do you mean?" Playing dumb, I try to buy myself some time to sift through what I can tell her and what I can't. She pokes me with her feet until I relent.

"Fine. Yes, I'm seeing someone, Cooper, the guy who I rescued, the same guy who stopped James," I say reluctantly, and she sits up straighter and starts clapping her hands excitedly. Groaning, I cover my face with my hands in frustration. It's way too early for her giddiness. She's always a ball of energy.

"So, tell me what's going on?" she encourages, staring at me wide-eyed, keen to hear all the gossip.

"He is a great guy, Leah. I've never met anyone like him," I gush, and she rolls her eyes at me being all mushy, before I lower my voice to a whisper to make sure my dad doesn't hear the next part.

"And the sex, holy shit Leah. HOLY SHIT." She chokes on a biscuit and coughs as she stares at me.

"He can't be *that* good?" She sounds unconvinced, but intrigued.

"Mm-hmm, really, *that* good." I nod vigorously and giggle, and she bursts out laughing, kicking her feet.

"Oh, I love it, Hayley, you lucky bitch. So, what's the problem?" She stops laughing and tries to pull back on a straight face. I think for a second about how much I can tell her before trying to give her a vague version of what's going on.

"He is basically the town mayor and his family's businesses are big in the area. He doesn't want anyone to know about us because he says it will draw a lot of attention to me immediately. He is worried that it'll be too much stress for me with everything that's gone on lately. He says I shouldn't be making any serious decisions right now." I huff the last bit out angrily. It's like he thinks I'm on the verge of a meltdown or something. "But it just makes me feel like he's not as into this as I am." I look at her for support, but she's just staring at me wide-eyed.

"You love him," she says in a stunned whisper and gives me a little smile. Pausing, I consider lying, but my little sister is shrewd, and I know there is no point, so I nod in agreement.

I love him, and if I hadn't been certain before, I know it now when I haven't even been away from him for 24 hours and I am itching to get back and just breathe him in.

"Has he told *anyone* about you?" she asks me, tilting her head to the side as if she is trying to work out some complicated math problem.

"Well, his brother and sister know, and Ethan, obviously. I think his dad does too."

"So, basically the most important people to him know about you dating, just not everyone else," she continues, being annoyingly reasonable when I'm set on remaining angry.

"Yes, but..." She cuts me off before I can finish.

"You said he's a decent guy. Do you think he'd lie to you about liking you? That he's playing you?" she presses, her fingers tapping the arm rest as she thinks.

"Well, no, but..."

Ethan appears in the doorway, stuffed to the brim by my mother, and finished charming my father, who is thrilled by the appearance of my own personal bodyguard. I see Leah do a double-take when she sees him as if stunned afresh at his good looks and presence in our home.

"Leah, this is Ethan, Ethan, my sister Leah," I say, introducing them properly. He drifts into the sitting room and lowers himself into the empty armchair that's beside Leah, turning to face her.

"Cooper is a great man. He would *never* lie to Hayley," he assures her, fixing her with those piercing blue eyes and I roll my eyes, praying to God he's not going to hit on my little sister right in front of me.

"And he's been taking care of you since the attack? He put himself in danger to save you?" She drags her eyes away from Ethan and back to me after giving him a quick, blatant once over.

"Yes," I confirm. "Actually, he got shot." Wincing, I'm starting to hear how bad this all sounds.

"And he sent me here to watch her, just in case there are any more of James' buddies looking to cause trouble for Hayley," Ethan supplies helpfully. "If Hayley would have let him, he'd be here himself."

Leah gives me a withering look.

"And he's not jerking her around?" She doesn't even ask me this time, just directs it straight at Ethan as if he is the fountain of all knowledge and my take means nothing.

"Absolutely not. He just doesn't want her to deal with any extra stress right now. But he adores her, and he's all about keeping Hayley happy and satisfied." He shoots me a wink as he all but admits that he heard me complimenting Cooper's sexual prowess. Shoot me now. I blush furiously and try not to think about that.

"Hayley, you're an idiot," Leah says to me bluntly. My jaw drops.

"What? You're supposed to be on my side!" I shout, indignant.

"There is no side. Let me ask you something. If Chase was here when you were attacked, what do you think would've happened?" she asks, daring me to lie.

"He would never let me leave the house ever again." I can see Ethan squinting at me slightly, confused and concerned. "My brother," I say to him before he worries about another ex of mine crawling out of the woodwork.

"And would that make you think he doesn't love you?" Leah continues.

"Of course not," I sigh.

"Because him being an overprotective ass would be his messed-up way of showing how much he cares. And this is Cooper's way of trying to protect you. He's not trying to hide you; he's trying to shield you. And he's not wrong. You have had a crappy few months. If it's coming from a good place. Maybe you need to give the guy a break." She sits back after giving me her little speech. "Just enjoy the sexy times and being spoiled, and stop complaining."

When I open my mouth to argue with her a few times but then close it again, she smirks. So does Ethan.

"I like you," he says to her, and she grins back at him, thick as thieves already. They're enjoying ganging up on me, just as she would with my brother.

"He wants me to miss the conference. It's not happening," I say to both of them. I know that will irk my sister. She's not a fan of anyone being expected to stay at home, barefoot in the kitchen.

"Only because he thinks you should be resting. I, for one, agree with you, Hayley, but there will be plenty more. Why not just skip this one and go to the next?" Ethan says reasonably. It's very annoying.

"Because I don't want him to see me as some delicate flower that he has to wrap up in cotton wool. If I give in, he'll just keep doing it. And everyone else will see me as weak, too. So, what do I do?" I ask myself more than anyone else.

If I am supposed to help him lead a pack of wolves, I can't be seen as some helpless little girl that he needs to mind all the time.

"You break him," she says simply, tucking a stray strand of blonde hair back behind her ear.

"Sorry, I do what?"

Leah is completely straight-faced. I must have heard her wrong.

"You... break... him," she says again slowly and sighs, as though I'm daft for not catching on to what she means.

"You need to get him to see you for you again, and not as a victim. You need to stop him thinking with his brain, get him to listen to another part of his anatomy, and won't be able to stay away." She winks at me before shoving another biscuit into her smug mouth.

"Ooh, that sounds like fun." Maybe she's right. With all this drama with James, Cooper has been treating me so carefully. It's time to remind him I'm not as fragile as he thinks I am.

"Break out naughty Hayley, look smoking hot at this conference... he'll be begging to have you on his arm."

"Oh no, that's not a good idea... I've changed my mind. I don't like you. You're trouble," Ethan says, concern etched across his handsome features as he frowns at Leah, but we completely ignore him.

"Great idea. And you don't say anything for now. He's assuming I'm staying behind; it'll be a nice little surprise when I tell him." I point a finger at Ethan, who is now shaking his head vigorously as he stands and rubs his hand over his face.

"No, no, this is *bad*, Hayley," Ethan pleads, but now he knows what it's like to be ganged up on.

"It's genius. We'll see who has the most willpower now. How did you get to be so wise?" I give her a quick hug, laughing at Ethan, who groans, looking paler than I have ever seen him before.

"Easy. I've learned exactly what NOT to do by watching you two idiots." She laughs, right before I smack her in the face with a pillow to hide her self-satisfied smirk.

CHAPTER 47
COOPER

The rumble of a suitcase being dragged down the hall catches my attention, and then a heavenly smell drifts through the open door of my office, teasing my senses.

She's back.

I step out from behind my desk, happy to get away from the never-ending unread emails waiting for my attention. Hayley is hauling a small cabin bag on wheels across the wooden floor, while Ethan trails behind her with a large duffel bag. She looks relaxed and happy.

"What's going on?" I ask, glancing down at the bag, stopping just short of Hayley, my fingers itching to reach out and pull her to me for a kiss, but there are always people watching in the packhouse.

"Cooper I... em," Ethan stutters, looking at me wide-eyed and slightly terrified, "sorry man. I know nothing."

The hairs on the back of my neck stand up as I realise I won't like whatever this is one bit. Hayley looks delighted with herself as she steps into my personal space, a little too close for an employer and employee situation and smiles up at me seductively. I clear my throat and edge back a bit, and Hayley chuckles.

Now I'm nervous.

"Leila and I are doing a little house swap," she says as she starts up the stairs, Ethan snatching the bag from her before she tries to lift it herself with her cast still on her arm. I go still as I absorb her words.

"I'll just bring these up for you," he offers, before basically running away to escape from the argument he knows is coming.

"What do you mean house swap?" I ask cautiously, trying not to jump to conclusions. Maybe I never asked her outright, but I thought I had made it pretty clear that her staying at the cabin was not a temporary arrangement.

"Leila is going to stay in my place, and I'm staying here. For a little while anyway." She keeps walking and I clench my fists to stop myself from grabbing her and carrying her straight back out the front door.

"I can't face staying there, and I can't stay in your cabin again, or the rumour mill will go back into overdrive. And you did say that I need to spend time around the packhouse before you'll mark me. This is perfect." She is suspiciously cheery about this when just two days ago she stormed out, furious with me for not marking her or making our relationship public.

Deep breaths.

Focusing on taking deep calming breaths, I follow her into Leila's one-bed apartment, which is next door to my own. And just one flight of stairs up from a floor full of horny, unmated wolves.

Over my dead body will she be staying here.

Ethan bolts out the door and shoots me another apologetic glance before shutting it behind him. I stride across the room to where Hayley is placing her purse down on the sideboard and whirl her around to face me. She looks up at me, stunned with lips parted and I can't help myself.

Grabbing her around the waist, I haul her to me, smashing my lips to hers in a bruising, possessive kiss.

"I missed you. I've been going out of mind while you've been gone," I admit, burying my head into the crook of the neck and sucking in a big lungful of her beautiful scent to calm myself.

"I missed you too." She relaxes into my embrace, running her hands up my back and into my hair. Her pale pink nails scratch across my scalp and it sends shivers down my spine.

"Hayley, there is absolutely no fucking way you are staying here," I say firmly, lifting her ass onto the sideboard and pulling her hips to the edge so our hips are perfectly lined up. Cupping her face in my hands, I lean down to kiss her, those full lips irresistible to me.

"I can't stay with you, Cooper, so it's either here or with Marcus. He offered me his spare room if I want it. You know I'll be safe there," she says all innocently, cutting off my argument before I can make it.

Fucking Marcus.

Growling, I push my hips against her, rubbing my cock along her pussy. I can already catch the faint smell of her arousal; she missed me too.

"Fine, but I'm staying here too. I don't trust these fuckers not to hit on you as soon as my back is turned. You're mine," I grumble sulkily. She's gorgeous. They'll be perving on her and trying to charm their way into her pants in no time.

"In your place," she clarifies. "You wanted us to pretend we're not together, remember?" Nodding, I completely distracted by her small soft hands which are underneath my shirt, trailing up my abdomen and chest, her nails dragging across my sensitive skin, making me shiver.

"And I'll need to book my room for the conference..." she says quietly, before kissing along my jaw and down my neck. I nearly forget what she just said when she bites down on my shoulder, and I feel my dick twitch.

Then I go stock-still as her words penetrate my lust-addled brain.

"You're not going to the conference," I state the obvious, and Hayley's head whips up to look at me with a stern expression on her face.

"Excuse me?" She narrows her eyes at me, and I see anger flare in the depths of those brown eyes. I cage her in with one arm on either side of her and lean in close. She's hot even when she's pissed off.

"You are NOT going to that conference. I won't allow it," I grind out, using every ounce of my Alpha aura to get her to submit to my will, but nada. She slides to her feet and stares up into my eyes with obvious annoyance.

"Won't allow it? Who the hell do you think you are?" She scoffs at me, totally immune to my attempted Alpha order. It's so sexy to see this fiery side of her, but frustrating as hell.

"Do I need to remind you that you were almost killed just a few days ago? Someone tried to shoot you!" My hands clench into fists and my arms shake with the tension building inside of me. "I nearly lost you."

"They did shoot you, but you're not sitting at home!" She throws her hands up in the air in frustration and then shakes her head as she calms down a bit. "I am going to the conference, Cooper, because that is my job, and your dad wants me there," she says gently.

"No Hayley. You're still recovering. It's too much," I argue. "You are not listening to me, Cooper. I want to go; therefore, I

am going, that's it." She crosses her arms across her chest and stares at me defiantly. I let out a growl of frustration and pace away from her, pulling at my hair with my hands.

"Hayley, you should be resting. If you go, and people realise you're mine, but still unmarked, you'll be in danger. At the very least, you'll be on the receiving end of some unwanted attention, and you don't need that stress."

"I appreciate you looking out for me, Cooper, but what is your plan? You can't keep me locked up in your cabin. Unless you want me to stay here and get to know the rest of the pack while you're gone?" she says, and I can see the mischievous glint in her eye.

Damn it. She's got me and she knows it.

I don't want her at the conference.

It'll be torture to pretend we're not together. But I'll lose my mind thinking of her here with a pack of unmated males and jealous females, with none of my family to watch out for her. The conference is the lesser of two evils.

"Fuck. Fine," I concede, and she grins victoriously. "But you and Leila better stay out of trouble, and you stick to her like glue."

"Yes sir," she purrs, and the sultry sound goes straight to my balls. When she looks up at me from under her long dark lashes and she looks so hot, it's making me ache to touch her. She backs further away from me and kicks off her shoes, which land with a thud somewhere behind me.

I don't take my eyes off her for a second.

She gives me a sexy little smile before gripping the hem of her white top, pulling it up over her head, and tossing it carelessly to the side, giving me a tantalising view of her flat stomach and pert breasts hidden by some expensive-looking lingerie. Next, she pops the buttons on her jeans and shimmies them down over her hips, flicking them at me with her foot when they fall to the floor.

She's left in a pale blue silk bra and panties, and the sheer lace sets off her tanned skin to perfection. I can see her nipples straining against the thin material as she reaches behind herself and opens the clasp. The delicate straps slip off her shoulders as she wraps one arm over her breasts, keeping the cups of the bra from falling away completely.

"Fuck Hayley, you look so fucking sexy," I growl as I stalk towards her, my steps forward eating up the space between us as she continues to sashay backward, swaying her hips sexily from side to side.

"Come here," I demand, tempted to just pounce on her but also keen to see what will come of this little strip tease she is doing. My cock is straining uncomfortably against the front of my trousers, and I adjust it, giving it a firm squeeze as I see Hayley's eyes wander down to my hand and what it's holding. She licks her lips and stops back-tracking as her feet hit the cool tiles of the bathroom floor.

"See something you like, Princess?" I ask cockily. Ethan told me she had bragged to her sister that our sex life was unbelievable. It might have gone to my head a little. She nods, and her eyes devour my body as I reach behind me and pull my t-shirt up over my head one-handed while I open the fly on my trousers.

"Come here Hayley," I order again, but she shakes her head slowly, staring at where my trousers are open and the top of my boxers, and what is filling them, is on display. It's as if she's in a daze, but then suddenly she snaps her eyes up to mine. The scent of her arousal swirls around me, and it's intoxicating.

All I can think of and see is her, her sexy toned little body, her pretty face, her plump full lips, pupils blown wide with desire. It's heady and overwhelming, my wolf craves her, needs to reconnect after a couple of days apart.

"Nuh-uh," she teases, shaking her head as she takes a step inside,

"I'm feeling dirty. I'm going for a shower." She winks at me, and I grin back. Shower sex with my dirty mate sounds amazing.

I hear her heartbeat pick up and her breathing quicken as I prowl forwards to grab her and carry her towards the shower, already picturing burying myself inside her from behind with water streaming down her back.

But just as I reach for her, she flashes me a sexy little smirk and the door slams in my face.

"Hayley?" I ask, completely bewildered, pressing a hand to the wooden door. It opens a few inches, but only wide enough for her to fling her bra and panties out the door at me before it closes again, and a click sounds as she locks it.

"You can't have your cake and eat it, Cooper. I'm nobody's dirty little secret, and you, Alpha, won't be getting any more cake until we're officially together."

Well shit, I didn't see that coming.

"Jesus, what the fuck is going on?" I tip my head back and look up to the ceiling, hoping for divine inspiration, and I hear Hayley chuckle quietly before I hear the noise of the shower going on.

"You're killing me, baby," I moan, resting my head against the door and slapping it once with my open palm, before retrieving my t-shirt and dragging myself back to my room.

My mate is a sexy little minx but also pure evil. And I absolutely love it.

CHAPTER 48

COOPER

I sit in my office, my knee bouncing up and down with nervous energy, as I focus all my senses on working out where Hayley is and where she's going.

She just got rid of one stalker.

Turning into another wouldn't be a good look for me, but having Hayley sleep right next-door last night, especially after the little show she put on, was absolute hell. Then she was at breakfast this morning, chatting and laughing with everyone who said hello. And there were plenty. Not all of them were just being friendly.

It's exactly what I wanted, for her to see what pack life is like, but it's not how I pictured it at all. I need to see her alone. I tossed and turned until I finally gave in and took care of myself to the image, I had in my head of taking her in the shower before she shut that down. It's not even close to the real thing, but it took the edge off.

I'm fucked if she keeps this up.

I need to go to the resort this afternoon with my mother to set up for the conference which starts tomorrow. Hayley is following in the morning with Rex and Leila, and it's killing me to leave her here for even one night, even knowing Rex and Ethan are staying close by.

Between this and her trip to her parents, it's too much time away from my unmarked mate and my wolf is already anxious about it.

I slam my laptop shut and scrub my hands down my face. I'm getting no work done. There's no point in even pretending I can focus right now. Maybe a workout will help burn off this excess energy.

When I hear a gentle rap on the door, I shoot to my feet as Hayley slowly pushes it open halfway and sticks her head inside. Just seeing her smiling face makes my heart skip a beat. Grinning back at her, and it takes all my control to keep my feet planted where they are rather than rushing to her and taking her luscious lips in a savage kiss.

"Hey," she says shyly, as she pushes further into the room now that she can see I'm on my own.

"Hey," I say back because apparently my brain has stopped working, and it's all I can come up with.

"I just wanted to say goodbye before you go. And to apologise to you, you were right," she says.

"I always like hearing that I'm right, but what specifically was I right about?" I ask as she closes the door quietly behind her and turns back to face me.

"About waiting to tell people. If you say there are safety concerns around being open about us being mates, I need to trust you on that. And I do trust you, Cooper." Her voice is low and sultry, and my wolf preens at her placing her faith in us and trusting us to protect us. The man in me, however, already knows that I'm in trouble here. This is a complete 360.

What happened to not wanting to seem afraid?

She's up to no good again.

Hayley crosses the room slowly, never taking her eyes from mine. I can hear her heart beating so fast it reassures my wolf that she is still just as affected by me. She trails her fingers along the edge of my desk as she draws closer and I'm imagining her trailing those fingers along my chest, up my back, and I'm already growing hard for her again. I clench my fists by my side and her eyes drift to my hands as she catches the movement.

She stops in front of me, leaving only a few inches between us and it feels like there is an electric charge drawing us to close the final gap.

She reaches out and takes my fist softly into her hand and strokes her thumb back and forth across where my knuckles have turned white. The action calms me immediately, and I soften my grip, uncurling my hand slowly. She links our fingers together.

"Thank you, Hayley." I press my forehead to hers and our lips are only inches apart. She nods.

"So, you're right, we'll take a step back and after the conference, we can spend some time together as friends while you give me a crash course on wolf shifters."

For a moment, I'm speechless. She agrees with me and my reasons for not claiming her immediately, yet somehow it's backfired.

"Friends?" I ask. My voice has taken on a deeper timbre as I try to keep the growl out of my voice.

"Temporarily," she purrs. "Did you sleep?" She asks, knowing full well that I wouldn't have had a hope after her leaving me hanging like that.

"Not really," I reply bluntly.

"I'm sorry I left things like that," she whispers. "I should have taken care of you." Her voice calms me, while simultaneously wrapping around my cock, making me want to just haul her to me and lay her out on my desk. She still hasn't lifted her eyes to mine but reaches out to take my other hand and rubs her thumb back and forth over those knuckles.

"I couldn't sleep either," she states, and a flush spreads across her cheeks. Sweet Jesus, is she suggesting what I think she is? She finally lifts her gaze back to mine, and I could drown in those pools of golden brown.

"No? And what did you do about it, Princess?" I ask her, as I let my gaze take in her outfit properly for the first time. She's in a cream silk blouse and a black pencil skirt, black high heels, and barely-there stockings. Very sexy secretary.

I run my hands up over her hips and waist, continuing up to caress her breasts, pressing soft kisses to her skin above where her bra is peeking through some buttons that she's left strategically open at the top.

"Nothing," she lies, dipping her chin as the blush spreads.

"Don't lie to me, Princess," I rumble, tipping her chin up so that I can see her face, trying to coax her into telling me what I already know. I want to hear her say it.

"I... I touched myself," she admits with a gasp as I grab her roughly and spin us so that she's pinned with her back to my desk. She shivers in my arms as I growl into her ear.

"Did you now. Did you come?" She nods. "That pussy is mine Hayley. You only get to come when I say so. Do you understand me?" She nods again enthusiastically.

"Yes sir."

Fuck me, something about this fiery little lady suddenly acting all submissive makes me so hard. I know she's trying to tempt me, that she's still trying to prove a point. Leaning down, I whisper against her ear.

"Good, now you leave that pussy alone until we get back. You're going to have to wait and wait until you're begging me to take you. And I will Hayley, I am going to bend you over this desk and take you so fucking hard that you'll be screaming my name and nobody in this house will be under any illusions about what you are to me." She whimpers, and I can smell the arousal that floods between her legs. She loves dirty talk. I feel smug. She's not the only one who's going to be left frustrated around here.

"Then, every time I'm in here having boring meetings, I'll be able to picture you in this office, spread out for me, crying for me to fill you up." She moans softly. "Do you understand Hayley? No touching yourself," I order, satisfied that she is going to be the one left wanting more this time.

"Yes, Alpha sir," she says meekly, and I grin, cupping a hand to the side of her face. That's so hot.

"So ... you mean only you're allowed to do this?" She pulls my hand from her face and slips it between her thighs, swiping my fingers through her dripping wet pussy.

No panties. Fuck me. She's playing hardball.

Groaning, I swallow hard, and nod, realising the tables are swiftly being turned against me. She's not being meek, and she has no intention of obeying me. I'm not feeling so smug anymore. She knows that at this moment, she has all the power.

"Or this?" she asks innocently as she presses my finger up into her tight channel, letting her head fall back. Hayley allows a soft exhale to pass through her lips as she pushes it even further inside her and grinds her clit against my palm. I nearly come just from looking at the ecstasy on her face.

"Hayley... we can't..." My brain has stopped working entirely as my wolf urges me to spin her around, hike up that skirt, and sink myself deep inside her, pounding into her until she knows teasing me is not a good idea. But in some twisted way, I'm enjoying playing her game, in seeing what this little seductress has up her sleeve.

She shoves me backward into my leather chair and climbs up into my lap to straddle me. Her skirt hitches up and now I can see that she is wearing lace stockings and suspenders, with no fucking panties. She came prepared.

This woman is trying to kill me.

Gripping my rock-hard dick through my trousers, she rubs it, up and down, up and down, as she takes my lips in a deep, sensual kiss.

"Cooper, I want you, so bad it hurts. I miss you inside me. My body craves it. I'm burning up." Her words light my insides on fire and all I want is to be buried inside my mate. It's all-consuming.

I grip her ass in my two hands and squeeze hard, desperate to lift her onto the desk and show her just how much I want her too.

Hayley stops rubbing me and drops her hand to stroke between her legs. Panting and rocking her hips, she picks up speed as she touches her clit with just the right pace and pressure. She gasps as I stroke up her arms and shoulders, and grip her throat in my hand, adding slight pressure as I bring her face to mine, and make her meet my eyes.

"Are you enjoying yourself there, Princess?" My other hand grips her waist and drags her core over my hard cock, straining behind my now destroyed trousers. She groans and slips a finger inside her tempting pussy and rocks faster.

"Are you imagining that's me touching you, me inside you?" Nodding frantically, her body quivers as her release nears. I can feel the muscles in her stomach tighten as she gets closer and closer.

"You wait till I tell you to come," I growl, keeping my hand around her throat but using my other hand to pinch and roll her nipples between my fingers.

But she ignores me again and grips my biceps with her two hands as her back arches and her thighs clench on either side of my own. She calls out my name as her climax rushes through her, and she shakes and twitches in my lap. Throwing my head back, I pull at my hair with my two hands, knowing that if I touch her now, I won't be able to stop myself from taking her and marking her.

Fuck, I want her. I'm struggling to remember my reason for not just making her mine.

"Cooper, that was incredible," she mumbles incoherently, resting her head on my shoulder as she raises herself on her knees and smooths back down her skirt. I just groan and tentatively rub my hands down her back, before gripping her elbows to help her as she clambers off me and onto shaky feet. She looks down at me with a satisfied smile before leaning in to kiss me lightly.

"Amazing as that was, I'd much prefer the real thing. You can put us both out of our misery whenever you want, Alpha." Laughing lightly in my ear, she looks pointedly down at my lap where my now painfully hard erection is tenting the front of my trousers. "I better go."

"You are pure fucking evil, and I've never been so turned on in my life," I admit, keeping my hands clasped behind my head to stop myself from lunging at her. Looking thrilled with herself, she steps away from me and turns to leave, before stopping at the door and turning back with a wink.

"I'll see you at the resort, Cooper. You better have a shower before you go, though. Those wolves will smell me on you a mile away."

She's right, a shower is what I need. A freezing cold one.

CHAPTER 49

HAYLEY

"You wanted to stay in my house because you were in heat?" I ask Leila again, as I try to wrap my head around why she had wanted to clear out of the packhouse for the last few nights.

"Yes, even though I'm taking this horrendous herbal tea to mask the scent, it never hides it completely. I'd have to have stayed locked in my room to avoid all of them trying to hump me," she jokes. "They're afraid to go near me the rest of the time, but the heat would make them brave, horny, and stupid."

"It doesn't seem like the worst problem to have!" I laugh, thinking of how the shifter genes seem to make them all gorgeous compared to the rest of us mere mortals. "What would happen if you didn't take the herbs?" I ask, finding the whole thing completely fascinating.

"Well, given I'd be horny as hell too, I'd probably have days of passionate sex with whichever determined shifter took my fancy," she shrugs, her cheeks pink with embarrassment at the thought of it. "Don't tell my mother about my heat or the herbs. She'd kill me. All she wants are pups."

If I'm mated to a wolf, will I go into heat? As if I haven't got enough going on already.

I'm about to ask Leila more, but a car horn blares from outside and Leila carries our bags down the stairs to the porch where Rex immediately throws them into the back of this truck. I got my cast off yesterday and just need to wear a splint now, which is heaven in comparison.

Leila jumps into the back seat and immediately lays on her back across the full seat, closing her eyes. I guess there will be no more girly chat on the drive to the hotel then. Sliding into the passenger seat, I glance over at Rex, whose jaw clenches as we pull out of the driveway and onto the road.

"Dreading this thing that much?"

He briefly glances at me before turning his eyes back to the road. It doesn't look like he is going to answer me as the silence stretches on, but eventually, he looks at me again and shakes his head slightly.

Cooper mentioned Rex met his mate at this event before. Maybe it's dragging up some terrible memories for him.

"You have no fucking idea. Surprised to see you coming along..." He doesn't look too thrilled about my presence, and I feel like somehow, I am part of what is making the idea of this weekend so miserable for him rather than anything else.

"I never said I wasn't. That was Cooper's idea. And Cooper's not too keen on me staying in the packhouse with all of you away for the weekend." I shrug but don't elaborate more than that, before turning to stare out the window as the trees thin and we leave Grey Ridge behind.

"I bet he wasn't," Rex says wryly, one side of his mouth tipping up in an almost smile.

"So, what are you planning to do now that you're back? Are you going to get stuck into the family business again or do something completely different?" I ask, watching Rex shift slightly in the chair as if even just having this conversation makes him uncomfortable.

"I'm not sure really. I hate the office stuff that Cooper has to do. Couldn't do it, I'd go mad. And even Nathan. He's always stuck in project meetings and glued to his phone, trying to fix one problem after another. It's just not for me." His lips pull together in a tight line as if it physically pains him just thinking about stepping into one of their shoes.

"Okay, so you don't want to be the big boss. Do you think you'll stay working on the sites? Outside, fresh air, physical work," I venture. He was able to do all the work in my house. Nathan and Cooper pretty much left him to it.

"It might surprise you to hear this, Hayley, but I'm not great at being ordered around either," he says with a self-deprecating smile, and I laugh as an image of him growling and terrifying anyone who dared tell him what to do fills my head.

"So, you'd like to be the boss. You want to be outdoors most of the time, I guess, and not have loads of staff or paperwork to deal with." I tap my fingers on my knee as I think aloud. "Your family already has the construction and resort businesses, so it makes sense to tie in with one of those... didn't Cooper say you were in the military?"

"Well, yes, both me and Cooper. All Alpha's need to complete Alpha camp and do a stint on the Council security squad," he answers. Interesting. More questions for Cooper for another day.

"I don't understand what that is, but how about doing survival training and a fitness boot camp type thing? You could offer different levels, hardcore stuff for shifters or experienced humans, and then more basic fitness and self-defence stuff for weaklings like me? Add in some extra classes like yoga, or trail hikes and runs? A bit of kayaking."

"You're anything but a weakling Hayley," Rex says seriously.

"You could do packages, including accommodation and food. You can use the bed and breakfast. I definitely won't be using it and it seems a shame to leave it sitting empty. You could offer guests a deal on a couple of pamper nights in one of your resorts to recover afterward." He has his eyes narrowed in thought, but he hasn't dismissed the idea outright, so I continue on.

"All you'd need are a couple of people to come in and help with the classes or a bit of cooking. My sister Leah is just finishing college and is a qualified yoga teacher. She could come out and help you for a few weeks on a trial basis and see how it goes? The chefs in the packhouse would probably help and cook some extra food for you." He is nodding along, and I feel like we're on to something here. I'm getting more enthusiastic about my idea as we talk.

"Have a look and see if there is anything else similar in the area and talk to your dad's marketing team. I bet they could throw up a basic website with booking facilities in no time. Offer a free week to some of the local packs you get on with and use them as guinea pigs. Some local influencers, or hell, I'll drag some of my friends down from the city." I can already picture friends from back home or the city falling over themselves to sign up once I flash them a picture of their hot boot camp instructor.

"And where will you be?" he asks cautiously.

"What do you mean?" I ask baffled. Is he asking if I'd be willing to help?

"If I can take over your bed-and-breakfast, where will you be?" he asks, and I am reminded that this man is all Alpha, nothing slips past him.

"I can't stay in that house. I love it, but it just makes me think of James," I mumble, and it nearly kills me to admit it after putting my heart into the renovations. It is my dream house in every way, but he has ruined it for me, and it makes me so angry. "I wish I could get past it, but I don't think I'll ever be able to go up those stairs and not remember the feeling of being chased." I feel foolish getting emotional, but Rex just nods and reaches out to give my hand a quick squeeze.

"That's understandable Hayley, I think most people would feel the same. But where will you live?" I love that he doesn't sound like he pities me or makes me feel like I'm being overly dramatic.

"I don't want to sell it, not yet anyway. My sister lives an hour away, so I could easily do that drive back and forth for a while if I need to. I'm just staying in the packhouse now to prove a point." I try to picture living with Zoe. It is an option, but I just honestly can't imagine being that far away from Cooper. At the same time, I'm not staying in his bed again until we're a proper couple. I'm sticking to my guns on this one.

"Steel's territory," Rex mumbles, adjusting his grip on the steering wheel.

"Hmmm?" I ask absentmindedly, as I picture Zoe rattling around all on her own in the big house attached to the veterinary clinic that she bought. It would be good to spend some time together again. She'd probably appreciate the company since she has no social life. She's even more of a hermit than I am, and that's without a stalker to blame. She'd be happy for me to save, even for a few weeks.

"That's outside our pack's territory, Hayley, in Alpha Steel's lands. Have you mentioned this to Cooper by any chance?" He turns to meet my eye briefly, worry on his handsome dark features.

"Well, no, but why would I? I haven't even told my sister yet. Anyway, Cooper and I decided to just be friends for the moment since he's so determined not to claim me." Rex snorts in disbelief as he turns to look at me with those piercing hazel eyes, dancing with intrigue.

"Hmmm, has he now?" Feeling like I am under a microscope, I struggle to keep an innocent look fixed on my face.

"Well, we're not together anyway," I mutter, not wanting to get sucked into this conversation.

"Do me a favour. Wait until I'm there before you tell him you're moving out of Grey Ridge, please? I want to see his face when he realises exactly what he agreed to." Shaking his head, he laughs to himself.

"What's so funny?" I ask.

"Oh, you know! Don't even try to do that little Miss Innocent with me. He'll lose his mind. But he only has himself to blame." Shrugging as if I have no clue what he is talking about, Rex continues to grin to himself. I think it's the happiest I've seen him, and it's definitely at Cooper's expense.

Brothers.

CHAPTER 50

COOPER

A long cold shower and an evening completing seating arrangements, presentations, and dealing with daft requests was my self-inflicted penance for trying to be a good guy.

Rex mind-links me as their car is pulling up, telling me that the car journey was enlightening, but that's all he'll say. All his travelling the world has still left him a man of very few words. I dread to think about what's coming my way over the next few days.

The weekend hasn't even started and I'm already exhausted.

I am standing in the lobby, trying to make small talk with the other guests at the conference, including a spoiled little Alpha's daughter called Stephanie, who seems determined to drag me into a private conversation. Inside I feel like screaming, but instead I nod politely instead and edge away from her cloying perfume.

Rex: You are going to need to chill out when we come in, ok

Cooper: What do you mean?

Rex: Just take a deep breath

Rex walks through the automatic doors weighed down with bags just a second before Leila, and then Hayley. Suddenly, there is a lull in all the conversations going on in the busy foyer as everyone turns to watch their arrival. I know Leila is a beauty, even by wolf shifter standards. This, along with her alpha lineage, as well as her obvious disinterest in every male suitor who approaches her, has made her quite the prize, and she always attracts a lot of attention at these events.

However, the eyes of pretty much everyone in the room have zeroed in on my mate. How she ever thought she could hide anywhere is beyond me. Her beauty makes her stand out wherever she goes.

Ten seconds in and I'm already hating this.

Some are curious about the arrival of this stunning human, seemingly here with Rex. He's the last person many of them would have expected to see at the Alpha conference, considering he met his mate at the last one and it fell apart shortly afterward. They're also curious why she isn't the least bit nervous about being surrounded by powerful wolves. In fact, she owns the room.

The overpowering scent of want pours from most unmated males in the room, leaving no doubt as to their interest in her. And my wolf is pushing me to take their eyes out.

Hayley is dressed to kill in a pair of skin-tight leather-look leggings tucked into high-heeled black ankle boots. She has a cream silk top on which shows enough of her figure that her flat stomach and pert ass can be seen, but it has long sleeves and is loose enough that it's still appropriate for the venue. It also mostly covers the splint she's still wearing on one arm. A gold necklace drapes onto her chest, drawing attention to the deep v of the blouse and her cleavage. Subtle makeup sets her tanned skin and caramel eyes to perfection.

It's an outfit designed to torture me.

She looks like a supermodel on her way to a business meeting and I am torn between the desire to attack every male who is looking at her with lust in their eyes and wanting to drag her up to my room and make her scream, so they know exactly who she belongs to. I don't even realise I am growling until Stephanie, who had crept back over to my side and placed her hand on my forearm without me noticing, shrinks back from me.

Rex: Keep it together, Coop. Remember, this is your idea. You didn't want to claim her yet.

Cooper: This was not exactly what I had in mind.

Rex: Are you seriously telling me you thought she would stay home? She's your Luna.

Cooper: I am aware of that.

Rex: You know she's loving this. Cooper: Oh, believe me, I know.

I glare at Rex as they make their way over to where I am standing beside reception, and I swear he is actually grinning. It would be great to see if it wasn't at my expense. Hayley reaches me and after giving Stephanie a brief glare that lifts my spirits slightly, she leans up and gives me a peck on the cheek.

"Hi, Cooper," she says in greeting, grinning at me. I cough and try to pull myself together.

"Hayley," I say, it's all I can get out that sounds remotely normal. "Let me show you to your room." I need to get her out of here right now.

"No need. You look busy here. I'm sure Rex can get me settled." I frown at her as she directs a pointed look at Stephanie who is still hanging around beside me, before giving me a little wave before turning on her heels and heading for the lifts, offering me the perfect view of that sexy ass as she walks away.

I can hear both Rex and Leila laughing at me before I shut down the mind-link and concentrate on damping down the rage I feel after seeing all the other males watching Hayley as she leaves.

This is going to be a long weekend.

CHAPTER 51

HAYLEY

After unpacking my suitcase and having a last look over notes Marie gave me on the attending guests, I head downstairs to join Jonathan, Marie, and Leila for lunch in the bar.

When I arrive, the only seat left is one facing Cooper, who's having a meeting at another table. I try not to catch his eye as I slide into the chair, even though I can feel his gaze burning into me. I thought it would be fun to see his reaction, watching me all dressed up arriving here, but now that I'm close to him, his genuine fear and frustration are making me feel bad. Damn conscience.

"Alpha Jones, might we have a quick word?" I glance up from my meal to see two tall men standing beside our table. I recognise one of them immediately as being the future alpha of the Red Creek pack, Toby. The other must be the current leader, Alpha Anderson, who is in the process of handing over his pack to his son-in-law.

Why it's not being passed on to his daughter is beyond me, but maybe she's not interested in running a pack, like Leila.

Looking over to Jonathan, who is sitting back in his chair, I watch as he carefully places his knife and fork down on his plate, drawing attention to the half-finished meal in front of him. Jonathan looks displeased at the interruption, but that does not seem to have deterred Toby in his pursuit of an audience.

For a second, I think I see a flicker of amusement crossing Jonathan's face, replacing the earlier annoyance, as he gestures for the two men to go ahead with whatever they want to ask.

"Alpha Jones, we apologise for interrupting your meal. Marie, forgive us. I know you were in the middle of a conversation, but Toby tells me there is something we need to discuss urgently." The older Alpha's good manners help to ease the tension that has settled across the table. He tips his head at Marie in a respectful greeting, and Marie nods graciously before rising.

"Leila, join me on the terrace. I could do with some fresh air before the next course." Marie excuses them from the table, ever the perfect host, and leaves just me and Jonathan to speak with the two men privately, gesturing for them to take the vacated seats.

"I believe we already have some time in the diary before we leave on Sunday to discuss the deal..." Jonathan trails off, suggesting he doesn't see any reason there needs to be a conversation right now.

"You were supposed to sign on Wednesday! This was supposed to have closed already, and now I'm getting stone-walled by your lawyers. It's bullshit!" Toby exclaims, and I feel, rather than hear, low rumble coming from Jonathan beside me, but his face remains perfectly calm.

"I want to know what the hell is going on, or we'll pull the deal and go straight to the next bidder." Toby is pushy, rude, and bluffing. I may not have enhanced shifter senses, but even I can see his nervousness and agitation. His colour is high and his grip on the table is tight, as if he's having trouble staying in his seat. Jonathan takes him in for a second before responding calmly, although there is no mistaking the annoyance in his voice at the tone with which he is being spoken to.

"I don't believe you will do that, Toby, and I suspect we both know the reason. Alpha Anderson, perhaps we should move somewhere more private to have this discussion?" Jonathan suggests, essentially dismissing Toby and it's clear how much the snub has rankled the already irate young man, who now looks like he's about to explode.

"No, I want to know now!" he shouts, thumping the table. Cooper is clenching his jaw at the table across from me, and I can see the knuckles in his fists have gone white. The blatant disrespect for his father and the volatile nature of Toby's behaviour is rubbing Cooper the wrong way, but he's trying to stay composed and not create more of a scene.

I glance up and see Rex watching closely from the terrace door, obviously ready to step in if needed. Jonathan eyes Toby for a second, shrugging and turning to me.

"As you wish. Hayley, could you explain? Given you were working on it more closely than me." Jonathan fixes me with an encouraging look, and I can almost feel the faith he has in me flowing towards me, calming my nerves and letting me know I've got this. His public show of support means a lot. I follow Jonathan's lead and address the Alpha instead of his would-be successor.

"Alpha, in the course of my due diligence, I uncovered a potential issue which you may not be aware of." The Alpha's eyebrows draw together slightly in confusion, and I am already convinced that he doesn't know what's coming.

"Stratton, who built the resort, is part of a larger group which is currently under investigation for deliberately cutting corners on health and safety measures, particularly fire safety requirements.

We intended to ask for an extension on the signing deadline to allow us to conduct a thorough inspection. If there are issues, it's likely the costs to fix them will be significant, and we'll have to pull out."

I have finished delivering the potential bad news, and look to the son-in-law, who Jonathan never took his eyes off. It's obvious that he knew all along. He's barely breathing. And furious.

I wonder whether he knows there is actually a problem with the building, or just that there is potentially one? When he finally looks up and fixes me with a glare, he's so angry that I know it's the latter. His face is almost purple with rage as he leaps to his feet and bumps the dining table, sending a glass toppling over the side to smash on the floor.

"You interfering bitch! This is your doing!" he roars. For a second, I wonder if he's going to shift right there at the table.

Cooper is already on his feet, but suddenly my view is blocked by a broad back as someone places their body between me and Toby, an arm pressing me behind and shielding me from Toby's view.

"You say another word to her, and I'll end you right now." A deep voice warns in front of me, and as he looks over at Jonathan, I realise I know this man.

It's none other than Alpha Reynolds, the angry guy from the party. Today his anger isn't directed at one of the Joneses, it's being used to defend me, and I'm grateful.

I glance over at Cooper, who has edged closer and is now looming dangerously over Toby. He looks like a completely different man from the one I normally see. Gone is the strong but relaxed attitude, the charming smile, and the glint in his eye; in its place is intimidating power and dangerous masculine energy. You would not mess with this Cooper.

You could hear a pin drop as the attention of every shifter in the lounge turns to the scene unfolding at our table. Toby moves to lunge around Reynolds, who doesn't even flinch. Alpha Anderson growls deeply and puts a hand on Toby's shoulder, which seems to have the effect of turning him into a statue – albeit one that is still trembling with anger.

I slowly step out from behind Alpha Reynolds and place my hand on his forearm gently to let him know that I'm okay.

"Alpha, I apologise for telling you like this, we had hoped to discuss it in a more appropriate setting. I do sincerely hope that your property is not affected," I address Alpha Anderson, who moves slowly around the table towards me.

"No need for you to apologise, dear," he says warmly, shooting a look that could kill towards his son-in-law. "It shouldn't have been you that had to tell me in the first place." He grasps my good hand in his giant handshake and smiles kindly at me.

"It would appear," he turns to Jonathan, "as though I may need to take back the reins of my pack. This is not the way I do business, old friend; I hope you know that. I will undertake the inspections myself immediately and be in touch." He shakes Jonathan's hand firmly, and, as Jonathan nods in agreement, I realise why Jonathan was so insistent on doing this meeting face-to-face.

He needed to be sure that it was only the son- in-law who was trying to pull a fast one.

Toby is still staring at Jonathan and me with pure venom in his eyes. Alpha Anderson hauls him away, and the tension in the room gradually ebbs away. Although every hushed conversation that begins at the other tables is no doubt about what just went on. Dean Reynolds relaxes his stance beside me, satisfied that the young man won't be back, but doesn't take his eyes off Toby until he has left the room.

Cooper's deep brown eyes glaze over, which I now know is a sign he is mind-linking someone, and I'm not surprised when I see Rex move from his position to follow the two men out into the lobby.

"Thank you," I say sincerely to Dean, who nods once at me, tips his head at Jonathan in respect, and stalks out of the room. I let out a sigh as I sink back into my chair and reach for my glass of wine. Cooper sits down beside me and wraps his arm around my shoulder, giving me a gentle squeeze and moving back to a more professional distance.

"Are you okay?" he asks quietly. I nod, but he doesn't look convinced, and the frown on his face doesn't lift as he turns to face his father.

"Dad, could you not have done that quietly? Or at least warned the rest of us," Cooper grumbles, but his father just grins back at the two of us.

"Where would be the fun in that? Plus, I didn't know what would happen. They may have been just as shocked by Hayley's findings as we were," Jonathan says, but even I know he never believed that would be the case.

"It went better than I thought it would," I say honestly, downing the last of my wine.

"How was that better than you thought?" Cooper asks incredulously, staring at me as if I've lost my mind. I can sense his lingering tension from the confrontation through the bond and I now appreciate that everything he does, as daft as it sometimes seems, genuinely comes from a place of trying to mind me and protect me.

"He didn't eat me," I say simply with a wry smile, setting down my wine glass and pushing to my feet. Jonathan chuckles, and I hear a few sniggers from around the bar making it clear most of the wolves present have been using their super-hearing to eavesdrop on our conversation.

"If you'll excuse me, I think I could do with another drink," I say as I force my feet to step away from the table, from Cooper.

That mixture of caring and dominance within him does something to me I can't explain, and I need to get some space before I do something completely unprofessional, like jumping him in front of his parents.

"I'll come with you!" Leila announces, linking my arm as she drags me away. I don't look back, but I can feel Cooper's eyes on me as I move further away, and I can sense the pride coming from him. I can't help the giant smile that is plastered on my face.

Maybe Leah was on to something.

Maybe I just need to be me, and Cooper will see that just because I'm human, doesn't mean I'm not going to be able to handle all of this wolf stuff, too.

CHAPTER 52
COOPER

Leila and Hayley stand at the bar, heads close together as they whisper and laugh.

My heart swells to see this amazing woman is now thick-as-thieves with my little sister. I cannot believe what I just witnessed, and I don't think my brain has fully grasped the fact that my mate just went toe to toe with a powerful alpha and his next in line without batting an eyelid. I sensed a vague flutter of nerves over the bond, but nothing like the fear or intimidation that I would have expected, especially once things got ugly.

"Impressive," my mum murmurs as she follows my gaze to Hayley.

"Absolutely," my father concurs. "She has potentially saved the pack from financial ruin." He shakes his head and knocks back his whiskey.

It doesn't even bear thinking about it. We take our role in providing for the pack seriously. That deal could have destroyed not only our lives and our jobs, but everyone in the pack.

"That girl deserves the rest of the weekend off; if I see her at any of your boring talks, I'll send her away myself," my mum says. "And Dean Reynolds stood up for our girl. I told you he's different."

Leaving to make her rounds as hostess, smoothing over any unease the attendees may have over Toby's outburst, she's always the luna before all else.

My dad squeezes my shoulder and follows her, taking her hand and pressing a kiss to her temple as they face the other alphas and their families, who have been watching closely. A perfect team as always, a united front, supporting each other and leaving no room to doubt their leadership.

That's exactly what I want to build with my mate.

It's the only chance I have of leading the pack as well as they have for almost 40 years.

As a tall and intense, dark-haired wolf whom I recognise as the Steel Pack beta begins chatting to Leila, I see Hayley slip out to the terrace. Even though I know it's a terrible idea, I can't help myself from quietly following her outside.

While I'm telling myself any friend would check on her, to make sure she really is okay after that confrontation, I know I'm feeling decidedly more than friendly right now. She walks to the railing and leans over, resting her forearms on the smooth wood. Tipping her head forward, her hair hangs in waves around her face and shoulders, and she suddenly looks tired.

Her posture straightens as soon as she senses she's not alone anymore, and I know she knows it's me. She doesn't even glance around to see who it is, but I hear her heartbeat quicken and her breathing picks up as I step up behind her, placing my hands gently on her shoulders. I massage her tense muscles and she relaxes, letting out a soft sigh and a little groan that makes my mouth water. It's been almost a week since I've had her in my bed – far too long.

"Cooper." She sighs as she allows me to continue rubbing her shoulders. I move my hands up to tend the back of her neck and she groans again, quietly.

The noise reminds me of how she sounds when I'm inside her, and it's making me hard as a rock. I stroke my hands down her shoulders and along the tops of her arms, but when my lips press against her jaw and my thumbs graze the sides of her breasts, she starts. The moment is broken.

She steps away and wraps her arms across her chest.

"I'm sorry. I shouldn't have let you do that. It's a bad idea." She meets my eye steadily, and I can scent her desire, even as she's pulling back.

"Don't be, I'm just being friendly." I edge closer, cupping her cheek with one hand and gently resting my other on her hip.

"Friends do not touch each other like that," she quips, smiling up at me.

"I've never really had a friend who's a girl before, I'm just learning my way."

She rolls her eyes, laughing, but then stops and fixes me with a sharp look.

"Are you...?" she trails off as her frown deepens as she considers something.

"Unbelievably impressed and turned on by what I saw in there? Absolutely." I try to turn on the charm as I reach for her again, but she inches back further to stay out of my arms.

"Don't distract me. Have you changed your mind?" she asks, and I know she's referring to the marking.

"I... no... I still can't. Look at what happened with Toby. If he knew you were my mate, he could hurt you to get back at us. I can't chance it," I say. "And this is only the tip of the iceberg. You need to see it before you agree to stick with me forever."

"Then don't do this, Cooper. You're the one who wants us to keep this quiet. I know I was playing with you before we came but don't mess with my head."

"It's just... I need to touch you, to hold you. I can't stay away. My wolf is screaming to just take you right here, right now." I see her flush at my words as I press against her, showing her how much I mean it. Her arousal intensifies, but so does her annoyance.

"And you want everyone to think what, Cooper? That we're fuck buddies?"

Her disappointment in me is clear.

"Shit, no, Hayley. I just can't think clearly when I'm around you, and it's a million times worse with all these other alphas around."

She's right, that is what everyone would think. While I don't want any other men near her, I don't want her in that position either.

"If you can't control it, then you need to stay away from me. It's not fair. Do you think I enjoy seeing all these gorgeous she-wolves staring at you when all I want is to be with you? While you hide me away because you think I'm weak, less than them?" She looks up at me with bright, shiny eyes, and I can see how upset she is about this whole thing.

I curse myself as my sexy little mate turns to go back inside. She's a queen, and she shouldn't have to put up with anyone treating her like anything but, including me.

"Hayley, wait. Please, stay and talk to me for a while. I'll be on my best behaviour." I hold my hands up in surrender.

"Ok," she smiles weakly as something else flickers across her features, "but on one condition."

I nod eagerly. I don't care what it is.

"I want to see your wolf again."

"Your wish is my command, Princess." I take a little bow and begin to strip for her. As I unbutton my shirt, I can see the hunger in her eyes. Much as I would love to turn this into something more, it's not the right time, so I undress quickly. The transformation happens easily, bones snapping into place, teeth and claws lengthening, black fur covering my entire body.

Padding slowly toward her, my wolf is ecstatic about getting to finally meet her up close. She holds perfectly still as he circles her, sniffing and brushing up against her, relishing in her wonderful scent.

He adores her and would happily lay his life on the line for her – in retrospect, he has been since before I even knew who she was.

When I was younger, I tried dating both humans and she-wolves from outside the pack, to have a little fun and to calm the restlessness inside me. But my wolf wouldn't have any of it. If I tried to get physical with one of those other women, he would go berserk and make it impossible to enjoy. I gave up trying, relieved to stop battling with the guilt I felt.

I've heard it's not unusual for an alpha wolf. They won't settle for anyone less than their fated mate, and are powerful enough to make their feelings known.

She relaxes a little when he sits down in front of her, tilting his head to one side and pushing his snout under the hand. She chuckles, rubbing him along his back and the top of his head.

"You're magnificent," she whispers, to which he yips in delight.

Someone could come along at any minute, so I cut the introduction short and transform back, grabbing my clothes and covering my modesty, and my attraction to my mate. I wink at Hayley when I catch her staring as I tuck myself away. She tuts, stepping in close and smiling at me in wonder.

"That was amazing, thank you," she beams.

"Hayley, I know this is tough. The shifter thing, and all the pack politics that go with it, are new to you. And this relationship stuff is new to me. I'm just trying to look out for you." I cup her cheek tenderly and she leans into my touch.

"I know, Cooper, but hiding me away is not the way we're going to learn to navigate any of it. We should work together." She presses a gentle kiss to my palm, stepping away and wandering back inside.

CHAPTER 53

HAYLEY

My decision to make a quick pit stop in the ladies' room has proved to be a terrible one.

Leila warned that, after the little showdown earlier, people are asking questions, and I'd probably get a good grilling from other pack leaders throughout the evening.

Normally that wouldn't make this any different than any other networking event I've attended over the years, but these are actual wolves that I'm being thrown to. My nerves set in, and I feel as though I need to show Cooper, and his family, that I'm ready for this. That I can stand by Cooper's side.

So, now it feels like I'm part of the world's longest audition.

Which is why I'm here in the ladies' room, settling my nerves and trying to avoid the inevitable.

Just as I'm about to leave the stall, the door to the bathroom swings open, and two voices fill the air. I should just go out, but I hold on and wait for them to leave.

"Did you see that little hullabaloo earlier with the Jones pack? I thought Cooper was going to shift on the spot and tear Toby apart. God, that man is just sex on legs." The speaker sighs dreamily.

I agree with her, but her interest in my man makes my temper flare, and I have the urge to march out there and tell her exactly who he belongs to.

And maybe smash her face off the mirror while I'm at it.

"Who is that blonde chick with them, anyway? Reynolds was quick to defend her, and Cooper was coddling her afterward. Is she here with either of them?" annoying she-wolf number two asks.

"No, I heard she came with Rex." Voice One seems to have this all worked out. She's been paying attention.

"Maybe they're all just being overprotective, because she can't defend herself?" Voice Two doesn't seem as nasty, but I'm still offended by that one. I may not be a wolf like them, but I'm not completely helpless.

"Yeah, maybe. I've been waiting years for Cooper to give up on his fated mate. No way some human is sneaking in there to steal him."

Yep, I hate Voice One.

"I thought you were after Rex?"

"Oh, that man. My wolf is such a slut for him, but he's not home to take over the pack... and I want to be luna." She's nasty *and* a gold-digging social climber. Lovely. "Maybe we need to make it clear she should back off? Those Jones boys are too hot to be wasted on a girl like *that*."

She growls, snapping her teeth, and her companion giggles.

Cooper was right. Some of these she-wolves are vicious. When they've finished touching up their make-up, or whatever they were doing in the bathroom, and I hear them exit, I hang back for an extra minute then follow them out the door.

Out into the corridor, I'm surprised to see them still standing in the hallway, talking, flirting really, with an attractive man who is leaning casually against the wall on the far side of the corridor.

Why are these wolves so good-looking?

As soon as he sees me, he pushes off the wall and stands at his full height, fixing me with a warm, friendly smile. He reaches a hand past the two ladies towards me, and, despite not having a clue who he is, I surprise myself by immediately taking his hand and letting him pull me in close to his side.

"Ah, ladies. I'd like to introduce you to Hayley. As I'm sure you know, she works with the Jones pack, and she is a close friend of mine. I'm sure you'll make her feel very welcome this weekend, won't you?" He looks at each of them as if to emphasise what he has just said. They nod sullenly.

"I'd consider it a personal favour if you kept an eye out for her during the conference after the unpleasantness earlier today. We don't want her to think we're all animals, do we?" He hits them with a little wink, and I can see them practically swoon.

"Of course, Alpha Steel," they mutter. Bowing their heads to him, they stroll off when he turns his back on them, not so subtly cutting off any further conversation.

He fixes me with intense hazel eyes, rimmed by thick black lashes, and I can't seem to look away as he brings my wrist to his nose. He smiles as he inhales my scent, closing his eyes as he breathes deeply before frowning and looking at me in confusion, he lowers my wrist to my side.

What the hell was that?

CHAPTER 54

HAYLEY

"Hayley, allow me to introduce myself properly. I'm Alpha Blake Steel," he says, and I try not to react. I know who he is from Marie's 'who's who' cheat-sheets.

This is the most powerful wolf here. And he was waiting out here for me.

"I hope those ladies didn't upset you. You seem to have thrown the cat among the pigeons this weekend, and their noses are out of joint." He leans down and tilts his head slightly, so I don't get a crick in my neck looking up at him.

Gosh, he's tall.

Even in my high heels, he makes me feel teeny.

"Are they from your pack?" I ask, trying to get my head around how these pack politics work.

"Actually, no. But I'm currently the Head Alpha of the region, so they have to listen to me whether they like it or not." He grins and I can't help laughing. He's not what I expected. "You can rest assured they won't give you any trouble now."

He holds out the crook of his elbow for me, and I slip my hand through. Even though I have no idea what this massive guy wants, or where he's leading me, I feel at ease. My steps falter as I realise we're turning away from the back lawn where the marquee and BBQ are set up, but he places his hand lightly on top of mine to stop me from pulling back. He tips his head towards me and speaks quietly, even though there isn't anyone around to hear us.

"You seemed a little nervous about going out there, if you don't mind me saying, and I'd like to get you to myself for a moment. Will you join me for a quick drink?" he asks politely and steps back, leaning his large frame away from me, giving me space to decide.

I'm intrigued, and he's right. I don't want to go outside and socialise just yet.

"Lead the way, Alpha Steel," I return his smile and fall into step with him.

"Please, call me Blake." He steers me to a table in a quiet corner of the lounge, which is empty except for two other tables, and seats himself with his back to the wall as I slide into the seat beside him. I watch with fascination as a young girl behind the counter leaps to attention as soon as she spots him and practically runs over to take our order.

He smiles, running a hand through his jet-black hair, which falls below his ears but still looks immaculately groomed. I bet any hairstyle would look good on this man. He looks like a male model with his full lips and strong jawline, his perfection superficially marred by a scar, maybe two inches long, that runs down the side of his face. Running from his eyebrow to just above his ear on the right side, it probably makes him more gorgeous, helping him look less perfect and a bit dangerous.

"So now that you have me all to yourself, Blake, what did you want with me? You don't seem like the type who lurks around the ladies' bathroom just for the hell of it."

He barks out a surprised laugh, as though that was the last thing he expected me to say.

"I don't, if that puts your mind at ease." He sits back and looks at me curiously. "I wanted to see if what I heard was true; to meet the lady who put Toby back in his box."

"What did you hear?" I ask, interested to hear what these wolves were saying about me. "Leila is probably too kind to tell me the truth, but you don't seem like the type to pull punches. It wouldn't be fitting of the Head Alpha. You can't just be a pretty face and a sharp suit."

"Very observant," he takes a swig from his drink as he continues to eye me. "I'm not sure whether to take that as a compliment or an insult." He frowns in mock confusion, tutting at me, laughing, and turning to address the lounge girl, who looks like she might wet herself with nerves.

"What... what can I get you Alpha?" she asks breathlessly, looking at the table instead of meeting his eye, twirling the pen around and around in her fingers.

He glances at her name badge and then speaks.

"Sarah, I'll just have a beer, please, and whatever the lovely lady wants. Just stick it on my tab, ok?"

Sarah nods vigorously and seems relieved to turn her attention to me.

"Same for me, too. Thank you." I smile at her warmly and she relaxes a little, meets my eye, and smiles back; relieved that I've ordered something straightforward, she dashes off to get our order.

"Is that normal?" I ask, meaning the nervous server falling over herself to please him, turning into a stuttering wreck in his presence.

"Occupational hazard I'm afraid, particularly with the more submissive wolves. But you're not affected at all by my... alpha-ness. Are you?" He leans back and stretches a long, muscular arm along the back of his chair, eyeing me with fascination.

"Alpha-ness, is that the technical term?" I laugh. "No, it would appear not. I mean, you're a big guy, but other than being conscious of that, I don't seem to be affected the way others are."

"Interesting." He narrows his eyes thoughtfully while taking a long draw from the beer bottle Sarah placed in front of him before scurrying off again. "So, a brother in the Marines. How did he take the news of your recent troubles with your ex?" He glances down at my hand, still splinted.

"What? How?" I stutter, embarrassed that he knows about my brother, but he simply lifts a shoulder and smiles kindly. He did that on purpose, trying to throw me off balance by showing how much he knows about me, and I'm annoyed that I reacted.

"It's my job to know these things, but don't worry. I'm not a gossip, it's nobody else's business. I'm glad you're okay." He gives my hand a gentle squeeze.

"My brother doesn't know. To say he's protective is an understatement. He's going to go mad that we didn't tell him what was going on." When I think about how he will react, I cringe. I better tell him before he gets home from deployment; that would give him some time to calm down before I see him face to face.

"I don't blame him. If you were my sister, I'd be furious. I am furious, and I only just met you." He clenches his jaw and takes another long slug of beer to settle himself.

"He has three sisters. He's used to constantly worrying," I admit, and Blake grimaces, making me laugh.

"I bet your mate didn't take it any better," he whispers. I cough, nearly choking on my drink.

"What? I'm human." I try to maintain my best poker face.

Suddenly, I'm wondering what Blake's intentions are and whether I'm being naïve in assuming they're good. Cooper said that other alphas would see me as a potential weakness to exploit if they knew I was his mate.

"You haven't been marked, true, but that doesn't mean you don't have one. Don't worry, your secret is safe with me." He smiles, and, even though my brain is telling me I don't know this guy and to be cautious, I relax. My heart seems to know him, like when meeting an old friend that I haven't seen in a while. I neither confirm nor deny what he's saying.

"I'm another old romantic, waiting for my true mate to make an appearance. Or trying, anyway," he offers.

Another. Does that mean he's guessed who it is?

"I guess there's a lot of pressure on you if you're running your pack on your own," I empathise.

"Yes, that's part of it. But it's lonely, too. It would be nice to have some company like this, where I don't have to worry about what someone wants from me or wants to gain from me. Or, worse still, most are too intimidated to even have a proper chat with me."

I'm shocked at his open admission.

"Not that I should probably admit that as the Big, Bad Alpha," he says wryly, catching the surprise written all over my face.

"Your secret is safe with me," I say, and he lets out a laugh, eyes crinkling in amusement.

"There's something about you, Hayley. I'll admit, at first, I thought maybe you were her, that you were mine. But you're not, I'm sad to say. There's something strange there, though; not like a mate, but a connection. Maybe I'm losing my mind," he admits, trailing off, knocking back the rest of his beer.

If I didn't know better, I'd think he was embarrassed.

"No, you're not losing your mind. It's like we're family, or you're my new gay best friend." He tips his head back and lets out a loud laugh, slapping his hand down on the table and drawing the eyes of everyone in the bar towards us.

"That's definitely a new one for me. Jesus, Hayley, straight into the friend zone. That was brutal." He puts his hand to his heart, laughing heartily. I doubt he's ever been friend-zoned in his life.

"Come on, I better bring you back before your mate sends out a search party." He stands and holds out his hand for me, his eyes glinting mischievously. I take it. He helps me up and tucks my hand under his arm as he escorts me back through the hotel to where the festivities are well underway, music drifting through the open doors.

"How did you know I have a mate?" I whisper, curiosity getting the better of me. He smirks.

"It's the only explanation I can think of for why an Alpha Order wouldn't work on you. You are destined to be an alpha's equal in life, his luna." He faces me and tucks a loose strand of hair behind my ear, cupping my cheek for a brief second before sighing and dropping his hand. "I kind of wish it was me."

CHAPTER 55

COOPER

"**N**o, you don't. She's coming. You just need to wait a little longer. And it'll be worth it," I say with conviction, and I genuinely believe it. He nods at me and smiles but doesn't look as convinced as I feel.

"I hope you're right. Come on, let's go have some fun."

I break contact with those hazel eyes and realise he has positioned us just inside the doorway. When I look out, at least a dozen faces are staring our way, slack-jawed. I elbow him in the side, but it's like hitting a wall, and he laughs loudly, guiding me towards the bar. He's obviously not concerned in the slightest about angering my mate or causing trouble.

"I don't know if this is a good idea." I hesitate, not wanting to cause any more drama.

"Hayley, if your mate is daft enough to leave you unclaimed and unattended, he should be happy that I'm ensuring nobody with less honourable intentions bothers you. Don't worry about him, he'll come to his senses, and in the meantime, surely, you're allowed to have some fun." He looks at me pleadingly with big puppy dog eyes, and I can't help but smile.

"Fine, but I better go find Leila. She'll kill me for bailing on her," I relent.

"Even better, I'll send Max to go find her now. We can have a double date." I groan as soon as he says it. He's clearly finding this hilarious.

"Shut up, Blake," I chastise quietly, but I hear someone gasp beside us. Damn wolf super senses. Blake roars laughing, and continues to push us closer to the bar, his hand gently pressed against the middle of my back.

"I don't think anyone has told me to shut up since I was about 8 years old. This is brilliant. I like you, Hayley."

I've never seen anyone quite so thrilled at being told off, but I suppose being surrounded by yes men all day would get old quickly.

When we reach the bar, Leila is already there with another man who must be Max, chatting away. Her eyes go almost comically wide, and her mouth drops open when she sees me and catches Blake's hand on my back.

"Well, hello there, Hayley. I was getting worried about you, but you were obviously in very safe hands," she says, flicking her eyes back and forth between me and Blake.

"Leila, this is Blake, Blake this is Leila. Or do you guys know each other already?" I do the introductions and watch as her eyes nearly bug out of her head when I call him Blake.

"Yes, Hayley, I have met Alpha Steel before," she says, emphasising his formal title, which must be how everyone else addresses him, as she reaches out to shake his hand. "I didn't realise you guys were on a first-name basis?" She raises an eyebrow at the two of us and Blake smiles again.

"It's Blake to you too, Leila." He takes the two beers the barman hands him and places one into my hand, ordering for me without asking what I'd like.

It's a familiar gesture that doesn't go unnoticed by Leila, and I know she's itching to ask me a million questions. She doesn't get the chance, however, as Blake launches into a barrage of questions about her clinic in Grey Ridge, treating both humans and shifters, and how she manages both. Max is Blake's beta, second in charge, and they have been considering opening a similar operation somewhere on their pack's land.

The next hour goes by in a blur, and the conversation switches quickly from business to more informal topics, and I realise that other than my time with Cooper, I haven't had any proper fun in a long, long time.

A steady stream of people drifts by to give their greetings to Blake, and he makes time for them all, switching seamlessly back into serious Alpha mode whenever anyone else is around. I can see how it would be lonely. He and Max are like brothers as they joke and tease, but it's easy to see why he needs to keep himself distant in his role.

It must make it hard to just be normal.

"Well, ladies, I'm sorry to say I'm going to have to love you and leave you. I've hogged far too much of your time this evening, and I believe you have many others looking for some of your attention. Thank you for the best night I've had in a long, long time. See you tomorrow." Blake winks at me and leans to whisper into the shell of my ear so nobody can hear. "I'll be interested in hearing what your mate has to say."

To someone else watching, it would look intimate, and even though I haven't seen him, I feel Cooper's red, hot, fury like an echo in the back of my mind through the bond. Blake and Max head back into the hotel, everyone stepping out of their path as they pass, shooting furtive glances back toward Leila and me.

"Holy shit. Hayley, you sure know how to cause trouble. I can't leave you alone for two seconds," Leila whispers as she watches their retreating forms. "So, you're best friends with Blake Steel now?"

I laugh and nod, catching her hand in mine as we head through the party to find the rest of her family.

"Something like that. They were good fun though, weren't they?"

"Eh, I have never seen that man smile, let alone laugh. I don't think anyone has ever said "Blake Steel" and "fun" in the same sentence before. What on earth happened?" she asks incredulously.

"We just bumped into each other and went for a drink. Nothing exciting." I dismiss it, keeping what he said in confidence. She looks at me as if she knows I am lying through my teeth but doesn't get the chance to question me as Marie sweeps us up in a giant three-way hug.

"Leila, were those *men* I saw you talking to?" her mother says in mock surprise, as if she doesn't know exactly who they were.

"Ha, ha. Yes, Mum, I was talking to men. Don't start getting ideas." Leila rolls her eyes and tugs her arm out of her mother's grasp.

"I wouldn't dare," she jokes, "even if Max is one of the most eligible, handsome men here; and I know for a fact that he is in the market for a chosen mate." She winks and turns her attention to me, gripping my face between her two palms. "And you, you don't mess around." She whistles low, still smiling. Is she implying I hit on him?

"It's not like that..." I explain but she's gone again before I can finish, and my heart lurches as I meet Cooper's eyes from where he and Rex are standing on the other side of the room. His eyes look black from here, and he's not smiling, not frowning, just staring at me with so much intensity I swear it's like I am burning up from the inside. Passionate desire and possessiveness, scorching hot, flood across the mate bond, tempered by burning anger.

Well, I guess he saw me talking to Blake.

CHAPTER 56

COOPER

I f I thought that the weeks after I first found Hayley were hard, I had no clue what I was talking about.

One positive thing I can say about all this is that I have gained control over my wolf in a way I never thought possible. And I'm going to need every shred.

My mind is in chaos.

I can't concentrate on anything being said, and my wolf is ready to burn the world down to get to Hayley. He's already angry that I didn't mark her when I had the chance. When she was late arriving at the welcome drinks, he was freaking out, and the only thing that kept him calm was that we could sense through the bond that she was close by and enjoying herself.

It was like a dagger to the heart when I finally saw the reason behind her happiness, and the little show that Blake Steel put on as they arrived at the drinks was devastating. Seeing him touching her hair and leaning down to whisper in her ear, I wanted to charge across the room and rip his arms off. But given that Hayley didn't seem uncomfortable, I forced back my fury.

And I suppose, technically, in his eyes anyway, she's available. He hasn't done anything wrong.

I am the one who said I didn't want to come here as a couple, that I didn't want to claim her as my mate until she had some time to deal with her attack.

As the evening wears on and listen to countless other wolves asking about her, interested either for themselves or their unmated sons, I feel more and more sick, and I'm doubting my rationale.

Hearing her sparkling laughter as the normally cold and reserved Steel regales her with yet more stories of his antics as a teen wolf is winding me up.

Does she laugh that easily with me?

I'm struggling to remember why I was so convinced that she shouldn't come here when I see how comfortable she is. A little too comfortable for my liking, to be honest. When she finally comes back to join our group, my fingers itch to haul her close to me and kiss her, right here and now, so that everyone knows who she belongs with. I can't stop staring at her as she moves around, networking and charming like a pro.

"What on earth was Dad thinking?" I grumble to Rex as I sink another beer. I still can't understand why Dad put Hayley in the firing line like he did earlier. Toby could have lost control and hurt her. He should have told Alpha Anderson himself, and I know he would have thoroughly enjoyed putting that upstart Toby in his place personally.

So why didn't he?

It doesn't make any sense. And now she's firmly on the radar of every wolf at the conference.

"Because he's an evil genius, that's why," Rex says simply.

I frown, trying to understand what angle he thinks my father was working. I've had to field question after question about who the stunning little human is. Who not only worked out this attempt to defraud our pack, but also had the full confidence of our alpha in dealing with the perpetrators. Perpetrators who happen to be two powerful alpha wolves who she faced without fear.

To top it all off, now she's cozying up to the Alpha of all the Alphas in the region, who barely talks to his most powerful allies. And so, the gossip and intrigue intensify. Many are merely curious. Some of the she-wolves are seething with jealousy at the attention she's getting, particularly from Steel, and the interest from the unmated males has grown exponentially.

"Genius? He could have gotten her killed," I say grumpily.

"Pfft. He was right there to step in. You were right there. Reynolds was right there. And Alpha Anderson is old school. Dad knew nothing would happen to her." Rex dismisses my concern with a wave of his hand.

"If he's so clever, then what's his master plan?" I ask, getting irritated at his obvious smugness that he has it all figured out.

"To show you, and everyone else apparently, just how special she is. If you would stop looking at her like she's a victim, you would see what everyone else now sees," he eyes me seriously.

"You don't need to fucking tell me how amazing my mate is," I snap.

"Obviously, I do." He leans back in his chair and starts ticking off his fingers. "She's gorgeous. Funny. Smart; and not just book smart, like a lot of these alpha daughters that go to college but then just came home to spend Daddy's money." He tips his head, pointing to the very glamorous ladies around the room. They're highly educated but seem to be more interested in snagging a powerful husband than putting their brains to use.

"She has practical experience in a cutthroat business, that's rare in an alpha's mate, which means she's hard-working. And maybe most importantly, she doesn't bow to an alpha's command. It's like she doesn't even feel it. Toby told her to shut up, and she kept right on talking. That means that any Alpha who has her as a mate would have a truly equal partner. In short, your mate is a catch and a half." He finishes his little speech and tips his head towards where Hayley is standing, talking to two tall wolves, one of whom has just handed over his business card. "And it looks like you're the only one who sees a problem with claiming her."

"Fuck, he really is a diabolical bastard," I whisper as the reality of what Dad has done hits home.

He could have dealt with it all quietly. He could have had it all handled before we even got here and left Hayley out of it, but he wanted to show me what she's capable of. So that I'd stop thinking of her only as someone to be protected. He just took the opportunity to show every other male in the place at the same time. And to make my life a little harder.

Thinking I was going to be down at breakfast before anyone else, and hoping to get some time with Hayley, my heart sinks when I see she's here alright, but not alone.

Blake Steel joins Hayley in the line for the buffet and immediately takes the plate she's struggling with because of her awkward splint. Hayley is smiling at him as he teases her about the mountain of food she's asking him to pile up for her, and I feel like shit for not thinking about helping her myself.

What kind of mate am I when another male is looking after her better than I am?

I glance around the restaurant, and, much like last night, plenty of eyes are watching my little mate. No doubt wondering whether this is some kind of public declaration from Steel about his intentions.

I'm wondering the same thing myself.

He has always said he won't take anyone but his true mate, but ruling with no partner and no family can't be easy. And, like me, he's getting to an age where moon madness will start to become a real danger.

Maybe he's changed his mind. Hayley could tempt any man to rethink his plans.

I was watching closely last night, though. She was friendly and enjoyed his company, but she didn't encourage him. I sensed no desire from her. It was the only thing that kept me sane.

I'm shocked when, after spotting me arrive, he leads Hayley over to where I've sat down and holds out a chair for her to sit. She meets my eye and smiles awkwardly as she takes her seat, pushing in her chair and easing his huge frame into the one beside her.

"Morning, Hayley," I say softly. "Steel." I acknowledge him, but I can't help that the tone of my voice is less than welcoming, and Hayley scowls at me. I know full well I am behaving like a child. Steel, to his credit, doesn't bite; he grins, seeming amused, and holds out his hand for me to shake.

"Cooper, always good to see you. Sorry I didn't get the chance to catch up with you last night." He's completely relaxed, friendly even, while normally he's pleasant but reserved.

"You didn't look like you were busy talking to that many people," I respond pointedly, referring to the fact that he only spoke with Hayley and Leila.

"That's true," he laughs, "but I was having such a good time with the Jones girls. I make enough small talk with people I can't stand, who could blame me for wanting to enjoy myself a little for a change?" He pours some milk into Hayley's tea to save her trying to pick up the pitcher with her injured hand, and the gesture makes my blood pressure spike. Not only is he treating her like she's his mate, but he's doing a better job than me.

"So, what is your plan for the day?" Hayley asks, trying to steer the conversation into safer territory.

"I have to give a talk this afternoon, which hopefully Cooper will have time to attend," Blake says, leaning back casually in his chair while drinking his coffee, "and then a couple of mediation meetings with packs having succession issues. It can be tricky trying to work out who's best suited to take over. Many find it easier to let a third party decide, i.e., me." He shakes his head, making it clear he wishes they could sort these things out for themselves.

"I'll be there," I confirm, "Hayley, I was hoping I could nab you quickly this morning before my first meeting?" She looks confused, no doubt wondering whether it's business-related, but nods her agreement anyway.

"Well, on that note, I shall leave you to it. Hayley, I'm sure I'll catch up with you later." Blake leans over quickly and gives her a quick peck on the cheek, then strides out of the room, avoiding any attempts by other attendees to make eye contact and draw him into a conversation.

Hayley sits up straighter in her chair, less relaxed now that it's just the two of us, and clasps her hands together in her lap.

"I just wanted to check in with you and make sure you're alright?" I say honestly. She flicks her gaze up to mine.

"I'm fine. Thank you, Cooper." She smiles a proper smile at me, and I can't help grinning back. "I had a great time last night."

Well, that's taken my mood back down a notch. She had a great time without me.

"I saw that," I grumble. "You were in your element. You know how to work a crowd, Princess," I admit, and she grins again when I use my nickname for her.

"Did you doubt I would?" Hayley asks teasingly, "You wolves think you're all scary, but you are just a bunch of pussycats," she jokes.

"Hey!" I pretend to be horrified but can't help laughing, relieved to be joking light-heartedly with her after all the seriousness and drama of the last week or so. "I miss you, Hayley," I whisper, and her face instantly falls.

"Cooper, you can't do this. This was your idea," she says with obvious annoyance.

"And what if I changed my mind? What if I've realised that I'm an idiot?" I venture.

"Have you? Or are you just jealous?" she asks, eyebrows raised.

"I am fucking jealous," I growl.

"I'm not a toy Cooper. You don't want to play with me, but you don't want anyone else to, either?" she asks, standing and smoothing out her dress.

"Jeez, Hayley." I grumble, her analogy has put images of Blake 'playing' with her into my already jealous brain, and makes me want to claw my own eyes out. She drops her napkin onto the table with a shake of her head and leaves me alone, walking away with her head held high.

CHAPTER 57

HAYLEY

My annoyance with Cooper has reached an all-time high. I'm relieved that I have the day off today to clear my head, and Leila has a nice pamper day set up before the ball this evening.

"Good morning, hot stuff!" Leila squeals as she bursts into my room.

"Guess who had all the coffee this morning?" I tease, her bright mood a welcome distraction.

"Oh, I just can't wait to have all the chats with the most eligible lady in town!" She throws herself onto my bed, where I am packing a bag to take to the spa.

"That's a bit of an exaggeration." I look at her suspiciously. She seems a little too cheerful. Fake cheerful, like she's trying too hard.

"And yesterday was a bit dramatic, Hayley! Kicking some alpha butt, saving the pack, and having the always stoic, always sensible, always smoking hot Alpha Steel eating out of your hand."

"Hardly." I ignore her comments about Blake and keep tidying up, "But what about you? Max and you seemed to hit it off. What do you think?"

"He's great, but I don't think I was getting those vibes," she sighs and rolls onto her back to stare at the ceiling.

"Maybe he's just a decent guy and wasn't laying it on thick. Some of these shifter guys are full-on," I suggest, trying to convince her not to shut it down immediately, but I have a feeling a certain grumpy lawman is in the forefront of her mind.

"Hmm. He's invited me to come up to stay with the pack for a few weeks, to help set up their new clinic," she trails off, looking at me to see what I think of the idea.

"Leila, maybe a change of scenery would be good for you? I think you could do with a break. And it's not a million miles away," I hedge. I don't want to be rude, but I know she has been putting on this act of being fine when she's not.

"Yeah, you know what? I think you're right. But enough about me. Tell me what happened with you and Alpha Steel, or should I say Blake?" she says, again seeming to find great amusement in the fact that I was calling him by his first name.

"Leila, you do remember I am your brothers' mate, don't you? Why do you seem to be so excited about me talking to someone else?" I remind her.

"I love my brother, but Cooper is being an ass. You snooze, you lose. So did Alpha Steel ask you out?" she asks. I know she's joking, that she's just enjoying seeing her brother suffer.

"No! Jesus, Leila. These she-wolves were talking about scaring me off Cooper, and he politely put them in their place. And then he brought me for a drink to steady my nerves. That's all."

"Okay, okay. Look, obviously you and Cooper will end up together, but there's nothing to say you can't enjoy the attention of a handsome man in the meantime."

I sigh, but she's undeterred.

"So, there was no mention at all of you being gorgeous and him looking like a freaking model, or the sizzling hot connection between you?" She presses as she flips over onto her stomach on my bed and fishes my bikini out of my bag, holding up the top and wiggling her eyebrows at me.

"No." I deny it, but I feel my cheeks flame, and she tips her head back and laughs.

"I love it! Oh, this ball is going to be priceless." She takes pity on me and drops the subject. "Come on, you and I are going for a massage, then we're hitting the hot springs before hair and make-up." She tosses the bikini back in my bag and rolls off the bed.

"Hot springs sound amazing. I'm looking forward to this after last week." And it's true, a bit of rest and relaxation is exactly what I need.

"You deserve it, babe. A bit of girl time." She pulls me into a big hug. "I love you; you know that don't you? And that big dope of a brother of mine does too," she says, hugging me again, and I take a deep breath and blink away the tears that form in my eyes.

I can't even think that it won't work out. He'll come to his senses eventually, right?

CHAPTER 58

COOPER

The guy sitting beside me at Alpha Steel's talk pulls out his phone and glances at the text message he just received. He slips his phone into his back pocket with a slight smirk and, only 10 seconds later, slides out of his chair and makes a beeline for the exit.

Alpha Steel frowns at his departing back, turning to the remaining attendees.

"I think we'll take a break here to allow anyone else who needs to leave to do so without disturbing the rest of us." He looks out at the room but instead of looking angry, as I would have expected him to be at the departure of the sixth person in the last ten minutes, he appears to be holding back a smile.

As everyone gets up to stretch their legs, I approach the front, wondering about his strange reaction.

"Not offended that you aren't holding their attention, Steel?" I can't help but have a dig at him even though he's done nothing to deserve it, and, really, he doesn't have to take that kind of attitude from me. He quirks up one side of his mouth, and I have the awful feeling I am missing something.

"Even I know I can't compete with the Jones ladies. I believe they might have something to do with the sudden interest all these big bad alphas have in visiting the hot springs." Shaking his head, he chuckles to himself and watches me for my reaction.

"Fuck," I mutter, and when I spin on my heel and head for the door, I hear his laughter deepen behind me. I mindlink Rex on my way to my room and tell him where to meet me. He seems upset when we get to the changing rooms while I throw on a pair of swim shorts, barely-contained rage pouring off me. Rex rolls his eyes as we push outside to the network of hot pools connected by little waterfalls and lazy rivers that make up the outdoor springs area of the hotel.

"What's the problem, Rex? Just spit it out," I growl, grinding my teeth to stop myself from raising my voice.

"Cooper, I'm rapidly losing my patience with this bullshit. If you can't deal with her being in a stupid pool without you, then claim her already and put the rest of us out of our misery. It's getting really old," he says quietly, sighing deeply, and turning to look me dead in the eye.

"Have you any idea how sickening it is for me to see you blessed with an amazing mate, one who wants you to claim her, and to watch you throwing it all away?"

That hits home and immediately softens my cough, bringing me back to earth with a jolt. I'm such an ass. I've been so wrapped up in my drama that I've forgotten what it must look like to Rex and how hard it must be for him to watch.

"Rex, I'm so sorry, I didn't think. But this is different. I'm not rejecting her," I try to explain.

"But you're not claiming her either, and you're taking her for granted. You think she's going to wait around?" he asks.

Shaking my head, I'm ready to argue with him, but then I'm distracted by my mate's delicious scent. Soft footsteps pad across the stone floor behind me and I already know it's her by the grimace that flashes across Rex's face. I turn slowly and nearly drop to my knees at the vision in front of me.

Hayley is sauntering across the pool deck, all long toned limbs, glowing skin, flat stomach, and perky breasts, in a hot pink bikini that shows off her tan.

Drops of water run down her body, between her breasts, and down her perfect legs. She looks like a wet dream. Her hair is pulled up loosely into a high ponytail, and a few wavy tendrils hang down, ends damp from the water and begging to be touched. Her face is flushed from the combination of the cool air and hot water.

She's a goddess and just the sight of her makes me hard. I'm going to need to get into the water before my appreciation of her becomes too obvious. I can't help the growl that passes my lips as I see the other males blatantly checking her out. Steel was right. This is exactly where they were all sneaking off to.

Perverts.

"Cooper, what are you doing here?" Leila asks innocently as she approaches us, even though she knows exactly why I'm here. I ignore my sister completely as I walk straight up to Hayley, grip her firmly by the elbow, and steer her towards one of the grottos dotted around the spa. She yanks her arm back but walks with me willingly, seeming to know there is little point in protesting unless she wants to make a scene.

"What the hell, Cooper? Don't manhandle me," she complains as soon as we're in private, whirling around to glare at me with her arms propped on her hips. I know I should focus on how angry she is, but I can't stop thinking about how amazing she looks.

My wolf is driving me to claim her now, before any of these other circling males even get to look at her again. Nobody should see my mate in a bikini, especially when she's not marked, and he is not one bit happy. Sucking in a deep breath, I clench my fists to keep control.

"Jesus, Hayley, that fucking bikini," I press forward until her back is to the far wall of the shower, and I cage her in with a hand on either side of her head, leaning my forearms against the wall. "I can't stand all these guys ogling what's mine, turned on by this hot little body of yours." Lowering my nose to her neck, I rub it from her shoulder up to below her ear, inhaling her tantalising scent.

"You like the bikini, do you?" she teases me, ignoring the other part of what I said.

"I love it. I love it so much I want to rip it off you."

My voice is so deep and gravelly I barely recognise it. I run my fingers along the straps and grip her hips tightly, pulling her against me so I can feel her breasts pressed to my chest. She adjusts her stance so I can move my leg between hers and put pressure against her clit, grinding slowly, causing her to moan softly, her face buried in my chest.

She gasps as I grab her ass roughly in both hands and drag her core against my hard length to show her just how much I like it.

"Mine," I growl as she moans against my shoulder. Hayley wriggles to get free, and I reluctantly set her toes back down to the ground.

She smiles shyly as she turns us around and takes control, placing her hands on my pecs and pushing me back so I'm leaning against the wall. She runs her fingers down my chest and my breath catches as she uses her nails to trace the outline of my abs while kissing along my jaw and nibbling on my earlobe. My head is spinning and I'm in heaven. I have missed this so much, missed her so much.

"I'm not yours, Cooper Jones," she whispers, "or did you forget?"

What the fuck?

"You're mine, Hayley; you'll always be mine." My wolf is fuming at her denial of my claim. "We're meant to be together."

"Sure, but we're not. Are we?" she reminds me, and I wince. "You've barely spoken to me since we got here."

She's right, we're not together. I don't know what we are, friends or something stupid like that? I've been trying to be the good guy and yet I'm making my mate insecure.

"Hayley, I know I've gone about this all wrong. I'm sorry. I should have brought you here on my arm and shown everyone how fucking crazy I am about you. I miss you and I feel lost without you," I'm suddenly panicking that I've pushed her too far.

"How do I know you won't change your mind again? That we'll get home and you won't decide there's another reason I'm not enough?"

She's right. I haven't done anything to show her how much I admire her, how much faith I have in her to stand by my side as luna. She just hears more hollow words.

I go to step in and wrap my arms around her, my wolf wanting to comfort her, but she shrinks back as if touching me would be painful. My wolf whines, and I can feel his fear that we are screwing this up beyond repair. I can feel her uncertainty through the bond, and it's tearing me up.

"Hayley, don't think like that," I plead.

"I don't know what to think," she says dejectedly, and I'm about to tell her how I feel, to beg her to let me bring her to the ball this evening, when some douchebag with a six-pack and a tan sticks his head into the grotto, flicking his gaze back and forth between us. He senses the tension, but it's a bad type of tension, not the fun kind, so he thinks it's a good idea to interrupt.

"Hayley, you ok in here? Is he bothering you?" As if he needs to protect her from me, her mate.

I growl as he moves to step between us, and Hayley places a hand on my chest to stop me before I grab him.

"I'm fine," she says calmly, nodding back towards the pool, telling him to leave us alone. He fixes me with a serious look and puffs up his chest, peacocking for Hayley's benefit.

"Dude, you need to fucking chill. You're scaring her," the douchebag says, and I can't stop my wolf. The suggestion that we are a threat to our mate is enough to make him go berserk. In a split second, I have him up against the wall, and I'm snarling in his face.

"Cooper, for heaven's sake!" Hayley grips my arm in hers and the contact snaps me out of the descending red mist. I immediately let him go, running my hand through my hair in frustration. He rubs his throat with his hand and shoots me a filthy look.

"We're about to start a game of water polo if you and Leila want in," he says as he backs away, trying to retain some semblance of swagger about him, even though he isn't prepared to fight me.

Hayley gives me a sad little smile, leaving to join Leila in the pool. I punch the wall of the grotto and am strangely satisfied when I see the grazes on my knuckles, knowing this bit of pain is the least that I deserve.

Cooper: Rex, you're right. I'm making a mess of this.

Rex: I'll stay and keep an eye on things, make sure nobody steps out of line. You need to get out of here and get your head straight.

I nod numbly as I stumble back into the changing room and put my head in my hands.

What the hell am I doing?

CHAPTER 59

HAYLEY

Leaving Cooper in that grotto, fully clothed, was one of the hardest things I've ever done. I jumped straight into the water to hide how turned on I was from these shifters and their super-sensitive noses.

I want him, more than anything else I've ever wanted before. I know I'm pushing Cooper, but if I were a wolf, he would have claimed her already, and I'm not willing to accept anything less. I link my arm with Leila's as we walk into the ballroom, and my nerves disappear. It's some people's worst nightmare, but I know I'm good at this. Damn good. Mingling, chatting, making connections: it's a skill.

The ballroom looks amazing, bathed in soft pink tones and a million twinkling lights. We snag flutes of champagne from a passing server and bump into Max, who looks dashing in his tux. His dark hair is long on top and shaved at the sides, and tonight it's slicked back neatly in a man bun. Other than the hint of one tattoo peeking over the collar of his shirt, most of his ink is covered. He usually dresses like a sexy biker; somehow, he looks just as dangerous but more handsome in formal wear.

Blake arrives through the double doors, the complete opposite of Max: groomed and polished like a GQ model. He's stunningly handsome; it's impossible not to recognise, but my reaction to him is not the same as the one that I have with Cooper. One look into Cooper's deep brown eyes and I'm putty in his hands.

"Ladies, looking beautiful as always," Max says, bowing slightly. "I heard you caused quite a stir down at the pools today, and, yet, no lucky men are escorting you this evening?"

"Who needs men?" Leila quips, wincing as she takes a sip of the champagne and places the full glass back onto a tray of empties. "Yuck, not feeling that."

"I'll get you something else," I offer and sneak off to the bar to give her and Max some time to chat on their own. She has been putting on a brave face, but I know she's upset about whatever happened with Marcus – or didn't happen.

Perhaps Max will be the one to show her she has other options, and what a fine option he is.

As I reach the bar, the tall gentleman beside me inclines his head as he finishes his order. "And whatever the lady is having," he adds to the bartender in a gruff voice that I immediately recognise.

"Alpha Reynolds. That's very kind of you, thank you." I look up and he's studying me curiously.

"What?" I ask.

"I didn't think you'd accept," he mutters, looking mildly surprised.

"You're right, I should be the one buying for you after what you did earlier," I say.

"No, I didn't mean it like that." He looks genuinely a bit lost. "Usually, none of the Joneses want to speak to me – or be near me – apart from Marie, and that's just out of politeness."

I roll my eyes and sigh. "Well, I'll happily have a drink with you. It's the least I can do after you stuck up for me."

"You're probably the only person here to say that. You seem to have made quite the impression on everyone, I wouldn't want to tarnish your reputation by hanging around with me," he says with a serious expression on his dark features. His eyes are grey but they're light, and it's quite unnerving. It makes him look intense all the time.

"Why would that happen?" I ask, curious why he's considered persona non grata.

"My father was not a pleasant man, to put it mildly. He made a lot of enemies within these four walls. And packs have long memories." He grimaces and takes a long draw from his beer as he gazes around at the other groups of wolves, drinking and catching up like old friends.

"Are you the same as your father?"

He looks offended, eyes widening with outrage.

"No, I am nothing like my father. I'm trying to engage with the other packs, but nobody will even entertain it," he admits. "But I can't appear weak and desperate, either. It's a Catch 22."

"You need a big gesture then; show everyone that you're serious about undoing whatever your father has done. Do it without duress and it'll show strength, not weakness. Something like reversing the bans on moving between packs, something that is a win-win for everyone."

He eyes me curiously.

"You just need one pack to agree; once it's successful, the rest will follow."

"You rolled your eyes at me earlier" he not-so-subtly changes the subject. "I can't say I recall anyone ever doing that before." He frowns as though I am an alien species.

"It's the price for having a drink with me. My human-ness makes me immune to your wolfy scariness," I tease, and he smiles again.

"I'll give your suggestion some thought," he says, effectively ending the conversation.

It would be rude of anyone else, but he must really believe the dislike for him is contagious.

"Have a good evening, Alpha." I pat him gently on the arm and pick up my drink to leave, when suddenly Blake is by my side.

"Everything ok here?" he asks tightly, and Reynolds fixes him with a glare at the insinuation that I might not be safe in his company.

"Everything is perfect, just making new friends."

I flash a smile at them both as I walk away and towards the Jones' table, hopeful that Alpha Reynolds can undo the damage his father did to his pack's reputation. And that I might be able to help him.

CHAPTER 60

COOPER

Ethan saunters up beside me as I pretend to casually look around the room; I'm actually watching with trepidation as Hayley speaks to Alpha Reynolds at the bar, accepting a drink from him, and chatting away happily.

I'm about to push off the table I am leaning on and interrupt, but Ethan places his hand on my arm to stop me.

"Wait, Cooper. Trust that she can handle herself," he advises.

"Easy for you to say." I'm about to argue further, to shake out of his grip, when I see her heading toward our table, with Blake Steel in tow. Stopping in front of us, she pulls Ethan in for a big hug and a kiss.

"So, you skip the boring parts of the weekend and just come for the party, eh?" she teases him good-naturedly.

Hayley's a vision in a mid-length off-white dress that skims her curves. It's one- shouldered, so her bare marking spot is exposed, and it's calling out to me. She's radiant.

"I was called in as reinforcement. I heard you and Leila have been causing trouble." He winks. "And a room full of drunk alphas is a brawl just waiting to happen." He claps me and Blake on the shoulder as he says this, and the two of us frown as Hayley laughs.

"How is Reynolds?" I ask Hayley, unable to pretend I'm not dying to know what they were talking about.

"Indeed, how is the angriest wolf of them all?" Steel asks, equally intrigued.

"He seems nice."

We all raise an eyebrow at that.

"He's trying to undo the damage his father has done, but keeps getting stonewalled. I think he's genuine." She shrugs when she sees our shocked faces. "I might have an idea or two to help."

"I think that's enough work for the evening. How about a dance?" Blake commands, and he reaches out for her hand.

My stomach tightens. I have to grip the table to stop my wolf from surging forward and challenging Steel for what he sees as an attempt to steal our mate. Steel glances at me like he can sense my internal struggle.

Maybe he can.

"Oh, I'm not sure I'm ready for dancing..." Hayley starts to make an excuse, but Steel persists.

"Steel..." I grit out in warning, but he flashes me a big smile.

"Don't worry, Cooper, I'll bring your prized employee back in one piece."

He's baiting me, now I know he is. I swallow down my rage and force myself to stay silent.

"Come on, Hayley, someone has to kick things off, or it's going to be a very dull night. Max? Leila? What do you say?"

Max places an arm around Leila's waist and steers her toward the floor with a smile and a bow. Hayley looks at me with concern, but when I don't move, she hesitantly places her small hand in Blake's and lets him lead her away.

He's taking my mate away from me and I feel like someone is standing on my chest. I imagine this is what having a panic attack feels like.

"Rex told me you were making a mess of things, but I can't believe what I'm seeing. You're just going to stand here and let him have her?" Ethan says incredulously, grabbing my arm and turning me so I am facing him.

"Watch it," I warn him, but he just shakes his head.

"I'm done watching your pointless shit-show. She is your *mate*, Cooper. This noble idea of waiting until she has had time to adjust, when it looks like she's doing just fine? When are you finally going to stop dragging your feet and believe her? When she's back here next year, stomach round and full, with Steel's pups in her belly?" He gives me a little shove, and, if he wasn't my best friend, I'd lay him out.

Making no sound, but to prove just how close to the edge I am, I flash my canines at him.

"I'm your best friend, Cooper. I'm telling you now that you're going to lose her, and it'll be the biggest mistake of your life."

Pushing him off me, I go back to staring at the dance floor where Hayley and Blake have just taken the centre position.

"I don't want her to resent me later. She should have time. I don't want her to think she never had a choice," I argue, but it's a lame excuse, even to me.

"You're afraid she'll reject you later, but you guys are nothing like Rex and Stacey. What do you think is going to happen if you keep pushing her away, keep letting these charming bastards woo her?"

I stare at Ethan wondering if that's really what I've been doing. Trying to give Hayley space, because I've seen how much pain Rex went through, and I'm waiting for some kind of assurance that she'll never reject me.

When I look back at Hayley, she's laughing at something Steel said. His hand is resting lightly on her hip, the white silky material of her dress the only thing between his fingertips and her body, as he spins her around.

I cough to stifle a groan when my mother appears beside Ethan and me, wrapping an arm around us both and effectively trapping us beside her.

"Look at that, don't they make a stunning pair?"

My mother nods her head towards my mate and Steel – another man – and I reach up to tug at my hair in frustration.

Calm down, you trust Hayley.

It's not like that.

"They look like that perfect couple on the top of a wedding cake," she comments, and I can't take it anymore.

A loud growl comes out of my mouth before I can stop it, and a little grin tugs at the corner of her mouth.

"Mine!" I roar.

My mother flinches but looks strangely satisfied as everyone turns to see what's going on, and murmurs begin to ripple through the crowded ballroom.

Confronting the most dangerous wolf on the entire east coast might not be clever, but I'm not waiting another minute to take Hayley back.

CHAPTER 61

HAYLEY

As I place my hand in Blake's, I know that this is a terrible idea. Cooper must already be on the verge of losing it, if the maelstrom of emotions swirling through the bond is anything to judge by.

Will the sight of me dancing with another male push him over the edge?

I'm about to pull my hand away and turn back when Blakes's grip tightens.

"Trust me, Hayley." He speaks so quietly into my ear that I'm certain nobody else can hear.

"I just... this is a bad idea," I blurt, feeling genuinely afraid that Cooper will see this as a rejection.

"He'll be fine. He's trying to be a gentleman, to act like a human would in this situation. Giving you time and space, blah, blah, blah," he stops with a big grin on his face. "But he's not a human, and you are destined to be mated to a powerful wolf. The sooner he begins acting like himself, the sooner both of you can get on with being happy." Blake tips his head to me in a bow, wrapping one arm around my waist and leading me out onto the dance floor.

For such a big man, he's an effortless dancer. He takes care to leave some space between our bodies, knowing being too close would make me uncomfortable with the way I am feeling right now.

"He's going to lose it, Blake, I can feel it," I warn him, glimpsing Cooper's tense face while he speaks to Ethan as we glide by. They look like they're having an argument, and I have a sinking feeling in my stomach.

"Good. He needs to remember that primal feeling he had when he first scented you, to remember exactly what he has and what he wants. I'm impressed by the control he has over his wolf. There aren't many who could do what he has done."

Blake is talking about Cooper like this is all some sort of social experiment.

"I'm glad you're enjoying this, but let's see how impressed you are when he shifts in the middle of the ballroom," I mumble.

Blake laughs heartily.

"It won't come to that. I'm right, you'll see. I always am."

Glancing up at this handsome man who has made this weekend much more bearable for me, I shake my head at his cocky smirk. I try to relax and enjoy myself, smiling at Leila as she twirls past in Max's arms; her dark hair flows behind her, and her stunning green dress lifts gracefully as she spins by.

"Thank you, Blake," I say seriously, and he frowns as he looks down into my eyes.

"For looking out for the 'lost little human'. I know you have plenty of other people demanding your attention."

Hearing a growl and some commotion over to the side of the dancefloor, I try to look but Blake turns us away from it as if determined to keep my focus on enjoying our dance.

"What kind of man would I be if I didn't help one of my alpha's get his happily ever after? But you're a little early, you can thank me tomorrow," he whispers, spinning me so suddenly away from him that I struggle to stay on my feet.

Colliding with what feels like a brick wall, as soon as I feel the familiar tingles spread up and down my arms, I know exactly who has caught me.

My mate.

I tip my head back and his gorgeous face, just inches from mine, takes my breath away. It's like the first time we met, all over again.

CHAPTER 62

COOPER

Barging my way to within an arm's reach of Hayley and Blake Steel, gliding around the floor like a golden anniversary couple, I intended to grab Steel.

Instead, my arms wrap around Hayley, who has stumbled into my chest. I steady her as she teeters precariously on her high heels, and a current of electricity races through my body. She gazes up at me from underneath her long lashes and all thoughts of kicking Steel's ass are forgotten.

She melts into me, her body fitting perfectly against mine, and my entire world shrinks down to the two of us. I've stopped trying to hold back, and every one of my senses is finely attuned to my mate again. The hairs stand up on the back of my neck as my body remembers my desire to claim her. I feel like I did that first day at the hospital, anticipation making me tingle all over and the uncontrollable urge to be with her taking hold.

Curious stares turn towards us, wondering what on earth is going on. The human they thought would be the Alpha of Alpha's chosen mate, is now dancing in my arms.

"Mine!" I growl in Steel's direction, as I tuck Hayley against my chest possessively, annoyed at how perfectly they also seemed to fit together.

Gasps sound around us as people realise Hayley is my mate, my fated mate.

My wolf puffs out his chest in pride, delighted to finally tell everyone who she belongs to. Some are probably expecting a fight, like I'm here to challenge Blake's claim on her, but judging by his relaxed demeanour, they won't get what they're hoping for.

"It took you long enough to get your head out of your ass, Cooper. You better take care of her, if she'll still have you," Steel chides over Hayley's shoulder, nodding at her as he steps back.

Blake's smiling fondly at her, but when he meets my eye, there is a hard glint there which lets me know he's genuinely warning me to treat her well.

He shakes my hand with an iron-tight grip and ignores all the puzzled stares as he strides off the dance floor. He makes a beeline for Alpha Reynolds, who hasn't left the bar where Hayley sat with him, reaching out a hand and resuming his Alpha's duties without pause.

I dip my head to breathe in her delicious scent and pull her tight to me, seamlessly picking up where Blake left off, leading her around the now packed dance floor.

"Cooper," she sighs happily, holding me close. I can feel her relief and it makes me feel awful that my attempt at being gallant has been causing her so much anxiety.

"I've missed you so much. I'm a stubborn idiot. I thought I knew better, that you needed time before you could be sure you wanted me." I pause, but she stays quiet, staring up at me patiently. "I didn't want to rush you into something you might regret, but I wasn't listening to what you wanted."

"It's okay, Cooper." She reaches up and tenderly places her palm on my cheek.

"No, it's not. You've proven what I should have already known. You're the most amazing, beautiful, and capable woman I have ever met. And if you are willing to be with me, I should learn to keep my mouth shut and be grateful." She laughs at that as I spin her away then pull her back into my chest, lowering one arm so my hand grazes the dip of her lower back. I feel her body tense at the contact.

"Cooper, how do I know you're not going to freak out again? I won't stay at home and hide. Doing that once was enough," she whispers, her voice cracking.

I kiss her cheek lightly and trail my lips close to her ear.

"I was afraid, Hayley, but I'm not anymore," I admit. "I want you and I'm going to claim you right now." Her breath hitches and she lets out a soft moan as I kiss her neck, just behind her ear.

"Oh god, Cooper, I... I... you can't...," she groans again as I run my hand up her side and bite her earlobe gently. Keeping her body flush to mine as we move, I know she can feel how serious I am about this. I know this is getting too racy for a room full of people, but I can't help myself. I've been holding back for so long.

"Hayley, it's not just how amazing you have been here. It's everything. It's how shy you are when you're turned on," I tease, rubbing my thumb gently over her hip bone and dipping lower than is appropriate towards the top of her thigh.

"It's how you love being outdoors, how you would live barefoot if you could, how you always curl up beside me and tuck your feet up under your legs. I miss those things, and I love them all, Hayley. I love you," I admit, pulling my head back to look her in the eye so she knows I'm not trying to seduce her.

I feel warmth and contentment, like nothing I've felt before, sweeping through me from the bond, and I smile happily as she goes up on her tippy toes to plant a soft kiss on my lips.

"I love you, too, Cooper," she says softly. I lean down to kiss her tenderly, trying to show her exactly how happy I am, because I'm too caught up to get the words out.

"It's forever Hayley. If I mark you, there's no going back," I say into her hair when she places her head against my chest. I hold her tight and sway us from side to side, the emotions of finally sharing those feelings shocking me; the fear that she still might not go ahead with the mating, lingering.

She places her hands on my shoulders and stares up at me seductively, licking her plump lips in anticipation.

"Forever with you sounds amazing to me. What are we waiting for?"

My heart swells with pride that his little vixen is going to be my mate at last.

We need privacy and we need it fast.

I sweep Hayley up over my shoulder, careful to keep her dress covering her modesty, and she giggles in surprise as I carry her off the dancefloor. She kicks and squirms as I stride towards the doors opened to the gardens outside. I hear whooping and laughter behind us as we leave our friends and family, disappearing into the darkness. Carrying her through the silence of the unseasonably warm evening air, a little away from the noise, I set her gently on her feet.

"Cooper, I..."

I don't even give her a chance to finish whatever it was she was going to say. I'm on her, pressing her up against the wall, my mouth ravishing hers. I can't get enough. This week has been torture. Actually, the last month has been torture. I need to be as close as physically possible to her now that she is finally going to be mine. I'm not backing down now.

There are no doubts, no hesitation.

I should have done this as soon as she asked me to.

"Fuck, Hayley, I don't know if I can control myself. You feel too good," I say as I squeeze her breast roughly over her white dress with one hand and grip the back of her head with the other, going in for another searing kiss. Her little moans let me know she's as lost to this as I am, and I can feel the burning heat through our bond. I push back, panting, and try to wrestle back some control as I run a hand through my hair.

"I won't be able to stop myself from marking you, and I don't think I can be gentle," I warn, clenching and unclenching my fists to release some of my tension as I try to wrestle back control from my wolf.

"Then don't be," she says in that sultry little voice of hers as she leans back against the wall and brushes her mussed-up hair to the side, revealing the spot where I'll mark her. She bites her swollen lower lip between her teeth, and I growl, my lust for her shooting off the charts.

"Princess, I'm not marking you out the back of a hotel like some horny teenager. Come on." I take her hand and all but drag her along a narrow pathway through the gardens. Rounding a corner, a guest house comes into view. We normally reserve it for honeymooners or VIPs that require extra privacy and security, but it's empty tonight.

This will do nicely.

She grins at me as we get close, and I wrap an arm around her shoulder. My master key card opens the door, and I gently usher her through.

"Wow, Cooper, it's beautiful. Are we breaking and entering?" She stares around her in awe at the stunning Hamptons style white and pale blue décor and luxurious furniture, running her fingertips along a whitewashed oak sideboard.

"Fit for a queen, or soon to be queen," I quip, getting up close and using my size to walk her backward into the space. "I had planned to bring you here in a few weeks, maybe, with candles and romantic music, but I can't wait for a second longer. I promise I'll romance you some other time."

Hayley's heartbeat picks up and I can sense she is just as excited as I am; she nods in response, allowing me to push her further into the room with my body.

"You look so hot in this dress. It's perfect because this is our marriage, Hayley, and our happily ever after starts now. You can organise a big fancy wedding later, whatever you want – but, to me, this is it."

I drag the zip down at the side of her dress and slip it over her head. I nearly come on the spot when I see the delicate white lace panties and corset bralette she's wearing underneath. She looks like an angel standing there in her white lingerie and champagne high heels, tousled hair falling over her shoulders. Her lips are full and pink from our kissing.

Whistling quietly, I take it in, knowing that image will stay with me forever.

"I hope to God you aren't wearing that for Steel's benefit," I grit out, unable to stop my jealousy from surfacing when I wonder why she has this on under her dress when we weren't supposed to be together.

"Maybe I was hoping you'd change your mind about staying away. I like to be prepared," she teases. "You don't need to worry about Blake. I'm all yours, Cooper. Always have been. So, are you going to come here and take what's yours, Alpha?"

That snaps the last bit of control I have, and I lunge forward, hauling her up against me and gripping her tight. I'm trying not to be too rough, to move too quickly and scare her; but my wolf is in the driver's seat now, and he has lost all patience.

"I'm sorry, baby, but my wolf isn't going to wait any longer, and he's going to fight me for control," I whisper as my hands roam and squeeze every inch of her flesh that they can get to. I topple her backward onto the bed and take a second to stare at her before lowering myself down to cover her.

"It's always good with you Cooper," she murmurs, and then lets out a shriek as I rip the back of the corset open with my two hands and fling the ruined garment across the room, diving forward to suck and nip at her breasts. Her panties get the same treatment and hit the floor somewhere behind us while I circle one nipple with my tongue.

"That thing was sexy. I'll buy you as many of those as you want," I pant between kisses, as I use my knee to part her thighs and push her further up the bed. Reaching down between her legs, I sweep my fingers between her delicate folds, and she gasps. So wet for me.

I grab her, pushing the heel of my hand hard against her clit, eliciting a shiver, then plunge two thick fingers into her, entering her easily. I thrust them in and out as I use my free hand to grip her wrists and pull them up over her head. She's laid bare for me, naked except for the heels.

"Oh, Cooper," she groans, grinding her hips to increase the pressure on her clit from the palm of my hand, and I slap her pussy lightly in chastisement, leaning down to nip the inside of her thigh. She jerks from the unexpected sensation and a little moan passes from her lips, like she's surprised that she enjoyed that bit.

"I'm in charge here, Princess. You're going to come when I tell you to, and tonight that's going to be around my cock while I sink my teeth into your beautiful skin. The first time, anyway," I growl into her ear, as I go back to pumping my fingers inside her slowly but deeply, fingers curling to brush against that tight little bundle of nerves that drives her crazy.

Pressing her clit firmly, I watch as she arches her back in pleasure and writhes against the crisp white sheets, her release just out of reach. I flip her over in the blink of an eye, hauling her up to her hands and knees, and stand up, stripping off my clothes at record speed.

"Eyes forward," I say, delivering a sharp slap to her ass when she looks over her shoulder to see what I'm doing. She whimpers in plea-sure and drops her head, hair hanging down between her arms. I can sense her arousal and frustration increasing in equal measure, the anticipation of what's coming heightening every sense.

"But I want to see you, Cooper. I need..." She's cut off when I kneel back onto the bed behind her, entering in one swift, delicious stroke. Wrapping her hair around one fist and pulling her head backward, exaggerating the arch in her back and pushing her ass up higher, I deepen the angle.

"I know what you need, Princess." I fill her tight channel all the way to the hilt. I have to stop for a second, buried as far as I can go inside her, to steady myself or it'll all be over in a matter of seconds. She grips the sheets tightly in her hands, and I can tell she's off-kilter with this even more dominant side of me.

Once I stop seeing stars, I pull all the way out lazily, slamming home again, and she pushes back to meet me eagerly. I swat her ass, earning another rush of arousal through the bond. Gripping her hip tightly so she can't move, leaving her no choice but to take the pleasure she's given.

Pounding into her harder, the sound of flesh meeting flesh fills the room as my thrusts get faster. It's animal and raw and exquisite. I release her hair and trail a hand lightly down the back of her neck, along her spine softly and wrapping it around her middle, her skin coming up in goosebumps wherever I touch her.

Pulling her torso up against mine, I hold her tight to me as I continue to push us towards release, thrusting in and out. Gripping her shoulder gently in my teeth, I feel her pussy quiver, almost pushed over the edge in ecstasy at the thought of what's coming. But I won't give it to her yet.

I pull out and flip her over, laying her on the soft mattress, and she whimpers in frustration at the loss of contact.

"I want to see your face, Hayley, when we're mated at last and you feel my claim running through your veins. When you realise exactly what belonging to me forever really means." I look into her eyes as I push back inside her, her body just about able to take my size, the perfect fit.

Her eyes roll back as I move steadily and bring my head down to press kiss after kiss along her collarbone, shoulder, and neck.

"Cooper, Cooper, Cooper," she mumbles out on each thrust, closer and closer to coming. I lick her neck where my mark will go, allowing my teeth to lengthen, the serum containing my scent coating them as my wolf urges me to complete the mating.

"Are you ready, Princess?" I whisper against her skin, letting her feel the sharpness of my teeth as they scrape lightly across her neck. She sucks in a breath and nods, unable to speak, and I can tell she's holding on for me, waiting for me to join her. I bite down quickly, and, the second my teeth pierce her silky, perfect skin, she cries out in ecstasy. I feel the rush of pleasure flooding through the bond as it snaps fully into place, euphoric and exhilarating.

As her body tightens around me again and again, wave after wave of electrifying release, I drive deep and hold her to me. I am blinded by the strongest orgasm I've ever had and the rush of emotion that passes through me. Jets of come leave me as my cock continues to pulse inside Hayley and I rock gently in and out of her until we both stop shivering and shuddering with the delicious aftershocks.

Her eyes are shining with tears, but I know from the bond that they are tears of happiness. I kiss her softly on the forehead and rub them away with my thumb as they slide down her cheeks.

"What was that?" She looks up at me wide-eyed and I smile back, feeling just as astonished as she is at the power of the sensation that just washed over us. I feel stronger, invigorated, and happier than I can ever remember. It takes me a minute to answer, because I'm speechless at the strength of what just happened.

"The bond, Princess. It's fully in place now," I assure her, "and you're all mine."

"Wow. I mean that was..., this is..." she continues to stare at me, lost for words, and shakes her head gently. I laugh, rolling us over so I'm lying on my back, and she's curled into my side. I decide to give something a go and watch for her reaction:

Cooper: I wonder if we just made a pup. Hayley: What the hell?

She sits bolt upright in the bed and stares down at me, bringing a hand to touch her head at the strange sensation of hearing someone else's voice.

"Cooper, what did you just say?" she laughs, and I kiss the top of her head.

"I didn't say anything, Princess, that was a mindlink. Think of something and see if you can project it to me." I watch Hayley scrunch up her face in concentration and wait for her thought to appear in my head, and when it does, I can't help but burst out laughing at the same time as I haul her up and drag a leg across my body so she's straddling me.

"Did it work?" she says shyly, as she rubs her hands up and down my chest, over my stomach and sides.

"It did, but maybe a little too well," I respond, just as another link comes through.

Ethan: Ew. Jesus, Hayley, keep it clean until you learn to control that.

Hayley leans forwards and covers her face in her hands, as she hides her red cheeks in my chest in embarrassment.

"Maybe try to keep it PG 13 until you have a better handle on directing your thoughts to the right person," I laugh, unable to stop myself from enjoying her blushes. "But I like the way you're thinking. Let's give that a try." I growl as I lift her gently and push back up inside her while taking her lips in a passionate kiss.

Nothing has ever felt this right, and I can't believe she is finally mine.

CHAPTER 63

HAYLEY

Dazed, that's how I feel.

I sit up and stretch in the middle of the biggest, comfiest bed, and I'm deliciously sore everywhere. I gently run my fingers over the raised mark on my neck, Cooper's mark. Just touching it reminds me of the night we had and sends shivers down my spine.

Cooper was insatiable and woke me again and again to make love. It was as if he needed to prove to himself that this was real, over and over, until I was thoroughly satisfied and left in no doubt of whom my body belongs to. Sex was always hot with Cooper, but now I realise he was holding back before, hiding his dominant side; his raw need for me.

The bed points towards a wall of glass overlooking the tree-tops and valleys below; light spills into the room, past curtains that we never got around to closing last night. I run my hand across the space beside me where Cooper slept, leaning over to take a deep lungful of his masculine smell from the sheets.

Is it normal to be this obsessed with someone?

The tap in the bathroom turns off and the door swings open, revealing Cooper in a pair of black, skin-tight boxer briefs, toothbrush hanging out of his mouth, and mussed-up hair.

He leans an arm against the doorjamb lazily and studies me.

He has never looked better.

"Good morning, mate," I say, unable to keep the massive grin off my face.

He smiles around the toothbrush, then leans down to rinse out his mouth and spit. Strolling over to me, he leans down to press a minty kiss to my lips, a big smile on his ridiculously handsome face.

"Oh, I like the sound of that. Mornin' to you, too, Princess." He saunters over to the front door and hauls in two suitcases, his and mine, and rummages around in the front pocket of his.

"Did you go out?" I ask, swinging my legs out from underneath the sheets and standing at the side of the bed. Where did the bags come from?

"Ethan and Leila dropped them off for us. They figured we wouldn't want to walk through the hotel this morning in what's left of our formal wear."

My mind flashes back to my ripped lingerie, flung across the room, and I turn away to hide my blush.

He crosses to me quickly, "What was that you were thinking about little mate?" he murmurs against my shoulder, pressing behind me and wrapping his arms around me as I fish a nightie and pants from my bag. Turning in his arms to look him, I try to send him the image via the mindlink. I know I have succeeded when he growls and leans closer to suck over his mark, dragging his teeth along the sensitive spot. My legs turn to jelly as sparks course through my body.

"I like that you're getting creative with the mindlink, Hayley, but be careful. If you send an image of you in sexy lingerie to my pack, I'll have to kill them all," he growls.

"Yes, Sir; Alpha sir," I whisper as I pull back and step into my panties, pulling my nightie over my head, hiding my breasts from his view, much to his obvious disappointment.

"I like that coming from your lips. I need to think about what to call you from now on. Do I still call you Princess?" he teases, as he trails a finger along the delicate spaghetti straps of my top. I flash him another image of him doing the same thing to me in the bar back in Grey Ridge when he nearly made me come from a little stroking and teasing.

"Fuck, Hayley, that will never get old," he chokes out, looking at me with fire in his eyes.

"Do you feel what I'm feeling, or just see the image?" I'm amazed by how the mindlink works and am still trying to figure it out.

I'm waiting for his response when he sends me his point of view of the same moment; my legs almost go from underneath me with the strength of the pure lust that accompanies it.

"I get the whole nine yards, baby," he smirks, delighted with the fact that his little show-and-tell has left me a little stunned and shaky. "So, what do you think? Stick with Princess? Or maybe you've been promoted to Queen? You're soon-to-be luna, after all."

I laugh at that. The thought of being anyone's queen is too ridiculous to comprehend. And I'm definitely not going to try to pry the luna title away from Marie any time soon.

"No, that's your mother, Cooper. You don't really want to call me that, do you?" I joke.

"Heavens no. Good point. Hmm, how about fiancé then?" he asks quietly, dipping down gracefully onto one knee, producing a little black box from behind his back.

"What? Oh, Cooper, you don't have to do this," I gasp and sink to my knees in front of him on the soft carpet. He wraps his big, muscular arms around me as emotions well inside of me.

"Hayley, never for a second did I intend not to make you mine. I bought this right after I came to your house begging for work." He places a finger underneath my chin and tilts my head so he can look me in the eye.

I can't speak. I'm completely stunned.

"You were it for me the moment I met you, and now we're mated. I'm yours, and you're mine. But I want you to have the human side of this relationship, too. It can't be all my way." He opens the box and takes out a stunning ring. "Will you do me the honour of marrying me, Hayley?"

The brilliant round diamond, with a glittering halo, is set on a yellow gold band. He holds it out and slips it onto my finger, holding my hand steady.

I launch myself into his arms, nodding furiously.

"Yes, yes!" I pepper his cheeks and stubbly jaw with kisses. He laughs and reaches over to his bag to pull out another box. He opens it and takes out the slim band inside, placing it on his own ring finger.

"I know it's not the proper way to do it, but in my heart, I'm yours already, Hayley. You might not be able to mark me, but I want everyone, wolf or human, to know I'm taken, because I'm so damn proud to be yours," he says adorably, and I've never loved him more than in this moment.

"Thank you, it's beautiful. I love you, Cooper." I reach up and pull him in for a kiss…which quickly escalates into something more, there on the floor, beside the comfiest bed in the world.

CHAPTER 64

COOPER

Walking into lunch with my new mate on my arm is the best feeling in the world.

Breakfast was quickly forgotten when my proposal went as I had hoped, and I can't keep the smile off my face and beam with pride as guests greet us with cheering as we walk into the dining room. We can't get more than a few metres before we're stopped by well-wishers.

As we make our way to our table, Hayley squeezes my hand, and I can feel her joy through the bond, boosting my own. I'm relieved she can finally see for herself how celebrated fated mates are in our world.

"Well, well, well, look what the cat dragged in," Ethan teases. "Hayley, you're only allowed to sit beside me if you promise no more visions of Cooper naked."

He pulls Hayley into a friendly hug, and I swallow down the growl that tries to force its way out. Ethan laughs as he spots the look on my face over her shoulder. "Relax buddy. She's all yours. If we didn't spot the mark, that giant rock weighing her down would be a dead giveaway."

He sits back down as Leila pounces on Hayley, grabbing her hand and hauling it up so she can get a good look at the ring.

"Wowza, maybe I need to get mated so I get me one of these," she jokes as she hugs both of us. "Congratulations, guys. I'm so thrilled for you both."

"At last!" Marie exclaims, coming around the table to embrace us at the same time. Everyone at the table exchanges a look and then stares back up at my mother, who shakes her head in disappointment. "Hmph. You idiots always think I don't see what's going on, but you should know better by now."

I sigh, and Hayley giggles beside me.

"Hayley, I couldn't have asked for a better daughter-in-law. I have already booked out a couple of dates for the wedding, either here or at the packhouse, so you let me know when you'd like it to be," she ploughs on. "Although, of course, being human you'll be in heat every month instead of twice a year like wolf shifters, so probably best to do it quickly before... you know."

She makes a sweeping gesture in front of her, miming a pregnant belly, and Hayley goes deathly pale. That stopped her giggling.

"Not so funny now, is it?" I tease, wrapping my arm around her and pulling her against my side. "Don't worry, there's no rush, Princess," I reassure her.

"Give her a minute to enjoy it, dear. Welcome to the family, Hayley." Dad shakes my hand and gives me a wink, pulling Hayley into a big hug.

"Where's Rex?" I ask, looking around the table for my older brother.

"He's gone ahead, Cooper. Nathan needs a hand," Dad answers, but he doesn't meet my eye and I know he's lying. Either Rex left after struggling to watch me push my mate away, or it would have been too painful seeing a newly mated pair. Either way, I need to make sure I find him and make things right as soon as I get back.

Hayley: It'll be ok. I promise. I think I know where he's gone.

She seems to think Rex is alright, so I nod at her. This bond thing is amazing.

"A word, Alpha Jones, if you can spare a minute?"

I can sense the dominant wolf of Blake Steel before I even hear his voice. Turning, I see him smiling at me, but with the same glint in his eye that he had last night right before he handed my mate back to me. If he has changed his mind, it's too late now, but I'll gladly prove it to him if that's what's going on here.

"Hayley, congratulations. You both look so happy; I'm truly thrilled for you."

Okay, so maybe that's not where this is going.

"I'll be back in a second, Princess," I whisper in her ear before I head outside with Steel.

"I just wanted to make sure you aren't carrying any ill will towards me after the last couple of days?" Steel says sincerely, leaning back against the rough stonewall surrounding the patio.

"Once you understand she's my mate, and respect that, I have no issues with you." I'm curious about why he cares.

"I knew from the second I spoke to her she was some other alpha's mate, and it only took seeing the way she looks at you one time to know who that was. You're a lucky man." He sighs and clasps his hands together in his lap. "There is something there. Maybe we are distantly related or something. I can't explain it, but part of me feels she is something to me. That she belongs to me, too, in some way."

Growling, I step toward him, but he stands to his full height and puts his hands up in front of him immediately.

"Not in that way. But I feel protective of her. Which is why I did all that I could to make sure nobody bothered her." He looks into the distance thoughtfully.

I'm stunned by his admission. I thought he enjoyed winding me up, but it was more than that all along? I owe him.

"I don't know what to say except thank you, Alpha," I say sincerely, shaking his hand.

"You're welcome. Now go, enjoy." He smiles, but it doesn't quite reach his eyes.

"You'll come to the mating ceremony?" I ask, even though my wolf is not too keen on having this man too close to my mate.

"Perhaps," he says noncommittally as he turns toward the woods, deep in thought. I'm pretty sure that means no. He's normally a closed book, but I can tell he's genuinely troubled. Not by our mating. He's happy for us, but I know what it's like to long for your mate, and he has no family to speak of.

It must be hard.

He reminds me a little of Rex, trying to act fine when he isn't. It brings home just how fortunate I am to have found Hayley. I wish that for them both.

"Cooper, just a heads up, Toby was here again yesterday, despite being escorted off the premises on Friday. Trying to get in to speak to Alpha Anderson to smooth things over. He might not let this lie so easily," he warns, strolling off slowly, hands clasped behind his back.

With that thought, I go back inside to find Hayley, not wanting to leave her alone for too long when the fully formed bond is so new. I'll deal with Toby and what his presence might mean later.

When I step back into the room, my eyes immediately go to her, sitting elegantly beside Ethan, caramel hair pulled up to reveal her tanned slender neck. She's showing off her mark proudly as she laughs with my family. I never thought I'd be this lucky. I re-join them and teasing flows easily around the table. Pressing a kiss to the top of her head, I sigh contentedly, knowing we are finally right where we are meant to be.

Together.

EPILOGUE
HAYLEY

A flat, white, shiny box with a pale pink bow tied around it is sitting in the middle of my bed. I glance back towards the bedroom door, but nobody is there watching. Surely if one of the gaggle of girls currently laughing and boozing it up in my sitting room had left it here for me to find, they would have come to watch me open it.

I drift closer and take the small envelope from underneath the ribbon, opening it carefully to read the message inside.

Hayley,

I am so sorry that I'm not there to pour shots down your neck on this, the most sacred of days. Although I'm more than confident Leah will take care of that for me!

I am so happy you are joining our family. I could never have dreamed that I would be lucky enough to end up with a sister like you. I wanted you to have this, maybe for the Luna Ceremony? It was just too pretty to leave behind.

I love you so much, and I promise I will come back for the wedding. Enjoy the hen!!

P.P.S. Please send some pics of the dick paraphernalia. I need a laugh and it's probably as close to getting some action as I'm going to get any time soon.
    Leila xxx

Sitting down on the bed, I wipe the tears from my eyes carefully, trying to avoid ruining my makeup. I miss Leila. While there is a room full of fabulous women outside, waiting to make a show of me tonight, it won't be the same without her. She's been away from the pack for almost two months now and it's too damn long.

Once this hen party is done, I'm going to drag her ass back here. I'll need her to fend off Marie if I'm going to get through the Luna Ceremony and our wedding with my sanity intact.

I lift the lid on the box and the waterworks start again as I run my fingers over the delicate champagne material. It's the dress I tried on while shopping for the conference with her. The one that I refused to buy. It's probably the most thoughtful gift anyone has ever given me.

"Everything ok?" Zoe asks, leaning against the doorframe and studying me closely. She looks like a knockout in a little sparkling, silver dress and high heels. It's always such a shock to see her glammed-up when she spends most of her time in old clothes and wellies, covered in muck and God knows what else.

"You know, if you're having second thoughts, if this is all too fast, nobody will mind if you want to slow things down." She crosses the room and sits beside me, pulling me into a hug. I sigh and push her back, looking her in the eye to make sure she's hearing me this time.

We've had this conversation before, over and over. I know she's concerned, so I'm trying to be patient, but at some point, the second-guessing needs to stop.

"Zoe, I know you think this is crazy, that we only just met each other, but I love Cooper. I do. And I've been through enough to know what I want, and I want to marry him," I assure her. She shakes her head slightly and then takes a deep breath.

"I just... it's so fast, Hayley! Are you sure it's not some weird cult or something? They're all super-hot and intense here." I give her a look and she sighs, resigned that she won't change my mind.

"Fine. If you're happy, I'm happy. I'll get my head around it eventually." Zoe is by far the more steady, sensible one of the two of us. While I did well in college, I also made the most of my time there. Work hard, play hard, was my motto. Zoe had more of a work hard, and then work even harder type of mentality.

I know she's struggling with my engagement to a man she had never even met, only months after fleeing the city to get away from James, and mere weeks after my attack. Anything that isn't completely logical is outside of her comfort zone, but I know she just wants the best for me.

"Thank you. You do like him, don't you?" I ask her, because even though it would never change how I feel about Cooper, her approval means a lot to me.

"I mean, I suppose." She rolls her eyes and I know we're past it. "Handsome, funny, totally into you. I don't see it but ... if you must marry someone, he's not the worst." She grins then and gets back to her feet. "Chase is going crazy; you know that, right?"

She was there when I face-timed our brother from my parent's house to share the good news. Everyone else was hugging and congratulating me while he cursed and slammed stuff around.

"I know, there's not much he can do from the other side of the world, though." I laugh thinking of the threats he levelled at Cooper, who nodded along patiently when he could have slammed the laptop shut.

"This is beautiful." Zoe points to the dress. "Is it from Cooper?"

"No. Leila," I answer with a little shrug, and my sister smiles at me sympathetically.

"You said she'll come home for the wedding?"

"So, she says, but honestly, I'm not sure. She might never come back." I sigh, trying to not let the sadness at her sudden departure creep back in around me. This is a celebration. If I don't get a grip, it'll be the most depressing hen party ever.

"She'll be there if she said she would," Zoe assures, flashing me a big smile that lights up her pale silvery-grey eyes. Those eyes get her noticed everywhere she goes. Different eye colour in identical twins is unusual, but it can happen, and it's the only way people have been able to tell us apart for most of our lives.

An obnoxious novelty car horn sounds from outside, and I frown at Zoe, who looks equally confused. We rush to the front windows of Cooper's cabin, our cabin now I suppose, and stare outside with the other hens. A white stretch hummer is parked outside with pink balloons and streamers tied to it; a lady chauffeur with a black cap is climbing out to open the door.

This had to be Cooper. The female driver is a dead giveaway.

Hayley: Did you do this?

Cooper: Do you like it? You ignored my attempts to convince you that a nice relaxing spa retreat was the perfect hen party. So, I figured if you were going tacky and rowdy, you may as well go all-in.

Hayley: I love you.

Cooper: I love you, too, Princess. Now go have fun. Those hens will kill me if they think we've been talking.

Hayley: You know, my hen party is today. Technically, after midnight, you're no longer banished.

Cooper: Oh, really?

Hayley: Yep, those are the rules.

I flash him a mental image of the pale pink lingerie and garter I have underneath my dress and earn a growl through the link.

Cooper: You tell me the minute you're home, and your sisters are back in the guest house. I want to be the one to rip those off you.

Hayley: Yes, sir, Alpha.

Growling again, he cuts the mindlink, and I can't help but chuckle to myself. This mindlink thing is outstanding. I don't use it for emergencies as it was probably intended, but whatever. Cooper seems to appreciate my take on it.

I can't stop laughing as I watch Leah hoisting Marie into the back of the limo band placing a lei of pink and white flowers, interspersed with plastic dicks, over her head. Leah flashes me a wink, obviously delighted that Marie hasn't cottoned on to what she's wearing... yet.

Lord, help me. She has the luna wearing a necklace of penises.

This is going to get very messy.

The rest of the girls are already inside the limo, music blaring and lights flashing, when I close the front door of the cabin behind me.

"You didn't lock it!" Zoe yells through the open window, and there are a few giggles from the surrounding girls who know just how stupid someone would have to be to break into the alpha's house.

"Don't need to," I reply, much to her shock. "It's safe around here. I'm safe here." I climb in beside her and squeeze her hand while she eyes me dubiously.

My sisters aren't in the loop yet about the whole wolf-shifter thing, so they don't get how ludicrous that sounds to the pack here. No one messes with the luna.

"This place is weird," Sam states, clearly not understanding the open-door policy either. It reminds me just how much life has changed in the last couple of months. I feel so secure compared to the fearful wreck I was when I arrived. "But you promised me shots and a bar full of hot mountain men, so let's go!" she cheers.

Leah thrusts a plastic glass full of warm prosecco into my hand, banging on the glass partition to let the driver know we're ready to roll. Marie eyes me closely as I take a big swig and her face pinches in disappointment. She has appointed herself my personal baby whisperer, and I swear if she tells me when I'm ovulating by sniffing me one more time, I'm going to lose it.

Yeah, I need Leila back. I need to wrap my head around becoming luna before I add any pups to the mix. No matter how cute a few little Coopers running around the place would be. Gosh, they would be cute.

The late afternoon patrons of Taaffe's look stunned and a little frightened by the stream of dolled-up, tipsy, loud-and-laughing ladies that pour in the front door. I know we could have gone further afield, and somewhere fancier, but I wanted my sisters and my friends to see my new home.

Sean, the barman, shakes his head as the cackling reaches an ear-splitting level within ten minutes of our arrival.

Kim raises her glass to lead a toast.

"Hayley, I know how you arrived here might not have been the best start, but we are so grateful that you landed in our little town.

It was written in the stars that you and Cooper would find each other, and it's a truly special thing that you have together. To the future Mrs. Jones, welcome to your new forever home!"

Hollers and shouts mix in with awes and dreamy sighs as the girls all clink their glasses together. Even Sean raises a glass and gives me a little wink.

Kim's right, everything happens for a reason; without James, I would never have found my way to Grey Ridge. Or Cooper. Wherever he is, that's my forever home.

And I couldn't be happier.

———

Thank you for reading!!

If you want to know just why Marcus is staying away from Leila, read The Alpha's Inferno here now.

If you're not ready to leave Hayley and Cooper, and want to read the bonus epilogue about Hayley's first heat here or at www. reecebarden.com/bonus-content.

THE ALPHA'S INFERNO
SHIFTERS OF GREY RIDGE: BOOK 2

READ ON FOR A SNEAK PEEK...

CHAPTER 1
LEILA

'm going to die a virgin. It's official. I have obviously done something to anger the fates. My mate, the sexiest man I have ever seen, and the one I was just about to suggest do unspeakable things to me, is currently doing some serious back-pedalling despite the scorching heat between us. And I know exactly why.

"Leila Jones, as in Alpha Jonathan Jones's daughter?" He asks again, his deep masculine voice laced with concern. It's as if he is hoping the answer will have miraculously changed from the first time he asked me.

His deliciously chocolate brown eyes are shaded by his thick black brows, drawn down heavily under the weight of his frown. I wish I could rewind to thirty seconds ago. Before he knew who I was. Before he decided I wasn't worth the hassle. Before he realised he was better off making his excuses and calling a halt to the evening.

Another person who is all too quick to write me off as nothing more than the pack princess. I should have refused to give him my name. Maybe I would have seemed mysterious and sexy rather than terrifying.

It had been the best evening of my life until now, with easy laughter, smouldering glances, and subtle touches that have been sending my pulse racing. I know bears don't feel the mate bond the same way wolves do, but I know he's feeling something powerful between us.

He doesn't seem like the type of man who lets loose too often, but from the second I sat down beside him, he had a glint in his eye and a witty remark at the ready. Just one tumble in the hay with this mountain of man would be enough. I pray to the Moon Goddess to at least let me have that, and I'll be happy.

But I already know that's a lie. One taste and I'd be hooked.

In all honesty, I was under his spell from the second I walked through the door and caught his woodsy scent. I wonder, if I leaned forward and kissed him with all I have, could stop him from doing what he's about to do.

But I don't. Instead, I just nod like a coward. If he's about to run away from me, it won't be quite as mortifying if he doesn't have to physically pry me off of himself.

"So, you know my father?" I ask casually, already knowing the answer. My father, as the alpha of the local pack, is widely known and respected, and more than a little feared. Which translates to avoiding his daughter like the plague for pretty much every unmated male in the area.

Except for alpha males. It's the only reason they seek me out. They want the prestige that comes from mating an elusive alpha female, but they're only interested in good breeding, not me. Not love. Most of them think a big bank account and a fancy house are enough to turn any woman's head. Personality and genuine feelings seem to be way down the list of qualities they are looking for, but that's not what I want. My parents are fated mates, and, all my life, I've hoped and prayed that I'd be fortunate enough to find my own.

And here he is. Presented to me on a silver platter, appearing like some sort of hunky mirage, sat atop a barstool in my hometown dive bar. Like he was waiting here just for me.

A bear as my mate makes perfect sense. I had never considered it before, but when I saw him, I thought how clever the fates were, giving me a man who doesn't care about any of those alpha things. A solitary animal who doesn't feel the need to bow and scrape to others. A dominant bear like this wouldn't be concerned with trivial things like pack politics and scary fathers.

Or so I thought.

Except now, I'm starting to wonder if the fates are just screwing with me. Dangling this delicious specimen in front of me just to whip him away from me again.

I realise now that the reason this handsome stranger was in town and knew about our pack was something I should have paid more attention to before. Instead of mentally drooling over the powerful thigh muscles I can see flexing under his jeans and the bulging biceps stretching his shirt whenever he moves.

"I haven't met him yet." He says cautiously, sitting back in his chair and looking at me seriously.

Yet. Interesting.

I sigh and do the same, feeling the increased physical distance he is putting between us like a blast of ice-cold air. I want to be back in his arms on the dancefloor, face pressed to his warm muscular chest, swaying slowly together to the music, and basking in the happiness I had felt as he held me tight.

"What are you in town for, Marcus?" I ask, getting straight to the point. I clasp my hands in front of me to stop myself from fidgeting and looking as nervous as I feel. The alpha wolf within me is torn between despairing over what is transpiring, and anger that our mate is pulling back from us. Particularly over who I'm related to, given it's clear he is no pushover. I've met plenty of bears before, and stubborn-ness is a common trait. I can't imagine there is much that can change this man's mind.

"I'm the new Sheriff." He watches me closely for my reaction, but I simply smile and offer him my congratulations.

"That's brilliant. Someone needs to get these rowdy shifters back in line. They've lost the run of themselves since Madeline retired." I pick up my beer and take a long draw, both of us eyeing each other like chess players, not willing to give anything away. If he's the new law in town, that means he'll be working closely with my father. I can already see where this is going. He doesn't want to get involved with some needy little daddy's girl who's going to go running to the alpha when she gets her heart broken, sending a whole heap of drama his way.

"So, I don't think... maybe this isn't the best idea," he says coolly, and my wolf's hackles immediately go up. He narrows his eyes at me as he senses some of my alpha power when my anger flares. Either he didn't expect that, or he doesn't like it. Or both. Well, tough luck. He's my mate. He's not supposed to think as all the others do and assume that I'm some pampered brat.

"Fine." I stand up and yank my leather jacket off the back of my chair, throwing down a twenty on the bar to cover my drinks. I'm not letting the guy who's rejecting me pay for my drinks. I have my pride.

Marcus lifts his eyes to heaven, rubbing a hand down his neatly trimmed dark beard.

"Leila, don't go. Not like this," he pleads quietly, and I can hear the genuine regret in his voice.

I don't want his pity, though. I want him to want me as I want him: with an all-consuming need that should be impossible to deny.

My wolf whimpers, anger shifting back to hurt, and I need to get out of here fast if I want to keep my dignity intact. I turn away from him, letting my dark hair fall around my face as I go to leave. His big hand catches my wrist, and a soft gasp escapes my lips as electricity shoots up my arm from his touch. His eyes jerk up to meet mine, and I know he felt it, too.

This is just too unfair and I'm on the verge of breaking down. He pulls me back towards him gently, using his obvious strength to stop me from pulling away, but doing it carefully rather than aggressively. He tips my head up so I'm forced to meet his eyes and flinches when he sees the tears glistening there.

"Just let me go, Marcus. I just want to go home. Please don't make this worse than it already is," I whisper, looking down at where his large rough hand holds mine, unable to look into his soulful eyes for another second. The pain there seems to mirror my own and I can't wrap my head around why he has completely shut down.

He doesn't say a word, just slowly lets my hand drop. I pull in a deep breath and turn on my heel, head held high as I push through the crowded bar towards the rear entrance. As soon as I get outside, I slam the door behind me and sink to the ground, letting the tears come as big sobs rack my body.

The best day of my life has now officially become the worst.

CHAPTER 2

MARCUS

Taaffe's Bar is hopping. Before I even open the door, the sounds of old school 80s rock music and laughter spill out onto the street. When I step inside, the atmosphere is buzzing with the uplifting energy of shifters and humans all having a good time. The décor is rustic, wood and some exposed brick, nothing fancy, nothing that can't be replaced or wiped down. The smell of hops and deep-fried bar food fills my nostrils as I survey the full booths, and the small groups gathered around the tall tables dotted around the place.

I edge my way past the Saturday evening crowd and head straight for the bar, sliding onto an empty stool in the corner and turning to observe the patrons. This place seems to attract a friendly crowd. When I enquired at the local diner where would be the best place to go for a drink, I was told that this was really the only place. I'm relieved that it's not a complete dive. I don't doubt that there's the odd bar fight. There always is in a shifter town where tempers are shorter and emotions run higher, but I don't see any evidence of a rough element in town. A bonus point for Grey Ridge. It'll be a welcome change to have a good pub to frequent that I won't have to get called to every other night.

I should probably already know a little more about my new hometown, but I had just been so grateful to get the job and the excuse to move away from home, that I didn't care where I was going. Anywhere was better than there. I have badly needed a change for far too long.

A very large, very bald, very serious-looking barman stops in front of me with a clean dish towel tossed over his shoulder and eyes me carefully. Tattoos adorn his forearms and knuckles, but he's clean-shaven and wears a blue shirt. The owner, I'm guessing, given the rest of the staff are dressed casually in just black t-shirts and jeans. He probably knows everyone in this town, and a big grizzly bear shifter like me sticks out like a sore thumb. He's serving me himself to mind his staff and check me out, and truth be told, he's right to watch me. Any bear shifter has the potential to wreak havoc, and there are plenty of them that like to throw their weight around just for the hell of it. Make that two bonus points for Taaffe's. It's also a well-run bar. Maybe life in Grey Ridge won't be too bad at all.

"Hey, how are you doing? Can I just get a bottle of beer, please?" I ask, and he nods, reaching into the cooler behind him before flipping the lid off and handing the chilled bottle to me. He settles his enormous frame against the fridge and folds his arms in front of him like he has all the time in the world, as if there aren't five other people trying to catch his attention to get served.

"New in town or just passing through?" The tone is friendly, but there's no beating around the bush, and I like a man who's straight to the point, just like me. He seems to suggest that passing through is the better answer. He's a shifter too, but I can't place exactly what kind. Not a bear like me, but not a wolf like most customers here.

"New in town. Marcus Lennox, Madeline's replacement." I half stand from my stool and lean across the bar, offering my hand to the man to put his mind at ease. He visibly relaxes and pushes forward off the fridge, moving in closer.

"Sean," he says, a broad smile cracking his face. His intimidating demeanour is quickly replaced by a relaxed one as he shakes my hand enthusiastically. "No shit. A bear running a wolf town. They must think this place has gone to hell if they're sending in the big guns."

I have to laugh at that. Any bear working in law enforcement is well used to people thinking we're only brought in to quell trouble; our animals are large and dominant enough to put most shifters back in line.

"No, no, nothing like that. I was just looking for a change of scene when this came up," I reassure him as I settle back onto my stool.

"Well, I hope you like things quiet." He wipes down the counter as he talks, completely at ease now. "The pack here is a good one, well run, and we rarely have any trouble. You might be twiddling your thumbs, Sheriff Lennox."

"Oh, believe me, I can live with that." I give him a nod as I settle back into watching the crowd, and he moves on to serve his other customers. My eyes drift around the room, and I catch the eyes of a few she-wolves eyeing me with blatant interest. Wolves love power, which makes my sheer size and the dominance of my bear attractive to most.

Technically, I don't start my new job until Monday morning, so tonight, I can have a bit of fun and enjoy myself, and blow off some steam if I see someone who takes my fancy. My bear is agitated just at the thought and has been tense since we got here. Our last home was isolated and I'm not a people person. Maybe after coming from somewhere where it's all bears, the sheer number of other shifters around has him all antsy.

Whatever it is, he's driving me crazy.

Even despite that, the hungry glances are doing nothing for me. When one particularly brazen bottle blonde she-wolf licks her painted red lips and winks at me, I snort and turn back to face the bar. No thanks, not my type.

I take a long swig and gesture at Sean to bring me another when I sense rather than see someone walking up behind me. The breeze blowing through the door as it shuts softly behind her carries the delicious scent of cherry blossoms, even with the overpowering scents mingling in the bar, and I take a deep swallow as my mouth literally waters.

My optimism escalates another notch when a slim, olive-skinned hand grips the bar right next to my own, and a curtain of glossy chestnut hair swishes past my shoulder as my new companion slips gracefully onto the stool next to mine. I can only see the back of her head as she chats easily with Sean, and he places a beer in front of her without her even asking. He waves away the cash she holds out, as if offended she is even attempting to pay him for it.

She laughs as she tips her bottle to him, and it lifts my soul with how light and happy it sounds. She takes her black leather jacket off and stands to hang it on the back of the stool, exposing silky skin and toned arms. Her skin-tight black jeans show off a curvy, firm backside and tiny waist, the perfect combination for a bear who likes a bit of something to grab onto.

Naturally dark-pink lips wrap themselves around the mouth of the bottle and my dick twitches in my pants as she pours some of the amber liquid down her neck. She lets out a contented sigh, and I fight back a growl as desire floods my veins.

I haven't even seen her face and I'm already imagining that mouth wrapped around me.

What the hell is up with me and my bear tonight?

I clear my throat as I try to bring my brain back online, and she tenses, as though she's only just noticing my presence now. Her long fingers grip the counter tightly as she turns around slowly to face me straight on, and I'm rewarded with my first glimpse of the most exquisite creature I have ever seen. Thick black eyelashes frame sparkling hazel eyes. High cheekbones and clear tan skin make her look bright and healthy, and those lips, full and pouty, just begging to be kissed. She's a goddess.

One side of her mouth tips up in a shy smile and her cheeks flush slightly. She's blushing, a goddamn, sex on legs she-wolf, is blushing at me and I'm done for. I just stare at her, mutely, for what I'm sure is far too long to be cool or appropriate, but she stares back, seemingly equally enthralled by the crackling energy filling the space between us.

"Eh, Marcus, this is Leila, local doc and all-round pack legend." Sean introduces us, watching our interaction carefully. When neither of us responds, he shakes his head slightly and moves along the bar.

"All-round legend? What do you have to do to earn that title around here?" I finally ask, and my voice comes out deep and gravelly, like I'm having to force the words out. Which I am. My bear seems content to just ogle like some sort of weird creeper.

She blinks rapidly, trying to snap herself out of whatever spell is wrapped around us, and smiles at me.

"Sean's definition is a little different to most people. Stitching up a few brawling shifters on the QT is probably a bad thing in most people's books," she admits with a mischievous twinkle in her eyes, and I can't help but laugh. She has no clue that I'm the new sheriff in town.

"That all sounds dodgy," I tease, and she grins back at me. "Well, it's a boring town, Marcus, a girl has to get her kicks somehow."

She winks at me, and it's all I can do to stop myself hauling her to me and kissing the fuck out of her right here and now. I've lost my damn mind. Thirty seconds after meeting might be a bit too soon to be ravishing her in a crowded bar, so I distract myself by checking for a ring or a mark, and am very grateful to see neither.

A bit more flirting, a few touches here and there, and I'm on fire. My fingertips burn to touch her, but despite the chemistry between us, I can tell that she's a classy lady and I don't want to crash and burn here by coming on too strong. She's smart too, and witty. Too good for me, but she seems to be just as attracted to me as I am to her if her dilated pupils and elevated heart rate are anything to go by. This isn't any ordinary wolf. This is not the type of woman you just want one night with.

I know I'm in big trouble because when she asks me to dance; I don't refuse as I would anyone else. Instead, I stand and move out to the side of the dance floor with her and seize the chance to hold her body tight against me, one hand on her waist, the other holding her hand loosely to my chest as we sway side to side.

I have a flash of us doing this in a kitchen, when we're old, laughing and smiling as we stay pressed close together, and the vision is like a kick in the gut. It knocks the wind out of me, and I'm stunned. I'm normally the grumpy bear that grunts at everyone until they leave me alone, but she has me hooked already. I'd do anything to get more. More of her, more of her time, and definitely more of that body.

I glance down at the little dark-haired firecracker the gods have been kind enough to drop into my lap and grin when I see her looking up at me adoringly.

What the hell is this? I've never felt an instant connection with someone like this before.

We're back at the bar and I'm trying to find a way to tactfully broach the subject of getting out of here because I need to be alone with her more than I've ever needed anything else. Every time we touch, my bear is getting more and more worked up and pushing me to just haul her out of there in the most ungentlemanly manner imaginable. How to do it in a way that lets her know that it's not just tonight I want? Because for the first time in a long time, I can see something serious starting here.

But just like the story of my life, nothing good ever lasts. As she speaks the five words that will change the rest of my life forever, I curse the heavens, because nothing can ever be easy.

"My name is Leila Jones."

The alpha's daughter. Way too good for a bear like me, and the one person I can't mess around with without getting kicked out of the town. And where would I go then? Home? Fuck that. Either my father will kill me, or that town will destroy what little of my soul it hasn't tainted already.

No matter what, if I take this woman home with me tonight, that'll be the end of us. We'll have no chance. I'm dead in the water if I show up to my first meeting with him, having already bedded his daughter – having done all the seriously filthy things to her that I'm imagining. I already know that having her and losing her will break me. A woman like this is like a drug, one taste and I'll be addicted.

I'll never fit into her world, but maybe, just maybe, if I wait and prove to her, and the alpha, that I can be a good provider, we'd have a shot.

I want to roar; I want to tear this place apart, but I'm the new sheriff, so I can't be the one causing a scene, and this isn't Leila's fault, either. I pause and look at her, and I see it. She's too quick, she's copped my hesitation and I see a bit of the sparkle in her eyes fade, and it kills me. She already has my heart, but it's not meant to be.

Not yet anyway.

ALSO BY REECE BARDEN

ABOUT THE AUTHOR

Reece is a bestselling author of steamy paranormal romance books.

Her favourite stories to write are about sexy alphas, from diehard bad boys to cinnamon roll heroes, who don't just fall in love first, they fall hard and for keeps.

From Ireland , she loves leafy green forests, lakes, and rolling hills, and while she doesn't get to spend as much time outdoors as her characters, her stories are all set in wild, untamed locations with cozy small-town vibes.

The stories she writes are for people just like her who love a little light-hearted fun with their naughty heroes and edge-of-your-seat storylines.

🅕 🅞 🅑🅑 🅐

Made in United States
Orlando, FL
24 March 2025

59822869R00182